THE SKULL MANTRA

Eliot Pattison is a world traveller and frequent visitor to China, whose numerous books and articles on international policy issues have been published on three continents. *The Skull Mantra* is his first work of fiction and won him the Edgar award for Best First Novel from the Mystery Writers of America.

'A cocktail of action adventure . . . a great read.'
Guardian

'A captivating thriller.'   *Choice*

'Complex, crammed with Tibetan and Buddhist lore and legend, and utterly fascinating.'   *Daily Telegraph*

'Vivid, absorbing, intriguing.'   *Sunday Telegraph*

'The physical background, ranging from the barren hills of the gulag to the achingly beautiful mountains just out of reach, also helps to mark this as a thriller of laudable aspirations and achievements.'   *Chicago Tribune*

'Does for Tibet what *Gorky Park* did for Russia. A colourful, moving portrayal of a strange and complex Tibet under an iron fist. Pattison's novel is as suspenseful as it is beautiful and tragic.'   *Portsmouth Herald*

'My favourite novel of the year . . . I loved it.'
The Poisoned Pen

'[A] superb whodunnit . . . [and] breathlessly suspenseful tour of a dangerous and exotic landscape, where opposing forces, political and magical, give way to an eerie mystical truth.'   *Kirkus Reviews*

It's a riveting story but it's also a great deal more. Pattison's narrative . . . somehow imbues the harsh Tibetan gulag with moments of eerie beauty and serenity.'
Booklist

'Set against a background that is alternately bleak and blazingly beautiful, this is at once a topnotch thriller and a substantive look at Tibet under siege.'
Publisher's Weekly

'A stark and compelling saga. Pattison writes with a confident knowledge and spare, graceful prose.'
Library Journal

'As distinctive in its own way as *Gorky Park*, this is a powerful, fascinating thriller which grips right from the start. It would also make a splendid film.'
Publishing News

'Demands to be noticed amidst all the competition . . . the complex narrative (owing not a little to Eco's *The Name of the Rose*, and none the worse for that), has a heady plot, lashings of atmosphere and a strong investigator.' *Good Book Guide*

'Few [thrillers] can match the power and poetry of this debut novel . . . a rare combination of excitement and enlightenment.' Amazon.com

'A full-tilt thriller that exhibits a profound feel for Buddhism . . . not only an exhilarating read, but an important one.' *Tricycle: The Buddhist Review*

Very nearly perfect . . . I missed deadlines, trains, dinners, dates, appointments and chores reading this great book, and so will you!' *London Student*

THE SKULL MANTRA

Eliot Pattison

ARROW

Published by Arrow Books 2000

1 3 5 7 9 10 8 6 4 2

Copyright © Eliot Pattison 2000

First published in the United Kingdom in 2000 by Century.

Arrow Books Limited
20 Vauxhall Bridge Road, London, SW1V 2SA

Random House Australia (Pty) Limited
20 Alfred Street, Milsons Point, Sydney,
New South Wales 2061, Australia

Random House New Zealand Limited
18 Poland Road, Glenfield
Auckland 10, New Zealand

Random House (Pty) Limited
Endulini, 5a Jubilee Road, Parktown 2193, South Africa

Random House Group Limited Reg. No. 954009
www.randomhouse.co.uk

A CIP catalogue record for this book
is available from the British Library

Papers used by Random House are natural,
recyclable products made from wood grown in sustainable forests.
The manufacturing processes conform to the environmental
regulations of the country of origin

ISBN 0 09 940979 8

Typeset by Deltatype Limited, Birkenhead, Merseyside
Printed and bound in Australia by
Griffin Press, Pty Ltd

For Matt, Kate, and Connor

ACKNOWLEDGEMENTS

This book would not have been possible without the sage advice and encouragement of Natasha Kern and Michael Denneny. I am also grateful for the valuable assistance of Laura Conner, Christina Prestia, Ed Stackler, and Lesley Payne.

T)

CHOMOLUNGMA
(Mt. Everest)

NEPAL

BHUTA

INDIA

THE SKULL
MANTRA

Chapter One

They called it *taking four*. The tall, gaunt monk hovered at the lip of the five-hundred-foot cliff, nothing restraining him but the raw Himalayan wind. Shan Tao Yun squinted at the figure to see better. His heart clenched. It was Trinle who was going to jump – Trinle his friend, who just that morning had whispered a blessing on Shan's feet so they would not trample insects.

Shan dropped his wheelbarrow and ran.

As Trinle leaned outward, the updraught pushed back, ripping away his *khata*, the makeshift prayer scarf he secretly wore around his neck. Shan weaved around men swinging sledgehammers and pickaxes, then stumbled in the gravel. Behind him a whistle blew, followed by an angry shout. The wind played with the dirty scrap of white silk, dangling it above Trinle's reach, then slowly twisting it skyward. As it rose, the prisoners watched the *khata*, not in surprise but in reverence. Every action had a meaning, they knew, and the subtle, unexpected acts of nature often had the most meaning.

The guards shouted again. But not a man returned to his work. It was a moment of abject beauty, the white cloth dancing in the cobalt sky, two hundred haggard faces looking upward in hope of revelation, ignoring the punishment that would surely come for even a minute's lost time. It was the kind of moment Shan had learned to expect in Tibet.

But Trinle, hanging at the edge, looked downwards again with a calm, expectant gaze. Shan had seen others take four, all with the same anticipation on their faces. It

1

always happened like this, abruptly, as if they were suddenly compelled by a voice no one else could hear. Suicide was a grave sin, certain to bring reincarnation as a lower life form. But opting for life on four legs could be a tempting alternative to life on two in a Chinese hard labour brigade.

Shan scrambled forward and grabbed Trinle's arm just as he bent over the rim. Instantly he realized he had mistaken Trinle's actions. The monk was studying something. Six feet below, on a ledge barely wide enough to accommodate a swallow's nest, lay a glittering gold object. A cigarette lighter.

A murmur of excitement pulsed through the prisoners. The *khata* had scudded back over the ridge and was plummeting to the slope fifty feet in front of the road crew.

The guards were among them now, cursing, reaching for their batons. As Trinle moved back from the edge, now watching the prayer cloth, Shan turned back to his upset wheelbarrow. Sergeant Feng, slow and grizzled but ever alert, stood beside the spilled rocks, writing in his tally book. Building roads was in the service of socialism. Abandoning one's work was one more sin against the people.

But as Shan plodded back to accept Feng's wrath, a cry rang out from the slope above. Two prisoners had gone for the *khata*. They had reached the pile of rocks where it had landed but were on their knees now, backing away, chanting feverishly. Their mantra hit the prisoners below like a gust of wind. Each man dropped to his knees the instant he heard it, taking up the chant in succession until the entire brigade, all the way to the trucks at the bridge below, was chanting. Only Shan and four others, the sole Han Chinese prisoners in the brigade, remained standing.

Feng roared in anger and shot forward, blowing his whistle. At first Shan was confused by the chant, for there had been no suicide. But the words were unmistakable. It

2

was the invocation of Bardo, the opening recitation for the ceremonies of death.

A soldier wearing four pockets on his jacket, the most common insignia of rank in the People's Liberation Army, trotted uphill. Lieutenant Chang, the officer of the guard, spoke into Feng's ear, and the sergeant shouted for the Han prisoners to clear the stack of rocks discovered by the Tibetans. Shan stumbled forward to where the *khata* lay and knelt beside Jilin, the slow, powerful Manchurian known only by the name of his province. As Shan stuffed the scarf up his sleeve, Jilin's surly face took on an air of expectation. With a surge of new energy he shoved aside the rocks.

It was not unusual for the lead work team, assigned to clear the largest boulders and loose surface rocks, to encounter the unexpected. A discarded pot or the skull of a yak was often discovered along the routes surveyed by the engineers of the PLA. In a land where the dead were still offered to vultures, it was not uncommon even to encounter the shards of human beings.

A half-smoked cigarette appeared in the rubble. As Jilin snatched it with a purr of delight, a pair of brightly polished boots appeared beside them. Shan leaned back on his haunches and watched as Lieutenant Chang's expression changed to alarm. His hand jerked to the pistol at his belt. A shrill outburst died on his lips, and he stepped behind Feng.

This time, the People's 404th Construction Brigade had beaten the vultures. The body lay outlined by the rocks that had covered it. Its shoes, Shan saw at once, were of real leather, in an expensive Western fashion. Under a red V-necked sweater, a freshly laundered white shirt glistened.

'American,' Jilin whispered with awe, not for the dead but for the clothing.

The man wore new blue jeans – not the flimsy Chinese denim for which street vendors sold pirated Western labels, but the real thing, made by a company in the United States. On the sweater was an enamel pin of two crossed flags, American and Chinese. The man's hands were folded over his belly, giving the impression of a man lying in repose at a guesthouse, waiting to be called for tea.

Lieutenant Chang quickly recovered. 'The rest, dammit,' he snarled, shouldering Feng forward. 'I want to see the face.'

'An investigation,' Shan said without thinking. 'You can't just –'

The lieutenant kicked Shan, not hard, but with the motion of one accustomed to dealing with troublesome dogs. Beside Shan, Jilin flinched, reflexively shielding his head with his hands. Lieutenant Chang impatiently stepped forward and grabbed the exposed ankles. With a peevish glance at Feng, he jerked the body away from the remaining rocks. Instantly the colour drained from Chang's face. He turned away and retched.

The body had no head.

'Idolatry is an attack on the socialist order,' a young officer barked into a bullhorn as the prisoners were marched towards a line of decrepit grey troop trucks long ago retired from army service. 'Every prayer is a blow against the people.'

Break the Chains of Feudalism, Shan silently bet himself, or *Honouring the Past Is Regression*.

'The dragon has eaten,' called out a voice from the ranks of prisoners.

A whistle blew for silence.

'You have failed to make quota,' the political officer continued in his high-pitched drone. Behind him was a red truck Shan had never before seen at the construction site. MINISTRY OF GEOLOGY, it said on the door. 'You have shamed the people. You will be reported to Colonel Tan.' The officer's amplified words echoed off the slope.

Why, wondered Shan, would the Ministry of Geology need to be there? 'Visiting rights suspended. No hot tea for two weeks. Break the Chains of Feudalism. Learn the will of the people.'

'Fuck me,' an unfamiliar voice muttered behind Shan. '*Lao gai* coffee again.' The man stumbled into Shan's back as they waited to climb into one of the trucks.

Shan turned. It was a new face to the squad, a young Tibetan whose small rugged features marked him as a *khampa*, from the herding clans of the high Kham plateau to the east.

As the man saw Shan his face instantly hardened. 'You know *lao gai* coffee, your highness?' he snarled. The few teeth he had left were blackened with decay. 'A spoonful of good Tibetan dirt. And half a cup of piss.'

The man sat on the bench opposite Shan and studied him. Shan turned the collar up on his shirt – the tattered canvas that covered the rear of the truck did little to shield them from the wind – and returned the stare without blinking. Survival, he had learned, was all about managing fear. It might burn your stomach. It might sear into your heart until you felt your soul smouldering. But never let it show.

Shan had become a connoisseur of fear, learning to appreciate its many textures and physical reactions. There was a vast difference, for example, between the fear of the torturer's bootsteps and the fear as an avalanche descended on an adjacent work crew. And none compared to the fear that kept him awake at nights as he searched through his miasma of exhaustion and pain, the fear of forgetting the face of his father. In the first days, during the haze of hypodermics and political therapy, he had come to realize how valuable fear could be. Sometimes only the fear had been real.

The *khampa* had deep scars, blade marks, on his neck. His mouth curled with cold scorn as he spoke. 'Colonel

Tan, they said,' he growled, looking about for acknowledgment. 'No one told me this was Tan's district. From the Thumb Riots, right? The biggest son of a bitch in an army of sons of bitches.'

For a moment it seemed as though no one had heard, then a guard suddenly leaned through the flap and slammed his baton against the man's shins. A grimace of pain twisted the *khampa*'s face, fading into a spiteful laugh as he made a small, twisting gesture towards Shan, as though with a knife. With studied disinterest, Shan shut his eyes.

As the flap was tied shut behind them and the truck groaned into movement, a low murmur rose in the darkness. It was nearly imperceptible, like the sound of a distant stream. During the thirty-minute ride to their camp, the guards were in the truck cabs, and the prisoners were alone. The fatigue in the squad was almost palpable, a weary greyness that dulled the ride back to camp. But it did not relieve the men from their vows.

After three years, Shan was able to identify the men's *malas*, their rosaries, by sound. The man to his left fingered a chain of buttons. On his other side the bootleg *mala* was a chain of fingernails. It was a popular device; one let the nails grow, then clipped and collected them, until reaching the required one hundred and eight, on thread pulled from blankets. Some rosaries, made only of knots tied from such thread, moved silently through callused fingers. Others were made of melon seeds, a prized material that had to be carefully guarded. Some prisoners, especially the recent arrivals, were more concerned with the rituals of survival than the rituals of Buddha. They would eat such rosaries.

With each seed or fingernail, knot or button, a priest recited the ancient mantra, *Om mani padme hum*. Hail to the Jewel in the Lotus, the invocation to the Buddha of Compassion. No priest would recline on his bunk until

6

his daily regime of at least one hundred cycles was completed.

The chants worked like a salve on his weary soul. The priests and their mantras had changed his life. They had made it possible for him to leave behind the pain of his past, to stop looking back. At least, most of the time. An investigation, he had said to Chang. The words had surprised him more than they had the lieutenant. Old ways died hard.

As fatigue pushed his consciousness back, an image pounced on him. A headless body, sitting upright, fidgeting with a gold cigarette lighter. The figure somehow took notice of him, and reluctantly extended the lighter towards Shan. He opened his eyes with a gasp, suddenly short of breath.

It was not the *khampa* who was watching him now, but an older man, the only prisoner with a genuine rosary, an ancient *mala* of jade beads which had materialized months earlier. The man who used it sat diagonally across from Shan, with Trinle, on the bench behind the cab. His face was worn smooth as a cobblestone except for the ragged scar at the left temple where a Red Guard had attacked him with a hoe thirty years earlier. Choje Rinpoche had been the *kenpo*, the abbot of Nambe gompa, one of the thousands of monasteries that had been annihilated by the Chinese. Now he was *kenpo* of the People's 404th Construction Brigade.

As Choje said his beads like the others, oblivious to the lurching of the truck, Trinle dropped a small object wrapped in a rag into his lap. Choje lowered his rosary and slowly unwrapped it, revealing a stone covered with a rust-coloured stain. The old lama held it reverently, studying each facet, as if it held some hidden truth. Slowly, as he discovered its secret, a great sadness filled his eyes. The rock had been drenched with blood. He looked up and met Shan's stare again, then nodded

7

solemnly, as if to confirm Shan's sense of foreboding. The man in the American jeans had lost his soul there, in the middle of their road. The Buddhists would refuse to work the mountain.

As the trucks pulled to a stop inside the compound, the rosaries disappeared. Whistles blew and the canvas was untied. Through the grey light of dusk the prisoners plodded in silence into the squat plank buildings that housed them, then quickly emerged with the tin mugs that served each man as wash basin, food plate, and teacup. They filed through one side of the mess shed to have their mugs filled with barley gruel and stood in the dusk, coming to life as the warmth of the gruel reached their bellies. Prisoners silently nodded to each other, offering tired smiles. If anyone spoke, he would be sent to the stable for the night.

Back in the hut, Trinle stopped the new prisoner, the *khampa*, as he moved across the room. 'Not here,' the monk said, pointing to a rectangle drawn in chalk on the floor.

The wiry *khampa*, apparently familiar with the invisible altars of prison barracks, shrugged and moved around the rectangle to an empty bunk in the corner.

'By the door,' Trinle announced quietly. He always spoke in the same worshipful tone, as though in awe of his every waking moment. 'Your bunk would be by the door,' he repeated, and offered to move the man's kit.

The man seemed not to have heard. 'Buddha's breath!' he gasped, studying Trinle's hands. 'Where's your thumbs?'

Trinle cocked his head towards his hands. 'I have no idea,' he said with a tinge of curiosity, as though he had never considered the question.

'The bastards. They did it to you, didn't they? To keep you from your rosary.'

'I still manage. By the door,' Trinle repeated.

8

'There's two empty bunks,' the man snapped. He was no priest. He leaned back on the straw pallet as though challenging Trinle to move him. The fiercest resistance fighters ever to oppose the People's Liberation Army had been those from Kham. They were still being arrested in the remote ranges for random acts of sabotage. Outside, a *khampa* from the southern clans, which had resisted the army long after the rest of Tibet was subdued, was still prohibited from possessing any weapon, or carrying a blade of more than five inches.

The man removed one of his tattered boots and with great ceremony removed a slip of paper from his pocket. It was a sheet from one of the guards' tally pads, which sometimes blew open in the wind. He held it up with an exaggerated smile and pushed it into his boot for added insulation. Life in the 404th was measured by the thinnest of victories.

As he rewrapped the rags that served as socks, the new arrival studied his cellmates. Shan had seen the routine more times than he could count. Each new prisoner first looked for the chief priest, then looked for the weak who would make no trouble. For those who had given up and those who could be informers. The first was easy. His eyes quickly settled on Choje, who sat lotus fashion on the floor beside one of the central bunks, still studying the rock in his hand. No one in the hut, no one in the entire brigade, emitted such serenity.

One of the young monks produced a pocketful of leaves, sprouts of the weeds that had begun to emerge on the mountain slopes. Trinle counted them out and distributed them, one leaf to each prisoner. Each of the monks accepted his leaf solemnly and whispered a mantra of thanks towards the man whose turn it had been to risk punishment for gathering the greens.

Trinle turned back to the *khampa* as the man chewed his leaf. 'I am sorry,' he said. 'Shan Tao Yun sleeps there.'

9

The *khampa* looked about and settled his gaze on Shan, who sat on the floor near Choje.

'The rice eater?' he snarled. 'No *khampa* lets a damned rice eater beat him.' He laughed and looked around. No one joined.

The silence seemed to inflame him. 'They took our land. They took our monasteries. Our parents. Our children,' he spat, studying the monks with growing impatience.

The monks looked at each other uncomfortably. The hatred in his voice was like an alien presence in their hut.

'And that was just the beginning, just giving them the time they needed for the real fight. Now they take our souls. They put their people in our cities, in our valleys, in our mountains. Even in our prisons. To poison us. To make us like them. Our souls shrivel up. Our faces disappear. We become nobody.'

He turned abruptly to face the opposite bunks. 'It happened at my last camp. They forgot all their mantras. One day they woke up, their minds are blank. No prayers left.'

'They can never take the prayers from our hearts,' Trinle said, with an anxious look towards Shan.

'Shit on them! They *take* our hearts. No one passes on then, no one goes to Buddha. They only go down, drifting from one form to a lower one. An old monk at the last camp, they fed him politics. One day he woke up and found he had been reborn as a goat. I saw him. The goat got in line for food, just where the old priest had been. I saw it with my own eyes. Just like that. A goat. The guards bayoneted him. Roasted him on a spit in front of us. Next day they brought a bucket of shit from the latrine. Said look what he's become now.'

'You do not need the Chinese to lose your way,' Choje said suddenly. 'Your hate will be enough.' His voice was soft and fluid, like sand falling on a stone.

The *khampa* shrank back. But the wildness stayed in

10

his eyes. 'I'm not waking up as a damned goat. I'll kill someone first,' he said, glaring again at Shan.

'Shan Tao Yun,' Trinle observed quietly, 'was reduced. He cannot sleep on his bunk until tomorrow.'

'Reduced?' the *khampa* sneered.

'A punishment,' Trinle replied. 'No one explained the system?'

'They just pushed me out of the truck and gave me a shovel.'

Trinle nodded to one of the young monks sitting nearby, a man with one milky eye who instantly dropped his prayer beads and moved to the *khampa's* feet.

'Break one of the warden's rules,' the man explained, 'and he sends you a clean shirt. You appear before him. If you are lucky, you are reduced. The immediate elimination of everything that provides comfort except the clothes on your back. The first night is spent outside, in the centre of the assembly square. If it is winter you will leave your body that night.'

In Shan's three years he had seen six of them, carried away like altar statues, frozen in the lotus position, clutching their makeshift beads.

'If it is not winter, the next day you may return to the shelter of your hut. The next your boots are returned. Then your coat. Next your food cup. Then the blanket, the pallet, and finally the bed.'

'You said that's the lucky. What about the others?'

The young priest suppressed a shudder. 'The warden sends them to Colonel Tan.'

'The famous Colonel Tan,' the *khampa* muttered, then abruptly looked up. 'Why a clean shirt?'

'The warden is a fastidious man.' The priest looked back to Trinle as though uncertain what more to say. 'Sometimes those who go are sent to a new place.'

The *khampa* snorted as he recognized the hidden meaning of the priest's words, then warily circled Shan. 'He's a spy. I can smell it.'

Trinle sighed and picked up the *khampa's* kit, moving it to the empty bunk by the door. 'This one belonged to an old man from Shigatse. It was Shan who got him out.'

'I figured he took four.'

'No. Released. He was called Lokesh. He had been a tax collector in the Dalai Lama's government. Thirty-five years here, then suddenly they call his name and open the gate.'

'You said this rice eater got him out.'

'Shan wrote some words of power on a banner,' Choje interjected with a slow nod.

The *khampa* studied Shan with a gaping mouth. 'So you're some kind of sorcerer?' The venom was still in his eyes. 'Going to work some magic on me too, shaman?'

Shan did not look up. He watched Choje's hands now. The evening liturgy would soon begin.

Trinle turned with a sad smile. 'For a sorcerer,' he sighed, 'our Shan hauls rocks well.'

The *khampa* muttered under his breath, and threw his boot to the bunk by the door. He was conceding not for Shan, but for the priests. To be certain, he turned to Shan. 'Fuck your mother,' he grunted. When no one took any notice, a gleam entered his eyes. He moved to the bare planks of Shan's bunk, untied the string at his waist, and urinated on the boards.

No one spoke.

Choje slowly rose and began cleaning the bunk with his own blanket.

The sheen of victory left the *khampa's* face. He cursed under his breath, then, nudging Choje aside, pulled off his shirt and finished the job.

There had been another *khampa* in their hut two years earlier, a tiny, middle-aged herder jailed for failing to register with one of the agricultural co-operatives. Alone for nearly fifteen years after a patrol picked up his family, he had finally wandered into a valley town after his dog died. He had been the closest thing to a caged animal

Shan had ever seen, always pacing back and forth in the hut like a bear behind bars. When looking at Shan his face had been like a small fist clenched in fury.

But the little *khampa* had loved Choje like a father. When one of the officers, known as Lieutenant Stick for his affinity with the baton, had beaten Choje for spilling a barrow load, the *khampa* had leapt on the Stick's back, pounding him, screaming profanity. Stick had laughed and pretended not to notice. A week later, released from the stable with a limp from something they did to his knee, the *khampa* had ripped strips from his blanket and begun sewing pockets to the inside of his shirt. Trinle and others had told him that even if he stored up enough food in his new pockets for a flight across the mountains, it was futile to consider escape.

One morning, when he had finished his pockets, he asked Choje for a special blessing. At their mountain worksite he began filling the pockets with rocks. He kept working, singing an old herder's song, until Lieutenant Stick moved near the edge of the cliff. Then, without a second's hesitation, the *khampa* had charged, hurling himself at Stick, locking his arms and legs around the officer, using the extra weight to convey them both over the cliff.

Suddenly the night bell rang. The single naked bulb that lit the room was extinguished. No talking was permitted now. Slowly, like a chorus of crickets claiming the night, the liquid rattle of rosaries filled the hut.

One of the young monks stealthily moved to watch by the door. From a hiding place under a loose board Trinle produced two candles and lit them, placing them at either end of the rectangle of chalk. A third was placed in front of Choje. The flame was too dim even to reach the *kenpo's* face. His hands appeared in the light, and began the evening teaching. It was a prison ritual, with no words and no music, one of the many that had evolved

13

since Buddhist monks began filling Chinese prisons four decades earlier.

First came the offerings to the invisible altar. Choje's palms were pressed together facing outward, his index fingers curled under his thumbs. It was the sign for *argham*, water for the face. Many of the *mudra*, the hand symbols used to focus inner power, still eluded Shan, but Trinle had taught him the offering signs. The bottom two fingers of Choje's disembodied hands withdrew into the palms and the hands aimed downward. *Padyam*. Water for the feet. Slowly, gracefully, Choje deftly moved his hands to offer incense, perfume, and food. Finally he closed his fists together, the thumbs extended upward like wicks from a bowl of butter. It was *aloke*. Lamps.

From outside a long moan of pain punctuated the silence. A monk in the next hut was dying of some internal ailment.

Choje's hands gestured towards the invisible circle of worshippers, asking what they brought for the glory of the inner deity. A pair of thumbless hands appeared in the light, the index finger of each hand touching at the tip, the other fingers folded. A tiny murmur of approval moved through the room. It was the golden fish, an offering for good fortune. New hands appeared, each after sufficient time to silently recite the dedication prayer that accompanied the prior offering. The conch shell, the treasure flask, the coiled knot, the lotus flower. It was Shan's turn. He hesitated, then extended his left index finger upward and covered it with his right hand flattened. The white umbrella, another prayer for good fortune.

The room filled with the tiny, remarkable sound, as if of rustling feathers, that had become a fixture of Shan's nights, the sound of a dozen men silently mouthing mantras. Choje's hands returned to the circle of light for the sermon. He began with a gesture Shan had not often seen, the right hand raised with palm and fingers pointing

14

up. The *mudra* of dispelling fear. It cast an uneasy silence on the room. One of the young monks audibly sucked in his stomach, as though suddenly aware that something profound was happening. Then the hands shifted, clasping together with the middle fingers pointing upward. The diamond of the mind *mudra*, invoking cleansing and clarity of purpose. This was the sermon. The hands did not change. They floated, unmoving, as though carved of pale granite, while the devotees contemplated them. The message could not have been more intensely communicated if Choje had shouted it from a mountaintop. The pain was irrelevant, the hands said. The rocks, the blisters, the broken bones were inconsequential. Remember your purpose. Honour your inner god.

It wasn't clarity that Shan lacked. Choje had taught him how to focus like no teacher before. Through the long winter days when the warden kept them in – not for fear of losing prisoners, but for fear of losing guards – Choje had helped him reach an extraordinary discovery. To be an investigator, the only job Shan had ever known before the gulag, one had to have a troubled soul. The exceptional investigator could have no faith. Everything was suspect, everything transitory, moving from allegation to fact to cause to effect to new mystery. There could be no peace, for peace only came with faith. No, it wasn't clarity he lacked. In moments like this, with dark premonition weighing heavy, with his prior life pulling him like a man tangled in an anchor line, what he lacked was an inner god.

He saw there was something on the floor below Choje's hands. The bloody rock. With a start, Shan realized that he and Choje were thinking about the same thing. The *kenpo* was reminding his priests of their duty. Shan's tongue went dry. He wanted to blurt out a protest, to beg them not to put themselves at risk over a dead foreigner, but the *mudra* silenced him like a spell.

He clamped his eyes shut but still Shan could not focus

on Choje's message. He kept seeing something else each time he tried to concentrate. He kept seeing the gold cigarette lighter hanging five hundred feet above the valley floor. And the dead American who had beckoned to him in his daylight nightmare.

Suddenly a low whistle came from the door. The candles were extinguished, and a moment later the ceiling light was switched on. A guard slammed open the door and moved to the centre of the room, a pick handle cradled in his arm. Behind him came Lieutenant Chang. With mock solemnity Chang extended a piece of clothing so that no prisoner could mistake it. It was a clean shirt. He jabbed it towards several men as though feinting with a blade, laughing as he did so. Then he abruptly flung it at Shan, who lay on the floor.

'Tomorrow morning,' he snapped, and marched out.

A sharp, chill wind slapped Shan's face as Sergeant Feng escorted him through the wire the next morning. The winds were harsh to the 404th, which sat at the base of the northernmost ridge of the Dragon Claws, a vast rock wall rising nearly vertically behind it. Updraughts sometimes ripped roofs from huts. Downdraughts sometimes pelted them with gravel.

'Already reduced,' Sergeant Feng muttered as he locked the gate behind them. 'Nobody already reduced ever got the shirt.' He was a short, thick, bull of a man, with a heavy stomach but equally heavy shoulders, his skin as leathery as that of the prisoners from years of standing guard in sun and wind and snow. 'Everyone's waiting. Making bets,' Feng added with a dry croak Shan took to be a laugh.

Shan tried to will himself not to listen, not to think of the stable, not to remember Zhong's white-hot fury.

Zhong's temper was in control for once. But the warden's gloating smile as he paced around Shan scared him more than the expected tantrum. He gripped his upper right arm, which often twitched in Zhong's presence. Once they had connected battery wires there.

'If he had bothered to consult with me,' Zhong said in the flat nasal tone of Fujian province, 'I would have warned him. Now he will have to find out for himself what a damned troublemaker you are.' Zhong lifted a piece of paper from his desk and read it, shaking his head in disbelief. 'Parasite,' he hissed, then paused and scribbled on the paper to record the insight.

'It won't be for long,' he said, looking up expectantly. 'One wrong step and you'll be breaking rocks with your bare hands. Until you die.'

'I constantly endeavour to fulfil the trust the people have bestowed in me,' Shan said without blinking.

The words seemed to please the warden. A perverse gleam rose on his face. 'Tan's going to eat you alive.'

Sergeant Feng had an unfamiliar look, an almost festive air about him. A drive into Lhadrung, the ancient market town that served as county seat, was a rare treat for the 404th guards. He joked about the old women and goats who ran from the side of the road, spooked by the truck. He peeled an apple and shared it with the driver, ignoring Shan, who was wedged between the two men. With a spiteful grin, he repeatedly moved the key for Shan's manacles from one pocket to the next.

'They say the chairman himself sent you here,' the sergeant finally said as the low, flat buildings of the town came into view.

Shan didn't reply. He bent in his seat trying to roll up his cuffs. Someone had produced a pair of worn, oversized grey trousers for him to wear, and a threadbare soldier's jacket. They had made him change clothes in the middle of the office. Everyone had stopped his work to watch.

'I mean, why else would they put you in with them?'

Shan straightened. 'I'm not the only Chinese.'

Feng grunted as though amused. 'Sure. Model citizens, every one. Jilin, he killed ten women. Public Security would have put a bullet in him except his uncle was a party secretary. That one from Squad Six, he stole the safety gear from an oil rig in the ocean. To sell in the black market. Storm came and fifty men died. Letting him have a bullet was too easy on him. Special cases, you from home.'

'Every prisoner is a special case.'

Feng grunted again. 'People like you, Shan, they just keep for practice.' He stuffed two slices of apple into his mouth. *Momo gyakpa*, he was called behind his back, *fat dumpling*, for the curve of his belly and the way he was always scavenging food.

Shan turned away. He looked over the expanse of heather and hills rolling like a sea towards the high ice-clad ranges. It offered the illusion of escape. Escape was always an illusion for those who had no place to escape to.

Sparrows flitted among the heather. There were no birds at the 404th. Not all the prisoners were fastidious in respecting life. They claimed every crumb, every seed, nearly every insect. The year before there had been a fight over a partridge that was blown into the compound. The bird had narrowly escaped, leaving two men with a handful of feathers each. They had eaten the feathers.

The four-storey building that housed the government of Lhadrung County had a crumbling synthetic marble façade and filthy windows in corroded frames that rattled in the wind. Feng pushed him up the stairs to the top floor, where a small grey-haired woman led them to a waiting room with one large window and a door at each end. She scrutinized Shan with a twist of her head, like a curious bird, then barked at Feng, who shrank, then sullenly removed the manacles from Shan's wrists and retreated into the hallway.

18

'A few minutes,' she announced, nodding at the far door. 'I could bring you tea.'

He looked at her dumbfounded, knowing he should tell her of her mistake. He had not had tea, real green tea, for three years. His mouth opened but no sound came out. The woman smiled and disappeared behind the near door.

Suddenly he was alone. The unexpected solitude, however brief, overwhelmed him. The imprisoned thief suddenly left alone in a treasure vault. For solitude had been his real crime during his years in Beijing, the one for which no one had ever thought to prosecute him. Fifteen years of postings away from his wife, his private apartment in the married quarters, his long solitary walks through the parks, the meditation cells at his hidden temple, even his irregular work hours had given him a hoard of privacy unknown to a billion of his countrymen. He had never understood his addiction until that wealth had been wrenched away by the Public Security Bureau three years before. It hadn't been the loss of freedom that hurt most, but the loss of privacy.

Once in a *tamzing* session at the 404th he had confessed his addiction. If he had not rejected the socialist bond, they said, there would have been someone there to stop him. It wasn't friends that mattered. A good socialist had few friends, but many watchers. After the session he had stayed behind in the hut, missing a meal just to be alone. Discovering him there, Warden Zhong had dispatched him to the stable, where they broke something small in his foot, then forced him back to work before it could heal.

He examined the room. A huge plant extending to the ceiling, occupied one corner. It was dead. There was a small table, polished brightly, with a lace doily on top. The doily caught him by surprise. He stood before it with a sudden aching in his heart, then pulled himself away to the window.

The top floor gave a view over most of the northern quarter of the valley, bound on the east by the Dragon Claws, the two huge symmetrical mountains from which ridges splayed out to the east, north, and south. The dragon had perched there and taken phantom form, people said, its feet turned to stone as a reminder that it still watched over the valley. What was it someone had shouted when the American's body was found? 'The dragon has eaten.'

He pieced together the geography until at last, across an expanse of several miles of windblown gravel and stunted vegetation he discerned the low roofs of Jade Spring Camp, the county's primary military installation. Just above it, and below the northernmost Claw, was the low hill that separated Jade Spring from the wire-enclosed compound of the 404th.

Almost without thinking Shan traced the roads, his work of the past three years. Tibet had two kinds of road. The iron roads always came first. The 404th had laid the bed for the wide strip of macadam that ran from Lhasa, beyond the western hills, into Jade Spring Camp. Iron roads were not railways, of which Tibet had none. They were for tanks and trucks and fieldguns, the iron of the People's Liberation Army.

The thin line of brown that Shan traced from an intersection north of town towards the Claws was not such a road. It was far worse. The road the 404th was building now was for colonists who would settle in the high valleys beyond the mountains. The ultimate weapon wielded by Beijing had always been population. As in the western province of Xinjiang, the home of millions of Moslems belonging to central Asian cultures, Beijing was turning the native population of Tibet into a minority in their own lands. Half of Tibet had been annexed to neighbouring Chinese provinces. Population centres in the rest of Tibet had been flooded with immigrants. Endless truck convoys over thirty years had turned Lhasa into a Han Chinese city. The roads built for such convoys were called *avichi* trails at the 404th, for the eighth level of hell, the hell reserved for those who would destroy Buddhism.

A buzzer sounded. He turned to find the birdlike woman standing with a cup of tea. She extended the cup, then scurried through the far door, disappearing into a darkened room.

Shan gulped down half the cup, ignoring the pain as it scalded his throat. The woman would realize her mistake and take it back. He wanted to remember the sensation, to relive the taste in his bunk that night. Even as he did so he felt demeaned, and angry at himself. It was a prisoner's game that Choje warned against, stealing bits of the world to worship back in the hut.

The woman reappeared and gestured for him to enter.

A man in a spotless uniform sat behind an unusually long, ornate desk lit by a single gooseneck lamp. No, it was not a desk, Shan realized, but an altar that had been converted to government use.

The man silently studied Shan while lighting an expensive American cigarette. *Loto gai*. Camels.

Shan saw the familiar hardness. Colonel Tan's face looked like it had been chiselled out of cold flint. If they were to shake hands, Shan thought, Tan's fingers would probably slice through his knuckles.

Tan exhaled the smoke through his nose and looked at the teacup in Shan's hands, then to the grey woman. She turned to open the curtains.

Shan did not need the sunlight to know what was on the walls. He had been in scores of such offices all over China. There would be a photograph of the rehabilitated Mao, pictures of military life, photos of a favourite command, a certificate of appointment, and at least one Party slogan.

'Sit,' the colonel ordered, gesturing to a metal chair in front of the desk.

Shan did not sit. He examined the walls. Mao was there, not the rehabilitated one but a photo from the sixties, one that showed the prominent mole on his chin. The certificate was there, and a photograph of grinning army officers. Above them was a picture of a nuclear missile draped with the Chinese flag. For a moment Shan did not see a slogan, then he saw a faded poster behind Tan. 'Truth,' it said, 'Is What the People Need.'

Tan opened a thin, soiled folder and fixed Shan with an icy stare.

'In Lhadrung County the state has entrusted the re-education of nine hundred and eighteen prisoners to me.' He spoke with the smooth confident voice of one accustomed always to knowing more than his listeners. 'Five *lao gai* hard labour brigades and two agricultural camps.'

There was something Shan had not seen at first, fine wrinkles below the close-cropped greying hair, a trace of weariness around the mouth. 'Nine hundred and seventeen have files. We can tell where each was born, their class background, where each was first informed against, every word uttered against the state. But for the other one there is only a short memorandum from Beijing. Only a single page for you, prisoner Shan.' Tan folded his palms over the folder. 'Here by special invitation of a member of the Politburo. Minister of the Economy Qin. Old Qin of the Eighth Route Army. Sole survivor of Mao's appointees. Sentence indefinite. Criminal conspiracy. Nothing more. Conspiracy.' He pulled on the cigarette, studying Shan. 'What was it?'

Shan held his hands together and stared at the floor. There were things far worse than the stable. Zhong didn't need Tan's permission to send him to the stable. There were prisons where inmates never left their cells except in death. And for those whose ideas were truly infectious, there were secret medical research institutes run by Public Security Bureau doctors.

'Conspiracy to assassinate? Conspiracy to embezzle state funds? To bed the Minister's wife? Steal his cabbages? Why does Qin not trust us with that information?'

'If this is some sort of *tamzing*,' Shan said impassively, 'there should be witnesses. There are rules.'

Tan's head did not move, but his eyes shot up, transfixing Shan. 'The conduct of struggle sessions is not one of my responsibilities,' he said acidly, and considered Shan in silence for a moment. 'The day you arrived, Zhong sent your folder to me. I think it scared him. He watches you.'

Tan gestured to a second folder, an inch thick. 'Started his own file. Sends me reports on you. I didn't ask, he just started sending them. Results of *tamzing* sessions. Reports of work output. Why bother? I asked him. You're a phantom. You belong to Qin.'

Shan gazed at the two folders, one with a single yellowed sheet, the other crammed with angry notes from an embittered jailkeeper. His life before. His life after.

Tan drank deeply from his teacup. 'But then you asked to celebrate the chairman's birthday.' He opened the second folder and read the top page. 'Most creative.' He leaned back and watched the smoke wisping towards the ceiling. 'Did you know that twenty-four hours after your banner we had handbills circulating in the marketplace? In another day an anonymous petition appeared on my desk, with copies being passed around the streets. We had no choice. You gave us no choice.'

Shan sighed and looked up. The mystery was over. Tan had decided he had not been punished sufficiently for his role in Lokesh's release. 'He had been imprisoned for thirty-five years.' Shan's voice was little more than a whisper. 'On holidays,' he said, not knowing why he felt the need to explain, 'his wife would come and sit outside.' He decided to address Mao. 'Not allowed closer than fifty feet,' he said to the photograph. 'Too far to talk, so they waved to each other. For hours they just waved.'

A narrow smile, as thin as a blade, appeared on Tan's face. 'You have balls, Comrade.' The colonel was mocking him. A prisoner did not deserve so hallowed a title as comrade. 'It was very clever. A letter would have been a disciplinary offence. If you had tried to shout it out you would have been beaten into silence. Your own petition would have been burned.'

He inhaled deeply on his cigarette. 'Still, you made Warden Zhong look like a fool. He will always hate you for it. He asked for your transfer out of the brigade. Said you were a saboteur of socialist relations. Couldn't guarantee your safety. The guards were furious. An accident could happen to Minister Qin's special guest. I said no. No transfer. No accident.'

Shan looked into Tan's eyes for the first time. Lhadrung was a gulag county, and in the gulag, prison wardens always had their way.

'It was his embarrassment, not mine. Releasing the old man was the right thing. Gave him a double ration book.' Smoke drifted out of the colonel's mouth. He shrugged as he caught Shan's stare. 'To correct the oversight.'

Tan closed the folder. 'Still, I grew curious about our mysterious guest. So political. So invisible. I wondered, should I worry about the next bomb you might throw our way?' He took another drag on his cigarette. 'I made my own inquiries in Beijing. No more information, they said at first. Qin was not available. In the hospital. No more data on Qin's prisoner available.'

Shan stiffened and looked back at the wall. The chairman seemed to to be staring back now.

'But it was a quiet week. My curiosity was aroused. I persisted. I discovered that the memo in the file was prepared by the headquarters of the Public Security Bureau. Not the office in Xinjiang that arrested you. Not in Lhasa where your sentence was entered. Over nine hundred prisoners, only one has a file prepared by the Bureau's Beijing office. I think we never appreciated just how special you are.'

Shan stared into Tan's eyes again. 'There's an American saying,' he said slowly. 'Everyone is famous for fifteen minutes.'

Tan froze. He cocked his head and continued to stare at Shan, as if he wasn't sure he had heard right. The knife-edge smile slowly reappeared.

There was a rustle of small feet behind Shan.

'Madame Ko,' Tan said, the cold smile still on his face. 'Our guest needs more tea.'

The colonel was too old to be on the promotion lists, Shan decided. Even at his exalted level, a post in Tibet was a post in exile.

'I found more about this mysterious Comrade Shan,' Tan continued, shifting into the third person. 'He was a Model Worker in the Ministry of Economy. Commendations from the chairman for special contributions to the advancement of justice. He was offered Party membership, an extraordinary reward for someone halfway through his career. Then he did something even more extraordinary. He declined. A very complex man.'

Shan sat. 'We live in a complex world.' He saw that his hands, unconsciously, had made a *mudra*. Diamond of the mind.

'Especially when you consider that his wife is a highly regarded Party member, a senior official in Chengdu. Former wife, I should say.'

Shan looked up in alarm.

'You didn't know?' Tan asked with a satisfied smile. 'Divorced you two years ago. Annulled, actually. Never lived together, she said.'

'We' – Shan's mouth was suddenly bone dry – 'we have a son.'

Tan shrugged. 'Like you said. It's a complex world.'

Shan closed his eyes to fight the sudden pain in his gut.

They had finished the final chapter in their rewriting of his life. They had managed to take away his son. It wasn't that they were close. Shan and his son had spent maybe forty days together in the thirteen years since the boy was born. But one of the prisoner's games he played was fantasizing about the relationship he might have someday with the boy, about somehow creating the sort of bond Shan had shared with his own father. He would lie awake, wondering where the boy might be, or what he would say when he met his father again. The imagined relationship had been one of Shan's last slender reeds of hope. He pressed his palms against his temples and leaned over in his chair.

When he opened his eyes Tan was staring at him with a pleased expression. 'Your brigade found a body yesterday,' he said abruptly.

'*Lao gai* prisoners,' Shan said woodenly, 'are acquainted with death.' No doubt they had told the boy that Shan had died. But died how? As a hero? As a disgrace? As a slave used up in the gulag?

Tan opened his mouth and watched the smoke rise languidly to the ceiling. 'Attrition in the work brigades is always to be expected. Finding a decapitated Western visitor is not.'

Shan looked up, then turned away. He did not want to know. He did not want to ask. He stared into his cup. 'You have confirmed his identity?'

'The sweater was cashmere,' Tan said. 'Nearly two hundred American dollars in his shirt pocket. A business card for an American medical equipment firm. He must have been an unauthorized Western visitor.'

'His skin was dark. Black hair on the body. Could have been Asian, even Chinese.'

'A Chinese of such a rank? He would have been missed. And there was the business card from an American company,' Tan reported victoriously. 'The only Westerners allowed in Lhadrung are those operating our foreign investment project. They are too conspicuous not to be missed. In two more weeks American tour groups will begin to visit. But none yet.' Tan pulled on his cigarette one last time before crushing it out. 'I am pleased to see your interest in the case.'

Shan's eyes drifted past Tan to the slogan. Truth Is What the People Need. It could be read more than one way. 'Case?' he asked.

'There will have to be an inquest. A formal report. I am also responsible for judicial administration in Lhadrung County.'

Shan considered whether the statement was intended as a threat. 'My squad did not make the discovery,' he said tentatively. 'If the prosecutor needs statements he should talk to the guards. They saw as much as we did. All I did was clear a few rocks.' He shifted to the edge of his seat. Could he have been called in error?

'The prosecutor is on a month's leave in Dalian, on the coast.'

'The wheels of justice are accustomed to moving slowly.'

'Not this time. Not with American tourists on the way, and an inspection team from the Ministry of Justice arriving the day before. Their first inspection in five years. An open death file could give the wrong impression.'

A knot began to tie itself in Shan's gut. 'The prosecutor must have assistants.'

'There is no one else.' Tan leaned back, studying Shan. 'But you, Comrade Shan, were once the Inspector General of the Ministry of Economy.'

There had been no mistake. Shan stood and moved to the window. The effort seemed to sap him of strength. He felt his knees shaking. 'A long time ago,' he said at last. 'A different life.'

'You were responsible for compiling the two biggest corruption cases Beijing has ever known. In your time

27

you sent dozens of party officials to hard labour camps. Or worse. Apparently there are some who still revere your name, even those who fear it. Someone in your old ministry said it was obvious why you were in prison, because you were the last honest man in Beijing. Some say you went to the West and you're still there.'

Shan stared out of the window, seeing nothing. His hand was shaking.

'Some say you went, and the Bureau brought you back because you knew too much.'

'I was never a prosecutor,' Shan spoke towards the glass, his voice cracking. 'I collected evidence.'

'We're too far from Beijing to split such fine hairs. I was an engineer,' Tan said to his back. 'I commanded a missile base. Someone decided I was qualified to administer a county.'

'I don't understand,' Shan said hoarsely, leaning against the window, wondering if he could ever find strength again. 'That was another life. I'm not the same man.'

'Your entire career was spent as an investigator. Three years in the camp is not so long.'

'Someone could be brought in.'

'No. That might demonstrate a certain . . .' Tan searched for the words, '. . . lack of self-sufficiency.'

'But my file,' Shan protested. 'I have been proven . . .' His words drifted away. He pressed his hands against the glass. He could break it and jump. If your soul was in perfect balance, Choje said, you would just float away to another world.

'Proven what? A thorn in Zhong's side? I grant you that.' Tan opened the thick file and rifled through the papers. 'I'd also say you have proven yourself shrewd. Methodical. Responsible, in your own way. And a survivor. For men like you, surviving is the supreme skill.'

Shan did not have to ask what Tan meant. He stared

into his callused, bone-hard hands. 'I have been warned against regression,' he protested. 'I am a road labourer. I am supposed to think in new ways. I build for the prosperity of the people.' It was the last refuge of the weak. When in doubt, speak in slogans.

'If none of us had a past, political officers would have no work,' Tan observed. 'Failure to confront the past, that is the real sin. I want you to confront yours. Let the inspector live again. For a short while. I do not know the words the Ministry expects. I do not speak the language. No one here does. I want a file prepared that can be quickly closed. I am without the benefit of the prosecutor's thinking. It is not something I will discuss with him on the phone two thousand miles away. I need the matter framed in terms the Ministry of Justice understands. Terms that will not attract further scrutiny. I wager you still have the Beijing tongue.'

Shan sank into the chair. 'You can't do this.'

'It's not much I'm asking,' Tan said with false warmth. 'Not a full investigation. A report to support the death certificate. Explaining the likely accident that led to such an unfortunate demise. It could be your opportunity for rehabilitation.' Tan gestured toward Zhong's file. 'You could use a friend.'

'Must have been a meteorite,' Shan muttered.

'Excellent! Precisely what I mean. With that kind of thinking we can wrap this up in a day or two. We will think of an appropriate reward. Say, extra rations. Light duties. Assignment to a repair shop, perhaps.'

'I won't,' Shan said in a very still voice. 'I mean, I cannot.'

Amusement lifted Tan's face. 'On what grounds do you refuse, Comrade Prisoner?'

Shan did not reply. On the grounds that I cannot lie for you, he wanted to say. On the grounds that my soul has been worn to a few thin threads by people like you. On

29

the grounds that the last time I tried to find the truth for someone like you I was sent to the gulag for my trouble.

'Perhaps you have been confused by my hospitality. I am a Colonel in the People's Liberation Army. I am a party member of rank 17. This district belongs to me. I am responsible for educating the people, feeding the hungry, constructing civil works, removal of waste, custody of prisoners, supervision of cultural activities, movement of the public buses, storage of communal food. And eradication of pests. Of any variety. Do you understand me?'

'It is impossible.'

Tan slowly drained his tea and shrugged. 'Still, you are not permitted to refuse.'

Chapter Two

Shan sat silently in the cold, dim room they assigned him in the prison administration building at the 404th camp, staring at the telephone. At first he was convinced it wasn't real. He tapped it with a pencil, half expecting it to be made of wood. He pushed it, wondering if the wire would drop off. It was a thing of the past, of another world, like radios and televisions, taxis and flushing lavatories. Artefacts from a life he had left behind.

He stood and paced around the table. It was a storage room without windows, the room where small groups met for struggle sessions, the *tamzing* where antisocialist spasms were diagnosed and treated. Ammonia wafted from cleaning supplies stacked in one corner. A small notepad sat beside the phone, and three pencil stubs pocked with toothmarks. Feng sat in a chair by the door, peeling an apple. His smug face did little to alleviate Shan's suspicion that he had been led into an elaborate trap.

Shan returned to the table and picked up the phone receiver. There was a dialling tone. He dropped it back on its cradle, pressing his hand against it as though to restrain it. For whom was the trap intended? Choje and the monks? Himself? If, after so long, neither Beijing nor Tan would tell him what his crime was, then perhaps they had decided to create one they could better understand. And whom did they expect him to call? Minister Qin? His party functionary wife who had erased their relationship? The son whose face he would not recognize even if he ever saw him again?

He picked the phone up again and dialled five random digits.

'*Wei*,' a woman said impassively, with the ubiquitous, meaningless syllable used by everyone to answer phones. He hung up and stared at the telephone. He unscrewed the mouthpiece and found, as expected, an interceptor microphone, standard Public Security issue. Such devices had also been part of his prior incarnation. It could be active or inactive. It could be for him, or standard issue for all prison phones.

He replaced the mouthpiece and surveyed the room again. Every object seemed to have an added dimension, a heightened reality, as to a dying man. He turned to the pad, marvelling at the clean, bright paper. Such brightness was not a part of the universe he entered three years earlier. The first page held a list of names and numbers, the rest were blank. With a slight tremble he turned the empty pages, pausing over each one as though reading a book. On the last page, in a top corner where it was least likely to be discovered, he made the two bold strokes that comprised the ideogram for his name. It was the first time he had written it since his arrest. He looked at it with an unfamiliar satisfaction. He was still alive.

Below his name he made the ideograms for his father's name then, with a pang of guilt, abruptly closed the pad and looked to see if Feng was watching.

From somewhere came a low moan. It could have been the wind. It could have been someone in the stable. He moved the pad away and discovered a folded sheet of paper under it. It was a printed form with the heading REPORT ON ACCIDENTAL DEATH.

He picked up the phone and dialled the first name on the list. It was the clinic in town, the county hospital.

'*Wei*.'

'Dr Sung,' he read.

'Off duty.' The line went dead.

Suddenly he realized someone was standing in front of

his desk. The man was Tibetan, though unusually tall. He was young, and wore the green uniform of the camp staff.

'I have been assigned to you, to help with your report,' the man said awkwardly, glancing about the room. 'Where's the computer?'

Shan lowered the phone. 'You're a soldier?' There were indeed Tibetans in the People's Liberation Army but seldom were they stationed in Tibet.

'I am not –' the man began with a resentful flash, then caught himself. Shan recognized the reaction. The man did not understand who Shan was, and so could not decide where he belonged in the strata of prison life or the even more complex hierarchy of China's classless society. 'I have just completed two years of re-education,' he reported stiffly. 'Warden Zhong was kind enough to issue me clothing on my release.'

'Re-education for what?' Shan asked.

'My name is Yeshe.'

'But you are still in the camp.'

'Jobs are few. They asked me to stay. I have finished my term,' he said insistently.

Shan began to recognize an undertone, a quiet discipline in the voice. 'You studied in the mountains?' he asked.

The resentment returned. 'I was entrusted by the people with study at the university in Chengdu.'

'I meant a gompa.'

Yeshe did not reply. He walked around the room, stopped at the rear and arranged the chairs in a semicircle, as if a *tamzing* were to be convened.

'Why would you stay?' Shan asked.

'Last year they were sent new computers. No one on the staff was trained for them.'

'Your re-education consisted of operating the prison computers?'

The tall Tibetan frowned. 'My re-education consisted

33

of hauling night soil from the prison latrines to the fields,' he said, awkwardly trying to sound proud of his work, the way he would have been taught by the political officers. 'But they discovered I had computer training. I began to help with office administration as part of my rehabilitation. Looking at accounts. Rendering reports to Beijing's computer formats. On my release, they asked me to stay for a few more weeks.'

'So as a former monk your rehabilitation consists of helping imprison other monks?'

'I'm sorry?'

'It's just that I never cease to be amazed at what can be accomplished in the name of virtue.'

Yeshe winced in confusion.

'Never mind. What kind of reports?'

Yeshe continued pacing, his restless eyes moving from Sergeant Feng at the door back to Shan. 'Last week, reports on inventory of medicines. The week before, trends in the prisoners' consumption of grain per mile of road constructed. Weather conditions. Survival rates. And we've been trying to account for lost military supplies.'

'They didn't tell you why I am here?'

'You are writing a report.'

'The body of a man was found at the Dragon Claws worksite. A file must be prepared for the Ministry.'

Yeshe leaned against the wall. 'Not a prisoner, you mean.'

The question didn't need an answer.

Yeshe suddenly noticed Shan's shirt. He stooped and looked under the table at Shan's battered cardboard and vinyl shoes, then back at Feng.

'They didn't tell you,' Shan said. It was a statement, not a question.

'But you're not Tibetan.'

'You're not Chinese,' Shan shot back.

Yeshe backed away from Shan. 'There was a mistake,'

he whispered, and moved over to Sergeant Feng with his hands outstretched, as though beseeching his mercy. Feng's only answer was to point towards the warden's office. Yeshe retreated with mincing steps and sat in front of Shan. He absently stared at Shan's shoes again then, apparently marshalling his strength, looked up. 'Are you to be accused?' he asked, unable to hide the alarm in his voice.

'In what sense of the word?' Shan marvelled at how reasonable the question sounded.

Yeshe stared at him wide-eyed, as if he had stumbled upon some new form of demon. 'In the sense of a trial for murder.'

Shan looked into his hands and absently picked at one of the thick calluses. 'I don't know. Is that what they told you?' Perhaps that had been the plan all along. The old ones, like Tan and Minister Qin, enjoyed playing with their food before eating.

'They told me nothing,' Yeshe said bitterly.

'The prosecutor is away,' Shan said, struggling to keep his voice calm. 'Colonel Tan needs a report. It is something I used to do.'

'Murder?' Yeshe's voice sounded almost hopeful.

'No. Case files.' Shan pushed the list towards Yeshe. 'I tried the first name. The doctor was not available.'

Yeshe looked back toward Sergeant Feng, then sighed as the sergeant refused to acknowledge his stare. 'This is only for the afternoon,' Yeshe said tentatively.

'I did not ask for you. You said it was your job. You get paid to compile information.' Shan was confused at Yeshe's hesitation. He thought he had understood the reason for his new assistant. If the Bureau was watching, it would not rely simply on one bug in a phone.

'We are warned against collusion with prisoners. I am looking for a better job. Working with a criminal, I don't know. It could be seen as –' he paused.

'Regression?' Shan suggested.

'Exactly,' Yeshe said, with a hint of gratitude.

Shan studied him for a moment, then opened the pad and began writing. *Before this date I have never met the clerical assistant named Yeshe of the Central Prison Office of Lhadrung County. I am acting on the direct orders of Colonel Tan of the Lhadrung County government.* He paused, then added *I am deeply impressed by Yeshe's commitment to socialist reform.* He signed and dated the note, then handed it to the nervous Tibetan, who solemnly read it and folded it for his pocket.

'Only for today,' Yeshe said, as if reassuring himself. 'I just get assignments for a day at a time.'

'No doubt Warden Zhong would not want such a valuable resource to be wasted for more than a few hours.'

Yeshe hesitated, as if confused by Shan's sarcasm, then shrugged and retrieved the list. 'The doctor,' he said, suddenly all business. 'Don't ask for the doctor. Call the office of the director of the clinic. Say Colonel Tan needs the medical report. The director has a fax machine. Tell them to fax it immediately. Not to you. The warden's secretary. The warden left. I will talk to her.'

'He left?'

'Picked up by a driver for the Ministry of Geology.'

Suddenly Shan remembered the unfamiliar red truck he had seen the day the body had been found. 'Why would the Ministry of Geology visit the 404th worksite?' he wondered out loud.

'It's on a mountain,' Yeshe replied stiffly.

'Yes?'

'The Ministry regulates mountains,' Yeshe said distractedly, reviewing the list of names. 'Lieutenant Chang. His desk is down the hall. The army ambulance crew who took custody of the body from the guards. Their records will be at Jade Spring Camp,' he said, referring to the county's only military base, located three miles away on the road to Lhadrung Town.

'I will need an official weather report from two days ago,' Shan said. 'And a list of foreign tour groups cleared for entry into Tibet during the past month. China Travel Service in Lhasa should have it. And tell the sergeant we may be going back to town.'

Five minutes later Yeshe began delivering the reports, still warm from the machine. Shan read them quickly, and began to write. He had nearly finished when a claxon sounded in the corridor, a siren he had heard only once before in all his months at the 404th. It was the signal for rifles to be issued to the prison guards. A chill crept down his spine. Choje had begun his resistance.

Colonel Tan eyed Shan suspiciously as he stood with the report in front of Tan's desk an hour later, then grabbed the papers and read.

The building seemed nearly empty. No, not just empty, Shan considered, but deserted, abandoned, the way small mammals abandon their roosts when a predator at the top of the food chain moves in. The wind rattled the windows. Outside, a crow appeared, mobbed by small birds.

Colonel Tan looked up. 'You've given me the ancillary reports. But the form is incomplete.'

'You have all of the direct investigation facts. And such conclusions as are available. It is all I can do. You will need to make some decisions.'

Tan folded his hands over the pages. 'It has been a very long time since anyone mocked my authority. In fact, I don't recall it happening since I took over the county. Not since I was given the black chop.'

Shan stared at the floor. The black chop was the authority to sign death warrants.

'I had hoped for more, Comrade Prisoner Shan. I expected you would want to do a thorough job. Take time to embrace the opportunity I offered to you.'

'On consideration,' Shan said, 'it seemed that certain things should be said quickly.'

Tan picked up the report and read. 'At 1600 hours on the fifteenth a body was discovered. Five hundred feet above the Dragon Throat Bridge. The unidentified victim was dressed expensively, in cashmere and Western denim. Black body hair. Two surgical scars on his abdomen. No other identifying marks. The victim walked up a dangerous ridge at night and suffered a sudden trauma to the neck. No direct evidence of third party involvement. Since no missing person reports have been filed locally, victim was likely a stranger to the area, possibly of foreign origin. Attachments of the medical report and security officer incident report.'

He turned the page. 'Possible explanations accounting for the trauma. Scenario one. Victim stumbled on rocks in darkness, fell upon razor-edge quartz known to be geologically present in the area. Two. Fell onto tool left by the construction brigade. Three. Unused to high mountain atmosphere, suffered sudden attack of altitude sickness, passed out and incurred injuries as described in one or two.' Tan paused. 'No meteorite? I liked the meteorite. A certain Buddhist flavour. Predestination from another world.'

He folded his hands over the report. 'You have failed to give me conclusions. You have failed to identify the victim. You have failed to give me a report I can sign.'

'Identify the victim?'

'It is awkward to have strangers in the morgue. It could be misinterpreted as carelessness.'

'But that is precisely why the Ministry should not trouble you. You cannot be blamed if his family is negligent.'

'A tentative identification would attract less attention. If not a name. A hat.'

'A hat?'

'A job. A home. At least a reason for being here.

Madame Ko called the American company on the business card. They sell X-ray equipment. Let's say he sold X-ray equipment.'

Shan looked into his hands. 'There can be nothing but speculation.'

'One's man speculation may become another's judgement.'

Shan gazed over the shadows that were beginning to cover the slopes of the Dragon's Claw. 'If I gave to you the perfect scenario,' he said slowly, hating himself more with every word, 'one the Ministry would embrace, would you release me back to my unit?'

'This is not a negotiation.' Colonel Tan considered, then shrugged. 'I had no idea breaking rocks was so addictive. I would be pleased to return you to the warden, Comrade Prisoner.'

'The man was a capitalist from Taiwan.'

'Not an American?'

Shan returned Tan's gaze. 'How do you think the Public Security Bureau will react at the mention of the word *American*?'

Tan raised his brow and nodded, conceding the point.

'Taiwanese. It will explain his money and clothing, even why he could travel without being noticed. Say a former Koumintang soldier who had served here, had sentimental ties. Came to Lhasa with a tour group, broke away on his own and travelled to Lhadrung illegally. The government could not be responsible for the safety of such a person.'

Tan contemplated Shan's words. 'Such things could be verified.'

Shan shook his head. 'Two groups from Taiwan visited Lhasa over the last three weeks. The report from China Travel Service is attached. If you wait three days to check, the groups will all be home. Officially, nothing can be done to verify anything in Taiwan. It is well known by Public Security that such groups are often used for illegal purposes.'

Tan offered one of his knife-edge smiles. 'Perhaps I judged you too hastily.'

'It will be sufficient to complete a file,' Shan explained. 'After the inspection team leaves, your prosecutor will know what to do.' As he spoke, he recalled Tan had another reason to close the matter soon. Before referring to the inspection team, he had mentioned Americans, on their way for a visit.

'What will the prosecutor know to do?'

'Convert it to a murder investigation.'

Tan pursed his lips together as if he had tasted something bitter. 'Only a Taiwanese tourist, after all. We must guard against overreaction.'

Shan looked up and spoke to the photograph of Mao. 'I said it was the perfect scenario. Do not confuse it with the truth.'

'Truth, Comrade?' Tan asked with an air of disbelief.

'In the end, you will still have a killer to find.'

'That will be a matter for the prosecutor and myself to decide.'

'Not necessarily.'

Tan raised an eyebrow in question.

'You can complete a file sufficient to divert the matter for a few weeks. Maybe even send the file without all the signatures. It might sit on a desk for months before someone notices.'

'And why would I be so negligent as to send the file without signatures?'

'Because eventually the accident report will have to be signed by the doctor who performed the autopsy.'

'Dr Sung,' Tan said in a low, sour voice, as though to himself.

'The medical report was rather thorough. The doctor noticed the head was missing.'

'What are you saying?'

'The doctor has other authorities to whom she reports to. They do their own audits. Without the head, I doubt your accident report will be signed by the medical officer. Without the report the Ministry will eventually examine the case and classify it as a murder.'

Tan shrugged. 'Eventually Prosecutor Jao will return.'

'But meanwhile a killer is out there. Your prosecutor should be considering the implications.'

'Implications?'

'Like how this man was killed by someone he knew.'

Tan lit one of his American cigarettes. 'You don't know that.'

'The body was unmarked. No evidence of a struggle. He smoked a cigarette with someone. He walked up the mountain voluntarily. His shoes were clean.'

'His shoes?'

'If he was dragged, they would have been scuffed. If he had been carried, he would not have picked up the fragments of rock that were found on his soles. It's in the autopsy report.'

'So a thief found a rich tourist. Forced him to walk up at gunpoint.'

'No. He wasn't robbed – a thief would not have overlooked two hundred American dollars. And he didn't drive to the South Claw on a whim, or at the request of someone he did not know.'

'Someone he knew,' Tan considered. 'But that would make it local. No one is missing.'

'Or someone who knew someone here. An old feud rekindled by a sudden visitor. A conspiracy unravelled. An opportunity for settling a score presented itself. Have you tried to contact the prosecutor? One of the troubling questions I didn't write down is why the murderer waited until he left town.'

'I told you. I don't want to speak about this on the phone.'

'What if something else is planned for his absence? Before the inspection team arrives.'

He had Tan's attention now. 'I don't know. I don't even know if he's reached Dalian yet.' Tan studied the ember of his cigarette. 'What would you have me ask?'

'Ask him about pending cases. Was he putting pressure on someone?'

'I don't see –'

'Prosecutors look under rocks. Sometimes they stir up a nest of snakes.'

Tan blew a stream of smoke towards the ceiling. 'Did you have a particular breed in mind?'

'Potential informers get killed. Partners in crime lose trust. Ask if he was compiling a corruption case.'

The suggestion stopped Tan. He crushed his cigarette and walked to the window. Staring out the window for a moment, he absently picked up a pair of binoculars and raised them towards the eastern horizon. 'On a clear day when the sun is right, you can see the new bridge at the bottom of the Dragon Throat. You know who built that? We did. My engineers, without any help from Lhasa.'

Shan did not reply.

Tan set down the binoculars and lit another cigarette. 'Why corruption?' he asked, still facing the window. Corruption was always a more important crime than murder. In the days of the dynasties, those who killed sometimes simply paid fines. Those who stole from the emperor always died by a thousand slices.

'The victim was well dressed,' Shan observed. 'Had more cash than most Tibetans earn in a year. Statistics are kept in Beijing. Cross-references between cases. Classified, of course. Murders typically are the result of one of two underlying forces. Passion. Or politics.'

'Politics?'

'Beijing's way of saying corruption. Corruption always involves a struggle for power. Ask your prosecutor when you reach him. He will understand. Meanwhile, ask him

42

to recommend a real investigator, to start the field work now. I can finish the form, but the real investigation needs to start while the evidence is fresh.'

Tan inhaled and held the smoke in his lungs before speaking again. 'I'm beginning to understand you,' he said, letting the smoke drift out. 'You solve problems by creating a bigger one. I wager that has a lot to do with why you are in Tibet.'

Shan did not answer.

'The head rolled off the cliff. We will find it. I'll send squads out tomorrow. We'll find it and I'll persuade Sung to sign the report.'

Shan continued to stare at Tan in silence.

'You're saying if the head isn't found the Ministry will expect me to offer up a killer.'

'Of course,' Shan agreed. 'But that will not be their primary concern. First you must offer up the antisocial act. Your responsibility is detailing the socialist context. Provide a context and the rest will follow.'

'Context?'

'The Ministry will not care about the killer as such. Suspects are always available.' Shan waited for a reaction. Tan did not even blink. 'What they always seek,' he continued, 'is the political explanation. Murder investigation is an art form. The essential cause of violent crime is class struggle.'

'You said passion. And corruption.'

'That was the classified data. Private, for use by investigators. Now I am talking about the socialist dialectic. Prosecution of murder is usually a public phenomenon. You must be ready to explain the basis for prosecution here. There is always a political explanation. That will be the concern. That is the evidence you need.'

'What are you saying?' Tan growled.

Shan spoke to Mao's photograph again. 'Imagine a house in the country,' he said slowly. 'A body is found, stabbed to death. A bloody knife is found in the hands of

43

a man asleep in the kitchen. He is arrested. Where does the investigation start?'

'The weapon. Match it to the wound.'

'No. The closet. Always look for the closet. In the old days you would look for hidden books. Books in English. Western music. Today you look for the opposite. Old boots and threadbare clothes, hidden away with a book of the chairman's sayings. In case of a new resurgence of Party enforcement. Either way it shows reactionary doubts about socialist progress.

'Then you check the Party's central files. Class background. Find out that the suspect previously required re-education or that his grandfather was an oppressor in the merchant class. Maybe his uncle was a Stinking Ninth.' Shan's father had been in the Stinking Ninth, the lowest rank on Mao's list of bad elements. Intellectuals. 'Or maybe the murderer is a model worker. If so, look at the victim,' he continued. He realized with a shudder that he was repeating words he had last spoken to a seminar in Beijing. 'It's the socialist context that's important. Find the reactionary thread and build from there. A murder investigation is pointless unless it can become a parable for the people.'

Tan paced in front of the window. 'But to get this behind us all I really need is a head.'

A chill crept down Shan's spine. 'Not just any head. *The* head.'

Tan laughed without smiling. 'A saboteur. Zhong warned me.' He sat and studied Shan in silence. 'Why do you want so badly to return to the 404th?'

'It is where I belong. There's going to be trouble. Because of the body. Maybe I can help.'

Tan's eyes narrowed. 'What trouble?'

'The *jungpo*,' Shan said very quietly.

'*Jungpo?*'

'It translates as *hungry ghost*. A soul released by a violent action, unprepared for death. Unless death rites can be conducted on the mountain, the ghost will haunt the scene of the death. It will be angry. It will bring bad luck. The devout will not go near the place.'

'What trouble?' Tan repeated sharply.

'The 404th will not work at such a site. It is unholy now. They are praying for the release of the spirit. Prayers for cleansing.'

Anger was building in Tan's eyes. 'No strike was reported.'

'The warden would never tell you so soon. He will try to end it on his own. There will have been stoppages by the crews at the top first. There will have been accidents. Guns have been issued.'

Tan abruptly moved to his door and called for Madame Ko to dial Warden Zhong's office. He took the call in the conference room, watching Shan through the open door.

His eyes were blazing when he returned. 'A man broke a leg. A wagon of supplies fell off the cliff. The brigade refused to move after the noon break.'

'The priests must be permitted to perform the ceremonies.'

'Impossible,' Tan snapped, and strode back to the window. He pulled the binoculars from the sill, futilely looking through the gathering greyness for the worksite on the distant slope. When he turned, the hardness was back in his eyes. 'You have a context now. What did you call it? A reactionary thread.'

'I don't understand.'

'Smells like class struggle to me. Capitalist egoism. Cultists. Acting to relieve their revisionist friends.'

'The 404th?' Shan said, horrified. 'The 404th was not involved.'

'But you have convinced me. Class struggle has once again impeded socialist progress. They are on strike.'

Shan's *heart lurched*. 'Not a strike. It's just a religious matter.'

Tan sneered. 'When prisoners refuse to work, it is a strike. The Public Security Bureau will have to be notified. It's out of my hands.'

Shan stared helplessly. A death in the mountains might be overlooked by the Ministry, but never a strike at a labour camp. Suddenly the stakes were far higher.

'You will compile a new file,' Tan explained. 'Tell me about class struggle. How the 404th caused this death as an excuse to halt their work. Something worthy of an inspector general. The kind that the Ministry will not challenge.' He scrawled something on a sheet of onion-skin paper, then studied Shan for a moment. With a slow, ceremonial motion, he fixed his seal to the paper. 'You are officially on detail to my office. I'll give you a truck, and the warden's Tibetan clerk. Feng will watch. Permission to go to the clinic for interviews. If asked, you are on trusty duties.'

It felt as if someone was rolling a massive rock onto his back. Shan found himself bending, frantically looking towards the Dragon Claws. 'My report would be worthless,' he murmured, the words nearly choking in his throat. He had rushed his work to return to the 404th, to help Choje. Now Tan wanted to use him to inflict greater punishment on the monks. 'I have been proven untrustworthy.'

'The report will be in my name.'

Shan stared at a dim, vaguely familar ghost, his reflection in the window. It was happening. He was being reincarnated into a lower life form. 'Then one of our names will be dishonoured,' he said in a croaking whisper.

Chapter Three

The drab three-storey building that housed the People's Health Collective proved far more sterile outside than inside. The odour of mildew wafted through the lobby. On the lobby wall, a collage of bulldozers and tractors mounted by beaming proletarians was cracked and peeling. The same bone-dry dust that filled the 404th barracks covered the furniture. Brown and green stains ran across the faded linoleum floor and up one wall. Nothing moved but a large beetle that scuttled towards the shadows as they entered.

Madame Ko had called. A short, nervous man in a threadbare smock appeared and silently led Shan, Yeshe and Feng down a dimly lit flight of stairs to a basement chamber with five metal examination tables. As he opened the swinging doors, the stench of ammonia and formaldehyde broke over them like a wave. The aroma of death.

Yeshe's hands shot to his mouth. Sergeant Feng cursed and fumbled for a cigarette. More of the dark stains Shan had seen upstairs mottled the walls. He followed one with his eyes, a spatter of brown spots that arced from floor to ceiling. On one wall was a poster, tattered from repeated folding that announced a performance, years earlier, of the Beijing Opera. Their escort gestured towards the only occupied table with a mixture of disgust and fear, then backed out of the room and closed the door.

Yeshe turned to follow the orderly.

'Going somewhere?' Shan enquired.

'I'm going to be sick,' Yeshe pleaded.

'We have an assignment. You won't get it done waiting in the hall.'

Yeshe looked at his feet.

'Where do you want to go?' Shan asked.

'Go?'

'Afterwards? You're young. You're ambitious. You have a destination. Everyone your age has a destination.'

'Sichuan province,' Yeshe said, distrust in his eyes. 'Back to Chengdu. Warden Zhong told me he has my papers ready. Says he's arranged for me to have a job there. People can rent their own apartments now. You can even buy televisions.'

Shan considered the announcement. 'When did the warden say this?'

'Just last night. I still have friends back in Chengdu. Members of the Party.'

'Fine.' Shan shrugged. 'You have a destination and I have a destination. The sooner we get done, the sooner we can move on.'

Resentment still etched on his face, Yeshe found a wall switch and illuminated a row of naked lightbulbs hanging over the tables. The centre table seemed to glow, its white sheet the only clean, bright object in the room. Sergeant Feng muttered a low curse towards the far side of the room. A body was slumped in a rusty wheelchair, covered with a soiled sheet, its head slung over the shoulder at an unnatural angle.

'They just leave you like that,' Feng growled in contempt. 'Give me an army hospital. At least they lay you out in your uniform.'

Shan looked back at the arc of bloodstains. This was supposed to be the morgue. Corpses had no blood pressure. They did not spray blood.

Suddenly the body in the chair groaned. Revived by the light, it swung its arms stiffly to pull down the sheet, then produced a pair of thick, horn-rimmed glasses.

Feng gasped and retreated towards the door.

It was a woman, Shan realized, and it wasn't a sheet that covered her but a vastly oversized smock. From its folds she produced a clipboard.

'We sent the report,' she declared in a shrill, impatient tone, and stood. 'No one understood why you needed to come.' Bags of fatigue shadowed her eyes. In one hand she held a pencil like a spear. 'Some people like to look at the dead. Is that it? You like to gawk at the corpses?'

A man's life, Choje taught his monks, did not move in a linear progression, with each day an equal chit on the calendar of existence. Rather it moved from defining moment to defining moment, marked by the decisions that roiled the soul. Here was such a moment, Shan thought. He could play Tan's hound, starting here and now, trying somehow to save the 404th or he could turn around, as Choje would want, ignoring Tan, being true to all that passed as virtue in his world. He clenched his jaw and turned to the diminutive woman.

'We will need to speak to the doctor who performed the autopsy,' Shan said. 'Dr Sung.'

Inexplicably, the woman laughed. From another fold of her smock she pulled a *kiajiou*, one of the surgical masks used by much of the population of China to ward off dust and viruses in the winter months. 'Other people. Other people just like to cause trouble.' She tied the mask over her mouth and gestured towards a box of *kiajiou* on the nearest table. As she walked, a stethoscope appeared in the folds of the smock.

There was still a way, a narrow opening he might wedge through. He would have to get the accident report signed. An accident caused by the 404th would answer Tan's needs without the agony of a murder investigation. Sign the report, then find a way to conduct death rites for the lost soul. To answer the political dilemma, the 404th could be disciplined for negligent behaviour. A month on cold rations, perhaps a mass reduction of every prisoner.

It was summer; even the old ones could survive a reduction. It was not a perfect solution, but it was one within his reach.

By the time the three men fastened their masks, she had stripped the sheet from the body and pulled a clipboard from the table.

'Death occurred fifteen to twenty hours before discovery, meaning the evening before,' she recited. 'Cause of death: traumatic simultaneous severance of the carotid artery, jugular vein, and spinal cord. Between the atlas and the occipital.' She studied the three men as she spoke, then seemed to dismiss Yeshe. He was obviously Tibetan. She paused over Shan's threadbare clothes and settled on addressing Sergeant Feng.

'I thought he was decapitated,' Yeshe said hesitantly, glancing at Shan.

'That's what I said,' the woman snapped.

'You can't be more specific about the time?' Shan asked.

'Rigor mortis was still present,' she said, again to Feng. 'I can guarantee you the night before. Beyond that . . .' She shrugged. 'The air is so dry. And cold. The body was covered. Too many variables. To be more precise would require a battery of tests.'

She saw the expression on Shan's face and threw him a sour look. 'This isn't exactly Beijing University, Comrade.'

Shan studied the poster again. 'At Bei Da you would have had a chromatograph,' he said, using the colloquial expression for Beijing University, the reference most commonly used in Beijing itself.

She turned slowly. 'You are from the capital?' A new tone had entered her voice, one of tentative respect. In their country, power came in many shapes. One could not be too careful. Maybe this would be easier than he'd thought. Let the investigator live just a few moments, long enough to make her understand the importance of the accident report.

'I had the honour of teaching a course with a professor of forensic medicine at Bei Da,' he said. 'Just a two-week seminar, really. Investigation Technique in the Socialist Order.'

'Your skills have served you well.' She seemed unable to resist sarcasm.

'Someone said my technique involved too much investigation, not enough of the socialist order.' He said it with an edge of remorse, the way he had been trained to do in *tamzing* sessions.

'Here you are,' she observed.

'Here you are,' he shot back.

She smiled, as though he were a great wit. When she did so the bags under her eyes disappeared for a moment. He realized that she was slender beneath the huge gown. Without the bags, and without her hair tied so severely behind her, Dr Sung could have passed for a stylish member of any Beijing hospital staff.

Silently she made a complete circuit of the table, studying Sergeant Feng, then Shan again. She approached Shan slowly, then suddenly grabbed his arm, as if he might bolt away. He did not resist as she rolled up his sleeve and studied the tattooed number on his forearm.

'A trusty?' she asked. 'We have a trusty who cleans the toilets. And one to wipe up the blood. Never had one sent to interrogate me.' She paced about him with intense curiosity, as though contemplating dissection of the strange organism before her.

Sergeant Feng broke the spell with a sharp, guttural call. It was not a word, but a warning. Yeshe was attempting to ease the door open again. He stopped, confused but obsequious, and retreated to the corner, where he squatted against the wall.

Shan read the report hanging at the end of the table.

'Dr Sung.' He pronounced her name slowly. 'Did you perform any tissue analysis?'

The woman looked to Feng as though for help, but the sergeant was inching away from the corpse. She shrugged. 'Late middle-aged. Twenty-five pounds overweight. Lungs beginning to clog with tar. A deteriorated liver, but he probably didn't know it yet. Trace of alcohol in his blood. Ate less than two hours before death. Rice. Cabbage. Meat. Good meat, not mutton. Maybe lamb. Even beef.'

Cigarettes, alcohol, beef. The diet of the privileged. The diet, he comforted himself, of a tourist.

Feng found a bulletin board, where he pretended to read a schedule of political meetings.

Shan moved slowly around the table, forcing himself to study the truncated shell of the man who had stopped the work of the 404th and forced the Colonel to exhume Shan from the gulag, whose unhappy spirit now haunted the Dragon Claws. With his pencil he pushed back the lifeless fingers of the left hand. It was empty. He moved on, paused and studied the hand again. There was a narrow line at the base of the forefinger. He pushed it with the eraser. It was an incision.

Dr Sung donned rubber gloves and studied the hand with a small pocket lamp. There was a second cut, she announced, in the palm just below the thumb.

'Your custodial report said nothing about removing an object from the hand.' It had been something small, no more than two inches in diameter, with sharp edges.

'Because we didn't.' She bent over the incision. 'Whatever was there was wrenched free after death. No bleeding. No clotting. Happened afterwards.' She felt the fingers one by one and looked up with a blush of embarrassment. 'Two of the phalanges are broken. Something squeezed the hand with great force. The death grip was broken open.'

'To get at what it held.'

52

'Presumably.'

Shan considered the woman. In Chinese bureaucracies, there was a grey line between humanitarian service to the struggling colonies and outright exile. 'But can you be so sure of the cause? Perhaps he died in a fall and later, for unrelated reasons, his head was removed.'

'Unrelated reasons? The heart was still pumping when the head was severed. Otherwise there would have been much more blood in the body.'

Shan sighed. 'With what then? An axe?'

'Something heavy. And razor-sharp.'

'A rock, possibly?'

Dr Sung responded with a peevish frown and yawned. 'Sure. A rock as sharp as a scalpel. It wasn't a single blow. But no more than three, I'd say.'

'Was he conscious?'

'At the time of death he was unconscious.'

'Surely you cannot know, without the head.'

'His clothes,' Dr Sung said. 'There was almost no blood on his clothes. Which means no broken nails. No skin or hair under the nails. No scratches. There was no struggle. His body was laid out so the blood would drain away from it. Face up. We extracted soil and mineral particles from the back of his sweater. Only the back.'

'But it's just a theory, that he was unconscious.'

'And your theory, Comrade? That he died by falling on a rock and someone who collected heads happened along?'

'This is Tibet. There is an entire social class dedicated to cutting up bodies for disposal. Perhaps a *ragyapa* happened along and began the rite for sky burial, then was interrupted.'

'By what?'

'I don't know. The birds.'

'They don't fly at night,' she grumbled. 'And I've never seen a vulture big enough to carry a skull away.' She pulled a paper from the clipboard. 'You must be the fool

53

who sent me this,' she said. It was the accident report form, ready for her signature.

'The colonel would feel better if you just signed it.'

'I don't work for the colonel.'

'I told him that.'

'And?'

'It's a subtle point for a man like the colonel.'

Sung threw him one last glare, nearly a snarl, then silently ripped the form in half. 'How's this for subtle?' She tossed the pieces on the naked corpse and marched out of the room.

Jilin the murderer was obviously invigorated by his new status as the leading worker of the 404th. He loomed like a giant at the front of the column, slamming his sledgehammer into the boulders, pausing occasionally to turn with a gloating expression towards the knots of Tibetan prisoners seated on the slope below. Shan studied the others, a dozen Chinese and Moslem Uyghurs not usually seen on the road crews. Zhong had sent the kitchen staff to the South Claw.

Shan found Choje, sitting lotus fashion, his eyes closed, in the centre of a ring of monks near the top. Their idea was to protect him when the guards eventually moved in. It only meant that the guards would be all the more furious when they eventually reached him.

But the guards sat around the trucks, smoking and drinking tea brewed over an open wood fire. They were not watching the prisoners. They were watching the road from the valley.

Jilin's jubilance faded when he saw Shan. 'They say you're a trusty now,' he said bitterly, punctuating the sentence with a slam of the hammer.

'Just a few days. I'll be back.'

'You're missing everything. Triple rations if you work. Damned locusts gonna get their wings broken. Stable gonna be full. We'll be heroes.' Locusts. It was a label of contempt for the Tibetan natives. For the droning sound of their mantras.

Shan studied the four small cairns that had been raised to mark where the body had been found. He slowly walked around the site, sketching it in his notebook.

Sung was right. The killer had done his work here. This was the butchering ground. He had killed the man, and thrown the contents of his pockets over the cliff. But why had he missed the shirt pocket, under the sweater, which held the American money? Because, Shan mused, his hands had been so bloody and the white shirt so clean.

'Why come this far from town and not throw the body over the cliff? It would never have been found.' The query came from behind. Yeshe had followed Shan up the slope. It was the first time Yeshe had shown any interest in their assignment.

'It was supposed to be found.' Shan knelt and pushed away the remaining rocks from the rust-coloured stain.

'Then why cover it with rocks?'

Shan turned and studied Yeshe, then the monks who had begun to watch him nervously. *Jungpos* only came out at night. But by day the hungry ghosts hid in small crevasses or under rocks.

'Maybe because then the guards would have seen it from a distance.'

'But the guards did find it,' Yeshe argued.

'No. Prisoners found it first. Tibetans.'

Shan left Yeshe staring uneasily at the cairns and walked over to Jilin. 'I need you to put me over the edge.'

Jilin lowered his hammer. 'You're one crazy shit.'

Shan repeated the request. 'Just a few seconds. Over there,' he pointed. 'Hold my ankles.'

Jilin slowly followed Shan to the edge, then smirked. 'Five hundred feet. Lots of time to think before you hit. Then you're just a melon fired from a cannon.'

'A few seconds, then you pull me back.'

'Why?'

'Because of the gold.'

'Like hell,' Jilin spat. But then, with a suspicious gleam he leaned over the edge. 'Shit,' he said as he looked up in surprise. 'Shit,' he repeated, then quickly sobered. 'I don't need you.'

'Sure you do. You can't reach it from the top. Who do you trust to lower you?'

A spark of understanding kindled on Jilin's face. 'Why trust me?'

'Because I'm going to give you the gold. I'm going to look at it, then I'll give it to you.' Jilin could only be relied upon for his greed.

A moment later Shan was upside down, suspended by his ankles over the abyss. His pencil fell out of his pocket and plunged end over end through the void. He closed his eyes as Jilin laughed and bobbed him up and down like a child's marionette. But when he opened them the lighter was directly in front of him.

Seconds later he was back on top. The lighter was Western-made but engraved with the Chinese ideogram for long life. Shan had seen such lighters before; they were often tokens distributed at party meetings. He breathed on it, letting his breath fog the surface. No fingerprints.

'Give it to me,' Jilin growled. He was watching the guards.

Shan closed his hand around it. 'Sure. For a trade.'

Jilin's eyes went wild. He raised his fist. 'I'll break you in half.'

'You took something from the body. Pulled it out of the hand. I want it.'

Jilin seemed to be considering whether he would have time to grab the lighter while he pushed Shan off the edge.

Shan stepped out of his reach. 'I don't think it was valuable,' Shan said. 'But this –' he lit the flame. 'Look.

Wind-resistant.' He extended it, increasing the risk the guards would see it.

Instantly Jilin reached into his pocket and produced a small tarnished metal disc. He dropped it into Shan's palm and grabbed the lighter. Shan held onto it. 'One more thing. A question.'

Jilin snarled and looked back down the slope. As much as he might wish to crush Shan, the first sign of struggle would bring the guards.

'Your professional perspective.'

'Professional?'

'As a murderer.'

Jilin swelled with pride. His life, too, had its defining moments. He eased his grip.

'Why here?' Shan asked. 'Why go so far from town but leave the body so conspicuous?'

An unsettling longing appeared in Jilin's eyes. 'The audience.'

'Audience?'

'Someone told me once about a tree falling down in the mountains. It don't make a sound if no one's there to hear. A killing with no one to appreciate it, what's the point? A good murder, that requires an audience.'

'Most murderers I've known act in private.'

'Not witnesses, but those who discover it. Without an audience there can be no forgiveness.'

It was true, Shan realized. The body had been discovered by the prisoners because that was what the murderer intended. He paused, looking into Jilin's wild eyes, then released the lighter and looked at the disc. It was convex, two inches in width. Small slots at the top and bottom indicated that it had been designed to slide onto a strap for ornamentation. Tibetan script, in an old style that was unintelligible to Shan, ran along the edge. In the centre was the stylized image of a horse head. It had fangs.

As Shan approached Choje, the protecting circle parted. He was uncertain whether to wait until the lama finished his meditation. But the moment Shan sat beside him, Choje's eyes opened.

'They have procedures for strikes, Rinpoche,' Shan said quietly. 'From Beijing. It's written in a book. Strikers will be given the opportunity to repent and accept punishment. If not, they will try to starve everyone. They make examples of the leaders. After one week a strike by a *lao gai* prisoner may be declared a capital offence. If they feel generous, they could simply add ten years to every sentence.'

'Beijing will do what it must do,' came the expected reply. 'And we will do what we must do.'

Shan quietly studied the men. Their eyes held not fear, but pride. He swept his hand towards the guards below. 'You know what the guards are waiting for.' It was a statement, not a question. 'They are probably already on the way. This close to the border, it won't take long.'

Choje shrugged. 'People like that, they are always waiting for something.' Some of the monks closest to them laughed softly.

Shan sighed. 'The man who died had this in his hand.' He dropped the medallion in Choje's hand. 'I think he pulled it from his murderer.'

As Choje's eyes locked on the disc, they flashed with recognition, then hardened. He traced the writing with his finger, nodded, and passed it around the circle. There were several sharp cries of excitement. As the men passed it on, their eyes followed the disc with looks of wonder.

There had been no real struggle between the murderer and his victim, Shan knew. Dr Sung had been right on that point. But there had been a moment, perhaps just an instant of realization when the victim had seen, then touched the demon, had reached out and grabbed the disc as he was being knocked unconscious.

'Words have been spoken about him,' Choje said.

'From the high ranges. I wasn't sure. Some said he had given up on us.'

'I don't understand.'

'They were among us often in the old days.' The lama's eyes stayed on the disc. 'When the dark years came they went deep inside the mountains. But people said they would come back one day.'

Choje looked back to Shan. 'Tamdin. The medallion is from Tamdin. The Horse-Headed, they call him. One of the spirit protectors.' Choje paused and recited several beads then looked up with an expression of wonder. 'This man without a head. He was taken by one of our guardian demons.'

As the words left Choje's mouth, Yeshe appeared at the edge of the circle. He studied the monks awkwardly, as though embarrassed or even fearful. He seemed unwilling, or unable, to cross into the circle. 'They found something,' he called out, strangely breathless. 'The colonel is waiting at the crossroads.'

The first road built by the 404th had been the one that ringed the valley, connecting the old trails that dropped out of the mountains between the high ridges. The road the two vehicles now followed up the Dragon Claws had been one of those trails, and was still so rough a path that it became a streambed during the spring thaws. Twenty minutes after leaving the valley, Tan's car led them onto a dirt track that had been recently scoured by a bulldozer. They emerged onto a small, sheltered plateau. Shan studied the high, windblown bowl through the window. At its bottom was a small spring, with a solitary giant cedar. The plateau was closed to the north. It opened to the south, overlooking fifty miles of rugged ranges. To a Tibetan it would have been a place of power, the kind of place a demon might inhabit.

A long shed with an oversized chimney came into view as Feng eased the truck to a stop. It had been built recently, of plywood sheets torn from some other structure. The sections of wood displayed remnants of painted ideograms from their prior incarnation, giving the shed the appearance of a puzzle forced together from mismatched pieces. Several four-wheel-drive vehicles were parked behind it. Beside them half a dozen PLA officers snapped to attention as Tan emerged from his car.

The colonel conferred briefly with the officers and gestured for Shan to join him as they walked behind the shed. Yeshe and Feng climbed out and began to follow. An officer looked up in alarm and ordered them back into the truck.

Twenty feet behind the shed was the entrance to a cave, riddled with fresh chisel marks. It had been recently widened. Several officers filed towards the cave. Tan barked an order and they halted, yielding to two grim-faced soldiers with electric lanterns who stepped forward at Tan's command. The others stood and watched, whispering nervously as Shan followed Tan and the two soldiers into the cave.

The first hundred feet was a cramped, tortuous tunnel, strewn with the litter of mountain predators, which had been kicked to the sides to make way for the barrows whose wheel tracks ran down the centre. Then the shaft opened into a much larger chamber. Tan stopped so abruptly Shan nearly collided with him.

Centuries earlier, the walls had been plastered and covered with murals of huge creatures. Something clenched Shan's heart as he stared at the images. It wasn't the sense of violation because Tan and his hounds were there. Shan's entire life had been a series of such violations. It wasn't the fearsome image of the demons which, in the trembling lights held by the soldiers, seemed to dance before their eyes. Such fears were nothing compared to those Shan had been taught at the 404th.

No. It was the way the ancient paintings awed Shan,

and shamed him, made him ache to be with Choje. They were so important, and he was so small. They were so beautiful, and he was so ugly. They were so perfectly Tibetan, and he was so perfectly nobody.

They moved closer, until fifty feet of the wall was awash in the soldiers lights. As the deep, rich colours became apparent, Shan began to recognize the images. In the centre, nearly life-size, were four seated Buddhas. There was the yellow-bodied Jewel Born Buddha, his left palm open in the gesture of giving. Then the red-bodied Buddha of Boundless Light, seated on a throne decorated with peacocks of extraordinary detail. Beside them, holding a sword and with his right hand raised, palm outward in the *mudra* of dispelling fear, was the Green Buddha. Finally there was a blue figure, the Unshakeable Buddha, Choje called him, sitting on a throne painted with elephants, his right hand pointed down in the earth-touching *mudra*. It was a *mudra* Choje often taught to new prisoners, calling for the earth to witness their faith.

Flanking the Buddhas were figures less familiar to Shan. They had the bodies of warriors, wielded bows and axes and swords, and stood over the bones of humans. To the left, closest to Shan, was a cobalt blue figure with the head of a fierce bull. Around his neck was a garland of snakes. Beside him was a brilliant white warrior with the head of a tiger. Around them were the much smaller figures of an army of skeletons.

Suddenly Shan understood. They were the protectors of the faith. As he moved forward he saw that the feet of the tiger demon were discoloured. No, not discolored. Someone had crudely attempted to chisel out a piece of the mural and failed. A small pile of coloured plaster lay on the ground below the figure.

His light began to fade. The soldiers were moving down the wall to the far side of the huge chamber. Two more demons came into focus, a green-bodied one with a huge belly and a monkey's head, holding a bow and waving a bone, then finally a red beast with four fangs set in a furious expression and, on an appendage above its golden hair, the small green head of a savage horse. A tiger skin was draped over one shoulder. The beast stood in blazing flames surrounded by bones. Shan's hand clamped around the disc in his pocket, the ornament torn from the murderer. He resisted the temptation to pull the disc from his pocket. He was certain the images of the fanged horse matched.

The lights shifted away from the wall and focused on Colonel Tan's boots, giving him the eerie, larger-than-life appearance of yet another demon. 'Things have changed,' he announced suddenly.

Shan studied the grim faces of their escort. His heart lurched again. He knew what men like Tan did in such places. Deep in the mountain nothing would be heard outside. Not a scream. Not a gunshot. Nothing could be heard, and nothing would be found afterwards. Jilin was wrong. Not all murders were done for forgiveness.

Tan handed Shan a piece of folded paper. It was his copy of Shan's accident report. 'We won't be using this,' he said.

His hand trembling, Shan accepted it.

Tan followed the soldiers towards a side tunnel. Before he entered it he turned and impatiently gestured for Shan to join them. Shan looked back. There was nowhere to run. Another twenty soldiers waited outside. He looked again at the painted images, empty with despair. Wishing he knew how to pray to demons, he slowly followed.

There was a vague odour in the tunnel. Not incense, but the dust that remains when the scent of incense has long settled. Ten feet into the passage, past a small pair of demon protectors painted on either wall like sentinels, shelves appeared. They had been constructed of stout timber decades, maybe centuries, earlier, over a foot wide, four shelves on each wall connected to vertical risers with pegs. For the first thirty feet along the passage they were empty. After that they were packed full, from floor to ceiling, their glittering contents extending beyond the reach of the lamps.

A deep chill wracked Shan's gut. 'No!' he cried, in pain.

Tan, too, halted suddenly, as though physically struck. 'I had read the report of the discovery weeks ago,' he said in a near whisper. 'But I never imagined it like this.'

They were skulls. Hundreds of skulls. Skulls as far they could see. Each sat in a tiny altar created by a semicircle of religious ornaments and butter lamps. Each skull was plated with gold.

Tan touched one of the skulls with a tentative fingertip, then lifted it. 'A team of geologists found the cave. At first they thought they were sculptures, until they turned one over.' He flipped the skull and rapped the inside surface with a knuckle. 'Just bone.'

'Don't you understand what this place is?' Shan asked, aghast.

'Of course. A gold mine.'

'Sacred ground,' Shan protested. He put his hands around the skull in the colonel's hands. 'The holiest of artefacts.' Tan relented, and Shan returned the skull to its shelf. 'Some monasteries preserved the skulls of their most revered lamas. The living Buddhas. This is their shrine. More than a shrine. It has great power. It must have been used for centuries.'

'An inventory was taken,' Colonel Tan reported. 'For the cultural archives.'

Suddenly, with horrible clarity, Shan understood. 'The chimney.' The word came out in a dry croak.

'In the fifties,' Tan declared, 'an entire steel mill in Tientsin was funded with gold salvaged from Tibetan temples. It was a great service to the people. A plaque was erected thanking the Tibetan minorities.'

'It's a tomb you're –'

'Resources,' Tan interrupted, 'are in tight supply. Even

63

the bone fragments have been classified a by-product. A fertilizer plant in Chengdu has agreed to buy them.'

They stood in silence. Shan fought the urge to kneel and recite a prayer.

'We're going to initiate it,' Tan declared. 'Officially. The murder investigation.'

Shan suddenly remembered. He looked at the report in his hand, his heart racing. Tan had a real investigator. He wanted to eliminate traces of his false start.

'The investigation will be in my name. You're not just a trusty now,' Tan said slowly, distracted by something ahead. 'In fact, no one is to know. You will be my –' he searched for a word '– my case handler. My operative.'

Shan took a step back, confused. Had Tan actually brought him to the cave simply to taunt him? 'I can rewrite the report. I spoke to Dr Sung. But the 404th is the problem. I can be better used there.'

Tan held up his hand pre-emptively. 'I have thought about it. You already have a truck. I can trust my old comrade Sergeant Feng to watch you. You can even keep your tamed Tibetan. An empty barracks at Jade Spring is being readied where you will sleep and work.'

'You are giving me freedom of movement?'

Tan continued to survey the skulls. 'You will not flee.' When he turned to Shan there was a savage flash in his eyes. 'Do you know why you will not flee? I have had the benefit of Warden Zhong's advice.' He turned to Shan with a sour, impatient countenance. 'There is still snow in the highest passes. Soft snow, melting fast. Threat of avalanche. If you run, or if you fail to produce my report on time, I will assign a squad from the 404th. Your squad. No rotation. On the cliffs above the roads, testing for collapse. The 404th has some of the old lamas arrested in '65. Some of the originals. I will order Zhong to start with them.'

Shan stared at him in horror. Nothing about Tan made

sense except his compulsion for terror. 'You misunderstand them,' he said in a near whisper. 'My first day at the 404th, a monk was brought in from the stable. For making an illegal rosary. Two ribs cracked. Three fingers had been broken. You could still see the lines in his flesh where the pliers had gripped his knuckles. But he was serene. He never complained. I asked why he felt no rage. Do you know what he said? "To be persecuted for travelling the correct path, to be able to prove your faith," he said, "is an event of fulfilment for the true believer."'

'It is you who misunderstand,' Tan snapped. 'I know these people as well as you. We will never physically force them into submission. Otherwise my prisons would not be so full. No. You will do it, but not because they fear death,' Tan said with bone-chilling assurance. 'You will do it because you fear being responsible for their deaths.'

Tan stepped another twenty feet down the tunnel to where the lanterns had stopped. The two guides wore wild, frightened expressions. One of them was shaking. As Shan stepped beside him, Tan grabbed the soldier's lamp and held it up to the third shelf. There, between two of the golden skulls, sat another head, a much more recent arrival. It still held its thick black hair and flesh and lower jaw. Its brown eyes were open. It seemed to be looking at them with a tired sneer.

'Comrade Shan,' announced Tan, 'meet Jao Xengding. The Prosecutor of Lhadrung County.'

Chapter Four

The high-altitude sunlight exploded against his retinas as Shan left the cave. Stumbling forward, his hand covering his eyes, he heard rather than saw the argument. Someone was shouting at Tan with the unrestrained anger that could issue from a Westerner. As he moved towards the sound Shan's vision cleared and he froze.

Tan had been ambushed. He had his back to a corner formed by the shed and one of the trucks. Like every other man in the compound, Tan seemed utterly paralysed by the creature that had attacked him.

It was not just that his assailant was female, or even that she was speaking in English, but that she had porcelain skin, auburn hair, and stood taller than any of the Chinese in front of her. Tan looked up to the sky as though searching for the unlucky whirlwind that must have deposited her.

Shan, still numb from the discovery in the cave, took a step closer. The woman was wearing heavy hiking boots and American blue jeans. A small, expensive Japanese camera hung around her neck.

'I have a right to be furious,' she shouted. 'Where's the Religious Bureau? Where's your permit?'

Shan moved around the shed. A white four-wheel-drive truck was parked beside Tan's Red Flag limousine. He moved to the far side of the truck, where he was out of the colonel's sight but where he could still hear the woman plainly. He relished her words. In his Beijing incarnation he had read a Western newspaper once a week to maintain the language skills taught him in secret by his father. But it had been three years since he had heard or read an English word.

'The Commission was not notified!' she continued. 'There is no Religious Bureau posting! I'm calling Wen Li! I'm calling Lhasa!' Her eyes flashed in anger. Even from twenty feet away Shan saw they were green.

Shan moved around the white truck. It was an American Jeep. At the wheel was a nervous looking Tibetan wearing wire-rimmed spectacles. On the driver's door was a symbol, a drawing of crossed American and Chinese flags, flanked top and bottom by the words *Mine of the Sun*, in Chinese and English.

'Ai yi, she's beautiful when she's angry,' someone said over his shoulder. The words were spoken in perfect Mandarin but their rhythm was not Chinese.

Shan slipped to the side to get a look at the man. He was a lean, tall Westerner with long, straw-coloured hair tied in a short tail at the nape of his neck. He wore gold wire-rimmed spectacles and a blue nylon down vest with an emblem that matched that on the truck. Throwing an amused sidelong glance at Shan, he turned back towards the woman, pulling an odd rectangular object from his pocket and raising it to his mouth. It was a mouth organ, Shan suddenly realized, as the American began to play a song.

He played quite well, but loudly. Deliberately loudly, Shan realized. Many traditional American songs were popular in China, and Shan recognized his tune instantly. 'Home on the Range.'

Several of the soldiers laughed. The American woman cast a peeved glance at her companion. But Tan was not amused. As the woman raised her camera and aimed it at the cave, Tan snapped from his spell. He muttered a command and one of his men leapt forward to cover the lens with his hand. The American with the mouth organ kept playing, but his eyes hardened. He took several steps towards the woman, as though she might need his protection. Shan watched as two of Tan's officers quietly adjusted their position, so they remained between the American and the cave.

'Miss Fowler,' Tan said in Mandarin, back in control, 'defence installations of the People's Liberation Army are strictly classified. You have no right to be here. I could order your detainment.' It was the most credible of bluffs. Tibet housed more of China's nuclear arsenal than any other region of the country.

The woman stared silently, defiance still in her eyes. The American man lowered the mouth organ and replied in English, though he had obviously understood Tan. 'Great,' he said, extending his wrists, 'arrest us. That will guarantee the attention of the United Nations.'

Colonel Tan threw a petulant glance at the American man, bent to the ear of one of his aides, then offered a hollow smile to the woman. 'This is no way for friends to behave. It's Rebecca, isn't it? Please, Rebecca, understand the problem you are creating for yourself and your company.'

Someone grabbed Shan by the arm and pulled him towards the truck where Yeshe and Feng still sat. 'Colonel Tan says you must go. Now,' the soldier said.

Shan let himself be led to the truck, but at the door pulled away to stare once more at the strange woman. She gave him a fleeting glance, then turned again and locked gazes with him as she realized perhaps that Shan was the only Chinese there without a uniform. Her green eyes had a wild, restless intelligence. A question appeared on her face. Before he could tell if it was directed towards him, he was pushed into the truck.

A file was already on his desk at the prison administration office. It had been delivered personally by Madame Ko, and was captioned 'Known Hooligans/Lhadrung County.' It was an old file, dog-eared from use, and was separated into four categories. *Drug cultists* was the first.

It was a quaint notion, abandoned by the police in China's large cities years earlier, that drug use was driven by fanatic rituals. *Youth gangs.* The fifteen individuals listed were all over thirty years of age. *Criminal recidivists.* The list had everyone in Lhadrung who had previously served time in a *lao gai* prison, nearly three hundred names. *Cultural agitators.* It was by far the longest list. For every name either a gompa or the label 'unregistered' was listed. They were all monks. Many had been detained during the Thumb Riots five years earlier. A dozen of the unregistered monks had an added notation. Suspected *purba.* He puzzled over the label. A *purba* was a ceremonial dagger used in Tibetan rituals. He scanned to the end. No list for homicidal protector demons.

He picked up the phone. Madame Ko answered on the third ring. 'Tell the colonel there will need to be more autopsy work. He'll need to tell Dr Sung at the clinic about it.'

'Wish I had known,' she sighed. 'I just got back from there.'

'You went to the clinic?'

'He had me make a delivery. I just walked over there. All wrapped up in newspaper and plastic bags. Said he wanted her cabbage to stay fresh.'

Shan stared at the receiver. 'Thank you, Madame Ko,' he mumbled.

'You're welcome, Xiao Shan,' she said brightly, and hung up.

Xiao Shan. The words brought a sudden loneliness. He had not heard them for years. It was what his grandmother called him, the old-style form of address for a younger person. Little Shan.

He found himself staring out into the central office at a worker sharpening pencils. He had forgotten about sharpening pencils and the thousand other tiny acts that made up a day on the outside. He clenched his jaw, fighting back the question that no prisoner in the gulag dared ask: Was he capable of ever having a life on the outside again? Not *would* he be released, for every prisoner had to believe he would someday be released, but who would he be when he was released? Everyone knew stories of former prisoners who never adjusted, who were too scared to leave their beds, or who stayed bent forever as if chained, like the horse which, once hobbled, never tries to run again. Why were there never stories of prisoners who succeeded after release? Perhaps because it was so hard to understand what success was for a survivor of the gulag. Shan remembered Choje's last words to Lokesh, after thirty years of sharing a prison hut. 'You must teach yourself to be you again,' Choje had said, as Lokesh cried on his shoulder.

He opened his notepad. They were still there, on the last page. His father's name. His name. Without thinking he drew another character, a complex figure, beginning with a cross with small slashes in each quarter pointing to the centre. Thrashed rice, these first lines meant. They connected to the pictograph of a living plant over an alchemist's stove. Together they meant *life force*. It had been one of his father's favourite ideograms. He had drawn it in the dust of the window the day they came to take away his books. Choje had taught him its counterpart in Tibetan characters. But Choje always referred to it differently: the Indomitable Power of Being.

There was a movement in front of the desk. He slammed the notebook shut, his hands reflexively covering it. It was only Feng, standing as Lieutenant Chang approached.

Chang pointed at Shan and laughed, then leaned towards Feng and spoke in a low voice. Shan stared past them out into the office, watching the monochromatic figures move through their paces.

Opening the pad again, he remembered Passage Twenty-one of the Tao Te Ching and wrote it at the end of his investigation notes. *At the centre is the life force*, it said. *At the centre of the life force is truth.*

He propped the pad upright in front of him, open to the verse, and studied it. Every case has its own life force, he had once told his own deputies, its essence, its ultimate motive. Find that life force and find the truth. At the centre there was a murdered prosecutor. Shan tilted his head and stared intensely at the verse. Or perhaps at the centre was the 404th and a Buddhist demon.

He became aware of a small noise in front of him. 'What are you doing?' Yeshe asked with a self-conscious glance back at Sergeant Feng. 'I've been standing here for five minutes.' He was holding a plate with three large *momo* dumplings. Beyond him, the office outside was empty. It was dark.

The *momos* were the only food Shan had seen all day. He waited until Feng turned his back and stuffed two into his pocket, then gulped down the third. It was rich, with real meat inside, prepared by the guards' kitchen. In the prisoner's mess the *momos* were stuffed with coarse grain, with a heavy portion of barley chaff always mixed in. His first winter, after drought had shrivelled the fields, the *momos* had been filled with the ground corncobs used to feed pigs. Over a dozen monks had died of dysentery and malnutrition. The Tibetans had a word for such deaths by starvation, which had taken thousands in the days when almost the entire monastic population of Tibet had been imprisoned. Killed by the *momo* gun. After the drought the Tibetan Friends Association, a Buddhist charity, had won the right to provide meals twice a week to the prisoners. Warden Zhong had announced it as a gesture of conciliation, and done so so cheerfully that Shan was confident that the warden was pocketing the money that would have otherwise fed the prisoners.

'I have compiled notes of our interview with Dr Sung,' Yeshe said stiffly, and pushed two pages of typed text across the desk.

'That's all you have been doing?'

Yeshe shrugged. 'They're still working on the supply records.'

'The lost supplies you mentioned?'

Yeshe nodded.

Shan considered the notes and looked up absently. 'What kind of lost supplies?'

'A truck of clothing. Another of food. Some construction materials. Probably just some bad paperwork. Somebody counted too many trucks when they left the depot in Lhasa.'

Shan paused to make a note in his book.

'But it's nothing to do with this,' Yeshe protested.

'Do you know that?' Shan asked. 'Most of my career in Beijing I spent on corruption cases. When it involved the army, I always went to the central supply accounts first, because they were so reliable. When they counted trucks, or missiles, or beans, they didn't do it with one man. They assigned ten, each counting the same thing.'

Yeshe shrugged. 'Now they use computers. I came for my next assignment.'

Shan considered Yeshe. He wasn't much older than his own son, and like his son was so smart, and so wasted. 'We need to reconstruct Jao's activities. At least the last few hours.'

'You mean talk to his family?'

'Didn't have any. What I mean is, we need to visit the Mongolian restaurant in town where he had dinner that night. His house. His office, if they let us.'

Yeshe had his own notepad now. He feverishly took notes as Shan spoke, then spun about like a soldier on drill and departed.

Shan worked another hour, studying the lists of names, writing questions and possible answers in his pad, each seeming more elusive than the last. Where was Jao's car? Who wanted the prosecutor dead? Why, he considered with a shudder, did Choje seem so perfectly assured that the demon existed? How is it that the prosecutor of Lhadrung County had appeared to be a tourist? Because he was preparing to travel? No. Because he had American dollars in his pocket, and an American business card. What kind of rage did this killer possess, to carefully lure his victim so far just to decapitate him? Not an instantaneous animal rage. Or was it? Could it have been a meeting turned sour, escalating to a fight? Jao was knocked unconscious and in a panic his assailant picked up – what, a shovel? – to finish the job and destroy Jao's identity in a single grisly act. But then to carry the head five miles to the skull shrine? Wearing a costume? That was not animal rage. That was a zealot, someone who burned with a cause. But what cause? Political? Or was it passion? Or had it been an act of homage, to lay Prosecutor Jao in such a holy place? An act of rage. An act of homage. Shan threw his pencil down in frustration and moved to the door. 'I have to go back. To my hut,' he told Sergeant Feng.

'Like hell,' Feng shot back.

'So you and I, Sergeant, we are going to spend the night here?'

'No one said anything. We don't go to Jade Spring until tomorrow.'

'No one said anything because I am a prisoner who sleeps in his hut and you are a guard who sleeps in his barracks.'

Feng shifted uneasily from foot to foot. His round face seemed to squeeze together as he gazed towards the row of windows on the far wall, as though hoping to catch an officer walking by.

'I can sleep here, on the floor,' Shan said. 'But you. Are you going to stay awake all night? That's what you would need orders for. Without orders the routine must stand.'

Shan produced one of the *momos* he had saved and extended it to Feng.

'You can't bribe me with food,' the sergeant grunted, eyeing the *momo* with obvious interest.

'Not a bribe. We're a team. I want you in a good mood tomorrow. And well nourished. We're going for a ride in the mountains.'

Feng accepted the dumpling and began to consume it in small, tentative nibbles.

Outside, the compound was gripped in a deathly silence. The crisp, chill air was still. The forlorn cry of a solitary nighthawk came from overhead.

They stopped at the gate, Feng still uncertain. From the rock face came the echo of a tiny ringing, a distant clinking of metal on metal. They listened for a moment and heard another sound, a low metallic rumbling. Feng recognized it first. He pushed Shan through the gate, locked it, and began running towards the barracks. The next stage of the 404th's punishment was about to begin.

Shan offered the remaining *momo* to Choje.

The lama smiled. 'You are working harder than the rest of us. You need your food.'

'I have no appetite.'

'Twenty rosaries for lying,' Choje said good-naturedly and laid the *momo* on the floor, between the altar marks. The *khampa* sprang forward, knelt and touched his head to the floor. Choje seemed surprised. He nodded, and the *khampa* stuffed the dumpling into his mouth. He rose and bowed to Choje, then squatted by the door. The catlike *khampa* was the new watcher.

Suddenly Shan realized the other prisoners were not doing their rosaries. They were bent over their bunks, writing on the backs of tally sheets or in the margins of the rare newspapers that were sometimes brought by the Friends Association. A few wrote with the stubs of pencils. Most used pieces of charcoal.

'Rinpoche,' Shan said. 'They have arrived. By morning they will have taken over from the guards.'

Choje nodded slowly. 'These men – I am sorry, what is the word I hear for the Public Security troops?'

'Knobs.'

Choje smiled with amusement. 'These knobs,' Choje continued, 'they are not our problem. They are the problem of the warden.'

'They have identified the dead man,' Shan announced. Several of the priests looked up. He looked around as he spoke. 'His name was Jao Xengding.'

A sudden, silent chill fell over the hut.

Choje's hands made a *mudra*. It was an invocation of the Buddha of compassion. 'I fear for his soul.'

From the shadows a voice called out. 'Let him stay in hell.'

Choje looked up in censure, then turned back with a sigh. 'He will have a difficult passage.'

Trinle suddenly spoke. 'He will be in struggle for his deeds. And for the violence of his death. He could not have been prepared properly.'

'He sent many to prison,' Shan observed.

Trinle turned to Shan. 'We have to get him off the mountain.'

Shan opened his mouth to correct his friend, then realized he was not speaking of Jao's body.

'We will pray for him,' Choje said. 'Until his soul has passed we must pray.'

Until his soul has passed, Shan reflected, he will continue to punish the 404th.

A monk brought one of the tally sheets for Choje to examine. He studied it, then spoke in low tones to the man, who took the scrap back to his bunk and began working on it again.

Choje looked at Shan. 'What is it they are doing to you?' He spoke very quietly, so no one heard but Shan.

In that moment Shan saw Choje as in their first meeting; Shan kneeling in mud, Choje striding across the compound, oblivious to the guards, as serenely as if he were strolling across a meadow to retrieve an injured bird.

Shan had been in fragments when his jailers first released him into the 404th compound, shattered physically and mentally from three months of interrogation and twenty-four-hour political therapy. Public Security had intercepted him at the end of his last investigation, just as he was about to dispatch a very special report to the State Council instead of his official superior, the Minister of Economy. At first they had simply beaten him, until a Public Security doctor had expressed concern about brain damage. Then they used bamboo splints, but that had built such an inferno of pain he could not hear their questions. So they had progressed to subtler means, eventually shifting from hardware to chemicals, which were far worse because they made it so difficult to remember what he had already told them.

He had sat in his cell in Moslem China – once in a room with a window he had seen the endless expanse of desert that could only mean western China – and recited the Taoist verses of his youth to keep his mind alive. They had constantly reminded Shan of his crimes, sometimes reading like professors from blackboards in *tamzing*, or shouting from statements of witnesses he had never heard of. Treason. Corruption. Theft of state property, in the form of files he had borrowed. He had smiled dreamily, for they had never understood the nature of his guilt. He had been guilty of forgetting that certain anointed members of the government were incapable of crime. He had been guilty of mistrusting the Party, because he had refused to reveal all his evidence – not only to protect those who had given it to him but also, and this shamed him, to protect himself, for his life would be worthless once they thought they had everything. In the end, the only lesson of those months of endless, shredding pain, the one resolute truth Shan had learned about himself, and the great handicap that kept the pain alive, was that he was incapable of giving up.

Perhaps that was what Choje had seen that first hour when Shan had stumbled from a Public Security van into the compound, dazed, wondering if they had decided to risk shooting him after all.

The prisoners had at first seemed just as dazed, staring at him as if he were some dangerous new species. Then they seemed to decide he was just another Chinese. The *khampas* spat on him. The others mostly shunned him, some making a *mudra* of cleansing as though to spurn the new devil in their midst.

Shan had stood unsteadily in the centre of the compound, knees shaking, considering what sort of hell his handlers had found for him, when one of the guards shoved him. He had fallen into a cold puddle face first, and splattered mud on the guard's boots. As Shan struggled to his knees, the furious guard had ordered Shan to lick his boots clean.

'Without a people's army the people have nothing,' Shan had said with a doleful smile. A direct quote from the Inestimable Chairman, from the little red book itself.

The guard had knocked Shan back into the mud and was slamming Shan's shoulders with his baton when one of the older Tibetan prisoners walked towards them. 'This man is too weak,' the prisoner had said quietly. When the guard laughed the prisoner had bent over Shan's prostrate body and taken the blows on his own back. The guard administered the punishment intended for Shan with great relish, then called for help to drag the unconscious man to the stable.

The moment had changed everything. In one blinding instant Shan forgot his pain, even forgot his past for a moment as he realized he had entered a remarkable new world, and that world was Tibet. A tall monk who introduced himself as Trinle helped Shan to his feet and led him into the hut. There had been no more spitting, no more angry *mudras* cast against him. Only eight days later, when the stable released him, did Shan meet Choje. 'The soup,' Choje had said with a crooked smile on seeing Shan, referring to the 404th's thin barley gruel, 'always tastes better after a week away.'

Shan looked up as he heard Choje's question again.

'What is it they are doing to you?'

He knew Choje did not expect an answer. It was simply the question he wanted to leave with Shan. The 404th would never be the same after the knobs took over. With a sudden aching in his heart, he realized Choje would probably be taken from them. He stared at a new *mudra* formed by the lama's hands. It was the sign of the mandala, the circle of life.

'Rinpoche. This demon called Tamdin —'

'It is a wonderful thing, is it not?'

'Wonderful?'

'That the guardian would appear now.'

Shan wrinkled his brow in confusion.

'Nothing that happens in life is random,' Choje explained.

True, Shan thought bitterly. Jao was killed for a reason. The killer wanted to be perceived as a Buddhist demon, for a reason. The knobs were there, prepared to destroy the 404th, for a reason. But Shan understood none of it. 'Rinpoche, how would I recognize Tamdin if I find him?'

'He has many shapes, many sizes,' Choje replied. 'Hayagriva, they call him in Nepal and the south. In the older gompas they call him the Red Tiger Devil. Or the horse-head demon. He wears a rosary of skulls around his neck. He has yellow hair. His skin is red. His head is huge. Four fangs come from his mouth. On top is another head, much smaller, a horse's head, sometimes painted green. He is fat with the weight of the world. His belly hangs down. I have seen him in the festival dances many years ago.' The *mudra* collapsed as Choje clasped his hands together. 'But Tamdin will not be found unless he desires it. He will not be controlled unless he is empowered.'

Shan considered the words in silence. 'He carries weapons?'

'If he needs it, it will be in his hand,' Choje said engimatically. 'Speak to one of the Black Hat sect. There was once an old Black Hat *ngagspa* in the town. A sorcerer. Khorda, he was called. Practised the old rites. Frightened the young monks with his spells. From a Nyingmapa gompa.'

The Black Hats comprised the most traditional of the Tibetan Buddhist sects, of which the Nyingmapa was the oldest, the one most closely linked to the shamans who once ruled Tibet.

'He could no longer be alive. When I was a boy he was already old. But he had apprentices. Ask who does Black Hat charms, who studied with Khorda.'

Choje stared deeply at Shan, the way a father might contemplate a son departing on a long and dangerous journey. He gestured with his fingers. 'Come closer.'

As Shan moved within his reach Choje placed a hand on the back of Shan's head and pushed it down. He whispered to Trinle, who handed him a pair of rusty scissors, then snipped a lock of Shan's inch-long hair from just above his neck. It was what they did in initiation rites, for students being admitted to monasteries, to remind them of how Buddha had sacrificed to attain virtue.

The action, inexplicably, made Shan's heart race. 'I am not worthy,' Shan said as he looked up.

'Of course you are. You are part of us.'

A deep sadness welled up within him. 'What is happening, Rinpoche?'

But Choje only sighed, suddenly looking very tired. The old priest rose and moved to his bunk. As he did so,

Trinle handed Shan a stained piece of paper on which an ideogram had been inscribed. 'This is for you.'

Shan futilely studied the paper. The characters were in the old style, like those on the medallion. Drawn on it was a series of concentric circles, encompassing a central lotus flower, each petal of which bore secret symbols. 'Is it a prayer?'

'Yes. No. Not exactly. A charm. A protector. Blessed by Rinpoche. Written on a fragment of an old holy book. Very powerful.' He grasped the lower corners. 'Here,' Trinle explained, 'you must fold it and roll it into a small roll. Wear it around your neck. We should find an amulet for it, on a chain. But there are none.'

'Everyone is writing protection charms?'

'Not like this. Not so powerful. There was only this one fragment. And the invocation of the symbols. These are not words made by the hands or the lips. They are never spoken. Rinpoche had to reach up and capture them. It takes several hours to empower it. He worked all day. It has exhausted him. It is one that will be recognized by Tamdin, one that can be detected from this demon's world, so he knows you are coming. It is not simply protection. It is more like an introduction, so you can commune with him. Choje says you are walking the path of protector demons.'

Meaning they are about to attack me, Shan was tempted to ask, when another question occurred to him. How had Choje obtained a fragment of an ancient manuscript?

Some monks placed their charms on the altar, looking expectantly towards Choje. Others carried theirs to a bunk at the rear. Shan stepped towards it. One of the old monks sat in the bed with a strange patchwork of charms. He was joining the tally sheets into a larger charm, deftly tying them together with tiny braids of human hair.

Shan realized Trinle was staring at the thick pad of

paper in his pocket. He ripped off a dozen blank pages and handed them to Trinle, with his pencil.

'The others. What are the other charms?'

'Each of us does what he can. Some are trying to prepare Bardo rites for the *jungpo*. Others are just protection charms. I do not know if Rinpoche will bless them. Without the blessing from one of power, they will be useless.'

'He will not bless the protection charms? He does not want them protected from the *jungpo*?'

'Not the *jungpo*. These are for the evils of this world. *Tsonsung* charms. For protection from batons. From bayonets. From bullets.'

Chapter Five

A sleek young man in a white shirt and a blue suit was waiting outside Tan's office the next morning. Pacing in front of the window, he paused to examine Sergeant Feng scornfully, then noticed Shan and threw him a knowing nod, as if they shared some secret.

Shan moved to the window, desperate to discern activity on the slopes of the South Claw. The stranger mistook his movement for an invitation to converse.

'Three out of five,' the man said. 'Sixty percent request to go home before their tour is up. Did you know that, Comrade?' He had Beijing written all over him.

'Most of those I know serve their full terms,' Shan said quietly. He leaned forward, touching the glass. The 404th should be on the slope by now. Would the warden even bother to take them out today?

'They can't take the cold,' the man continued, giving no evidence that he had heard Shan. 'Can't take the air. Can't take the drought. Can't take the dust. Can't take the stares on the street. Can't take the two-legged locusts.'

The stranger sprang to Madame Ko's side as she moved through the waiting room. 'There is nothing more important!' he insisted, speaking slowly and loudly as if she were somehow incapacitated. 'I must see him now!' She smiled coolly at him and pointed to the chairs along the wall.

But the man continued pacing, repeatedly glancing back at Tan's door. 'I've been here two years. Love it. Could do ten. How about you?'

Shan looked up, slowly, hoping the man was not speaking to him. But his eyes were like two gun barrels, aimed directly at Shan. 'Three so far.'

'A man of my own heart!' the stranger exclaimed. 'I love it here,' he repeated. 'The challenges of a lifetime. Opportunity at every crossroad,' he said, looking at Shan for confirmation.

'At least surprise. Surprise at every crossroads,' Shan offered judiciously.

The man replied with a short, restrained laugh and settled into the seat beside Shan. Shan covered his file with his hands.

'Haven't seen you before. Assigned to a unit in the mountains?'

'In the mountains,' Shan grunted. The outer office was not heated, and he had not removed the anonymous grey coat Feng had found for him that morning in the back of the truck.

'Old man's got his bowl too full,' the man confided, with a nod towards Tan's door. 'Reports for the Party. Reports for the army. Reports for Public Security. Reports on the status of reports. We don't let bureaucracy interfere like that. No way to get things done.'

Feng's head lurched backward. He began to snore.

'We?' Shan enquired.

With a theatrical air the man opened a small vinyl case and handed Shan an an embossed card.

Shan studied the card. It was made of paper-thin plastic. Li Aidang, it said. The name had been a favourite of ambitious parents a generation earlier. Li Who Loves the Party. Shan's gaze drifted to the title and froze. Assistant Prosecutor. Tan had done it, he thought, he had summoned an investigator from outside. Then he read the address on the card. Lhadrung County.

He rubbed his fingers over the words in disbelief. 'You are very young for such a responsibility,' Shan said at last, and studied Li. The assistant prosecutor could not have been much past thirty. He wore an expensive backdoor watch and, oddly, some kind of Western sporting shoes. 'And a long way from home.'

'Don't miss Beijing. Too many people. Not enough opportunity.'

There was that word again. It was odd to hear an assistant prosecutor speak of opportunity.

Madame Ko reappeared.

'Obviously he doesn't understand –' Li began in a patronizing tone. 'It's about the arrest. He needs to sign authorizations. He will want to inform the –'

Madame Ko moved out of the room without acknowledging Li. As Li stared after her a sneer grew on his face, as though he had made some mental note of particular delight. He leaned forward and studied Feng's slumped figure. 'If this were my office, they'd show some respect,' he began, his voice thick with contempt. Then Madame Ko emerged, opened the door to the adjoining conference room, and nodded for Li to enter.

Li gave a tiny snort of triumph and strode into the room. Madame Ko silently pulled out a chair for him at the table, then left him staring at the side door that opened into Tan's office, closing the door behind her as she re-entered the waiting room.

'I wonder,' Shan said, 'if the colonel is planning to go in there.' He wasn't sure she had heard as she moved into an alcove, but she answered with an amused nod as she returned with two cups of tea. She handed Shan one and sat beside him.

'He is a rude young man. There're so many like that today. Not raised well.'

Shan almost laughed. It was how his father would have described the generations of Chinese raised since the middle of the century. Not raised well. 'I wouldn't want him to be angry with you.'

Madame Ko gestured for him to drink his tea. She had

the air of an elderly aunt readying a boy for school. 'I've worked for Colonel Tan for nineteen years.'

Shan grinned awkwardly. His eyes wandered to the lace doily on the table. It had been a long time, much longer than just his three years imprisonment, since he had drunk tea with a proper lady. 'At first I wondered who it was who had the courage to give the petition about the release of Lokesh to the Colonel,' Shan said. 'I think I know now. You would have liked him. He sang beautiful songs from old Tibet.'

'I am old-fashioned. Where I came from we were taught to honour the elderly, not imprison them.'

What distant planet was that, Shan almost asked, then saw the way she was looking into her cup and realized that she needed to say something.

'I have a brother,' she abruptly confessed. 'Not much older than you. A teacher. He was arrested fifteen years ago for writing bad things and sent to a camp near Mongolia. No one talks about him, but I think about him a lot.' She looked up with an innocent, curious expression. 'You don't suffer, do you? I mean, in the camps. I wouldn't want him to suffer.'

Shan took a long swallow of tea and looked up with a forced smile. 'We just build roads.'

Madame Ko nodded solemnly.

In the next moment a buzzer sounded and Madame Ko pointed toward the colonel's door. Li burst out of the conference room, staring uncertainly at Shan. As Madame Ko herded Shan into the colonel's office, he heard Li exclaim, 'You're him!' in disbelief, just as she closed the door.

Tan was at his window, his back to Shan. The curtains were fully opened now, and in the brilliant light Shan could see the details of the back wall for the first time. There was a faded photograph of a girl with a much younger Tan beside a battle tank. To its left hung a map with the words *nei lou*, classified, printed boldly across the top. It was of the Tibetan border zones. Over the map an ancient sword was hung, a *zhan dao*, the stout, two-handed blade favoured by executioners of earlier centuries.

'Our man was picked up this morning,' Tan announced without turning.

About the arrest, Li had said.

'In the mountains, where they usually hide. We got lucky. Fool still had Jao's wallet.' Tan moved to his desk. 'Public Security has an active file on him.' He shot an impatient glance at Shan. 'Sit down, dammit. We have work to do.'

'The assistant prosecutor is already here. I assume I will be turning over my work to him.'

Tan looked up. 'Li? You met Li Aidang?'

'You never said there was an assistant prosecutor.'

'It wasn't important. Li isn't capable, just a pup. Jao did all the work in the office. Li reads books. Goes to meetings. Political officer.' Tan pushed forward a folder bearing the red stripes of the Public Security Bureau. 'The killer was a cultural hooligan since his youth. 1989 riots in Lhasa. You know about the '89 Insurrection?'

Officially, the riot that had started when monks occupied the Jokhang Temple in Lhasa had not occurred. Officially, no one knew how many monks had died when the knobs opened fire with machine guns. In a country that practised sky burial, it was easy to lose evidence of the dead.

'Several years later there was an incident here,' Tan continued. 'In the marketplace.'

'I have heard. Some priests had been mutilated. The local people call them the Thumb Riots.'

Tan ignored him. Was it true, Shan wondered, that Tan indeed had been the one to order the amputation of thumbs?

'He was there. Most of them got three years hard labour. He got six years, as one of the five organizers of the disturbance. Jao prosecuted him. The Lhadrung Five, the people called them.' Tan shook his head in disgust. 'They keep proving my point – that we were too easy on them the first time. And now, to lose Jao to one of them –' His eyes smouldered.

'I could make a list of the witnesses the tribunal will expect,' Shan said woodenly. 'Dr Sung of the clinic. The soldiers who found the head. They will want a spokesman from the 404th guards, to talk about discovering the body.'

'They?'

'The team from the prosecutor's office.'

'To hell with Li! I told you.'

'You can't stop him. He works for the Ministry of Justice.'

'I told you. He's political. Just doing his rotation to build up chits back home. No experience with serious crime.'

Shan caught Tan's eye to be certain he had heard correctly. Did Tan consider that there was part of the Ministry of Justice that was not political? It was no coincidence the Chief Justice of their country's supreme court was also the chief disciplinarian of the Party. 'He works for the Ministry of Justice,' he said again, slowly.

'I'll say he's too close. Like investigating the murder of his father. Judgement blinded by grief.'

'Colonel, at first we had the death of a stranger which might have been covered up by an accident report. Maybe no one would have noticed. Then we had a strike at the 404th because of the death. A lot more people will notice. Now, you not only have a crime against a Public Security official, but also the arrest of a recognized public enemy. Everyone will notice. There will be intense political observation.'

'I don't believe you, Shan. The politics don't scare you. You hold politics in contempt. That's why you're in Tibet.'

He expected to find amusement on Tan's face. But it wasn't there. His expression was one of curiosity. 'You want to withdraw because of your conscience, am I right?' Tan continued. 'Do you believe our inquiries will be less than honest?'

Shan pressed his hands together until the knuckles were white. He had lost again. 'There used to be struggle sessions, in my department in Beijing. I was criticized for failing to understand the imperative of establishing truth by consensus.'

Tan stared at him in silence, broken at last by a sharp guttural laugh. 'And they sent you to Tibet. This Minister Qin. He has some sense of humour.' Tan's amusement faded as he studied Shan's face. He rose and moved back to the window. 'You are wrong, Comrade,' he said to the window, 'to think men like me have no conscience. Do not hold me responsible for your failure to understand my conscience.'

'I couldn't have said it better.'

Tan turned with a look of confusion that quickly soured. 'Don't twist my words, dammit!' he spat, and marched back to his desk. He folded his hands over the Public Security file. 'I will say it only once more. This investigation will not be the responsibility of young pups in the prosecutor's office. Jao was a hero of the revolution. He was my friend. Some things are too important to delegate. You will proceed as we discussed. It will be my signature on the file. We will not have this discussion again.'

Shan followed Tan's gaze to the door. It wasn't simply that Tan didn't trust the assistant prosecutor, Shan suddenly realized. He was frightened of Li.

'You cannot avoid the assistant prosecutor,' Shan observed. 'There will be questions about Jao that will have to be answered by his office. About his enemies. His cases. His personal life. His residence will need to be searched. His travel records. His car. There must have been a car. Find the car and you may find where Jao met his murderer.'

'I knew him for years. I myself may have some answers. Miss Lihua, his secretary, is a friend. She will also help. For others you will prepare written questions which I will submit. We will dictate some to Madame Ko before you go.'

Tan wanted to keep Li busy. Or distracted.

The colonel pushed the Bureau's file towards Shan. 'Sungpo is his name. Forty years old. Arrested at a small gompa called Saskya, in the far north of the county. Without a licence. Damned negligent, to let them return to their home gompas.'

'You intend to try him for murder and then for practising as a monk without a permit?' Shan could not help himself. 'It might seem –' he searched for a word. 'Overzealous.'

Tan frowned. 'There must be others at the gompa who could be squeezed. Going rate for wearing a robe without a licence is two years. Jao used to do it all the time. If you need to, pick them up, threaten to send them to *lao gai* if they don't talk.'

Shan stared at him.

'All right,' Tan conceded with a cold smile. 'Tell them *I* will send them to *lao gai*.'

'You have not explained how he was identified.'

'An informant. Anonymous. Called Jao's office.'

'You mean Li made the arrest?'

'A Public Security team.'

'Then he has his own investigation underway?'

As if on cue there was a hammering on the door. A high-pitched protest erupted, and Madame Ko appeared. 'Comrade Li,' she announced, her face flushed. 'He has become insistent.'

'Tell him to report back later today. Make an appointment.'

A tiny smile betrayed Madame Ko's approval. 'There's someone else,' she added. 'From the American mine.'

Tan sighed and pointed to a chair in the corner shadows. Shan obediently sat down. 'Show him in.'

Li's protests increased in volume as a figure flew through the door. It was the red-haired American woman Shan had seen at the cave.

'There's really nothing else to say about the cave, Miss Fowler,' Tan said with a chill. 'That business is concluded.'

'I asked to reach Prosecutor Jao,' Fowler said hesitantly as she surveyed the office. 'They told me to come here. I thought perhaps he had returned.'

'You are not here about the cave?'

'You and I have said what we could. I will file a complaint with the Religious Bureau.'

'That could be embarrassing,' Colonel Tan retorted.

'You have reason to be embarrassed.'

'I meant for you. You have no evidence. No grounds for a complaint. We will have to state that you encroached on a military operation.'

'She asked to see Prosecutor Jao,' Shan interjected.

Tan shot Shan a cold glare as Fowler walked to the window only a few feet from Shan. She wore blue jeans again, and the same hiking boots. Sunglasses hung on a black cord around her neck, over a blue nylon vest identical to the one Shan had seen on the American man at the cave. She wore no make-up and no jewellery except for tiny golden studs in her ears. What was the other name Colonel Tan had used? Rebecca. Rebecca Fowler. The American woman glanced at Shan, and he saw recognition in her eyes. You were there too, her eyes accused him, disturbing a holy place.

'I'm sorry. I didn't come to argue,' she said to Tan in a new, conciliatory tone. 'I have a problem at the mine.'

'If there were no problems,' Tan observed unsympathetically, 'they wouldn't need you to manage the mine.'

Her jaw clenched. Shan could see she was struggling not to argue with Tan. She chose to speak towards the sky. 'A labour problem.'

'Then the Ministry of Geology is the responsible office. Perhaps Director Hu –' Tan suggested.

'It's not that kind of problem.' She turned and faced Tan. 'I would just like to speak with Jao. I know he's supposed to be away. A phone number would do.'

'Why Jao?' Tan asked.

'He helps. When I have a problem I can't understand, Jao helps.'

'What sort of problem can't you understand?'

Fowler sighed and moved back to sit at Tan's desk. 'My pilot production has begun. Commercial production is scheduled for next month. But first my pilot batches have to be analysed and qualified by our lab in Hong Kong.'

'I still don't –'

'Now the shipping arrangements have been accelerated without consulting me. Airport freight schedules have been changed without notice. Increased security. Increased red tape. Because of tourists.'

'The season has started early. Tourism is becoming Tibet's strongest source of foreign exchange. Quotas have been increased.'

'Lhadrung was closed to tourists when I took this job.'

'That's right,' Colonel Tan acknowledged. 'A new initiative. Surely you will be glad to see some fellow Americans, Miss Fowler.'

The sullen cast of Rebecca Fowler's face said otherwise. Was the mine manager merely disinterested in tourists, or actually unhappy about the prospect of visiting Americans, Shan wondered.

'Don't patronize me. It's all about foreign exchange. If you would only let us, we will produce foreign exchange as well.'

Tan lit a cigarette and smiled without warmth. 'Miss

Fowler, Lhadrung County's first visit of tourists from your country must go perfectly. But still I don't –'

'To get my containers out on time I need double shifts. And I can't even put together half a shift. My workers won't venture to the back ponds. Some won't leave the main compound.'

'A strike? I recall that you were warned about using only minority workers. They are unpredictable.'

'Not a strike. No. They are good workers. The best. But they're scared.'

'Scared?'

Rebecca Fowler ran her fingers through her hair. She looked like she had not slept in days. 'I don't know how to say this. They say our blasting woke up a demon. They say he is angry. People are scared of the mountains.'

'These are superstitious people, Miss Fowler,' Tan offered. 'The Religious Affairs Bureau has counsellors experienced with the minorities. Cultural mediators. Director Wen could send some.'

'I don't need counsellors. I need someone to operate my machinery. You have an engineering unit. Let me borrow them for two weeks.'

Tan bristled. 'You are speaking of the People's Liberation Army, Miss Fowler. Not some wage labourers you can pull off the street.'

'I am speaking of the only foreign investment in Lhadrung. The largest in eastern Tibet. I am speaking of American tourists who are scheduled to visit a model investment project in ten days. They are going to see a disaster unless we do something.'

'Your demon,' Shan said suddenly. 'When did he appear?'

'I don't have time to –' Fowler began sharply, then quieted. 'Does it matter?'

'A similar sighting was made on the South Claw. In connection with a murder.'

Tan stiffened.

Fowler did not immediately respond. She studied Shan as though just becoming aware of his presence. Her green eyes suddenly had a penetrating, hawklike quality.

'I was not aware of a murder investigation. My friend Prosecutor Jao will be interested.'

'Prosecutor Jao was quite interested,' Shan offered, ignoring Tan's glare.

'So he's been informed?'

'Shan!' Tan rose and slammed a button at the edge of his desk.

'Prosecutor Jao was the victim.'

A curse exploded from Tan's lips. He shouted for Madame Ko.

Rebecca Fowler sank back in her chair, stunned. 'No!' The colour drained from her face. 'Dammit, no. You're kidding,' she said, her voice breaking. 'No. He's away. On the coast, in Dalian, he said.'

'Two nights ago, on the South Claw,' – Shan watched her eyes as he spoke – 'Prosecutor Jao was murdered.'

'Two nights ago Jao and I had dinner,' Fowler whispered.

In that instant Madame Ko appeared. 'I think,' suggested Shan, 'we need some tea.'

Madame Ko nodded solemnly and moved back out of the door.

Fowler seemed to try to speak, then slumped forward, dropping her head into her hands until Madame Ko reappeared with a tray. The hot tea revived her sufficiently to find her voice. 'We worked together on the investment applications,' she began. 'Immigration clearances. All the approvals.' The words came out in a taut, nervous whisper. 'He was interested in our success. He said he would buy me dinner if we brought in production before June. We made it. At least, we thought so. He called up last week. In a celebratory mood. Wanted to do the dinner before his annual leave.'

'Where?' asked Shan.

'The Mongolian restaurant.'

'What time?'

'Early. About five.'

'Was he alone?'

'Just the two of us. His driver was in the car.'

'His driver?'

'Balti, the little *khampa*,' Fowler confirmed. 'Always hovering around Jao. Jao treated him like a favourite nephew.'

Shan studied Colonel Tan. Was it possible that Tan had actually forgotten such a vital point, had forgotten a possible witness?

'Where was he going after dinner?' Shan asked.

'The airport.'

'Is that what he said? Did you see him leave?'

'No. But he was going to the airport. He showed me his ticket. It was a late-night flight, but it can take two hours to the airport and it was not a flight he would risk missing. He was very excited about leaving.'

'Then why would he drive in the opposite direction?'

Rebecca Fowler did not seem to have heard. She appeared to be possessed by a new thought. 'The demon,' she said, her face suddenly gaunt. 'The demon was on the Dragon Claws.'

There was a hurried knock and Madame Ko appeared again, in front of the bespectacled Tibetan Shan had seen at the cave driving the Americans' truck. He was short and dark, with small eyes and heavy features that somehow distinguished him from most Tibetans Shan had known.

'Mr Kincaid,' the Tibetan blurted, extending an envelope. He saw Tan, and instantly turned his gaze to the floor. 'He said give you this right away, don't wait for anything.'

Rebecca Fowler stood and slowly, reluctantly, extended her hand. The Tibetan dropped the envelope into it and backed out of the room.

Tan watched him go. 'You have a flesh monkey working for you?'

That was it, Shan realized. The man was a *ragyapa*, from the ancient caste that disposed of Tibet's dead.

'Luntok is one of our best engineers,' Fowler said with a chill. 'Went to university.' Then her eyes moved to the paper and she started in surprise. She glared at Tan, then read it again. 'What's the matter with you people?' she demanded. 'We have a contract, for Christ's sake.'

She looked at Tan, then to Shan. 'The Ministry of Geology,' she announced in a tone that suggested Tan must already know, 'has suspended my operating permit.'

An empty barracks at Jade Spring Camp, in such disrepair Shan could actually see the tin roof shudder and lift with each gust of wind, had been made available to them. Sergeant Feng claimed the solitary bed typically occupied by the company's non-commissioned officer, and with a sweep of his hand offered Shan and Yeshe their choice among the twenty steel bunk beds that lined the remainder of the barracks. Shan ignored him, and began to spread his files on the metal table at the head of the columns of beds.

'I'll need a key to the building,' he announced to Sergeant Feng.

Feng, rummaging through a cabinet for bedding, turned for a moment to see if Shan was serious. 'Fuck off.' He discovered six blankets, kept three, handed two to Yeshe and threw one to Shan. Shan let it drop to the floor and paced along the beds, looking for a place to hide his notes.

Less than thirty yards across the parade ground was the guardhouse. A tumble of withered heather blew across the grounds. A loudspeaker, dangling by a wire from its broken mount, sputtered a martial air. Clusters of soldiers had gathered along the perimeter, resentfully studying the new guards posted at the brig.

'Knobs,' Yeshe warned Shan as they approached the structure across the yard, his voice filled with alarm. 'They don't belong here. It's an army base.'

'We were expecting you,' the Public Security officer in charge snapped to Shan at the entrance. 'Colonel Tan advised us you would commence interrogation of the prisoner.' He surveyed the three men as he spoke, not trying to conceal his disappointment. His eyes rested a moment on Sergeant Feng's grizzled face, passed over Yeshe, and fixed upon Shan, who still wore the anonymous grey pocketed jacket of a senior functionary. He hesitated a moment in front of the door, as though confused about his visitors, then finally shrugged.

'Get him to eat,' he said, and stepped aside. 'I can keep the bug from escaping,' he went on as he unlocked the heavy metal door to the cell block, 'but I can't keep him from starving himself. Gets too weak, we'll put a tube into his stomach. He'll have to be on his feet.'

Spoken, Shan considered, like one seasoned in the choreography of the peoples' tribunals. The prisoner was expected to stand in front of the court, head bent in remorse. The exquisite drama of a capital trial was always heightened by a show of physical strength on the part of the accused, so it could be more obviously broken by the will of the people.

The corridor, dank with the smell of urine and mildew, was lined with cells on either side, separated by concrete walls. The only light that reached the cells was from dim bulbs hung along the centre of the corridor. As his eyes adjusted to the greyness Shan saw that the cells were empty, containing only metal buckets and straw pallets. At the end of the corridor was a small metal desk at which a single figure slumped, his chair leaning against the wall, asleep.

The officer snapped out a single sharp syllable and the

man tumbled out of the chair with a disoriented salute. 'The corporal can attend to your needs,' the officer said, and wheeled about. 'If you need more men, my guards are available.'

Shan stared after him in confusion. More men? The corporal ceremoniously produced a key from his belt and opened a deep drawer in the desk. He gestured in invitation. 'Do you have a favoured technology?'

'Technology?' Shan asked distractedly.

The drawer contained six items resting on a pile of dirty rags. A pair of handcuffs. Several four-inch splinters of bamboo. A large C-clamp, big enough to go around a man's ankle or hand. A length of rubber hose. A ball peen hammer. A pair of needle nose pliers, made of stainless steel. And the Bureau's favourite import from the West, an electric cattle prod.

Shan fought the nausea that swept through him. 'What we need is to have the cell open.' He slammed the drawer shut. The colour had drained from Yeshe's face.

The corporal and Feng exchanged an amused glance. 'First visit, right? You'll see,' the corporal said confidently, and opened the door. Feng sat on the desk and asked the guard for a cigarette as Shan and Yeshe stepped inside.

The cell was designed for high occupancy. Six straw pallets lay on the floor. A row of buckets lay along the left wall. One held a few inches of water. Another, turned upside down, served as a table. On it were two small tin cups of rice. The rice was cold, apparently untouched.

The far wall of the cell was in deep shadow. Shan tried to discern the face of the man who sat there, then realized he was facing the wall. Shan called for more light. The guard produced a battery-powered lantern which Shan laid on an upturned bucket.

The prisoner Sungpo was in the lotus position. He had torn the sleeves from his prisoner's tunic to fashion a *gomthag* strap, which he had tied behind his knees and around his back. It was a traditional device for lengthy meditation, to prevent the body from tumbling over in exhaustion while its spirit was elsewhere. His eyes seemed focused somewhere beyond the wall. His palms pressed together at his chest.

Shan sat by the wall facing the man, folding his legs under him, and gestured for Yeshe to join him. He did not speak for several minutes, hoping the man would acknowledge him first.

'I am called Shan Tao Yun,' he said at last. 'I have been asked to assemble the evidence in your case.'

'He can't hear you,' Yeshe said.

Shan moved to within inches of the man. 'I am sorry. We must talk. You have been accused of murder.' He touched Sungpo, who blinked and turned to look around the cell. His eyes, deep and intelligent, showed no trace of fear. He shifted his body to face the adjoining wall, the way a sleeping person might roll over in bed.

'You are from the Saskya gompa,' Shan began, moving to face him again. 'Is that where you were arrested?'

Sungpo clasped his hands together in front of his abdomen, interlocking the fingers, then raised his middle fingers together. Shan recognized the symbol. Diamond of the Mind.

'Ai yi!' gasped Yeshe.

'What is he trying to say?'

'He isn't. He won't. They arrested this man? It makes no sense. He is a *tsampsa*,' Yeshe said with resignation. He rose and moved to the door.

'He is under a vow?'

'He is on hermitage. He must have seclusion. He will not allow himself to be disturbed.'

Shan turned to Yeshe in confusion. It had to be some kind of very bad joke. 'But we must speak to him.'

Yeshe faced the corridor. There was something new on his face. Was it embarrassment, Shan wondered, or even fear? 'Impossible,' he said nervously. 'It is a violation.'

'Of his vows?'

'Of everyone's.' Yeshe spoke in a whisper.

Suddenly Shan understood. 'You mean yours.' It was the first time Shan had heard Yeshe acknowledge the religious obligations he learned as a youth.

Shan placed his hand on Sungpo's leg. 'Do you hear me? You are charged with murder. You will be sent to a tribunal in ten days. You must talk with me.'

Suddenly Yeshe was back at his side, pulling him away. 'You don't understand. It is his vow.'

Shan thought he had been prepared for anything. 'Because of his arrest? As a protest?'

'Of course not. It has nothing to do with that. Look at his file. He was not taken from the gompa itself.'

'No,' Shan confirmed from his memory of the report. 'It was a small hut a mile above the gompa.'

'A *tsam khan*. A special sort of shelter. Two rooms. For Sungpo and an attendant. They seized him out of his *tsam khan*. I don't know how far into his cycle he is. Saskya gompa is orthodox. They would follow the old rules. Three, three, three is the usual cycle.'

Shan let himself be pulled to the cell door. 'Three?'

'The canonic cycle. Complete silence for three years, three months, three days.'

'He speaks to no one?'

Yeshe shrugged. 'The gompa would have its own protocol. Sometimes it is arranged that the abbot, or another esteemed lama, may communicate with a *tsamp-sa*.'

Sungpo was looking beyond the wall again. Shan was not sure the accused murderer had ever seen them.

Chapter Six

While the southern claws of the Dragon had not yet been tamed, their northern counterparts had been contained by a rough gravel road along their perimeter. Sergeant Feng drove along it fretfully, cursing the rocks that occasionally blocked the road, pausing to puzzle over the map despite the fact that before embarking he had laid out their route in red ink as if he were conducting a military convoy. At first he had ordered Yeshe to sit beside him with the map, with Shan at the door, then after ten miles stopped and ordered them out. He considered the seats as though they offered many confusing alternatives, then brightened. With a victorious grunt he moved his holster to his left hip and ordered Shan into the middle.

Shan ravenously consumed the map. The few times he had left the valley during the past three years had been in closed prison transports, exposing him to parts of the neighbouring geography in a disjointed fashion, as if they were pieces of an unexplained puzzle. Quickly he tied the pieces together, finding the worksite on the South Claw where Jao had been killed, then the cave where his head had been deposited. Finally he traced their route through the mountains, circuiting one ridge until they nearly intersected the deep gorge that separated the North and South Claws, then looping west to circuit another ridge before dumping onto a small, high plateau labelled by hand in black ink. *Mei guo ren*, was all it said. Americans.

As Feng eased the truck to a stop to clear more rocks, Shan discovered they were beside the central gorge, known by the Tibetans as the Dragon's Throat. Centuries earlier a rock slide had fallen down into the Throat from this spot, leaving a small gap that dipped down towards the gorge, exposing an open view of the South Claw. There was a small annotation on the map – three dots arranged in a triangle. Ruins. It was an all-encompassing term. It could mean a cemetery, a gompa, a shrine, a college. A path rose up the short slope of the rockfall and disappeared towards the chasm. Shan began to help Feng with the rocks, then paused and jogged up the path.

The ruin was a bridge, one of the spectacular rope suspension bridges that had been constructed in a prior century by monk engineers who laid out civil works according to pilgrimage paths. It was battered but not destroyed. The path that led to the bridge, and away from it on the far side, appeared to be well travelled. Nearly a mile away Shan spotted a small patch of red, conspicuous in the dried heather of the steep slope.

'Should be there in thirty minutes,' Feng said as Shan returned to the truck. He started the engine, then barked in protest as Shan grabbed a pair of binoculars from the back and moved back up the path.

He was still focusing on the red patch when Yeshe spoke at his shoulder. 'A pilgrim.'

Instantly Shan saw that Yeshe was correct. Although the distance was too great, he fancied that he heard the clump of wooden hand and knee blocks on the ground as the man kneeled, prostrated himself, and touched his forehead to the ground. Sometimes they travelled by the 404th, the prisoners breaking discipline to call out a quick word of encouragement or snippet of prayer. Every devout Buddhist tried to make a pilgrimage to each of the five sacred mountains in his or her lifetime. Sometimes a man or a woman would take a year off just for such a pilgrimage. By bus one could travel from Lhasa to the most sacred peak, Mt Kailas, in seven hours. For the prostrating pilgrim it could take four months.

Sergeant Feng appeared. 'The Americans! We are supposed to go to the Americans.'

'I am going across to the crest of the ridge on the other side,' Shan announced.

Feng put his hand to his forehead as though suddenly in great pain. 'You can't cross over,' he growled. He grabbed the map, then brightened. 'Look for yourself,' he said with a triumphant grin. 'It doesn't exist.' Years earlier Beijing had condemned all the old suspension bridges. Most, because they eased the movement of resistance fighters, had been bombed by the People's Air Force.

'Fine,' Shan said. 'I am going to walk across this imaginary bridge. You stay here and imagine I am right beside you.'

Feng's round face clouded. 'The colonel didn't say anything about this,' he muttered.

'And your duty is to assist me in the investigation.'

'My duty is to guard a prisoner.'

'Then let's return. We will ask Colonel Tan to clarify his orders. Surely the colonel would forgive a soldier who was confused by his orders.'

Sergeant Feng looked to the truck in confusion. But Yeshe's expression was one of impatience. He took a step towards the vehicle, as though anxious to move on. 'I know the colonel,' the sergeant said uncertainly. 'We served together a long time, before Tibet. He arranged my transfer when I asked to come to his district.'

'Hear me, Sergeant. This is not a military exercise. This is an investigation. Investigators discover and react. I have discovered this bridge. Now I will react. From the crest of that ridge I think I will see the 404th worksite. I need to know if it is possible for someone to have climbed down, if there is a route other than the road.' Climbed down, Shan thought, and climbed back up, carrying a human head. From where they stood the skull shrine was perhaps an hour's walk, and only a few minutes' drive.

Feng sighed. He made a show of checking the ammunition in his pistol, tightened his belt and started towards the bridge. Yeshe moved even more reluctantly than Feng.

'You can never help him, you know,' Yeshe said to Shan's back.

Shan turned. 'Help him?'

'Sungpo. I know what you think. That you must help him.'

'If he is guilty let the evidence show it. If he is innocent, doesn't he deserve our help?'

'You don't care because you don't mind being hurt. All you can do is get the rest of us hurt. You know you can't save someone who's already formally accused.'

'Who are you trying to be? A little bird looking for a chance to sing to the Bureau? Is that what you live for?'

Yeshe stared at him resentfully. 'I am trying to survive,' he said stiffly. 'Like anyone else.'

'Then it's all been a waste. Your education. Your gompa training. Your detention.'

'I have a job. I am going to get permits. I am going to the city. There's a place for everyone in the socialist order,' he said with a hollow tone.

'There's always a place for people like you. China is filled with them,' Shan snapped and pulled away.

Feng was already at the bridge, trying not to show his fear. 'It's not – we can't –' he didn't finish the sentence. He was staring at the frayed ropes that held the span, the missing foot-boards, the swaying of the flimsy structure in the wind.

There was a cairn of rocks nearly six feet high at the foot of the bridge. 'An offering,' Shan suggested. 'Travellers make an offering first.' He plucked a stone from the slope, placed it on the cairn, and stepped onto the bridge. Feng looked towards the road as though to confirm there were no witnesses, then hastily found his own stone and placed it on the cairn.

The boards creaked. The rope groaned. The wind blasted down through the funnel of the Throat. Three hundred feet below, a trickle of water flowed through jagged rocks. Shan had to will his feet forward with each step, force his hands to relinquish their white-knuckle grip on the guide ropes to find their next purchase.

He stopped at the centre, surprised to find a clear view of the new highway bridge, Tan's proud achievement, where the Throat emptied into the valley. The wind tore at his clothes and pushed at the bridge, giving it an unsettling swaying motion. He looked back. Feng was shouting, his words lost in the wind. He was gesturing for Shan to continue, not trusting the bridge with the weight of two men. Yeshe stood where Shan had left him, staring into the ravine.

On the other side of the gorge they walked up the steep slope for twenty minutes, with Shan in the lead as Sergeant Feng, older and much heavier, struggled to keep up. Finally the sergeant called out. When Shan looked back the pistol was out. 'If you run, I'll come for you,' Feng wheezed. 'Everyone will come for you.' He pointed the pistol at Shan but then quickly withdrew it with a startled look, as if the movement scared him. 'They will bring your tattoo back,' he said between gasps. 'That's all they need. The tattoo.' He seemed paralysed with indecision. He gestured with the pistol. 'Come here.'

Shan moved slowly to his side, bracing himself.

Feng pulled the binoculars from Shan's neck and began moving back down the slope.

Shan surveyed the long slope of the ridge to the south. The patch of red that was the pilgrim was nearly out of sight. Above him, over the ridge, would be the 404th. He kept climbing. As he reached the top of the ridge Shan felt a surprising exhilaration, a feeling so unfamiliar he sat on a rock to consider it. It wasn't just satisfaction from his discovery of another route to the worksite, which was in plain view below. It wasn't just the awesome top-of-the-world view that stretched so far he could glimpse the shimmering white cap of Chomolungma, highest mountain of the Himalayas, nearly two hundred miles away. It was the clarity.

For a moment it seemed he had not only reached the top, but entered a new dimension. The sky wasn't just clear, it was like a lens, making everything seem larger and more detailed than before. The clutter in his mind seemed to have been stripped away by the wind. His hand reached back and touched the spot where the lock of hair had been clipped. Choje would have said he was storming the gates of Buddhahood.

And then he realized: it was all because of the mountain. Jao could have been killed anywhere, certainly anywhere on the remote highway to the airport. He had been lured to the South Claw because someone wanted a *jungpo* to protect the mountain. Someone wanted to stop the road. Many had motives to kill Jao. But who had a motive to save the mountain? Or to stop the immigrants who would colonize the valley beyond? Jao had been with someone he knew and trusted. Those he knew and trusted would be interested in building, not blocking roads. The murder had an air of violent passion, yet obviously the killer had painstakingly planned his act. It was as if there were two crimes, two motives, two killers.

He unconsciously ran his fingers over his calluses. They were already getting soft, after just a few days. The hard shell of the prisoner was wearing away, which scared him, for he would need an even thicker one when he returned. His eyes wandered back to the 404th. The prisoners were on the slope. And below them, deployed at the bridgehead, was something new. The grim grey hulks of two tanks and the troop carriers used by the knobs. The prisoners were not working. They were waiting. The knobs were waiting. Rinpoche was waiting.

Sungpo was waiting. And now he was waiting. All because of the mountain.

But he couldn't wait. If he did nothing but wait, Tan would devour Sungpo. And the knobs would devour the 404th.

He followed the crest back to its abrupt dropoff into the Dragon's Throat. But the dropoff wasn't totally vertical. A steep narrow path, a goat path, led down in a series of switchbacks to a jumble of rock slabs a hundred yards below. Slowly, risking a fall to his death with any misstep, Shan moved down the path to the rocks. They had sheared off the mountain and collected on a small ledge, creating a barrier from the wind.

He climbed out onto a large flat slab and found himself looking directly at the new Dragon's Throat Bridge, close enough to hear the rumble of the diesel engines that had been kept running in the tanks, and even snippets of conversation from the guards on the slope.

Fearful of being seen, he began to push back when he suddenly noticed chalk markings on the slab. It was Tibetan script and Buddhist symbols, but unlike any he had ever seen. He copied them into his pad and stepped between two slabs which had fallen together in an inverted V to create a shelter. He froze. In the back of the enclosure a circular picture had been painted on the stone, an intricate mandala which had required many hours of work. In front of it was a row of small ceramic pots such as those used for butter lamps. They were all broken. But they had not been broken casually. They had been arranged in a row and broken where they stood, as if in a ritual.

He studied the chalk signs again. Had the pilgrim been here? Had the pilgrim been watching the 404th? He climbed back up to the crest, hoping to catch a glimpse of the red robe, but the pilgrim was out of sight. He moved southward again along the slope, looking for signs of the pilgrim's path. There was another goat path, but no sign of humankind, no sign of a demon.

He steered towards a rock outcropping that jutted from the side of the ridge, deciding that he would return to Feng and Yeshe when he reached it. But when he arrived at the huge rock formation he heard a bleating that carried him further. Behind the rocks, shielded from the wind, was a pool of water. A small flock of sheep lay beside the pool, basking in the warmth. They watched him as he approached, but did not shy away. Shan squatted at the water, washed his face, then lay back on a flat rock that had gathered the sun's heat.

Without the wind the sunshine was luxuriant. He watched the animals for several minutes, then, on a whim, grabbed a handful of the gravel at the bottom of the rock and began to count the stones. It was a trick his father had taught him. Place the stones in piles of six and the number left would be used as the bottom digit in the tetragram for reading the Tao Te Ching. Four stones were left after the first round, indicating a broken line of two segments. He grabbed three more handfuls, until he built a tetragram of two solid lines over a triple segment and the double segment. In the Tao ritual it mean Passage Eight.

The greatest good is like water. The value of water is that it nourishes without striving.

He spoke the words out loud, with his eyes closed.

It stays in places that others disdain and therefore is close to the way of life.

It was the way he had learned with his father. They would use stones or rice, or on special occasions the ancient lacquered yarrow sticks that had belonged to his grandfather, then close their eyes and speak the verse.

107

In his mind's eye he conjured his father. They were alone, the two of them, in the secret temple in Beijing that had nourished them through so many difficult years. His heart leapt. For the first time in over two years he could hear his father's voice, echoing the verse. It was still there, not lost as he had feared, waiting in some remote corner of his mind for such a moment. He smelled the ginger that was always in his father's pocket. If he opened his eyes he would see the serene smile, made forever crooked by a Red Guard's boot. Shan lay motionless, exploring an alien feeling he suspected might be pleasure.

When he at last opened his eyes, the sheep had been spirited away. He had not heard them leave and he could not see them on the slope. He rose with a peaceful expression, turned and froze. On a rock shelf above him sat a small figure bundled in an oversized sheepskin coat and wearing a red wool cap. He was smiling with great pleasure at Shan.

How had the man arrived so quietly? What had he done with the sheep?

'Spring sun is the best,' the figure said in a voice that was strong and calm and high-pitched. It wasn't a man – it was a boy, an adolescent.

Shan shrugged uncertainly. 'Your sheep are gone.'

The youth laughed. 'No. They are thinking I am gone. They will find me later. We only keep them so they will take us to high places. A meditation technique, in a way. It's always different. Today they brought me to you.'

'A meditation technique?' Shan asked, not sure he had heard properly.

'You're one of them, aren't you?' the boy asked abruptly.

Shan did not know how to answer.

'Han. Chinese.' There was no spite in the boy's words, only curiosity. 'I've never seen one.'

Shan stared at the boy in confusion. They were fifteen

108

miles from the county seat. Twenty miles from a garrison of the PLA, and the boy had never seen a Han.

'But I have studied the works of Lao Tzu,' the boy said, suddenly switching to fluent Mandarin.

So he had been there all the while. 'You speak well for one who has never met a Han,' Shan said, likewise in Mandarin.

The boy swung his legs out over the ledge. 'We live in a land of teachers,' he observed matter-of-factly. 'Passage Seventy-one,' he said, referring to the Tao Te Ching again. 'You know Seventy-one?'

'*To know that you do not know is best,*' Shan recited. '*To not know of knowing is a disease.*' He considered the enigmatic boy. He spoke like a monk but was far too young. 'Have you tried Twenty-four? *The way of life means continuing. Continuing means going far. Going far means returning.*'

Pleasure lit the boy's face again. He repeated the passage.

'Does your family live on the mountain?'

'My sheep live on the mountain,' the boy replied.

'Who does live on the mountain?' Shan pressed.

'The sheep live on the mountain,' the boy repeated. He picked up a pebble. 'Why did you come?'

'I think I am looking for Tamdin.'

The boy nodded, as though expecting the answer. 'When he is awakened the unpure must fear.'

Shan noticed a rosary on his wrist, a very old rosary carved of sandalwood.

'Will you be able to turn your face towards Tamdin when you find him?' the boy asked.

Shan swallowed hard and considered the strange boy. It seemed the wisest question anyone could ask. 'I don't know. What do you think?'

The serene smile returned to the boy's face. 'The sound of the water is what I think,' he said, and threw the pebble into the centre of the pool.

Shan watched the circles ripple the surface, then turned. The boy was gone.

Feng was asleep against the rock cairn when he returned. Yeshe was sitting at the bridge, not five feet from where Shan had left him. The rancour had left his face.

'See any ghosts?' he asked Shan.

Shan looked back over the slope. 'I don't know.'

As Sergeant Feng cleared the last ridge and began to descend onto the plateau, he slowed the truck to consult the map. 'Supposed to be a mine,' he mumbled. 'Nobody said anything about a fish farm.'

Stretching below them were acres of manmade lakes, vast, neat rectangles arrayed across the high plain. Shan studied the scene in confusion. Three long, low buildings sat at the end of the road, arranged in a line in front of the lakes.

There was no activity at the mine, but a military truck was parked in front of the buildings. Tan had sent his engineers. A dozen men in green uniforms were clustered around the entrance to the centre structure, listening to someone sitting on the step.

Shan and Yeshe were ignored as they ventured from the truck. But the moment Sergeant Feng emerged, the soldiers looked up. They quickly dispersed, studiously avoiding eye contact with their visitors. The figure sitting on the step was revealed, holding a clipboard. It was the American mine manager, Rebecca Fowler. Why, Shan suddenly wondered, would Tan send his engineers if the Ministry of Geology had suspended the mine's operating permit?

The American's only greeting was a frown. 'The colonel's office called. Said you want to speak to us.' She rose, holding the clipboard to her chest with folded arms as she spoke in slow, precise Mandarin. 'But I don't

110

know how to explain you to my team. He used the word *unofficial*.'

'Theoretically this is an investigation for the Ministry of Justice.'

'But you're not from the Ministry.'

'In China,' suggested Shan, 'dealing with the government is something of an art form.'

'He said it was about Jao. But he'd like to keep that secret. A theoretical investigation. Theoretical and secret,' she said with challenge in her eyes.

'A monk has been arrested. It is no longer much of a secret.'

'Then the matter is resolved.'

'There is the matter of developing evidence.'

'A monk was arrested without evidence? You mean he confessed?'

'Not exactly.'

The American woman threw her arms up in exasperation. 'Like getting my working papers. I applied from California. They said no working papers could be authorized because I wasn't here working. I said I would come here and apply. They said I couldn't travel here without working papers.'

'You should have told them the capital for your project would not be transferred unless you were here to verify receipt.'

Fowler flashed him a grimace that may have been part grin. 'I did better. After sending faxes for three months I bought a ticket with a Japanese tour group to Lhasa. Hitched a ride to Jao's office in a truck and asked him to arrest me. Because I was about to start managing the county's only foreign investment without my working papers.'

'That's how you met him?'

She nodded. 'He thought about it for a few minutes and burst out laughing. Had the papers for me in two hours.' She gestured towards the door and led them

111

inside, into a large, open room filled with desks arranged in two large squares. A few were occupied by Tibetans wearing white shirts. Most of them left the room as soon as they saw their visitors.

Fowler waited for them at the door to a conference room adjacent to the front door. But Shan moved to one of the desks. It was covered with strange maps of brilliant colours and no demarcation lines. He had never seen such a map before.

Fowler stepped to his side and threw a newspaper over the maps. An office worker called out that tea was ready in the conference room and Yeshe and Sergeant Feng followed him in.

Shan lingered at the desks. He spotted photographs of Buddhist artefacts, small statues of deities, prayer wheels, ceremonial horns, small *thankga* paintings on scrolled silk, all extended like trophies by anonymous arms. No faces were shown. 'I am confused. Are you a geologist or an archaeologist?'

'The United Nations makes inventories of antiquities deserving preservation. They are part of the heritage of mankind. They do not belong to political parties.' Her eyes flashed as she spoke.

'But you don't work for the United Nations.'

'Don't you believe there are things that are common to all mankind?' she asked.

'I'm afraid so.'

Rebecca Fowler stared at Shan uncertainly, then went for tea. Shan roamed around the square of desks. On the perimeter, behind walls of glass panels, there were two offices, labelled PROJECT MANAGER and CHIEF ENGINEER. Fowler's office was cluttered with files and more of the peculiar maps. The walls of the second office were hung with photos of Tibetans – candid, artful photos of children and ruined temples and windswept prayer flags. A shelf along one wall was filled with books about Tibet in English.

A group photograph of a dozen exuberant men and women hung on the wall outside Fowler's office. Shan recognized Fowler, the blond American with wire-rimmed glasses, Assistant Prosecutor Li, and Chief Prosecutor Jao.

'The dedication of this building,' Fowler explained, coming over to hand him a mug of tea. 'When we opened the facility officially.'

Shan pointed to an attractive young Chinese woman with a brilliant smile. 'Miss Lihua,' Fowler said. 'Jao's secretary.'

'Why were Prosecutor Jao and his assistant both involved in your operation?'

Fowler shrugged. 'Jao was more the broad oversight. He delegated the supervisory committee issues to Li.'

'You have telephones,' Shan observed with a gesture towards the desks. 'But I didn't see any wires.'

'A satellite system,' she explained. 'We have to talk to our labs in Hong Kong. Twice a week we call our offices in California.'

'And the UN office in Lhasa?'

'No. It's an internal system. Only authorized for designated receiving stations inside our company.'

'Not even Lhadrung?'

Fowler shook her head. 'I can contact California in sixty seconds. A message to Lhadrung means forty-five minutes' drive. Your country,' she said without smiling. 'It overflows with paradox.'

'Like putting American saccharine in buttered tea,' Shan said, watching a Tibetan woman in a white office smock pour pink packets into a bowl of the traditional milky brew.

There were bulletin boards with safety procedures in Chinese and English, and notices about staff meetings. There was a set of red double doors that were closed, with a sign that restricted entry to authorized personnel.

113

'Has the American staff been here long, Miss Fowler?' Shan asked.

'It's only me and Tyler Kincaid. Eighteen months.'

'Kincaid?'

'My chief engineer. Sort of second-in-command.' She gave him a pregnant glance, which Shan took to mean that she was reminding him that he had seen Kincaid with her at the cave. The lighthearted American who had played 'Home on the Range' to spite Colonel Tan; the man in the building-dedication photo.

'No other Westerners? How about visitors from your company?'

'None. Too damned far. Only Jansen from the United Nations office in Lhasa. But the week after next it all changes when the American tourists come. They're supposed to spend two hours here. After that we're a regular stop on the tourist circuit. Guess we'll show them empty offices and empty tanks, give them a lecture on Chinese bureaucracy.'

Shan refused the bait. 'The UN Antiquities Commission. How are you involved?'

'Sometimes they ask to borrow a truck. Or some ropes.'

'Ropes?'

'They explore caves. They climb mountains.'

'Do they take artefacts?'

Fowler stiffened. 'They record artefacts,' she said with a stern look. 'I guess you could say I am a member of the local committee.'

'There's a committee?'

Fowler did not respond.

'What of the conflicts? Without government support you could not operate. Your mining licence.'

'Please don't remind me.'

'And a permit to operate a satellite system, that is extraordinary. But you are opposing the government –'

Sergeant Feng appeared at Shan's side and made a sharp guttural sound, one of his warnings.

'– the government removal of artefacts,' Shan continued in English.

Rebecca Fowler's eyes flashed with surprise. 'You speak it well,' she said. 'We are not in a position to stop anything the government does. We just believe governments should act openly in dealing with cultural resources, especially resources of a different culture. The Antiquities Commission helps collect evidence.'

'So you have two jobs?'

Feng stepped between them with a resentful glare, but seemed uncertain what to do.

Fowler was six inches taller than Feng. She continued to speak, over his head. 'How about you, Inspector? How many jobs does an unofficial investigator have?'

Shan did not answer.

Fowler shrugged. 'My job is mine manager. But the Commission has only one expatriate, Jansen. A Finn. He asks other expatriates working in the remote areas to serve as his eyes and ears.'

'Your committee.'

Fowler nodded, looking uncomfortably at Sergeant Feng.

'You still didn't say why you were at the cave.'

'Didn't even know there was a cave. Until the PLA trucks got noticed.'

'By whom?'

'Army trucks are conspicuous. One of my Tibetan engineers saw them when he was climbing.'

'But army trucks can be explained in many ways.'

'Not really. There're two patterns of truck traffic in the high ranges. Manoeuvres. Or new construction for military camps or collectives. These weren't manoeuvres, and there was no construction equipment entering the site. The trucks weren't carrying things in. Not much, anyway.'

'So you decided they were carrying things out. Very clever.'

'I couldn't be sure. But as soon as I arrived I saw two things: your colonel, and a cave crawling with soldiers.'

'The colonel could have other reasons to be there.'

'You mean the murder?'

'I have had several American friends,' Shan observed. 'They are always quick to jump to conclusions.'

'There's a difference between jumping to conclusions and being direct. Why don't you just say no? Tan would just say no. Jao would just say no, if it suited.' She ran her fingers through her hair. Shan realized she did it when she was nervous. 'That day at Tan's office, you openly defied him. You're not like other Chinese I've known.'

It was going too fast. Shan drained his cup and asked for more. As Fowler went over to the conference room by the door he studied the bulletin board. There was a handwritten document in one corner, in Tibetan. With a start, Shan recognized it. It was the American Declaration of Independence. He led Sergeant Feng away from it, to the conference room, where Fowler sat on the table, waiting for him with the tea.

'So you are replacing Prosecutor Jao?' Fowler asked.

'No. Just a short assignment for the colonel.'

'He would have been disappointed. Jao used to read Arthur Conan Doyle. Loved his murder investigations.'

'You make it sound like a habit.'

'Half a dozen a year, I suppose. It's a big county.'

'He always solved them?'

'Sure. It was his job, right?' she asked in a taunting tone. 'And now you have already arrested the murderer.'

'I didn't arrest anyone.'

Fowler studied Shan. 'You sound like you don't think he did it.'

'I don't.'

Fowler could not conceal her surprise. 'I'm beginning to understand you, Mr Shan.'

'Just Shan.'

'I understand why Tan wanted you away from the cave when I was there. You're – what? Unpredictable, like he described the Tibetans. I don't think your government deals well with unpredictability.'

Shan shrugged. 'Colonel Tan prefers to deal with one crisis at a time.'

The American woman studied him. 'So what was his crisis, you or me?'

'You, of course.'

'I wonder.' She sipped her tea. 'If it wasn't your prisoner who killed Jao, then who was the murderer?'

'Your demon. Tamdin.'

Fowler's head snapped up. She looked around to see if her staff were listening. They were gathered at the far end of the room. 'No one jokes about Tamdin,' she said in a low voice, suddenly tinged with worry.

'I wasn't.'

'Every village, every sheepcamp around here has been telling stories of demons visiting for some time. Last month there were complaints about our blasting. They said it must have awakened him. There was a work stoppage for half a day. But I explained that we only began blasting six months ago.'

'Blasting for what?'

'Dykes. A new pond.'

Shan shook his head in bewilderment. 'But why build ponds? Why all this water? How can you produce minerals? There is no mine.'

Fowler smiled. 'Sure there is,' she said, seeming relieved to change the topic. 'Right out the front door.' She grabbed a pair of binoculars and gestured for him to follow. She led Shan outside along a path that rimmed the largest pond, walked briskly to the centre of the largest dyke, the one that was built across the mouth of

117

the valley, then paused for Yeshe and Sergeant Feng to catch up. 'This is a precipitation mine.'

'You mine rain?' Yeshe asked.

'Not what I meant. But I guess that's one way to describe it. We mine the rain of a hundred centuries ago.' She pointed across the ponds. 'This plain is the bottom of a bowl. No outlet but the Dragon Throat, and it was blocked up here by an ancient landslide. It's a volatile geology. The surrounding peaks were volcanic. Lava flowed down the slopes. Lava is filled with the light elements. Boron. Magnesium. Lithium. Over centuries rains dissolved the lava and washed the salts into the bowl. A salt lake would build up. In time of drought a crust would form over the lake. A foot thick. Sometimes five feet thick. Then a cycle of wet years would fill the basin with water again, with the dissolved minerals. Then another crust. Every few centuries another eruption would replenish the slopes. It's how the Great Salt Lake in America was formed.'

'But these lakes are manmade.'

'The natural salt lake is there. In fact, eleven of them. In layers, underneath us. We just moved clay to build surface ponds. We pump up the brine into our ponds for evaporation.' Fowler pointed towards three small sheds across the valley floor, ganglia in a network of pipes. 'Three wells do all the work.'

'But where is your plant?'

'In the ponds. With the right concentration we can precipitate out boron particles. Each lake is periodically drained and we harvest the product that has accumulated on the bottom. The trick is to maintain the concentration. Get it wrong and we wind up with table salt. Or a stew of metals too expensive to separate.'

She led them down the dyke to where it intersected the gully of the Dragon's Throat.

'But you said it was a landslide that blocked the valley,' Shan said.

'We moved it. Too unstable. The dam needs to be packed clay. Just finished this one, our last dyke.' Shan saw that the pond beside them, noticeably lower than the others, was still being filled by the wells. The American pointed towards the far end of the plateau and handed Shan the binoculars. 'The farthest pond is being harvested.'

There was a mound of brilliant white material near the pond.

'We have a crude processing unit, to refine the product slightly. Once we start production, we will seal it into one-ton bags and ship it to the world.' He realized she was looking elsewhere as she spoke, towards a cluster of workers in the middle of the pond complex. He turned the binoculars to the workers and saw that it was two separate groups. Neither seemed to be working.

'The world?' he asked.

'Some to factories in China,' she said distractedly. 'Much of it to Hong Kong for shipping to Europe and America.'

Shan studied the dull grey equipment beside the second group. 'Why would Tan send them when your permit is suspended?'

'The Ministry of Geology suspended the permit.'

'Who signed the order?'

Rebecca Fowler paused, as though considering whether to respond. 'Director Hu.'

'Of the local Ministry of Geology office?'

'Right. But I explained to Tan that if we shut down now, we lose all the material in the ponds. We design the process so our commercial products precipitate first. If we wait, they get contaminated. Could lose six months' work. He agreed we should continue to process our sample batches on the grounds that the permit is for commercial operations.'

'But then everything stops?'

'Unless we can figure out what's going on.'

119

'You're saying Hu gave no reason for the suspension?'

It was as far as Fowler would go. She took two steps away and looked up at a rock face at the end of the pond. Shan studied her for a moment, trying to understand if she was upset because of Prosecutor Jao, Director of Mines Hu, or himself, then followed her gaze to the rock. The cliff rose at least three hundred feet, nearly perpendicular. Suddenly he saw movement on the rocks, two white ropes dangling down the face from the top.

Fowler turned to face the gully. 'You can see all the way to the valley,' she observed.

But Shan did not turn. The ropes were moving. There were two figures at the top, in brilliant red vests and white helmets.

Suddenly Yeshe called out with surprise. He was still looking down the Dragon's Throat. 'The 404th! You can see –' he caught himself and cast an embarrassed glance towards Shan, who swung the binoculars around. It took only a moment to follow the Dragon's Throat to the base of the range. They were twenty miles away by tortuous mountain road, but there in plain view was the 404th's worksite, no more than three miles distant as a raven would fly. Adjusting the focus, he picked out Tan's bridge, the tanks of the knobs, and the long rank of prison trucks.

He felt the glare of the American and lowered the glasses.

'My chief engineer showed it to me,' she said with an accusing tone. 'It's one of your prison projects. Slave labour.'

'The government often assigns compulsory work crews to road construction,' Yeshe said, suddenly self-righteous. 'Beijing says it builds socialist awareness.'

'I've been talking to the UN about it.'

'Personally,' Shan said, 'I am in favour of international dialogue.' He felt a sharp gun-barrel jab in his back. Sergeant Feng had arrived behind him. Shan turned.

120

Feng's thumb was extended towards Shan and his eyes were smouldering.

The action was not missed by Fowler. She seemed about to say something when suddenly a loud whoop echoed across the rock face. They turned to see the two men dropping down the cliff on the ropes, kicking off the rock as they fell.

'Crazy fool,' Fowler muttered. 'It's Kincaid. He's teaching the young engineers. He's going to do Everest before his tour is finished. Wants to go up with a team of Tibetans.'

'Everest?' Yeshe asked.

'Sorry,' Fowler said. 'Chomolungma is what you call it. Mother mountain.'

'It means "goddess mother of the world",' Yeshe corrected.

As the figures landed at the base of the cliff, they made exhilarated leaps into the air and embraced. Moments later they began moving onto the long dyke, the lean man with brilliant eyes and ponytail Shan had seen at the cave and the young Tibetan driver Shan had seen driving the truck and later at Tan's office.

'I'm Tyler,' the American introduced himself. 'Tyler Kincaid. Just Kincaid will do.' His smile faded as he saw Sergeant Feng. His eyes settled on the sergeant's pistol. 'This,' he said with a distracted jerk of his thumb, 'is Luntok, one of our engineers.'

'Kincaid works the magic in the ponds,' Fowler explained.

'Nature does the magic,' Kincaid said impassively. He spoke with a slight drawl, the way Shan had heard characters speak in American westerns. 'I just give her the opportunity.'

He studied Shan, then lowered his voice. 'You were at the cave. With Tan,' he said with a tone of accusation. 'We want to know about that cave.'

'So do I. I need to know why you were there.'

'Because something is wrong there. Because it's a holy place,' he said.

'Why would you say that?' Shan asked.

'It is one of those places the Buddhists call a place of power. At the end of a valley. Facing south. A spring nearby. A large tree.'

'So you've been there before?'

Kincaid make a sweeping gesture towards the mountains. 'We climb a lot of ridges. Luntok saw the trucks. But we didn't need to see them to know it might be important. The topography shows it all.'

Suddenly an airhorn blew, a long unceasing howl that hurt the ears. A worker appeared beside Fowler, panting from a run across the dike. 'They're going to fight!' he shouted. 'They're going to destroy the equipment!'

'Goddamned MFCs!' Tyler snapped at Fowler. 'I told you!' He darted towards the trouble, Luntok close behind.

The Tibetan workers had formed a line in the middle of the valley. A huge grey bulldozer on which half a dozen of Tan's engineers perched had been stopped by a makeshift barricade of smaller trucks and earthmovers. The soldiers were firing the bulldozer's airhorn in staccato blasts, like a machine gun. The Tibetans sat cross-legged on the ground in front of the vehicles.

Kincaid appeared between the lines, standing with the Tibetans, haranguing the soldiers.

Shan offered Rebecca Fowler the binoculars. She seemed reluctant to take them. 'I never meant for this –' she began. 'If anyone got hurt I couldn't live with myself.' She turned to him, as if surprised to have said the words to Shan. Anguish filled her eyes. 'Make them leave.'

'Who?'

'The soldiers. Tell Tan we'll find some other way to meet the schedule.'

'I am sorry. I have no authority.'

'Of course you do,' Yeshe suggested. 'You are a direct

representative of Colonel Tan. You will report any impropriety to him.' Yeshe seemed torn by indecision, then bolted towards the soldiers. He was not about to have an incident at the mine delay completion of his assignment. He was, Shan reminded himself, a man with a destination.

The soldiers began raising and lowering the blade of their bulldozer, giving the machine the appearance of a hungry monster, impatient to chew its food. Kincaid moved back and forth, vigorously gesturing at the ponds, at the mountains, and the equipment sheds.

'Mr Kincaid,' Shan observed, 'is an unusually zealous man.' He saw Fowler's confused glance. 'For a mining engineer.'

'Tyler Kincaid is a treasure. Could have his pick of jobs in the company. New York. London. California. Australia. He chose Tibet. Is he zealous? We're eight thousand miles from home, trying to open a mine with unproven technology in an unproven location with an unproven workforce. Zealousness struck me as something of a credential.'

'Pick of his jobs. Because he is so qualified?'

'That, and his father owns the company.'

Shan watched Tyler Kincaid as he moved to the lead soldier and shook him by the shoulders. His father owned the company, and Kincaid was at what had to be the most remote, inaccessible outpost of the company anywhere on the planet. 'He said something. MFCs. What does it mean?'

'Just his way of talking.'

'Talking about what?'

'Bureaucrats, I guess.' She saw that he would not give up, and shrugged. 'An MFC is a Mother Fucking Communist,' she explained, and turned back towards the workers with an amused grin.

Yeshe arrived in front of the soldiers and began pointing towards Shan. The bulldozer blade stopped and the soldiers peered towards the dyke in obvious uncertainty. Kincaid used the reprieve to dart to the administration building, from where he reappeared at full speed carrying a black box. Fowler raised the glasses for a moment, gave a grunt of amusement, and handed them to Shan.

Kincaid had a portable tape player. He set it in front of the bulldozer and began playing American rock music, so loud Shan could hear it from the dyke. The American engineer began to dance.

At first both sides just stared. Then a soldier began to laugh. Another soldier joined the dance, then one of the Tibetans. The others all began laughing.

Fowler sighed. 'Thanks,' she said, as if Yeshe's intervention had been Shan's idea. 'Crisis averted. Problem still not solved,' she said, and began walking towards the office.

Shan moved to her side. 'Have you thought about a priest?' he asked.

'A priest?'

'The Tibetans won't work because they believe something has released a demon.'

Fowler shook her head sadly, surveying the valley. 'Somehow I can't believe it. I know these people. They aren't pagans.'

'You misunderstand. It's not that most of them believe a monster is roaming the hills. What they believe is that the balance has been disturbed, and an imbalance produces evil. The demon is just a manifestation of that evil. It could be manifested in a person, in an act. The balance can be restored with the right rituals, the right priest.'

'You're saying all of this is symbolic? Jao's murder wasn't symbolic.'

'I wonder.'

She turned to gaze down the Throat as she considered

Shan's suggestion. 'The Religious Bureau would never permit a ritual. The Director is on our board.'

'I was not suggesting a Bureau priest. You would need someone special. Someone with the right powers. Someone from the old gompas. The right priest would make them understand they have nothing to fear.'

'Is there nothing to fear?'

'I believe your workers have nothing to fear.'

'Is there nothing to fear?' the American woman asked, threading her fingers through her auburn hair.

'I don't know.'

They walked on in silence.

'It's not exactly something that was covered in my environmental impact statements,' Fowler observed.

'It was not necessarily the result of your mining work.'

'But I thought that was the whole.'

'No. Something happened here. Not Jao's murder because so few know about it. Something else. Something was seen. Something that scared the Tibetans, that had to be explained to their way of thinking. A ready explanation would be the excavation of the mountain. Every rock, every pebble has its place. Now the rocks and pebbles have been moved.'

'But the murder is involved, isn't it.' It was not a question. 'The demon. Tamdin.' Her voice was almost a whisper now.

'I don't know.' Shan studied her. 'I did not realize you were so upset about the murder.'

'It's got me spooked,' she said, looking back at the workers. The machines were backing away from each other. 'I can't sleep at night.' She looked back at Shan. 'I'm doing strange things. Like talking to total strangers.'

'Is there something else you need to tell me?' As they approached the compound, Shan noticed movement at the end of the furthest building. A line of Tibetans extended out of a side door, mostly workers but also old women and children in traditional dress.

Rebecca Fowler seemed not to notice. 'It's just that I keep thinking that Jao's murder and the suspension of my permit are connected. And there is something else, but now with my permit suspended it will just sound spiteful. Jao was on our supervisory committee. Before he left here on his last visit, Jao had a big argument with Director Hu of the Ministry of Geology. After the meeting, outside, Jao was yelling at Hu. It was about that cave. Jao said Hu had to stop what he was doing at the cave. He said he would send in his own team.'

'So you knew about the cave before this argument?'

'No. But Luntok mentioned the trucks he had seen. I didn't connect any of it until I went to the site that day. Even then I was so upset with Tan that it was only afterwards I remembered Jao's argument with Hu.'

They were nearly at the truck, where Yeshe and Sergeant Feng waited. She paused and spoke with a new, urgent tone. 'How do I find the priest I need?'

'Ask your workers,' Shan suggested. Was it possible, he wondered, that she would defy Hu, even Tan, to keep her mine open?

'I can't. It would make it official. Religious Affairs would be furious. The Ministry of Geology would be furious. Help me find one. I can't do it myself.'

'Then ask the mountaintops.'

'What do you mean?'

'I don't know. It's a Tibetan saying. I think it means pray.'

Rebecca Fowler grabbed his arm and looked at him desperately. 'I want to help you,' she said, 'but you can't lie to me.'

He responded only with an awkward, crooked smile then looked longingly towards the distant peaks. He would never lie to her but he would always believe the lies to himself if they were his only hope of escape.

Chapter Seven

'News flash,' Sergeant Feng muttered to the commando in battle fatigues who stood at the 404th gate. 'The Taiwan invasion is going to be on the coast, not in the Himalayas.'

The 404th had the appearance of a war zone. Tents had been erected along the perimeter. New wire had been strung on top of the barbed fence already in place, a vicious-looking strand with razor sharp strips of metal dangling from it. The electricity had been cut off, except for the wire leading to a new bank of spotlights at the gate. Bunkers of sandbags were being built for machine guns, as if the Bureau troops expected a frontal assault. A freshly painted sign declared that a fifteen-foot strip inside the fence was now the dead zone. Prisoners entering the zone without authorization could be shot without warning.

The commando raised his AK-47 rifle. There was a raw, animal quality in his countenance that made Shan shiver. Sergeant Feng shoved Shan violently through the gate, knocking him to his knees. The knob studied Feng a moment, then, with a reluctant frown, stepped back.

'Got to show them who's in charge,' Feng mumbled as he caught up with Shan. Shan realized it was meant to be an apology. 'Damned strutting cockbirds. Grab the glory and move on.' He stopped, arms akimbo, to survey the knobs' bunkers, then gestured towards Shan's hut. 'Thirty minutes,' he snapped, and moved back towards the brilliantly lit dead zone.

The air of the blackened hut was thick with the smell

of paraffin. There was a sound as though of mice scampering on a rock floor. Beads were being worked. Someone whispered Shan's name and a candle was lit. Several prisoners sat up and stared, breaking the count of their beads. Their faces were shadowed with fatigue. But on some there was also something else. Defiance. It scared Shan, and excited him.

Trinle was on his feet as soon as he saw Shan.

'I must speak with him,' Shan said urgently. Choje was on the bunk behind Trinle, as still as death.

'He is near exhaustion.'

Suddenly Choje's hands moved and folded over his mouth and nose. He exhaled sharply three times. It was the ritual of awakening for every devout Buddhist. The first exhalation was to expunge sin, the second to purge confusion, the third to clear away impediments to the true path.

Choje sat up and greeted Shan with a flicker of a smile. He was wearing a robe, an illegal robe, which had been sewn together from prison shirts and somehow dyed. Without speaking he rose and moved to the centre of the floor where he dropped into the lotus position, joined by Trinle. Shan sat between them.

'You are weak, Rinpoche. I did not mean to disturb your rest.'

'There is so much to be done. Today each hut did ten thousand rosaries. Many of the men have been prepared. Tomorrow we will try for more.'

Shan clenched his jaw, fighting his emotions. 'Prepared?'

Choje only smiled.

A strange scraping noise disturbed the stillness. Shan turned. One of the young monks was reverently spinning a prayer wheel, fashioned from a tin can and a pencil.

'Are you eating?' Shan asked.

'The kitchens were ordered closed,' Trinle explained. 'Only water. Buckets are left at the gate at midday.'

Shan pulled the paper bag that contained his uneaten lunch from his coat pocket. 'Some dumplings.'

Choje received the bag solemnly and handed it to Trinle to divide. 'We are grateful. We will try to get some to those in the stable.'

'They opened the stable,' Shan whispered. It was not a question but an anguished declaration.

'Three of the monks from a gompa to the north. They sat near the gate, demanding an exorcism.'

'I saw the troops outside. They look impatient.'

Choje shrugged. 'They are young.'

'They will not grow old waiting for striking prisoners.'

'What can they expect? There is an angry *jungpo*. It would be but the work of a day to restore the balance.'

'Colonel Tan will never allow an exorcism on the mountain. It would be a defeat, an embarrassment.'

'Then your colonel will have to live with them both.' There was no challenge in Choje's voice, only a trace of sympathy.

'Both,' Shan repeated. 'You mean Tamdin.'

Choje sighed and looked about the hut. There was another unfamiliar sound. Shan turned and saw the *khampa*, sitting by the door. The man had a frightening gleam in his eyes.

'Gonna get us out, wizard?' he asked Shan. He had removed the handle from his eating mug and was sharpening it on a rock. 'Another of your tricks? Make all the knobs disappear?' He laughed, and kept sharpening.

'Trinle has been practising his arrow mantras,' Choje observed as he watched the *khampa* with sad eyes. It was a charm of ancient legend, by which the practitioner was transported across great distances in an instant. 'He is getting very good. One day he will surprise us. Once when I was a boy I saw an old lama perform the rite. One moment there was a blur and he was gone. Like an arrow from a bow. He was back an hour later, with a flower that grew only at a gompa fifty miles away.'

'So Trinle will leave you like an arrow?' Shan asked, unable to disguise his impatience.

'Trinle knows many things. Some things must be preserved.'

Shan sighed deeply to calm himself. Choje was speaking as though the rest of their world would not survive. 'I need to know about Tamdin.'

Choje nodded. 'Some are saying that Tamdin is not finished.' He looked sadly into Shan's eyes. 'He will not show mercy if he strikes again. In the time of the Seventh,' Choje said, referring to the Seventh Dalai Lama, 'an entire Manchurian army was destroyed as they invaded. A mountain collapsed on them as they marched. The manuscripts say it was Tamdin who pushed the mountain over.'

'Rinpoche. Hear my words. Do you believe in Tamdin?'

Choje looked at Shan with intense curiosity. 'The human body is such an imperfect vessel for the spirit. Surely the universe has room for many other vessels.'

'But do you believe in a demon creature that stalks the mountains? I must understand if – if there is to be any chance of stopping all this.'

'You ask the wrong question.' Choje spoke very slowly, in his prayer voice. 'I believe in the capacity of the essence that is Tamdin to possess a human being.'

'I do not understand.'

'If some are meant to achieve Buddhahood then perhaps others are meant to achieve Tamdinhood.'

Shan held his head in his hands, fighting an overwhelming fatigue. 'If there is to be hope I must understand more.'

'You must learn to fight that.'

'Fight what?'

'This thing called hope. It still consumes you, my

friend. It makes you wrongly believe that you can strike against the world. It distracts you from what is more important. It makes you believe the world is populated by victims and villains and heroes. But that is not our world. We are not victims. Rather we are honoured to have had our faith tested. If we are to be consumed by the knobs then we are to be consumed. Neither hope nor fear will change that.'

'Rinpoche. I do not have the strength not to hope.'

'I wonder about you sometimes,' Choje said. 'I worry that you are too hard a seeker.'

Shan nodded sadly. 'I do not know how not to seek.'

Choje sighed. 'They are holding a lama,' he observed. 'A hermit from Saskya gompa.'

Shan had long ago given up trying to understand how information spread through the Tibetan population and across prison walls. It was as if the Tibetans practised a secret form of telepathy.

'Did this lama do it?' Choje asked.

'You think a lama could do such a thing?'

'Every spirit can lapse. Buddha himself wrestled with many temptations before he was eventually transformed.'

'I have seen this lama,' Shan said solemnly. 'I have looked into his eyes. He did not do it.'

'Ah,' Choje sighed, and then was silent. 'I see,' he said after a long time. 'You must obtain the release of this lama by proving that the murder was done by the demon Tamdin.'

'Yes,' Shan admitted at last, looking into his hands, his reply barely audible.

The two men sat in silence. From somewhere outside the hut came a long disembodied groan of pain.

Yeshe refused when Shan explained his task the next morning. 'I could get arrested just for asking about a sorcerer,' he complained.

Feng was driving them through the low rolling hills of

131

gravel and heather that led to town. A meandering line of willows and high sedges marked the path of the river that, having cascaded through the Dragon's Throat, moved at a more languid pace down the valley. They passed a field where bulldozers had flattened a hill, cultivated with rows of now dying plants, so twisted and contorted by the wind and dryness that they were unidentifiable. Another failed attempt to root something from the outside that Tibet neither needed nor wanted.

'What did they punish you for? Why were you sentenced to a labour camp?'

Yeshe would not reply.

'Why do you still fear them? You've been released.'

'Every sane person fears them.' Yeshe smirked pointedly.

'It's your travel papers, is that what troubles you? You think you won't get them if you work with me. Without new travel papers you'll never get out of Tibet, never get a job in Sichuan fitting your station, never get your shiny television.'

Yeshe seemed to resent the comment. But he didn't deny it. 'It's wrong to encourage these people who cast spells,' he said. 'They hold Tibet in another century. We will never progress.'

Shan stared at Yeshe but did not reply. Yeshe shifted in his seat and scowled out the window. A woman, enveloped in a huge brown felt cloak, walked down the road, leading a goat on a rope.

'You want a history of Tibet?' Yeshe asked sullenly, still facing the window. 'Just one long struggle between priests and sorcerers. The church demands that we strive for perfection. But perfection is so difficult. Sorcerers offer shortcuts. They take their power from the weakness of the people and the people thank them for it. Sometimes the priests rule, and they build up the ideal. Then the sorcerers rule. And in the name of the ideal the sorcerers ruin it.'

'So that is what Tibet is about?'

'It's what keeps society moving. China, too. You have your sorcerers. Only you call them secretary this and minister that. With a little red book of charms written by the chairman himself. The Master Sorcerer.'

Yeshe looked up, aghast, suddenly aware that Feng may have heard. 'I didn't mean –' he sputtered, then clenched his fists in frustration and turned to the window again.

'So these students of Khorda, they scare you?' Maybe they should all be scared, Shan thought. If you want to reach Tamdin, Choje had suggested, speak to the students of Khorda.

'Students? Who said students? No need. People are always talking about the old sorcerer. He lives. If that's what you call it. They say he doesn't need to eat. Some say he doesn't even need to breathe. But we'll have to find his lair. Could be a cave deep in the mountains. Could be in the marketplace. He is very secretive. He moves about, from shadow to shadow. They say he can disappear into thin air, like a wisp of smoke. It may take some time.'

'Good. The sergeant and I are going to the restaurant, then to Prosecutor Jao's house. After that, the colonel's office. Meet us there when you find your sorcerer.'

'This Khorda, he will never talk to an investigator.'

'Then tell him the truth. Tell him I am a troubled man badly in need of magic.'

They tried to close the restaurant when Shan arrived. 'You knew Prosecutor Jao?' he called to the head waiter through a crack in the door.

'I knew. Go away.'

'He ate here with an American four nights ago.'

'He ate here often.'

Shan put his hand on the door. The man moved as though to push it shut, then saw Sergeant Feng and relented, trotting back down the front hallway.

Shan stepped inside and followed the shadow of the fleeing waiter. In the hallway busboys cowered. In the kitchen no one would look at him.

He caught up with the man as he re-entered the dining room through a side door. 'Did someone bring a message that night?' Shan asked the waiter, who was still beating his awkward retreat, picking up trays and nervously setting them down a few steps later, then pulling a stack of plates from the counter.

'You!' Sergeant Feng shouted from the doorway.

As the man flinched, the plates slipped from his grip, shattering on the floor. He stared at the plates forlornly. 'No one remembers. It was busy.'

The man began shaking.

'Who has been here? Somebody was already here. Somebody said don't speak to me.'

'No one remembers,' the waiter repeated.

As Feng took a step inside the door, Shan raised a palm in resignation and walked away.

'Who's going to pay for the plates?' the waiter moaned behind him. He began sobbing like a child.

Prosecutor Jao had lived in a small cottage in the government compound on the new side of town, a square stucco structure with two rooms and a separate kitchen. In Tibet it was the equivalent of a grand villa.

Shan lingered at the entrance, making a mental note of the way the heather along the wall of the house had been recently trampled. The door was slightly ajar. He pushed it with his elbow, careful not to smudge any prints that might be on the handle. Here, he hoped, could be the answer to why Prosecutor Jao had detoured to the South Claw. Or at least, the picture of Jao the private man that would help Shan understand his motivations.

It was an orderly, anonymous room. A decorative mah-jongg set lay on a small table in the corner, under a poster of the Hong Kong skyline. Two large overstuffed chairs comprised the only furniture. Shan stopped, aghast. A young man was slumped in one of the chairs, deep in slumber.

Suddenly he heard voices from the kitchen, Li Aidang appeared, as sleek and well scrubbed as when Shan had first seen him in Colonel Tan's office. 'Comrade Shan!' he exclaimed with false enthusiasm. 'It is Shan, isn't it? You did not formally introduce yourself when we first met. Very clever.' The man in the chair stirred, blinked at Shan, stretched, and shut his eyes again.

Beyond Li, a team of Tibetan women was washing the walls and floor. 'You're cleaning his house before the investigation is completed?' Shan asked in disbelief.

'No need to worry. Already searched. Nothing here.'

'Sometimes evidence is not always obvious. Papers. Fingerprints.'

Li nodded as though to humour him. 'But of course the crime was not committed here. And the house belongs to the Ministry. It can't be left idle.'

'What if the murderer was looking for something? What if he came back here and searched the house?'

Li spread his arms. 'Nothing was taken,' he said. 'And we already know the movements of the killer. From the South Claw to the cave. From the cave back to his gompa.' He held up his hand to pre-empt further discussion, then called out to the man in the chair. The man stirred again, extending a folder. Li took it and handed it to Shan. 'I took the liberty of assembling Jao's schedule. Committees he served on. Details of the prosecution when the accused Sungpo was jailed as one of the Lhadrung Five.'

'I thought we would speak with his secretary.'

'Excellent idea,' Li said, and shrugged. 'But she always takes her leave concurrently with Jao. She is in Hong Kong. Left the same night as Jao. I took her to the airport myself.'

Outside Shan paused beside the truck and watched in

disbelief as the crew began hosing down the outside of the house.

'Little birds have big voices,' Feng said with amusement as he climbed behind the wheel.

Suddenly Shan remembered. The only person he had told about going to the house and the restaurant had been Yeshe.

Dr Sung appeared in the clinic hallway wearing a surgical gown and bloody gloves. A *kiajiou* mark hung around her neck. 'You again?'

'You sound disappointed,' Shan said.

'The nurse said there were two men with questions about Prosecutor Jao. I thought it was the others.'

'The others?'

'The assistant prosecutor. You two should engage in a dialectic.'

'I'm sorry?'

'Talk to each other. Do your own jobs right so I can do mine.'

'Li Aidang was here?'

'No,' Sung sneered. 'My mistake. Must have been the Minister of Justice himself.'

Shan clenched his jaw. 'So Li Aidang was asking about the body?'

Sung seemed pleased with Shan's discomfort. 'Asking about the body. Asking about you. Asking about your companions. They took the receipts for the personal possessions. You never asked for the receipts.'

'I'm sorry,' Shan said, without knowing why.

Doctor Sung stripped off her gloves. 'I have another surgery in fifteen minutes.' She began moving down the corridor.

'The colonel had the head sent here,' Shan said to her back, following her.

'A lovely gesture, I thought,' she said acidly. 'Someone

136

could have warned me. Just like that, out of the bag. Hello, Comrade Prosecutor.'

Surely the doctor should have known what to expect from Tan, Shan considered. Then he understood. 'You mean, you knew him.'

'It's a small town. Sure I knew Jao. Said goodbye last week, when he left on vacation. Then suddenly I'm unwrapping the colonel's package and he's staring right at me, as if we had unfinished business.'

'And what were your conclusions?'

'About what?' She opened a closet and scanned its nearly empty shelves. 'Great.' She put the gloves back on. 'I wrote to ask for more gloves. They said just sterilize the ones you have. The fools! Just what do they think would happen if I put latex gloves in an autoclave?'

'The examination of the head.'

'Ai yi!' she exclaimed, throwing her head back. 'Now he wants an autopsy of a head,' she said to the fly-specked ceiling.

Shan just stared at her.

'Okay. One skull, intact. One brain, intact. Hearing organs, sight organs, taste organs, smell organs all intact. One big problem.'

Shan moved closer. 'You found something?'

'He needed a haircut.' She moved down the corridor as Shan stared.

'You looked at his dental records?' he said to her back.

'There you go again. Thinking you're in Beijing. Jao had dental work, but it wasn't done in Tibet. No records to verify against.'

'Did you try to match the head to the body?'

'Exactly how large is your inventory of headless bodies, Comrade?'

Shan stared at her without reply.

Sung muttered under her breath, tightened her gloves, and threw him a *kiajiou* from the shelf.

They walked in silence to the morgue. Inside, the

137

stench was far worse now, nearly overwhelming. Shan pulled the mask tighter, looking over his shoulder. Sergeant Feng had refused to enter. He hovered in the hall, watching through the small window in the door.

A soiled cardboard box was on an examination table, resting on top of a covered body. Shan turned away as Dr Sung removed the contents of the box and leaned over the body.

'Amazing. It fits.' She made a gesture of invitation to Shan. 'Perhaps you would like to try? I know. We'll cut off the limbs and play mix and match.'

'I was interested in the nature of the cuts.'

Sung cast him a peeved look, then retrieved a bottle of alcohol and washed the flesh around the neck. 'One, two . . . I count three cuts. Like I said before, not violent blows. Precise, like slices.'

'How can you know?'

'If the killer had relied on force the tissue would have been crushed. These are very neat cuts with a razor sharp instrument. Like a butcher makes.'

A butcher. He had reminded Sung before that Tibet was the only land on the planet with butchers trained to cut up human bodies. 'Did you look for a bruise on the skull?'

Sung looked up.

'As you said,' Shan added. 'He was laid down before the incisions. No blood on his clothes. He must have been knocked unconscious. Then the cuts were made.'

'We seldom have a need for complete autopsies,' she muttered, and wheeled a lamp on rollers to the edge of the table. It was the closest she would come to an apology.

Shan could hear Sergeant Feng pacing in the corridor outside as Dr Sung examined the scalp.

'All right,' she said at last. 'Behind the right ear. A long ragged contusion. Some skin was opened.'

'A club? A baton?'

'No. Rough-edged. A rock could do it.'

Shan produced the card taken from the prosecutor's body. 'Do you know why Jao would have been talking to someone about X-ray equipment?'

Sung studied the card. 'American?' she asked, handing the card back. 'Too expensive for Tibet.' She pulled a pad from her pocket and began busily writing notes.

'Why would he want such equipment?'

She shrugged. 'Must have been for an investigation.' She turned the collar of her blouse up as if suddenly cold.

'What about the Americans at the mine? And their workers? Who provides medical care for them? Would someone need this type of equipment for them?'

Sung shook her head. 'They have to use the clinic like everyone else. Allocation of medical resources has been carefully planned.'

'Meaning what?' Shan asked.

'Meaning the most productive members of the proletariat must be supported first.'

Shan stared at her in disbelief. She was quoting something, as warily as if this were a *tamzing* session. 'The most productive members, doctor?'

'There is a memo from Beijing. I can show it to you. It states that Tibetans suffer permanent brain damage by spending their childhood in oxygen-deprived altitudes.'

Shan wouldn't let her get away with it. 'You're a graduate of Bei Da University, doctor. Surely you know the difference between medical science and political science.'

She returned his stare for a moment, then her gaze drifted to the floor.

'This must be difficult,' Shan offered. 'An autopsy on a friend.'

'Friend? Jao and I talked sometimes. Mostly it was just the investigations. And government functions. He told jokes. You don't often hear jokes in Tibet.'

'Like what?'

Sung thought a moment. 'There was one. Why do Tibetans die younger than Chinese?' She looked up expectantly, her mouth in a crooked shape that may have been a grin. 'Because they want to.'

'Investigations. You mean murders?'

'I get dead people. Murder. Suicide. Accident. I just fill out the forms.'

'But you wouldn't fill out our form.'

'Sometimes it's hard to ignore the obvious.'

'And the others? You're never curious?' he asked.

'Curiosity, Comrade, can be very dangerous.'

'How many traumatic deaths have you investigated over the past two years?'

'My job is to tell you about this body,' Sung frowned. 'Nothing else.'

'Right. Because that's what your forms are for.'

Sung threw her hands up in surrender. 'Anything to shut you up. Okay. I remember three who fell off mountains. Four in an avalanche. A suffocation. Four or five in auto accidents. One bled to death. Record-keeping is not my responsibility. And that's mostly the Han population. The local minorities,' she said with a meaningful glance, 'do not always rely on the facilities provided by the people's government.'

'Suffocation?'

'The Director of Religious Affairs died in the mountains.'

'Altitude sickness?'

'He didn't get sufficient oxygen,' Sung acknowledged.

'But that would be death from natural causes.'

'Not necessarily. He lost consciousness from a blow to the head. Before he recovered someone stuffed his windpipe with pebbles.'

'Pebbles?' Shan's head snapped up.

'Touching, really,' Sung said with a morbid smile. 'You know it was a traditional way to kill members of the royalty.'

Shan nodded slowly. 'Because no one was allowed to commit violence on them. Was there a trial?'

Sung shrugged again. It seemed to be her defining mannerism. 'I don't know. I think so. Bad elements. You know, protestors.'

'What protestors?'

'Not my job. I don't remember faces. If asked, I attend and read my medical reports to the tribunal. Always the same.'

'You mean you always read your reports. And a Tibetan is always condemned.'

Sung's only response was a sharp glare.

'Your dedication to duty is an inspiration.'

'Someday I'd like to return to Beijing, Comrade. How about you?'

Shan ignored the question. 'The one who bled to death. I suppose he stabbed himself fifty times.'

'Not exactly,' Sung said with a dark gleam. 'His heart was cut out. I have a theory on that one.'

'A theory?' Shan asked with a flicker of hope.

'He didn't do it himself.' On the way out she threw open the door so hard Sergeant Feng had to jump out of the way.

Twenty minutes later he was in Tan's office. He had passed Yeshe in the waiting room, ignoring his agitated whispering.

'You, Prisoner Shan,' Tan declared, 'must have balls the size of Chomolungma.'

'Do you know for certain the cases are not related?'

'Impossible,' the colonel growled. 'They're closed cases. You're supposed to be filling in one hole, not digging others.'

'But if they are related –'

'They are not related.'

'The Lhadrung Five, the people call them. You mentioned them two days ago. I didn't understand when you said the protestors keep proving your point, that you were too easy on them after the Thumb Riots. It's because they are being arrested again. For murder.'

'The minority cultists have difficulty complying with our laws. Possibly it has not escaped your attention.'

'How many of the Five have been arrested for murder?'

'It only proves it was a mistake to release them the first time.'

'How many?'

'Sungpo is the fourth.'

'Jao prosecuted them?'

'Of course.'

'The connections can't be ignored. The Ministry would not ignore such connections.'

'I see no connections.'

'The five were all here in Lhadrung. Convicted and imprisoned together. A connection. Then, one after another, four are charged with murder. A connection. First three prosecuted by Jao. The fourth charged with Jao's murder. A connection. I need to know about those three cases. Proving a conspiracy might finish the case.'

Colonel Tan eyed Shan suspiciously. 'Are you prepared to attack a conspiracy by the Buddhists?'

'I am prepared to find the truth.'

'Have you heard of the *purbas*?' Tan asked.

'A *purba* is a ceremonial dagger used in Buddhist temples.'

'It's also the name taken by a new resistance group. Monks mostly, though they don't seem to mind violence. A different breed. Very dangerous. Of course there's a conspiracy. By Buddhist hooligans, like the *purbas*, to kill government officials.'

'You're saying all the others were officials?'

Tan lit a cigarette and considered Shan. 'I'm saying don't let your paranoia conceal the obvious.'

'But what if it's something else? What if the Lhadrung Five themselves were the victims of a conspiracy?'

Tan gave an impatient wince. 'To what end?'

'Covering a larger crime. I could not suggest anything specific without analysing the other cases.'

'The other murders were all solved. Don't confuse the record.'

'What if there is another pattern?'

'A pattern?' When he exhaled smoke Tan had the appearance of a dragon. 'Who cares?'

'Patterns can't be seen in just two deaths. Sometimes not in three. But now we have four. Something may have been invisible that could be seen now. What if it were obvious to the Ministry, which will have access to the files? Four murders within a few months. Four of the five most prominent dissidents in the county are tried for those murders, but no effort is made to link the cases. And the victims include at least two of the most prominent officials in the county. Two or three, you might explain as a coincidence. Four murders feels like a crime wave. But five, that might seem negligent.'

A pattern, Shan repeated to himself as he followed Yeshe and Feng into the clutter of the market square. There was a pattern, he was certain. He knew it instinctively, the way a wolf might smell prey on the far side of a forest. But where was the scent coming from? Why did he feel so sure?

The market was a jumble of stalls and peddlers selling from blankets arranged on the packed earth. Shan's eyes opened wide as he absorbed the scene. Here before him was more life than he had seen in three years. A woman held out yak-hair yarn, another shouted prices for crocks of goat butter. He reached out and touched the top of a basket full of eggs. Shan hadn't tasted an egg since leaving Beijing. He could have stared at the basket for hours. The miracle of eggs. An old man tended an elaborate display of *torma*, the butter and dough effigies used as offerings. Children. His gaze settled on a group of children playing with a lamb. He fought the urge to walk over and touch one, to confirm that such youth and innocence still existed.

Feng bought a stick of roasted crab apples. A man with a milky eye whirled a prayer wheel and offered jars of *chang*, Tibetan beer made from barley. Yak cheese, hard, dry, and dirty, stood stacked beside a forlorn girl with waist-length hair braids. A boy offered plastic bags stuffed with yogurt, an old man some animal skins. Shan realized that most of the Tibetans wore sprigs of heather, tied or pinned to their shirts. A girl with one arm called for them to buy a rag of silk to use as a *khata*. The air was filled with the pungent traces of buttered tea, incense, and unwashed humans.

A squad of soldiers was checking the papers of a wiry, restless-looking man, who wore a dagger in his belt in the traditional *khampa* style. As the soldiers approached he gripped not the dagger but the amulet around his neck, the *gau* locket which probably contained an invocation to a protective spirit. They let him walk on. As the man gave his *gau* a pat of thanks, Shan suddenly remembered. The local inhabitants had complained about the blasting because it angered Tamdin. Fowler had said no, she started blasting only six months earlier. She meant Tamdin had been seen more than six months earlier. Tamdin had been angry earlier. A pattern. Had Tamdin killed earlier?

Yeshe stopped at the far end of the market, beside a shop whose door was a filthy carpet supported by two spindly poles. Sergeant Feng eyed the dark interior of the shop and frowned. More than one Chinese soldier had been ambushed in such places. He pointed towards a stall selling tea near the centre of the market. 'I'll have two cups, no more.' He reached into his shirt and pulled out a whistle on a lanyard. 'After that I'll call the patrol.' He pulled an apple from the stick with his teeth and walked away.

There was no window in the building, no doorway but the one they entered by. The interior was lit only by butter lamps, their meagre lights made even dimmer by the smoke of incense. As his eyes adjusted Shan discerned rows of shelves covered with bowls and jars. It was a herbalist's shop. An emaciated woman sat behind a wide plank laid across two upended crates. She cast a vacant stare at Shan and Yeshe. Three men sat on the earthen floor against the wall to the right, apparently in a state of stupor. Shan followed Yeshe's gaze to the left, into the darkest corner of the room. On a rough-hewn table sat a short, dirty conical hat with the bottom folded up. Behind it was a deeper shadow which had the shape of an animal, perhaps a large dog. 'An enchanter's cap,' Yeshe said with a nervous whisper. 'I haven't seen one since I was a boy.'

'You said nothing about Chinese,' the old hag barked. As she spoke one of the men on the floor sprang forward, grabbing a heavy staff that leaned against the shelves.

Yeshe put a restraining hand on Shan's arm. 'It's all right,' he replied nervously. 'He's not like that.'

The woman fixed Shan with a frigid stare, then pulled a jar of powder from the lowest shelf. 'You want something for sex, eh? That's what Chinese want.'

Shan shook his head slowly and turned towards Yeshe. Not like what? He took a step closer to the table in the corner. The shadow at the table seemed to have shifted. It was clearly a man now, who appeared to be asleep, or perhaps intoxicated. Shan took another step. The left half of the man's face had been crushed. Half his left ear had been cut away. A brown bowl sat in front of him, lined with silver. Shan studied the peculiar pattern on the vessel. It wasn't a bowl. It was the top half of a human skull.

Suddenly a second man leapt forward to hover at Shan's elbow. He muttered a threat in a dialect that was unintelligible to Shan. Shan turned and saw to his surprise that the man was a monk. But he had a wild, feral quality, a raw look that Shan had never seen in a monk.

'He says' – Yeshe looked at the sleeping man as he spoke – 'He says that if you take a photograph you will be sent immediately to the second level of the hot hell.'

No matter where Shan turned, people wanted to warn him of the great suffering that awaited him. He turned his palms outward to show that they were empty. 'Tell him,' he said wearily, 'that I am not acquainted with that particular hell.'

'Don't mock him,' Yeshe warned. 'He means Kalasutra. You are nailed down and your body is cut into pieces with a burning hot saw. These monks. They are from a very old sect. Almost none left. They will tell you it is real. They may tell you they have been there.'

Shan studied the monk with a chill.

Yeshe grabbed his arm and pulled. 'No. Don't anger him. This drunkard cannot be who we want. Let us leave this place.'

Shan ignored him and moved back towards the woman.

'I could read your omens,' the woman said in a voice like that of a hen.

'Not interested in omens,' Shan said. There was a brass piece, a plate the size of his palm on the table. It was inscribed along the perimeter with small images of Buddha. The centre was brilliantly polished.

'Your people like omens.'

'Omens just tell facts. I am interested in implications,' Shan said. He reached for the plate.

Yeshe's hand snapped up and grabbed his wrist before he touched it.

'Not for you,' the woman said with a chiding glance at Yeshe, as though she wished Shan had reached the disc.

'What is it?' he asked. Yeshe turned with his back to Shan, as though Shan needed protection.

146

'Much power,' the woman cackled. 'Enchantment. A trap.'

'Trap for what?'

'Death.'

'It catches the dead? You mean ghosts?'

'Not that kind of death,' she said enigmatically, and pushed his hand away.

'I don't understand.'

'Your people never understand. They fear death as an ending of life. But that is not the important one.'

'You mean it catches the forces that lay waste to the soul.'

The woman gave a slow nod of respect. 'When it can be focused correctly.' She considered him for a moment, then pulled a handful of black and white pebbles from a bowl and tossed them on the table. She solemnly arranged them in a line, then extracted several after careful deliberation. She looked at Shan sadly. 'For the next month you must not dig in the earth alone. You must light *torma* offerings. You must bow before black dogs.'

'I must speak with Khorda.'

'Who are you?' the woman asked.

Shan weighed her words. 'Right now,' he whispered back, 'I only know who I am not.'

She stepped around the table and took his hand as if he might lose his way if he tried to reach the corner alone. The monk moved to intercept him again, but was stopped with a sharp glance from the woman. He retreated to sit squarely in the entrance, facing outside. Yeshe squatted beside him at the door frame, facing Shan, as if he might need to spring to Shan's rescue at any moment.

Shan sat on a crate in front of the table and studied the old man.

As he did so the man's eyes burst open, instantly alert, the way a predator wakens.

Shan had the fleeting impression of looking into the face of an idol. The eye on the ragged side of the man's face looked at him with a supernatural intensity. The eyeball was gone, replaced with a brilliant red glass orb. The right eye, the living eye, seemed no more human. It too gleamed like a jewel, lit from the back.

'Choje Rinpoche suggested I speak with you.'

The eye seemed to turn inward for a moment, as though searching for recognition. 'I knew Choje when he was nothing but a brown-robe *rapjung*, an apprentice,' Khorda said at last. His voice was like gravel being rubbed against a rock. 'They took his gompa many years ago. Where does he study now?'

'The 404th *lao gai* brigade.'

Khorda nodded slowly. 'I've seen them take gompas.' The right side of Khorda's face twisted into a hideous grin. 'You know what it means?' the sorcerer asked. 'They eliminate it. They take it stone by stone. They eradicate its existence. They pound the foundation into the earth. Reclamation they call it. They take the stones and build barracks. If they could dig a hole deep enough they would bury all of Tibet.' Khorda stared at Shan. No, he stared at a point behind Shan that he seemed to see through Shan's skull. After a moment his eyelids shut.

'I touched a dead body,' said Shan.

Slowly the left eyelid opened. The red jewel stared at him. 'A common enough sin. Ransom a goat.' Khorda spoke with what seemed a shadow of a voice. It was hoarse and distant and gasping.

The penance was common among the herding people, who would buy a goat out of the herd to save it from the pot. 'Where I live there are no goats.'

The cheek curled in another half grin. 'Ransoming a yak would be even better.'

'The killer was wearing this.'

The sorcerer's face tightened. His good eye opened and

transfixed the disc that Shan held out. He pulled it from Shan's hand and held it closer.

'Once he was awakened,' Khorda nodded knowingly, 'he could not be expected to sit idle. When he sees everything he will have no more rest.'

'Everything? You mean the murders?'

'He means 1959,' the woman snapped from behind Shan. The year of the final Chinese invasion.

'I need to meet him.'

'People like you,' Khorda said, 'people like you cannot meet him.'

'But I must.'

Half of Khorda's face curled into a hideous smile. 'You will take the consequences?'

'I will take the consequences,' Shan said. He felt a tremor in his lips as he spoke.

'Your hands,' Khorda rasped. 'Let me see them.'

As Shan laid them on the table, palms upward, Khorda bent over each one, studying them a long time. His eyes rose to meet Shan's. As he did so, he pressed Shan's hands together and dropped a rosary into them.

The beads felt like ice. They seemed to numb his hands. They were made of ivory, and each was intricately carved in the shape of a skull.

'Repeat this,' Khorda said. There was something new in his voice, a bone-chilling tone of command that caused Shan to look into the sorcerer's eye. 'Look at me with the beads in your hands and repeat this. *Om! Padme te krid hum phat!*' he barked.

Shan did as he was told.

Behind him Yeshe gasped. The woman made a sound like the call of a raven. Was it laughter? Or fear?

They repeated the strange mantra at least twenty times. Then Shan realized Khorda had stopped and he was speaking alone. He felt light-headed, then an intense coldness clenched him and everything seemed to grow dark. The words came faster and faster, as though his voice was being controlled by another. Suddenly there was a brilliant flash that seemed to come from inside his head, and Khorda gave an immense roar. It was a sound of great pain.

Shan shivered violently. He dropped the beads and the room came back into focus. The shivering stopped, though his hands felt ice cold.

The sorcerer was gasping, as though from strenuous exercise. He looked warily around the chamber, especially into the shadows of the corners, as though expecting something to leap out. He reached and poked Shan's chest with a gnarled finger. 'You still alive?' he croaked. 'Is it still you, Chinese?' He retrieved the rosary and studied Shan's palms again.

Shan's heart was racing. 'How do I find Tamdin?' he asked.

'Follow his path. He won't be far now,' the sorcerer said with his crooked grin. 'If you are brave enough. The path of Tamdin is a path of ruthlessness. Sometimes only ruthlessness reaches his truth.'

'What –' Shan's mouth was as dry as sand. 'What if someone offended Tamdin? What would need to be done?'

'Offend a protector demon? Then expect to attain nothingness.'

'No. I mean a true believer did something in the name of Tamdin, pretending to be Tamdin. Maybe borrowing the face of Tamdin.'

'For the virtuous there are charms for forgiveness. Might work for the girl.'

'A girl has come to see you and asked to be forgiven by Tamdin?'

Khorda said nothing.

'Can they work for me?' If a non-believer used a costume, Shan realized, they would not ask for a charm. But surely a non-believer would have no reason to use the costume, unless they were framing the Buddhist monk.

And then they would not be concerned with forgiveness. Shan sighed. He wished he could simply settle for attaining nothingness.

Khorda lifted his enchanter's cap and set it on his head. As if it were a cue, the woman appeared with a sheet of rice paper, ink, and a brush. Khorda lifted the brush and began to work on the paper. He inscribed several large ideograms, then closed his right eye and raised the paper to the jewelled eye. He shook his head sadly, tore the paper into pieces and dropped it onto the floor. 'It won't stick to you,' Khorda grunted in frustration, fixing Shan with his unearthly stare. 'You require much more.' The sorcerer's hand, still clutching the rosary, began to shake.

'What do you see?' Shan heard himself say, as though from a distance. He massaged his fingers. They still seemed icy cold where they had touched the skull rosary.

'I have known men like you. Like a magnet. No. Not that. A lightning rod. If you are not careful your soul will wear out long before your body.'

Khorda's hand was shaking violently now. It began to move. Khorda seemed to fight it, to try to restrain it, but without avail. It leapt at Shan and grabbed his pocket. Two bony fingers pulled out a paper. It was the charm from Choje. The shaking hand unfolded it, then abruptly dropped it, as though burned.

The old man studied the paper and nodded deferentially. 'This Choje must love you well, Chinese, to give you such a thing,' he said solemnly. A hoarse laugh rose in his throat. 'Now I know why you survived,' he said, wheezing. 'But it cannot change the thing you did.' He gave a great sigh, as though he had been released from a powerful grip, and began to stare at the skull beads in his hand. An intense curiosity seized his face, as if he could not understand how they got there, or why.

'The thing I did? The mantra, with the skulls?' Shan asked.

But Khorda seemed not to hear. The woman pulled his

arm urgently. 'The summoning,' she hissed, pushing him out the door. 'You summoned the demon.'

As they moved back through the maze of stalls, a two-wheeled cart filled with young goats turned in front of them, pulled by two old women. The women stumbled and the cart flew upward, tipping its contents directly onto Sergeant Feng. Feng went down, entangled in bleating animals. The alley exploded with activity. Merchants angrily shouted to keep the goats from their wares. Herdsmen moved in to help, adding to the confusion.

Three men, dressed in the fleece vests and caps of herders, materialized at Shan's side. They pushed Yeshe and Shan into a doorway six feet away. One of them turned his back to them, blocking the view to Feng; he began shouting encouragement to the herdsmen.

'We know you have Sungpo,' one of them said abruptly. He pulled back his cap, revealing a familiar haircut. Several long scars crisscrossed his face.

'Isn't it a breach of the monastic rules not to wear your robe?' Shan asked.

The man gave him a sour look. 'When you do not hold a licence you are not so fastidious,' he said with a distracted tone. He was studying Yeshe. 'What was your gompa?' he demanded.

Yeshe tried to push away. The man at his arm responded by squeezing the top of his shoulder. The motion seemed to take Yeshe's breath away. He bent over, gasping. It was a traditional martial arts pincer movement against a pressure point.

'What kind of monks –' Shan began, then recognized the scars. They were the kind left by Public Security batons, from a beating so savage it ripped open long gutters of skin. Sometimes Public Security glued sandpaper to their batons.

The man's companion held Yeshe by the upper arm.

'*Purba!*' Yeshe warned.

'Some say you are among the *zung mag* protected by Choje Rinpoche,' the scarred-face man said. *Zung mag* was a Tibetan term. It meant prisoners of war. It was not a term Choje ever used. 'Others say you are protected by Colonel Tan. It cannot be both. It is a dangerous game you play.' He silently pulled up Shan's arm, unbuttoned the cuff and rolled up his sleeve. He pushed the flesh around the tattoo. It was a test used in the prisons for infiltrators. Recent tattoos would not lose their colour because of the bruising underneath.

The man nodded at his companion, who relaxed his grip on Yeshe. 'Do you have any idea of what will happen if you execute another of the Five?' Inside his sleeve another garment was visible. He was wearing a robe after all, Shan realized, under the herdsmen's clothes.

For some reason the man made Shan angry. 'Murder is a capital offence.'

'We know about capital offences in Tibet,' the *purba* snapped. 'My uncle was executed for throwing your chairman's quotations into a chamber pot. My brother was killed for conducting rites at a mass grave.'

'You are talking about history.'

'That makes it better?'

'Not at all,' Shan said. 'But what does it mean for you and me?'

The *purba* glared at Shan. 'They killed my lama,' he said.

'They killed my father,' Shan shot back.

'But you are going to prosecute Sungpo.'

'No. I am making an investigation file.'

'Why?'

'I am a *lao gai* prisoner. It is the labour assigned to me.'

'Why would they use a prisoner? It makes no sense.'

'Because I had a life before the 404th. I was an

investigator in Beijing. That is why Tan chose me. Why he decided to do an investigation outside the prosecutor's office I do not yet know.'

The rancour began to fade from the man's voice. 'There were riots before, the last time the knobs came to this valley. Many were killed. It was never reported.'

Shan nodded sadly.

'It seemed that they were beginning to move on. But then they started persecuting the Five.'

'Prosecution. There was a murder in each case.' As much as he disliked the man's violence, Shan desperately wanted to find common grounds with the *purbas*. 'At least accept that murderers must be punished. This is not some pogrom against the Buddhists.'

'Do you know that?'

No, Shan realized wearily, he didn't know that. 'But each started with a murder.'

'Strange words, for someone from Beijing. I know your kind. Murder isn't a crime. It's a political phenomenon.'

Shan felt an unfamiliar fire as he stared back at the young monk. 'What is it you seek? To warn me? To scare me away from a job I am forced to do?'

'There must be payment in kind. When you take one of ours.'

'Revenge is not the Buddhist way.'

When the monk frowned, the long gouts of scar tissue contorted his face into a gruesome mask. 'The story of my country's destruction. Peaceful coexistence. Let virtue prevail over force. It doesn't work when virtue has no voice left.' He grabbed Shan's chin and forced Shan to look as he turned his head slowly, to be certain Shan could see the ruin of his face. 'In this country, when you turn the other cheek they just destroy both of them.'

Shan pushed the *purba*'s hand away and looked into his smouldering eyes. 'Then help me. There is nothing that can stop this, except the truth.'

'We do not care who murdered the prosecutor.'

154

'The only reason they will release a suspect is because they have a better one.'

The *purba* stared at Shan, still suspicious. 'In the hut of Choje Rinpoche, there is a Chinese prisoner who prays with Rinpoche. They call him the Chinese Stone, because he is so hard. He has never broken. He tricked them into releasing an old man.'

'His name was Lokesh,' Shan acknowledged. 'He sang the old songs.'

The man nodded slowly. 'What are you asking of us?'

'I don't know.' Shan's eyes wandered toward Khorda's hut. 'I would like to know who has suddenly been asking for charms for forgiveness from Tamdin. A young girl. And I need to find Balti, Prosecutor Jao's *khampa* driver. No one has seen him or the car since the murder.'

'You think we would collaborate?'

'On the truth, yes.'

The monk did not reply. Sergeant Feng's voice could be heard now, calling for Shan and Yeshe above the bleat of the goats.

'Here –' the *purba* in front spun about and dropped a small goat into Yeshe's arms. His alibi.

Feng was raising the whistle to his lips as Shan and Yeshe stepped out of the doorway.

Shan glanced back. The *purbas* were gone.

Yeshe was silent as they returned to the truck. He sat in the back and stared at a piece of heather, like those worn by the people in the market. 'A girl gave it to me,' he said in a desolate tone. 'She said to wear it for them. I asked who she meant. She said the souls of the 404th. She said the sorcerer announced they were all going to be martyred.'

Chapter Eight

The lamp-posts leading out of town were being painted silver, no doubt for the honoured guests soon to arrive from Beijing and America. But a high wind was blowing, so that sand particles adhered to the poles as quickly as the workers applied the paint, making the poles appear even shabbier than before. Shan envied the proletariat its ability to embrace the most important lesson of their society, that the goal of any worker was not to do a good job, but to do a correct job.

The kiosks that housed public phones were being painted, too, although Sergeant Feng could not find a single phone that worked. He followed a wire to a musty tea shop at the edge of town and commandeered a phone.

'No one will stop you,' Colonel Tan replied when Shan told him he needed to inspect the skull cave. 'I closed it down the day we found the head. What took you so long? Surely you're not frightened of a few bones?'

As the truck climbed the low gravel foothills that led out of the valley, Yeshe seemed more restless than usual. 'You should not have done it,' he burst out at last. 'You shouldn't meddle.'

Shan turned in his seat. Yeshe's gaze moved unsteadily across the skyline as they headed towards the huge mass of the Dragon Claws. Giant cumulus clouds, almost blindingly white against the cobalt sky, had snagged on the peaks in the distance.

'Meddle with what?'

'What you did. The skull mantra. You had no right to summon the demon.'

156

'So you believe that's what I did?'

'No. It's just that these people . . .' Yeshe's voice faded away.

'These people? You mean your people?'

Yeshe frowned. 'Summoning is a dangerous thing. To the old Buddhists, words were the most dangerous weapon of all.'

'You believe I summoned a demon?' Shan repeated.

Yeshe cut his eyes at Shan, then looked away. 'It's not so simple. People will hear about the words you spoke. Some will say the demon will possess the summoner. Some will say the demon has been invited to act again. Khorda was right. Ruthlessness follows the name of the demon.'

'I thought the demon was already released.'

Yeshe looked with pain into his hands. 'Our demons, they have a way of becoming self-fulfilling.'

Shan considered his companion. He had never known anyone who could sound like a monk one moment and a party functionary the next. 'What do you mean?'

'I don't know. Things will happen. It will become an excuse.'

'For what? Telling the truth?'

Yeshe winced and turned back to the window.

Only one thing the sorcerer had said made sense. Follow the path of Tamdin. The Tamdin killer had gone from the 404th, then over the mountains to the skull cave. And Shan had to follow the path, had to return to the horrible, holy place of the dead lamas.

A single army truck with two drowsy guards sat at the turnoff to the skull cave, stationed there while Tan kept the project closed for the investigation. Startled by the sudden appearance of visitors, the soldiers grabbed their rifles, then relaxed as they saw Feng at the wheel.

The air was strangely still as they drove into the little valley. Overhead clouds scudded quickly by, but as they reached the small plateau with the solitary tree, Shan saw

157

that no wind touched its branches. He climbed out of the truck with a strange apprehension. There was also no sound. There was almost no colour other than the browns and greys of the rock and shed, except for a new sign in bright red characters. DANGER, it said, ENTRANCE FORBIDDEN BY ORDER OF THE MINISTRY OF GEOLOGY.

Yeshe exchanged an uneasy glance with Shan, then followed him towards the cave entrance. Feng hung back as they checked their flashlights, conspicuously examining the tyres as though they suddenly required his attention.

The two men walked silently through the entrance tunnel, Yeshe lagging farther behind Shan with each step.

'This is not –' Yeshe began nervously as he joined Shan at the edge of the main chamber. In the dim, shaking light of their handlamps the huge figures on the walls seemed to dance, staring angrily at them.

'Not what?'

'Not a place where –' Yeshe was struggling, but with what Shan was not certain. Had he been asked to stop Shan somehow? Had he perhaps decided to quit his assignment?

The figures of the demons and Buddhas seemed to be speaking to Yeshe. He cocked his head towards them, his face clouding, but it wasn't fear of the images, nor hatred of Shan. It was just pain. 'We should not go here,' he said. 'It is only for the most holy of people.'

'You're refusing to continue on religious grounds?'

'No,' Yeshe shot back defensively. He fixed his eyes on the ground, refusing to look at the paintings. 'I mean, this is only meaningful for the religious minorities.' He looked up, but refused to look Shan in the eyes. 'The Bureau of Religious Affairs has specialists. They would be better qualified to engage in cultural interpretations.'

'Odd. I thought a trained monk would be even better.'

Yeshe turned away.

'I think you're scared,' Shan said to his back, 'scared that someone will accuse you of being Tibetan.'

A sound something like a laugh came from Yeshe's throat, but there was no laughter in his eyes.

'Who are you?' Shan pressed. 'The good Chinese who craves losing himself with a billion others just like him? Or the Tibetan who recognizes that lives are at stake here? Not just one, but many. And we are the only ones who have a chance of saving them. Me. And you.'

Yeshe looked back as though with a question and froze. Shan followed his gaze. There were lights at the opposite side of the chamber, and voices raised in excitement.

Instantly they extinguished their own lamps and stepped back into the tunnel. Tan had shut down the cave. No one else was authorized to enter. There had been no other vehicles outside. Whoever the intruders were, they were running a grave risk if captured.

'*Purbas*,' Yeshe whispered. 'We must leave, quickly.'

'But we just left them back at the market.'

'No. Their ranks are large. They are very dangerous. There is a decree from the capital. It is a citizen's duty to report them.'

'So you want to get away from me to report them?' Shan asked.

'What do you mean?'

'We were with Sergeant Feng since seeing the *purbas* in the market. You said nothing to him.'

'They are outlaws.'

'They are monks. Are you going to report them?' Shan repeated.

'If we get caught working with them it will be conspiracy,' Yeshe said in anguish. 'At least five years *lao gai*.'

Shan realized the intruders were not in the skull tunnel, but a smaller alcove in the centre of the far wall. He pushed Yeshe towards them, moving silently along the perimeter of the huge chamber. Suddenly, when less than thirty feet separated them, a brilliant strobe exploded.

The camera flash was aimed towards the wall paintings beside him, but caught Shan in the face, blinding him. A high-pitched scream split the air, then was abruptly stifled. 'Son of a bitch,' someone else groaned in a lower voice.

Shan, shielding his eyes against another flash, switched on his light. Rebecca Fowler, her hand clutching her chest as though she had been kicked, stared at them numbly.

'Jesus, boys,' the man with camera said. 'Thought you were ghosts for sure.' Tyler Kincaid gave a quick, forced laugh and aimed a high-powered beam behind them. 'You alone?'

'The army is outside,' Yeshe blurted out, as though in warning.

'Sergeant Feng is outside,' Shan corrected.

'So here we are,' Kincaid said, and took another picture. 'Thieves in the night, you might say.'

'Thieves?'

'Just funny – I mean, you sneaking around without lights. Doesn't exactly feel official.'

'And when asked, how should I say this cave relates to your mining project, Miss Fowler?' Shan asked.

Kincaid's comment seemed to have restored her confidence. 'I told you. The UN Antiquities Commission. Who's going to ask?' She cocked her head. 'And why are you here?'

Shan ignored the question. 'And Mr Kincaid?'

'I asked him to come. For the photos.'

Shan remembered the photographs of Tibetans in the American's office.

'And how much have you seen?'

'This,' Rebecca Fowler gestured around the main chamber with a look of awe. 'And we're just getting to the records.'

'Records?'

She escorted him into the alcove, which was partially concealed by a canvas sheet hung over the entrance. Three makeshift tables had been erected on planks over wooden crates. One table held cartons of paper files, another empty beer bottles and ashtrays overflowing with cigarette butts. The third, much cleaner, had a cloth thrown over it, with small cartons containing computer disks, a pad to accommodate a portable computer, and an open ledger.

Kincaid kept snapping photos as Shan and Fowler examined the ledger. Beginning a month earlier, it recorded the removal of an altar and reliquaries, offering lamps and a statue of Buddha. Dimensions, weight and quantity were fastidiously recorded.

'What does it say?' Fowler asked. It was not unusual for foreigners learning Chinese to study only the conversational, not the written language.

Shan hesitated, then quickly summarized the contents.

'How about books?' Tyler Kincaid asked. 'The old manuscripts. Jansen says they are usually well preserved, the kind of thing that can easily be saved.'

There was a page recording the removal of two hundred manuscripts. 'I don't know,' Shan replied. He knew about recovered manuscripts. Once at the 404th a dump truck had deposited several hundred old religious tracts. Under gunpoint the prisoners had been forced to rip the volumes into small pieces which were boiled in big pots, then mixed with lime and sand to make plaster for the guards' new latrine.

'And on the first page?' Fowler asked.

'First page?'

'Who wrote this? Who is in charge?'

Shan turned to the overleaf. 'Ministry of Geology, it says. By order of Director Hu.'

Fowler shoved her hand forward to hold down the overleaf and called for Kincaid to photograph the page.

161

'The bastard,' she muttered. 'No wonder Jao wanted to stop him.'

Was it possible, Shan considered, that Fowler was in the cave not about the antiquities but about her mining permit?

Kincaid changed lenses and began photographing the pages, pausing over the detailed entries. 'They took an altar, you said. Where's it say that?'

Shan showed him.

Kincaid placed his finger on a column on the right side of the page. 'What's this?'

'Weights and dimensions,' Shan explained.

'Three hundred pounds, it says.' The American nodded. 'But look, here is something even heavier. Four hundred and twenty pounds.'

'The statue.'

'Can't be,' Kincaid argued, following the line of data. 'It shows it's only three feet high.'

Shan studied the entry again. The American was right.

Yeshe, over their shoulders, explained. 'In these old shrines,' he said in a brittle voice, 'the altar statue was often solid gold.'

Kincaid whistled. 'My god! It's worth millions.'

'Priceless,' Fowler said, excitement in her eyes. 'The right museum –'

'I don't think so,' Shan interrupted.

'No, really. Do you have any idea how rare this statue is? A major find. The find of the year.'

'No,' Shan shook his head slowly. He found himself almost angered by the Americans' passion. No, not their passion. Their innocence.

'What do you mean?' Fowler asked.

Shan answered by shining his light around the room. He found what he expected under one of the other tables, a pile of hammers and chisels. 'Four hundred pounds of gold would be inconvenient to transport in one large piece.' He picked up one of the chisels and showed the

Americans the flecks of brilliant metal embedded in its blade.

Rebecca Fowler grabbed the chisel, stared at it, then threw it against the wall. 'Bastards!' she shouted. Angrily she grabbed several of the computer disks and stuffed three of them into her shirt pocket, staring at Shan as she did so, as if daring him to defy her.

Kincaid gazed at the woman with obvious admiration, then began shooting photos again. Yeshe began leafing through the ledger, pausing at a loose sheet near the back. He looked up excitedly and handed the page to Shan. 'An audit page,' he whispered, as though he could keep the Americans from hearing. 'From the Bureau of Religious Affairs.'

'But it's blank.'

'Yes,' Yeshe said. 'But look at it. Columns to identify the gompa, date, relics found, distribution of relics. If Religious Affairs does audits, we could find if any gompas had a Tamdin costume.'

'And if so, when it was found, and where it is now,' Shan nodded, with an edge of excitement.

'Exactly.'

Shan folded the sheet and was about to put it in his pocket, then paused and handed it to Yeshe, who stuffed it in his shirt with a look that for the first time might have been satisfaction.

Shan slowly moved out of the alcove, leaving his three companions with the murals as he moved into the tunnel where Colonel Tan had taken him. He paused just before the circle of his light reached the first of the skulls, trying to find words to prepare the others. But no words came, and he forced his feet ahead.

Even the dead were different in Tibet. He had been in mass boneyards back home, after the Cultural Revolution. But there the dead had not felt holy, or wise, or even complete. They had just felt used.

As he moved along the shrine, he found himself

163

gasping. He stopped and surveyed the rows of empty eye sockets. They all seemed to be watching him, the endless lines of skulls like the endless rosary of skulls Khorda had pressed into his hands before making Shan call for Tamdin. With a start, he realized they had been witnesses. Tamdin had been there with Prosecutor Jao's head, and the skulls had seen it all. The skulls knew.

Behind him he heard a shudder. The others had discovered the tunnel. Fowler groaned. Kincaid cursed loudly. Something like a whimper escaped Yeshe's lips. Shan clenched his jaw and moved on to the shelf where Jao's head had been deposited. He tried to sketch the scene, but stopped. His hand was trembling too much.

'What is it you expect to find?' Yeshe whispered nervously over his shoulder. He stood with his back to Shan, as if expecting to be ambushed at any moment. 'This is not a place we should stay in.'

'The murderer came here with Jao's head. I want to find the skull that was moved from here to make room for Jao. Why was this particular shelf disturbed? Was there a reason for this particular skull to be moved? Where was its skull moved to?' Shan felt almost certain that Tan had given him the answer to the last question already. It would have been thrown into the shed with the other skulls being processed for the fertilizer plant in Chengdu.

Yeshe seemed not to have heard. 'Please,' he pleaded. 'We should go.'

As the Americans approached they were speaking of Tibetan history. 'Kincaid says this was probably a cave of Guru Rinpoche,' Fowler announced. She too was whispering.

'Guru Rinpoche?' Shan asked.

'The most famous of the ancient hermits,' Yeshe interjected. 'He inhabited caves all over Tibet in his lifetime, making each one a place of great power. Most were turned into shrines centuries ago.'

'I had no idea Mr Kincaid was such a scholar,' Shan observed.

'Jao wanted to stop them,' Fowler announced suddenly, her voice cracking. Shan looked up. A single tear rolled down her cheek.

'What's that?' Yeshe asked in an urgent whisper. 'I thought I heard something!'

There was something, Shan sensed. Not a sound. Not a movement. Not a presence. Something unspeakable and immense that seemed to have been triggered by Fowler's sadness. He lowered his pad and stood silently with the others, transfixed by the hollow sockets of the gleaming skulls. They weren't in the heart of the mountain. They were in the heart of the universe, and the numbing silence that welled around them wasn't silence at all, but a soul-wrenching hoarseness like the moment before a scream.

Choje was right, Shan suddenly knew, it was meaningless to ask whether Tamdin was indeed the grotesque monster he had seen painted on the wall. Whoever or whatever the killer had been, the killer had been a demon, not because it had decapitated Prosecutor Jao but because it had brought the ugliness of the act to such a perfect place.

He became aware of something new, a slight rustle of noise that became a chatter. It seemed to be coming from the skulls. Rebecca Fowler stepped closer to Kincaid, who turned and raised his camera towards Yeshe. He fired the strobe like a weapon and the noise stopped. Shan suddenly realized they had been hearing an echoing mantra, started by Yeshe.

The spell was broken.

'You could still help,' Shan suggested as he recovered.

Fowler looked up with a haggard expression. 'Anything.'

'We need a record. If Mr Kincaid could photograph all the shelves.' The skulls knew, Shan told himself again. Maybe he could make them talk.

Kincaid nodded slowly. 'I could get all three levels in one frame. Should have just about enough film.'

'I need the inscriptions for each skull included. After I study the photos maybe we could turn them over to your UN Commission.'

Fowler offered Shan a small, sad nod of gratitude, but lingered when Yeshe went to help Kincaid with the first row of skulls. She and Shan moved cautiously down the tunnel. The shelves ended, replaced by more images of demons painted on the walls.

'Is it true that you're being forced to do this, that you're a prisoner of some kind?' Fowler asked suddenly.

Shan kept walking. 'Who told you that?'

'Nobody. Tyler just said that nobody knows who you are. You were some kind of outside official, we thought. But outside officials – I don't know, outside officials get lots of respect.' She winced at her own words.

He was touched by her embarrassment.

'Tyler says it's funny, the way your sergeant watches you. He carries a gun, but he's not a bodyguard. A bodyguard would watch past you, around you. But your sergeant, he just watches you.'

Shan stopped and turned his light towards the American's face. 'When I am not investigating murders I build roads,' he confessed. 'In what they call a labour brigade.'

Fowler's hand went to her mouth. 'My god,' she whispered, biting a knuckle. 'In one of those awful prisons?' She looked away, towards the demons. Her eyes were bright and wet when she spoke again. 'I don't understand anything. How are you – why would you –' she shook her head. 'I'm so sorry. I'm such a fool.'

'A very senior Party member told me once that there're only two types of people in my country,' Shan observed. 'Masters and slaves. I don't believe it, and I would be saddened if you did.'

Fowler offered a weak smile. 'But how could you be investigating?'

'It was my talent before being elevated to road labourer. I used to be an investigator in Beijing.'

'But you defy Tan, I saw it. If he's your –'

Shan held up a hand, not wanting to hear the next word. *Prisonkeeper*, perhaps? Even *slavemaster*? 'Maybe that's why – because he can inflict no further harm.' It was the kind of half-truth an American would believe.

'Which is why you won't prove that monk is Jao's killer?'

'I can't. He's innocent.'

Fowler stared at him. Maybe, Shan considered, she knew too much about China to accept such a bold statement.

'Then what's going on? You're here like a thief. Li is conducting an investigation, too, but he's not here. What is Tan so worried about?'

So she did know more about China than Shan expected. 'I am confused about you too, Miss Fowler,' he countered. 'You are the manager, but you said Mr Kincaid's father owns the company.'

The American woman gave an amused grunt. 'Long story. Short version is that just because Tyler's father runs the company doesn't mean they get along.'

'They are not close? You mean for him Tibet is a punishment?'

'You know what a dropout is? Tyler went to mining school like his family wanted, so he could take over the company someday. But after graduation he announced he wanted none of it. Said the company ruined the environment, said it impoverished local populations. Spent several hundred thousand of his trust funds on a ranch in California, where he lived a few years, then gave it to a wildlife conservation group that was blocking a new mine his father wanted to build. Took a few years for things to cool down to where they would speak to one another, a few more before Tyler agreed to take a job in the company. But his father was still distrustful enough that he wouldn't put him in charge. Still, they're talking now. Tyler is serious about making a new life for himself. He's a damned good engineer. Tyler will be chairman one day, and one of the richest men in America.'

'And you? You're very young for such responsibilities.'

'Young?' Fowler shook her head slowly and sighed. 'I haven't felt young for a long time.' She stopped, looking ahead. The tunnel opened into another chamber. 'Guess I'm the opposite of Tyler. Never had two cents when I was growing up. Worked hard, saved, won scholarships. Worked like a dog for ten years to get here.'

'And you chose Tibet?'

She shrugged as she stepped forward. 'It's not what I expected.'

The paintings inside the chamber presented a tableau of Tibetan geography, images of mountains and palaces and shrines. On the floor at one end were shards of bone and a dozen skulls arranged in a triangle shape. Fifteen feet away was a row of skulls, surrounded by bootprints. The soldiers had been bowling.

Fowler picked up a skull and held it reverently in her palms, then began to retrieve the others as though to return them to the shelves. Shan touched her arm. 'You can't,' he warned. 'They will know you were here.'

She nodded silently, and turned back down the tunnel wearing a desolate expression. Joining Yeshe and Kincaid, waiting in the main chamber, the four moved quickly away. No one spoke until they were near the entrance.

'Wait a quarter of an hour,' Shan suggested, 'then return the same way you arrived.' He did not ask how they knew a secret route. 'I will come for the photos –'

He was interrupted by a gasp from Fowler. A figure had appeared in the entranceway, lit by the brilliant sunlight as though with a spotlight.

'It's him!' Fowler cried in a hoarse whisper and she and Kincaid faded into the shadows. But Shan needed no explanation. The man in the entrance could only be Director Hu of the Ministry of Geology.

Shan stepped out into the light.

'Comrade Inspector!' the short, stocky man called out. 'What a pleasure! I had hoped to find you still here.' On his wide face his tiny black eyes looked like beetles.

'We have not been introduced,' Shan observed slowly, surveying the compound as he spoke.

'No. But here I am, coming all this way to help you. And here you are, working so hard to help me.' He ceremoniously handed Shan his card. It was made of vinyl. Director of Mines, Lhadrung County, it read. Hu Yaohong. Hu Who Wants to be Red.

A red truck was parked beside their own; the same truck that had been parked at the worksite the day they had discovered Jao's body. He studied it more closely. It was a British Land Rover, the most expensive vehicle Shan had ever seen in Lhadrung.

'You came to help?'

'That, and for a security check.'

There was a man talking to Feng. With a twitch of his gut Shan realized Hu wasn't referring to security at the entrance. The second visitor was Lieutenant Chang, from the 404th. Chang looked at him with an indolent eye, the gaze of a shopkeeper confirming his inventory.

As Director Hu took a step towards the cave Shan moved in front of him. 'I do have some questions for you.'

'In my mine, I can show you –'

'No,' Shan pressed. Had Hu seen the Americans? He half expected Kincaid to step out for a photograph. 'Please. I'd rather not. He put his hand on his stomach and tried to look nauseated. 'It's very unsettling for me.'

'You're scared?' The Director of Mines looked amused. He wore a large gold ring. For a geologist he seemed extremely well dressed. 'We could sit in the car perhaps? It's British, you know.'

'I have to return to town. Colonel Tan.'

'Excellent! I'll drive you. I must explain my evidence.' Hu called out and Chang threw him the keys, then nodded as Hu instructed him to follow with Feng and Yeshe.

'Evidence?' Shan asked.

Hu seemed not to have heard. They spoke no more until they were on the main road. Hu drove hard, seeming to enjoy the rough road and the way Shan grabbed the dashboard as they bounced. On the curves he accelerated, laughing as the rear wheels skidded in the dirt.

'Civilization,' Director Hu said abruptly. 'It's a process, you know, not a concept.'

'You spoke of evidence,' Shan said, confused.

'Exactly. It's more than a process. It's a dialectic. A war. My father was stationed in Xinjiang, with the Moslems. In the old days they were even worse than the Buddhists. Bombings. Machine-gun raids. A lot of good government workers were sacrificed. The dynamic of civilization. New against old. Science against mythology.'

'You're speaking of the Chinese against Tibetans?'

'Exactly. It's progess, that's all. Advanced agricultural techniques, universities. Modern medicine. You think the advance in medicine wasn't a struggle? A battle against folklore and sorcerers. Half the babies born here used to die. Now babies live. Isn't that worth fighting for?'

Maybe not, Shan wanted to say, if the government won't let you have babies. 'You're saying Prosecutor Jao was a martyr for civilization.'

'Of course. His family will get a letter from the State Council, you know. The lesson is there for all of us. The challenge is making sure they get the lesson.'

'They?'

'This case must also be an opportunity for the minority

170

population to recognize how regressive, how backward, their ways are.'

'So you want to help with the evidence.'

'It is my duty.' Hu reached into his pocket and produced a folded paper. 'A statement from a guard stationed at the road into the skull cave. The night of the murder a monk was seen walking along the road near the entrance.'

'A monk? Or a man wearing a monk's robe?'

'It's all there. Matches this Sungpo's description.'

A monk was seen acting suspiciously near the entrance, the guard had written. He was of medium height, medium build. His head was shaven. He appeared antagonistic, and was carrying something in a cloth sack. The guard had signed the statement. Private Meng Lau. Shan put the paper in his pocket.

'When did this guard see this man?'

Hu shrugged. 'Later. After the murder. It happened at night, right?'

'How close was he? There was a new moon. Not much light.'

Hu sighed impatiently. 'Soldiers make good witnesses, Comrade. I expected more gratitude.'

He sped up as they reached the valley floor, laughing as he raised a cloud of dust around Feng, Yeshe, and Chang, still following closely. 'You said you had questions for me, Comrade Inspector?'

'Mostly about security. And how someone might get in the cave at night,' Shan replied.

'When we first discovered the cave we posted guards at its mouth. But after the contents were revealed they were all spooked. So we put a detail out on the road. Only way in and out. Seemed adequate.'

'But someone found another way.'

'These monks, they climb like squirrels.'

'Who discovered the cave?'

'We did,' Hu acknowledged. 'I have exploration teams.'

'So you found the Americans' brine deposits?'

'Of course. We issued their licence.'

'But now you want to cancel it.'

Hu looked at Shan, plainly peeved, then slowed the truck. They had reached the outskirts of Lhadrung. 'Not at all. What is being discussed is the operating permit, which assures that they comply with specified management systems. We are engaged in a dialogue about management. I am a friend of the American company.'

'By "management" you mean individual managers?'

'Pond construction technique, harvesting technology, equipment specification, utility consumption, and the conduct of their managers are all subject to permit criteria. Why do you ask?'

'So if you wanted a certain manager to leave you might suspend the operating permit.'

Director Hu laughed. 'And I thought your geological interests were confined to hauling rocks.'

Shan considered his words as they parked in front of the municipal building. 'I find it interesting that you knew I am a prisoner and still you came all the way out to the cave. I thought the Director of Mines would simply order me to appear.'

Hu replied with a wooden smile. 'I'm teaching Lieutenant Chang how to drive. When Colonel Tan told me where you were —' Hu shrugged. 'Chang must learn to navigate the mountain roads.'

'Is that why you were at the 404th worksite the day the body was found?'

Hu sighed, trying to control his impatience. 'We must be vigilant against faults.'

'Geological I presume.'

Hu grinned. 'The ranges are unstable. We must be careful about the people's roads.'

Shan was tempted to ask again if Hu was speaking of

geology. 'Comrade Director, would you please join me with the colonel?' he asked instead.

Director Hu's look of amusement did not fade. He tossed the keys to Chang, who had appeared behind them, and followed Shan inside.

Madame Ko gave Shan a nod of welcome and dashed into Tan's darkened room. The colonel's eyes were puffy. He was stretching. Shan glanced around the room. On the large conference table was a rumpled pillow.

'Colonel Tan, I would like to ask Director Hu a question.'

'You interrupted me for this?' Tan growled.

'I wanted to do it in your presence.'

Tan lit a cigarette and gestured towards Hu.

'Director Hu,' Shan asked, 'can you tell us why you suspended the American's permit?'

Hu frowned at Tan. 'He is intruding into Ministry business. It is counterproductive to engage in public dialogue about our problems with the American mine.'

Tan nodded slowly. 'You do not have to answer. Comrade Shan is sometimes too enthusiastic.' He fixed Shan with a sharp look of censure.

'Then perhaps,' Shan pressed, 'you could tell us where you were on the night Prosecutor Jao was murdered?'

The Director of Mines stared in disbelief at Shan, then, as a broad smile grew on his face, turned to Tan and began to laugh.

'Director Hu,' Tan explained with a cold grin, 'was with me. He invited me to dinner at his house. We played chess and drank some good Chinese beer.'

Hu's laughter became almost uncontrolled. 'Have to go,' he said between gasps and, throwing a mock salute at Shan, he disappeared through the door.

'You are fortunate he is so easygoing,' Tan warned. There was no amusement in his eyes.

'Tell me something, Colonel. Is the skull cave an official project?'

'Of course. You've seen all the soldiers there. A big operation.'

'I mean, does Beijing know about it?'

Tan exhaled a column of smoke. 'That would be the responsibility of the Ministry of Geology.'

'It's filled with cultural artefacts. The operation itself is the army's. How do Hu and the Ministry of Geology fit in?'

'They discovered it. They are responsible for exploitation. But they have only a small staff. As county administrator I offered the assistance of the army. A good field exercise.'

'Who benefits from the gold?'

'The government.'

'In this case, who is the government?'

'I don't know all the agencies which participate. Several of the ministries are involved. There are protocols.'

'How much does your office receive?'

Tan bristled at the suggestion. 'Not a damned fen. I'm a soldier. Gold makes soldiers soft.'

Shan believed him, though not for the reason he gave. Political office, not money, was the source of power for a man like Tan.

'Perhaps there are those in the government who would not support looting tombs.'

'Meaning what?'

'Did you know that Prosecutor Jao and Director Hu fought over the cave? The American woman was a witness. Now I believe Hu is trying to force her from the country.'

A narrow grin appeared on Tan's face. 'Comrade, you have been misled. You have no idea what Hu and Jao were fighting over.'

'Jao wanted to stop what Hu was doing.'

'Right. But not stop the cave, stop the accounting. He was arguing that a bigger share of the gold needed to go to the Ministry of Justice. His office. I have it on record. He wrote letters of complaint wanting me to mediate. Madame Ko can give you copies.'

Shan sank into a chair and closed his eyes. It was not Hu. 'What about his staff? Can we get their background files?'

Tan gave an indulgent nod. 'Madame Ko will make a call.'

'Whoever killed Jao was saying something about that cave.'

'So ask him.'

'The prisoner is not speaking.'

'Then go ask your damned demon,' Tan said irritably, moving to his desk.

'I would like to. Where do you suggest I look?'

'Can't help. I don't regulate demons.' He picked up a file and gestured towards the door.

Shan stood up and suddenly realized exactly where he had to go. There was indeed someone who regulated demons.

Like so much else in Tibet, the weather was absolute. It was seldom dry without drought, seldom wet without a downpour. The sun had been shining brightly when he left Tan's office, but by the time they reached the offices of the Bureau of Religious Affairs on the north side of town, it had reversed itself. The sky began throwing tiny balls of ice at them. Shan had read once that fifty Tibetans a year died in hailstorms. He handed Feng a piece of paper before he stepped out of the truck. 'Private Meng Lau. I need you to find if he was on the duty roster the night of the murder for guarding the road to the cave.'

Sergeant Feng accepted the paper without acknowledgment, uncertain how to respond to a request from Shan.

'You know who to ask. Even if I tried, they would never tell me. Please. Comrade Sergeant.'

175

Feng tossed the paper on the dashboard and began tugging at the wrapper of a roll of candy, taunting Shan with his disinterest.

Shan and Yeshe were ushered into an empty office on the second floor with a quick apology and the inevitable offer of tea. Shan wandered around the office. A tray on the desk held several magazines, the top of which was *China at Work*, a party organ that published glossy images of the proletariat. On the coffee table was a single book, entitled *Worker Heroes of Socialist Carpet Factories*. Shan lifted the magazines. On the bottom of the pile were several American news magazines, the most recent over a year old.

They were alone. 'Have you decided what you will do?' Shan asked. 'About the *purbas*.' And the Americans, he almost added.

Yeshe nervously looked back to the door. He hunched his thin shoulders forward, his face twisted as if he were about to weep. 'I am no informer. But sometimes questions are asked. What can I do? For you it is easy. I have my freedom to consider. My life. My plans.'

'Do you really understand what the warden has done to you?' Shan asked. 'You need to get out.'

'What he has done? He is helping me. He may be the only friend I have.'

'I am going to ask the colonel for a new assistant. You need to get out.'

'What has Zhong done?' Yeshe pressed.

'You misunderstand the organs of justice. For you, a Tibetan, to be offered a job in Chengdu immediately after re-education in a labour camp would not only be extraordinary, it would be impossible for Zhong to accomplish. Public Security in Chengdu would have to approve, after receiving an official request from Public Security in Lhasa. The new employer would have to approve without knowing you, which they wouldn't do. Travel papers would have to be issued, under the name of your new work unit, which doesn't exist. Zhong has no papers for you. He has no authority over such things. He lied to keep you talking with him, to tell about me. Then when it is finished, when they decide I have again failed the people by refusing to condemn Sungpo, he will accuse you of conspiring with me and have you detained again. Administration detention for less than a year requires nothing but the signature of a local Public Security officer. Zhong has his valued assistant back.'

'But he promised me.' Yeshe twisted his fingers together as he spoke. 'I have nowhere to go. I have no money. No recommendation. No travel papers. There is nowhere to go. The only real job I could get is at the chemical factory in Lhasa. They like to hire Tibetans, even without papers. I've seen the workers there. Their hair falls out after a few months. By the time you're forty you lose most of your teeth.' He looked up. Instead of the bitterness Shan expected to see, there was a hint of gratitude. 'Even if you're right, what could I do? And you, you are in the same trap, only worse.'

'I have nothing to lose. A *lao gai* prisoner on an indefinite sentence,' Shan said, trying hard to sound disinterested. 'For me it may be intentional. But for you, it's just bad luck. Maybe you should become sick.'

The wind slammed hail against the window. The lights flickered. The prisoners at the 404th always flinched when such weather began. Hailstones on their tin roofs sounded too much like machine guns.

'If they ask, I never saw the *purbas*,' Yeshe said to his back. 'But it's not just that. If the *purbas* are found to be helping Sungpo it will be taken as proof that the radicals were behind the murder, that Sungpo is one of them.' His voice trailed off. An old Red Flag limousine, no doubt retired from one of the eastern cities years before, had stopped below them. A man ran from the building with a tattered umbrella to the car to escort the occupant in the back seat.

Two minutes later the Director of the Bureau of Religious Affairs burst into the room. He was several years younger than Shan, and wore a worn blue suit and red tie that gave him the air of an earnest bureaucrat. His hair was cut short in military fashion. On his wrist was a watch, its face an enamel depiction of the Chinese flag, the kind presented to dedicated Party members.

'Comrade Shan!' the man greeted him loudly. 'I am Director Wen.' He turned to Yeshe. '*Tashi delay*,' he said clumsily.

'I speak Mandarin,' Yeshe said with obvious discomfort.

'Wonderful! This is what the new socialism is about. I gave a speech in Lhasa last month. We must focus not on our differences, I said, but on the bridges between us.' He spoke with great sincerity, turning to Shan with a sigh. 'That is why it is so tragic when hooliganism takes on cultural dimensions. It drives a wedge between the people.'

Shan did not reply.

'Colonel Tan's office called about the investigation.' Wen paused awkwardly. 'They requested my full compliance. Of course no one need ask.'

'You are responsible for all the gompas in Lhadrung County,' Shan began after the tea was served.

'They must all obtain licences from my office.'

'And each monk.'

'And each monk,' Director Wen confirmed, looking now at Yeshe.

'A heavy responsibility,' Shan observed.

Yeshe gazed at the floor in silence. He seemed unable to look at Wen. Slowly, stiffly, as though it caused him pain, he produced his notepad and began recording the conversation.

'Seventeen gompas. Three hundred ninety-one monks. And a long waiting list.'

'And the records of the gompas?'

178

'We have some. The licence applications are quite lengthy. A comprehensive review is required.'

'I mean of the old gompas.'

'Old?'

Shan fixed Wen with an unblinking gaze. 'I know monks who lived here decades ago. In 1940 there were ninety-one gompas in the county. Thousands of monks.'

Wen waved his hand dismissively. 'That was long before I was born. Before the liberation. When the church was used as a vehicle for oppressing the proletariat.'

Yeshe kept his gaze fixed on his notepad. It wasn't Shan's previous explanation of Zhong's true intentions that was causing Yeshe's reaction, it was Wen. And it wasn't pain in Yeshe's eyes, Shan realized. It was fear. Why did the Director of Religious Affairs disturb him so? 'In those days, some of the large gompas had special dancing ceremonies on festival days.'

Wen nodded. 'I have seen films. The costumes were symbolic, very elaborate. Deities. Dakinis, demons, clowns.'

'Do you know where such costumes would be today?'

'A fascinating question.' He picked up the phone.

Moments later a young Tibetan woman appeared at the door. 'Ah. Miss Taring,' Wen greeted her. 'Our – our friends were asking about the old festival costumes. How to find them today.' He turned to Shan. 'Miss Taring is our archivist.'

The woman acknowledged Shan with a nod and sat in a chair at the wall. 'Museums,' she began with a stiff, professional tone, removing her steel-rimmed glasses as she addressed Shan. 'Beijing. Chengdu. The cultural museum in Lhasa.'

'But artefacts are still being discovered,' Shan said.

'Perhaps,' Yeshe ventured, 'a costume was found in a recent audit.'

Miss Taring seemed surprised by the question. She turned to Wen. 'We do compliance checks, yes,' Wen said. Yeshe would still not meet his eyes. 'Licences are meaningless if they are not enforced.'

'And you list artefacts?' Shan asked.

'As part of the wealth redistributed from the church, the artefacts belong to the people. The gompas hold them in trust for us. Obviously, we must verify what is where.'

'And sometimes new artefacts are discovered,' Shan pressed.

'Sometimes.'

'But no costumes.'

'Not in the time I have served here.'

'How can you be certain?' Shan asked. 'There must be thousands of artefacts in your inventories.'

Wen smiled condescendingly. 'Esteemed Comrade, you must understand that these are irreplaceable treasures, these costumes. It would be quite a discovery, to find one now.'

Shan looked at Yeshe, to see if he was still writing. Had he heard correctly? Esteemed Comrade? He turned to the archivist. 'Miss Taring. You say all of the known costumes are in museums.'

'Some of the large gompas near Lhasa have been licensed to conduct the dances again. For certain approved events. Tourists come.' She studied him with an air of suspicion.

'Foreign exchange,' Shan suggested.

Miss Taring nodded impassively.

'Has your office authorized any for Lhadrung?'

'Never. The gompas here are too poor to sponsor such ceremonies.'

'I thought perhaps with the Americans coming –'

Director Wen's eyes lit up, and he glanced at the archivist. 'Why didn't we think of that?' He turned to Shan. 'Miss Taring is handling our arrangements for the Americans. Tour guide to cultural sites. Speaks English with an American accent.'

'An excellent idea, Comrade Director,' the archivist

said. 'But there are no trained dancers. Many of these costumes, they are not what you think – they are more like special machines. Mechanical arms. Elaborate fastenings. Monks were trained for months, just to understand how to operate them. To use them in a ceremony, to know the dances and movements – some dancers underwent years of training.'

'But a short show at one of the new projects,' Wen asserted. 'The Americans would not need the genuine dance. Just costumes. Some graceful swaying. Some cymbals and drums. They can take photographs.'

Miss Taring stared at Director Wen with a small, noncommittal smile.

'New projects?' Shan asked.

'I am pleased to say that some gompas have been rebuilding under our supervision. Subsidies are available.'

Subsidies. Meaning what, Shan considered. That they were looting ancient shrines to build pretend ones, destroying antiquities to pay for stage sets where Buddhist charades could be performed for tourists? 'Did Prosecutor Jao participate in reviewing the licences for such projects?' he asked.

The director set his cup on the table. 'Thank you Miss Taring.' The archivist rose and made a slight bow to Shan and Yeshe. Wen waited for her to leave before speaking. 'I am sorry. I believe you wanted to talk about the murder.'

'Comrade Director, I have been talking about the murder all along,' Shan said.

Wen stared at Shan with new curiosity. 'There is a committee. Jao, Colonel Tan, and myself. Each has a veto power over any decision.'

'For rebuilding only.'

'Permits. Rebuilding. Authorization to accept new novices. Publishing religious tracts. Inviting the public to participate in services.'

'Did Prosecutor Jao reject any such applications?' Shan asked.

'We all have. Cultural resources need to be allocated to avoid abuse. The Tibetan minority is only part of China's population. We cannot rubber-stamp every request,' Wen declared with a fuller, practised voice.

'But recently. Was there any particular one that Jao refused to support?'

Wen looked up at the ceiling, his hands tucked behind his neck. 'Only one in the last few months. Denied a rebuilding petition. Saskya gompa.'

Saskya was Sungpo's gompa. 'On what grounds?'

'There is another gompa in the lower end of the same valley. Larger. Khartok. It had already applied for rebuilding. Much more convenient for visitors, a better investment.'

Shan stood to go. 'I understand you are new in this job.'

'Nearly six months now.'

'They say your predecessor was killed.'

Director Wen nodded his head sadly. 'They consider him something of a martyr back home.'

'But don't you fear for your life? I saw no guards.'

'We cannot be bullied, Comrade. I have a job to do,' Wen declared sombrely. 'The minorities have a right to preserve their culture. But unless there is balance, there is danger from reactionaries. Just a few of us have been trusted by Beijing to stand in the middle. Without us there would be chaos.'

Chapter Nine

The seeds of the night sky grew in Tibet. There the stars were the thickest, the dark blackest, the heavens closest. People looked up and cried without knowing why. Prisoners sometimes stole from their huts, under threat of the stable, to lie on the ground silently watching the heavens. The year before at the 404th an old priest had been found in such a position one morning, frozen, his dead eyes fixed on the sky. He had written two words in the snow at his side. *Catch me.*

Shan leaned his head on the window as the truck climbed out of the valley on its long trip north, farther and farther into the sky. There was a test for novices at some gompas. Go out in the night and lie at a place of sky burial. Contemplate the heavens beside the bird-picked bones. Some did not come back.

'Everyone talks about this prisoner Lokhesh.' Yeshe's voice came out of the darkness behind Shan. 'You did something for him.'

'Did something?' Sergeant Feng interjected gruffly. 'Kicked us in the ass, that's what.'

'Just a harmless old man. A *tzedrung*,' Shan said, using the Tibetan term for a monk official. 'He had been a tax collector in the Dalai Lama's government,' Shan explained. 'It was long past time for his release.'

Feng snorted. 'Right. We just let the prisoners decide when we should open the gate.'

'But how could you –' Yeshe leaned forward. Having built up the courage to ask, he was not going to let go.

'I had seen a decree from the State Council ten years

before. In honour of Chairman Mao's birthday, amnesty was declared for all members of the former Tibetan government. The decree had been overlooked by Warden Zhong.'

'So you just instructed the warden about his duties?' Yeshe asked with disbelief.

'I reminded him.'

'Shit,' Sergeant Feng groused. 'Reminded him! Like a grenade down his pants he reminded him.' He slowed the truck and leaned towards Yeshe. 'What prisoner Shan does not say is that he couldn't remind anyone. Would have broken discipline. So instead he asked the political officer for materials to make a banner in honour of Mao's day.'

'A banner?'

'Big damned banner for all the world to see. Showed patriotic spirit, Lieutenant Chang bragged. Families were coming. Townsfolk were coming. Guards were on parade. Out comes the banner, on the roof of their hut. All honour to Mao, it said, in whose honour the State Council reprieved all former officials. Even showed the month and year of the decree, so no one would be confused. Political officer, he spent lots of time with Shan that week.'

'But this old man got released?'

'A petition was presented to Colonel Tan. It wasn't just a violation of law, it was a violation of a gift from Mao. Threat of demonstrations. So the colonel admitted to the world that Warden Zhong had made a mistake.'

On they drove, mile after mile, mingling with the stars. They were so high now the road seemed to have lost all connection to the planet. Only a few black patches along the edge of the sky showed they were still among the mountains.

'Why were you scared of Director Wen?' Shan heard himself asking Yeshe, unaware the question was even on his tongue.

'I did not intend to be scared,' came the disembodied reply a long time later. 'But he is the *kenpo*. For all of Lhadrung.'

The earnest young Director Wen an abbot? Then Shan understood. 'A priest would be scared of Wen.' Wen's chop made priests, or ruined priests. His chop ruined gompas.

'I am not a priest.'

'You were a priest.' Shan remembered Yeshe's haunting mantra in the skull cave.

'I don't know.' Yeshe's voice was hesitant, and pained. 'It was just a stage of my life. It was over long ago.'

You have no long ago, Shan almost said. Don't dare to speak of long ago, not until like the rest of us you have endured your ration of nightmares, not until you have memories so brittle they snap like twigs when the political officers scream for you to confess them. 'Then you went to school in Chengdu,' Shan said instead. 'But you were sent back for re-educating. Why?'

'It was a misunderstanding.'

'You mean a miscarriage of justice?' Shan challenged.

Yeshe made a sound that may have been meant as a laugh. 'Someone replaced a picture of Mao with a photo of the Dalai Lama in one of the classrooms. When no one would confess to the act, all six Tibetan students were sent home.'

'You mean it wasn't you?'

'I wasn't even at school that day,' Yeshe said forlornly. 'I skipped to get tickets for an American movie.'

'Did you get them?' Feng asked after a moment. 'The tickets.'

'No,' Yeshe sighed. 'They were sold out.'

The silence of the sky overwhelmed Shan again. A ghost appeared in the headlights and seemed to hover as it watched them. Feng gasped. Only as it slipped over the side of the mountain did Shan see its wings. An owl.

'My old man was a carpenter.' The words suddenly

floated into the air, like an uncontrolled thought. It took a moment for Shan to realize it was Feng. 'They took away his shop, his tools, everything. Because he owned them. Landlord class. Dug irrigation ditches for ten years. But at night he made things.' There was something new in Feng's voice. He had felt it too. The darkness.

'Out of cardboard. Out of dried grass. Sticks. Beautiful things. Boxes. Even cabinets.'

'Yes,' Shan said uncertainly, not because he knew such a carpenter but because he had known many such heroes.

'I asked him why. I was just a stupid kid. But he looked at me, all wise. Know what he said?'

A meteor shot across the sky. No one spoke.

'What he said,' Feng continued at last. 'He said you must always step forward from where you stand.'

Shan watched the stars for several more moments. 'He was very wise,' he said. 'I would have liked to have known your father.'

He heard Feng suck in his gut in surprise. Then he made the low gurgling noise that was his laugh.

Another meteor streaked by. 'Some of the old yaks say that each shooting star is a soul attaining Buddhahood,' Shan observed languidly.

'The old yaks?' Yeshe asked.

Shan didn't realize he had spoken aloud. 'The first generation of prisoners. The oldest survivors.' Shan smiled in the darkness. 'My first winter at the 404th we had snow removal duty in the high passes. Bitter cold. The winds, they would do strange things with the snow. Thirty-foot drifts in one spot, bare earth in the next. Boulders sculpted with ice and snow to look like huge creatures from your dreams. One day after a new snow we're digging out the road and there's a big boulder where there never was one before. Brought down by an avalanche, someone said.

'We shovelled snow. It blew back. We shovelled again. Later, behind us, one of the guards screams. The boulder's staring at him.' Shan smiled again. He had forgotten how fond he was of the memory. 'It was an old yak, letting the snow cover him to avoid the cold of the storm. He just stood there, like he was part of the mountain, watching the insanity of the world around him. On the way back one of the prisoners said it reminded him of the old monks in the 404th. Ageless, indestructible, like a mountain with legs, at peace in the most tormenting environment. The name just stuck.'

Later a strange sound arose, the buzz of a stadium filled with people. On the platform in the centre were three austere figures, seated at a table equipped with microphones. Behind them, off the platform, was an old woman with a mop and bucket. Shan jerked his head up. It was a dream. No, he realized with distress, it was a memory. He stared into the stars, but five minutes later was back in the stadium. A young, frightened man was on stage now, his eyes dull with drugs. A shrill, urbane woman behind him was reading a statement for him, an apology to the people.

Shan willed himself awake, shuddering at the recollection of the last murder trial he had attended. He forced himself to count the stars. He pinched himself. But in his fatigue he returned to the stadium. It was hushed now, and the defendant was on his knees before a Bureau officer. At the last minute, as the officer fired a bullet through his skull, the face changed to that of Sungpo. The old woman climbed the stairs and began mopping away the blood and tissue.

Shan groaned and was instantly in heart-pounding wakefulness. He did not drift off again.

Somewhere, much later, Sergeant Feng spoke again. 'That soldier Meng. He was on assignment to guard the cave. But not on the night of the murder.'

'You asked?'

'You needed to know, you said. He probably traded

187

duty hours. Happens all the time without the records being changed.'

'Could we see him? Back at the barracks.'

'Don't know,' Feng said uncomfortably. 'I'm assigned to the 404th. Those officers at Jade Spring – I don't know. They're tough as tiger's teeth,' he muttered, then leaned forward as though he had to give full attention to the road.

'Sergeant,' Yeshe ventured from the back seat. 'Comrade Shan says the warden is deceiving me. That he plans to detain me again, to work on his computers.'

A strained chuckle was Feng's only reply.

'Is it true?'

'Why ask me? The warden and I, we don't live on the same planet, you know what I mean? How would I know?'

'Just then, you laughed like you believed it.'

'What I believe is that Zhong is one prick son of a bitch. He's paid by the people to be a son of a bitch. He doesn't talk to sergeants when he seeks detention orders.'

'But you could find out. Ask the staff. Everyone talks to the *momo gyakpa*.'

Feng slowed the truck. 'What the hell did you say?' he barked, suddenly surly.

'I'm sorry. Nothing. Just if you could ask. Maybe I could do something for you in exchange.'

'*Momo gyakpa?* Fat dumpling?' Bitterness seemed to overtake his rage. 'I heard it before,' he said, much quieter. 'Behind my back. Thirty-five years in the People's Liberation Army and that's what I get. *Momo gyakpa.*'

'I'm sorry,' Yeshe muttered.

But Feng was no longer listening. He rolled down his window and reached into the bag of dumplings that was to serve as their breakfast and lunch. '*Momo.*' He picked up a dumpling and squeezed it as if it were something he was trying to kill. He hurled it out the window, then another, and another, throwing one with each protracted

188

syllable. 'Momo! Fucking! Gyakpa!' he yelled, with a choke of pain at the end. He stared out the window after the last *momo*. 'Used to be called the Axe, for the way I could break things in two with my hands. The Axe. Watch out boys, the Axe is coming they would say. Colonel Tan remembers those days. Run, the Axe is on leave tonight.'

As soon as the light was strong enough to read by, Shan reached into the canvas bag that Madame Ko had left at the barracks. Three files, the files of the cases which had resulted in the executions of three of the Lhadrung Five. Lin Ziyang, Director of Religious Affairs, killed by the cultural hooligan Dilgo Gongsha. Xong De, Director of Mines for the Ministry of Geology in Lhadrung County, killed by the enemy of the people Rabjam Norbu. Jin San, agricultural collective manager, killed by Dza Namkhai, leader of the infamous Lhadrung Five.

He read the records for nearly an hour. At the end of each file, pages had been ripped out. Witness statements.

Blushed with dawn, the peaks seemed to hover, more a part of the sky than the shadowy earth. Are the only religious people on the planet those who live near mountains? Trinle had asked him once. 'I don't know,' Shan had replied, 'but I know Tibetans would not be Tibetans without their mountains.'

They began descending into the head of a long valley. Below them, down a mile of winding road, a complex of stone buildings surrounded by long empty pastures could be discerned through the dim morning light. Shan tilted his head as he realized what it was, and that although he had spent three years living with Tibetan monks he had never until this moment seen an active Tibetan monastery. So few were left.

Yet countless monasteries had been constructed in his mind. On the most bitter winter days, when the trucks did not leave the compound and the prisoners huddled back to back under their thin blankets to conserve body heat, with words the old yaks guided them through the gompas of their youth. As the prisoners shivered, sometimes so violently that teeth were broken, Choje and Trinle or one of the others began the journey, describing how the dawn played on the distant stone walls of the gompa as the traveller approached, or how the sound of a particular bell resonated within the pilgrim long before the structure came into sight. The smell of jasmine on the path, the flight of a snowgrouse, the rustle of the musk deer that roamed unafraid in the gompa's shadow were not overlooked, nor the cheerful call of the watchful *rapjung*, a student monk, who first spied the visitor and opened the gates.

With the prisoners' gompas long ago annihilated and few memorialized in photographs, the only traces left were in the memories of a handful of survivors. But by the time the tale was told – and a visit to a single gompa could take days – the gompa had been rebuilt in the hearts and minds of another generation. Not just the visual images, for the old yaks revelled also in the sounds and smells of their former homes. Not just the physical, for the human rhythm too would be recreated, down to the rheumy eyes of the blind lama who rang the bell or how novices scrubbed the stone floors with wads of horsehair when they had grown too slippery from the butter offerings. There was a huge prayer wheel in a gompa that once stood in the southern mountains whose squeak reminded everyone of a flock of hungry magpies, and its kitchen mixed the flowers of a certain heather with barley for a fragrant *tsampa*.

Sergeant Feng slowed the truck. 'Probably got hot tea,' he suggested, nodding towards the buildings. 'Maybe we'll get better directions to Saskya. I don't know this road –'

'No.' Yeshe interrupted with unusual bluntness. 'Not enough time. Keep going. I know Saskya. Down the road twenty miles, up against the high cliffs at the end of the valley.'

Feng grunted non-committally and drove on.

Nearly an hour later Yeshe directed Feng into a forest of rhododendron and cedar. After a few minutes a long mound of stones became visible, running perpendicular to the road and disappearing into the thickets. Shan raised his hand for Feng to stop, then leapt out, ran to the pile of stones and halted. There was something he recognized, though he had never been there before. From somewhere nearby came the tiny ring of a *tsingha*, the small hand cymbal used in Buddhist worship.

He felt something inside, a flutter of excitement. He *had* been there before, or somewhere much like it, in the winter tales of the old yaks. Slowly his knees collapsed and for a moment he knelt, his hands on the stones. Then he began cleaning the detritus from the pile of rocks. He picked up one, then another, and another. They had been squared off by human hands, and each had a Tibetan inscription, either painted or crudely chiselled on its surface. He was in the middle of a *mani* wall, the walls of stones inscribed with prayers constructed over the course of centuries by devout visitors and pilgrims. Each stone was carried from far away, one at a time, for the glory of Buddha. A *mani* stone was said to continue the prayer after the pilgrim left. He looked at them, stretching into the forest as far as he could see, the mouldering, moss-covered prayers of generations.

Once Trinle had taken a beating for breaking from a work line to grab such a stone, abandoned on the slope above them. 'Why risk the batons?' Shan had asked as Trinle rubbed away the moss to release the prayer.

'Because this may be the prayer that changes the world,' Trinle had cheerfully replied.

Shan carefully rubbed away the dirt from the pr of five stones and laid out three, then stacked t one on top. The beginning of a new wall.

Ignoring Feng's scowl, he walked along the road in front of the creeping truck. The tinkle of the *tsingha* floated through the air again, and a high wall came into view. The cracks and seams and patchwork paint on the wall told of ordeal and survival. It had been battered and rebuilt and broken and patched more times than Shan could trace. Half a dozen shades of white and tan had been painted over the uneven surface, which here was stucco, there plaster, and elsewhere exposed rock.

Flanking the wall on either side were ruins, jagged piles of rocks overgrown with vines, shattered and charred timbers covered with lichens and mosses. The wall, he realized, had formed the inner courtyard of what once had been a far bigger gompa. The gate hung open, revealing several novices sweeping the courtyard with brooms of rushes tied to long sticks.

Shan surveyed the scene with unexpected joy. The buildings were familiar to him from the 404th's oral reconstructions, but nothing prepared him for the stark, powerful prescence of a working gompa.

In the centre of the yard was a huge bronze cauldron, so battered and dented the face of Buddha forged on its side had the appearance of a scarred warrior. Two monks were painstakingly polishing the vessel, which was one of the largest incense burners Shan had ever seen. Wisps of smouldering juniper rose from it as they worked.

On either side of the gate, following the wall halfway around the courtyard, were low structures with roofs made of overlapping flat stones, the quarters of the monks. Assembled of salvaged stone and scrap lumber, they looked suspiciously like unlicensed construction. What was it Director Wen had told them? Jao had denied Sungpo's gompa its building permits, cutting it off from official sources of material.

The buildings beyond were just as patchwork but somehow more majestic. On the left, up a small flight of stairs and past a porch of heavy timbers, was the *dukhang*, the hall of assembly where the monks took their lessons. To the right lay a parallel structure in front of which, under the overhanging roof, stood an upright prayer wheel as large as a man. A monk was slowly spinning it, each rotation completing the prayer inscribed on its side. Behind the wheel, past a pair of brightly painted red doors was the *lhakang*, the hall of the principal deity. On the wall above the hall was a circular mandala painting depicting the sacred path, the Wheel of Dharma, with a deer painted on either side, signifying Buddha's first sermon in India.

Between the two structures was a large chorten shrine, consisting of a plaster dome built over a square base, flattened at the top with a series of slabs of decreasing size. Above the slabs was a barrel-shaped stage capped by a conical steeple. Trinle had constructed a tiny chorten of wood scraps for Loshar, the new year holiday, once, and had explained its spiritual symbolism to Shan before it had been seized and stomped to splinters by Lieutenant Chang. There were thirteen levels to a chorten, representing the traditional thirteen stages of advancement to Buddhahood. The top of the chorten was crowned with sun and crescent-moon shapes worked in iron. The sun represented wisdom, the moon compassion. On the round, barrel-shaped level were two huge painted eyes, symbolic of the ever-watchful Buddha.

He stepped into the courtyard as the truck rolled to a halt behind him. The novices in the yard stopped and bowed low as they spotted their three visitors. Shan followed the gaze of one of the monks towards a door in the largest of the buildings. A middle-aged lama appeared.

'Forgive the intrusion,' Shan said quietly as the lama approached. 'May I speak to someone about the her *it* Sungpo?'

The lama did not seem to consider the question *i* answering. 'What is your purpose?'

'My purpose is to find the teacher of Sungpo.'

The man's face tightened. 'And what is his guru accused of?'

Yeshe stepped to Shan's shoulder. 'He is not the *kenpo*,' he whispered without moving his head. 'He is the *chotrimpa*.'

Shan looked up, trying to hide his surprise. The *kenpo*, the abbot, had chosen not to talk to Shan. He had sent the lama responsible for monastic discipline.

Shan looked back at the lama. 'Sungpo is with us. His tongue is not. I respectfully request an audience with his guru.'

The lama surveyed the curious young monks who were gathering beside the truck. A censuring sweep of his hand scattered them. In the same moment a deep-throated bell sounded from somewhere inside. The courtyard cleared.

'Will you join our instruction in *sunyata*?' he asked Shan and Yeshe. There was a small smile on his face, but he made the words sound like a taunt. *Sunyata* was one of five required studies of every monastic student; it was the study of voidness, of non-existence. Shan studied the lama as he disappeared into the nearest door. He had answered each of Shan's questions with another question, then turned away without waiting for a response.

Shan looked about the now empty courtyard. Without looking back to Feng or Yeshe he climbed the stairs into the *lhakang*. Inside was a small hall leading up another flight of stairs, which he followed into a large, empty chamber lit by butter lamps. He lit a stick of incense and sat at the altar, lotus fashion, before the life-size bronze statue of Maitreya Buddha, known as the future Buddha, that dominated the chamber. Before the statue were the seven traditional offering bowls, three filled with water, one with flowers, one with incense, one with butter, and one with aromatic herbs.

He sat for several minutes in silence, then picked up a broom at the back of the hall and began sweeping.

A silver-haired priest appeared and lit an offering of butter shaped into a small spire. 'It is not necessary,' he said, nodding towards the broom. 'This is not your gompa.'

Shan leaned on the broom for a moment. 'When I was young,' he said, 'I heard about a temple high in the mountains along the sea, where all the wisdom of the world was said to reside. One day I decided I must visit the temple.'

After a few strokes of the broom he paused again. 'Halfway up I began to lose my way. I met a man carrying a huge burden of wood on his back. I said I was looking for the temple of the saints, in order to find myself. He told me I didn't need the temple, he would show me all I needed to know. Here is what it takes, he said, and he set his burden on the ground and stood straight.

'But what do I do when I go home, I asked. Simple, he said. When you go home you do this – and he put the burden back on his shoulder.'

The old priest smiled, found another broom, and joined Shan in the sweeping.

When Shan emerged he walked to the gate and moved along the track that followed the outer wall. Halfway around he found a dirt path leading onto the slopes above the gompa. The grass on either side of the path had been crushed recently by the tyres of a heavy vehicle.

Ten minutes later he reached a clearing where the vehicle, unable to navigate the rocky terrain above, had been parked. He kept climbing. The path became tortuous, winding around wind-sculpted rocks, hugging the side of a precipitous cliff. It traversed a steep chasm across two logs which had been lashed together. At last the track opened into a large meadow. A carpet of tiny yellow and blue flowers led to a small stone structure built against a rock face. A raven screeched. He turned to see the black bird, a sign of wisdom and luck, gliding in the void barely a hundred feet away. Below the bird lay the entire world. A waterfall cascaded from the opposite slope into the conifer forest; beyond it a small lake gleamed like a jewel. To the south the valley stretched for miles with no visible sign of man. Beyond it, brushing a solitary cloud, he could discern the pass they had driven through at dawn.

Footsteps broke the spell. Feng and Yeshe were not far behind. Shan approached the building.

The door, painted with a small ideogram surmounted by the sun, a crescent moon, and a flame, swung open with a light touch. The entry chamber had the air of an austere but lovingly tended cabin. Fresh flowers stood in a can below a window. The second chamber had no windows. As his eyes adjusted to the darkness Shan discerned a straw pallet, a stool, writing implements, and several candles. Lighting a candle, he discovered he was not in a chamber, but in a cavern.

There was a noise outside. He extinguished the candle and moved back through the structure. The meadow was empty. A murmur of surprise came from overhead. He looked up to see a small squat man lying on the roof, his mouth stuffed with nails. The man's head jerked to the side, with the dull, inquisitive look of a squirrel. Suddenly he spat out the nails, grabbed the edge of the roof and pulled himself over, landing in a pile at Shan's feet.

He didn't rise, but extended his finger and poked at Shan's leg as though to test if he were real.

'Have you come to arrest me?' he said as he rose. There was a strange hopefulness in his tone.

His flat, light-coloured features were not Tibetan.

'I've come about Sungpo.'

'I know that. I prayed.' The man held his wrists together, as though for handcuffs.

'This is Sungpo's hermitage?'

'I am Jigme,' the man said, as though Shan should know him. 'Is he eating?'

Shan studied the strange creature. He seemed stunted somehow. His hands and ears were oversized for his body. His eyelids drooped, like those of a sad, sleepy bear. 'No. He is not eating.'

'I didn't think so. Some days I have to switch broth for his tea. Is he dry?'

'He has straw. He has a roof.'

The man named Jigme gave an approving nod. 'He has trouble remembering sometimes.'

'Remembering?'

'That he's still just a human.'

Yeshe and Feng appeared beside Shan. Jigme muttered a greeting. 'I am ready,' he said with an oddly cheerful voice. 'Just have to close up. And leave a little rice for the mice. We always leave food for the mice. Master Sungpo, he loves the mice. Maybe he can't laugh with his mouth but he laughs with his eyes when the mice eat from his fingers. Right from the heart. Have you seen him laugh?'

When no one replied, Jigme shrugged and began to move back to the hut.

'We didn't come to take you,' Shan said. 'I just have questions.'

Jigme stopped. 'You have to take me,' he said. He studied Shan in confusion. 'I did it,' he said in a new, desperate tone.

'Did what?'

'Whatever he did, I did it too. It is the way we are.' He lowered himself to the ground and put his arms around his knees.

'How often does Sungpo leave the hut?'

'Everyday. He goes to the edge of the cliff and sits, two or three hours every morning.' Jigme began rocking back and forth.

'I meant away from here, out of your sight.'

Jigme looked confused. 'Sungpo is on hermitage. He

started nearly a year ago. He can't leave.' He looked up, understanding his mistake. 'Not of his own will.' He seemed about to cry. 'It's okay,' he said apologetically. 'Grandfather says we'll start over when he returns.'

'But you aren't with him every hour. You sleep. He could go and come back before you wake.'

'Not me. I know. I always know. Is my job to know, to watch over him. Hermits can concentrate like –' his search for words seemed almost painful '– like a lump of coal in a wood fire.' He shrugged. 'They can fall off cliffs. It's happened. He belongs to me. I belong to him.' He looked into his hands. 'It's a good world.' But Shan knew he wasn't speaking of the world at large. He was speaking of a tiny plateau in a remote township in a forgotten corner of Tibet.

'There is one man he may speak with,' Shan suggested.

'Grandfather. Je Rinpoche.' Jigme spoke almost in a whisper.

'Is Rinpoche here?'

'The gompa.'

'The day they came for Sungpo. Tell me about it.'

Jigme began to rock again. 'They were six, maybe seven. Guns. They brought guns. I had been told about guns.'

'What colour were their uniforms?'

'Grey.'

'All of them?'

'All but the young one. Had a slice in his face. His name was Meh Jah. Everyone called him Meh Jah. He wore a sweater, and glasses with dark lenses. He sent for the abbot. He wouldn't do anything until the abbot arrived.'

'They said they found a wallet.'

'Impossible.'

'They didn't find it?'

'No. I mean they found it. I was there. In this cave. Meh Jah, he brought in the abbot. They had flashlights.

He turned over a rock and there it was. But it was impossible it could be there.'

'How long did they look for it?'

'The soldiers searched everywhere. Turned over my baskets. Broke my flowerpots.'

'But how long after this man named Meh was in your cave?'

'He took the abbot into the cave. Someone called out right away, all excited. Then Meh Jah is here and put chains on Sungpo's hands.'

'Show me the rock.'

It was fifty feet inside the cave, a flat rock large enough to serve as a stool. Shan asked Yeshe to take Jigme outside. He sketched the cave in his notepad then bent over the rock with a candle. He ran his fingers around the stone, and paused. On the side facing the entrance there was a stickiness, a small rectangular patch that pulled at his skin. He called for Feng to light three more candles. He found what he was looking for ten feet further in, where it had been thrown from the rock after it served its purpose. A wad of black electrician's tape. The rock had been secretly marked to ensure it could easily be found by those who came for the arrest.

'Were there other visitors?' Shan asked. 'Before the day Comrade Meh came?'

'None. None that I saw. Except Rinpoche.'

'Rinpoche. Where in the gompa will I find him?'

Jigme was looking away, towards the edge of the cliff. A raven was there again, this one with an odd patch of white on the back of its head. Jigme began waving. 'Visitors!' he shouted at the bird. 'Hurry up!'

Jigme shielded his eyes to study the bird. 'He's coming now,' he announced. 'The raven says he's coming now.'

Je Rinpoche was not coming. He was waiting. Shan found him on a ledge a hundred yards down the path. He was paper-frail. His head was nearly hairless, and his skin rough, as if covered with dust. But his eyes, wet and restless, were brilliantly alive. The effect was as though someone had set two jewels into corroded stone.

Shan pressed his palms together and bowed his head in greeting. 'Rinpoche. If I could ask –'

'There are so many things to consider,' the ancient one interrupted. His voice was surprisingly strong. 'This mountain. The dogs. The way the mist falls down the slopes, different each morning.' He turned to Shan. When he shifted his body the robe barely moved. 'Some days I feel like that. Like mist sliding down the mountain.' He looked back down the valley and pulled his robe tighter, as if cold. 'Jigme brings a melon sometimes. We eat it and Jigme will watch.'

Shan sighed and stared out over the landscape. He would never have a chance to speak to Sungpo. Je, his lama, had been Shan's only hope for an intermediary.

'When we climb to the top of the mountain, you know what we do?' Je asked. 'Just as I did when I was a novice. We make little paper horses and fly them away in the wind.' He paused as if Shan required an added explanation. 'When they touch the earth they become real horses to help travellers through the ranges.'

There was movement beside Je. The raven had landed an arm's length away.

'They are praying, my friends and teachers,' Je began again. 'All of them, and the bombs are beginning to fall. There is time to leave but they will not. I must take the young ones into the hills. The ones who stay are dying, just saying their rosaries and dying in the explosions. As I am leaving with the boys something is hitting me in the face. It is a hand, still holding its rosary.'

It was 1959, Shan calculated, or at the latest 1960, when the PLA bombed the gompas from the air.

'Was it right? That is always the temptation. To ask if it was right. It is the wrong question, of course.'

Suddenly Shan realized that the old man knew exactly why Shan was there.

'Rinpoche,' he began again. 'I would not ask Sungpo to break his vow. I only ask him to join me in finding the truth. There is a murderer somewhere. He will kill again.'

'The only one who can find the murderer is the murdered,' Je said. 'Let the ghost take its revenge. I am not worried about Sungpo. But Jigme. Jigme is lost.'

Shan realized he had to let the old man lead the conversation. The wind increased. He fought the temptation to grab Je's robe, lest he be lifted into the clouds. 'Jigme does not study at the gompa.'

'No. He abandoned studies to go with Sungpo. He never belongs. Being a gompa orphan, it is like being a small bird forced to live all its life in a rainstorm.'

A shiver of realization moved down Shan's spine. During the occupation of Tibet and again during the Cultural Revolution, monks and nuns had been forced, sometimes at bayonet point, to break their vows of celibacy, sometimes with each other, sometimes with soldiers. In some regions the offspring had been gathered into special schools. Elsewhere they formed gangs. There were several of the mixed-blood gompa orphans in the 404th, who had followed their priests to jail.

'Then for Jigme, help me bring Sungpo back.'

The old man's eyes were closed now. 'After the gompa was destroyed,' he murmured, 'I could see the rising moon better.'

The truck had already begun the long climb towards the pass when Shan asked the name of the gompa at the head of the valley, the compound they had passed at dawn. Yeshe did not reply.

Feng slowed and read the map. 'Khartok,' he said impatiently. 'They call it Khartok.'

Shan grabbed one of the files provided by Tan, glanced at it, and threw his hand towards Sergeant Feng. 'Stop. Now.'

'There isn't time,' Feng protested.

'You would rather leave before dawn tomorrow and come back here?'

'It is late. They will be preparing for last assembly, lighting the lamps soon,' Yeshe said insistently. 'We can try a telephone interview.'

Feng turned, looked into Shan's eyes, and without another word turned and moved back down the valley.

Yeshe groaned and covered his eyes with his hand, as if he could not bear to see more.

It wasn't pastures he had seen in front of the buildings. It was ruins, fields of stone that began half a mile from the gompa. There was no order to the stones. Some were in piles, others scattered as though they had been thrown from the overhanging mountains. But every stone had been squared by a mason.

Closer to the gompa the foundations of several buildings had been turned into gardens. A dozen figures in red robes leaned on their hoes to gaze at the unexpected vehicle. As they eased to a stop Shan saw that new construction lay beyond the foundations. The main wall was being rebuilt and extended. Stacks of fresh lumber and pallets of cement wrapped in plastic were arrayed along the treeline.

Yeshe lay on the back seat, an arm thrown over his eyes.

'You know gompas. You know the protocols,' Shan said impatiently. 'I need you.'

Feng opened the rear door. 'You're not sleeping, Comrade.' He pulled on Yeshe's arm. 'Hell, you're panting like a cornered cat.'

Shan ventured into the courtyard alone. The same structures he had seen at Saskya were there, but freshly painted and on a much larger scale. Not one but five chortens were arranged about the grounds, capped by suns and moons of newly worked copper.

A better investment, Shan remembered. Director Wen of the Religious Affairs Bureau had said Saskya was not permitted to rebuild because the gompa in the lower valley was a better investment.

A middle-aged monk with a row of gold embroidery on his sleeve appeared on the steps of the assembly hall. He threw his arms out in a gesture of welcome and trotted down the steps. Shan watched as the other monks looked up at the newcomer. Some nodded deferentially, others quickly averted their eyes. The man was a senior lama, probably the abbot. But why, Shan wondered, didn't the man seem surprised to see him? The lama interrupted a young student who was raking the gravel and dispatched him into the hall, then pointed towards a herb garden in the shelter of the wall. Shan silently followed him into the garden. Wooden benches were arranged in rows between the plant beds, as though for students receiving instruction. At the end of the garden an old monk was on his knees, pulling weeds.

'We will have the plans finished soon,' the lama announced as soon as Shan sat on the front bench.

'Plans?' The young monk appeared with a tray of tea, poured it for them, and retreated with a hurried bow of his head.

'For the first restoration of the college buildings. Tell Wen Li that the plans are almost finished.' There was something odd about the lama's demeanour. Shan searched for a way to describe it. Social, he decided. Almost urbane.

'No. We are here about Dilgo Gongsha.'

The lama did not relent. 'Yes, the plans are nearly complete,' he said, as though the topics were connected. 'The Bei Da Union is helping, you know. We are helping each other with our reconstructions.'

'The Bei Da Union?'

The lama paused and looked at Shan as though for the first time. 'Who are you then?'

'An investigation team. From Colonel Tan's office. I

am reviewing the facts of the Dilgo Gongsha matter. He was a resident here was he not?'

The lama's eyes slowly surveyed Shan, then shifted to Feng and Yeshe, who were inching along the shadows of the walls. As the two passed a small gathering of monks, someone called out in surprise, as if in greeting. Someone else called, in a tone Shan didn't recognize at first. Anger. Yeshe moved behind Feng.

'The last time we saw Dilgo,' a gentle voice announced from behind Shan, 'he was passing into that peculiar hell for souls taken by violence.' Shan's host stood and put his palms together in greeting. It was the old monk who had been tending weeds. His robe was stained from garden work, his fingernails filled with dirt. 'We performed the rights of Bardo. By now he is an infant. He will grow to bless those around him once again.' He had a twinkle in his eyes, as though the memory of Dilgo caused him joy.

'Abbot,' the lama said with a bow of his head. 'Forgive me. I thought you were in your meditation cell.'

Abbot? Shan looked in confusion at the first lama.

'You have met our *chandzoe*,' the abbot offered, noticing Shan's glance. 'Welcome to Khartok.'

'*Chandzoe*?' It was not a term Shan had heard in any of the winter tales.

'The manager of our secular affairs,' the abbot explained.

'Secular affairs?'

'Business manager,' the first lama interjected, pouring a cup of tea for the abbot and gesturing for him to sit.

'Why would you speak of our Dilgo?' The abbot asked the question the way a child might, with wide, innocent eyes.

'He was found guilty of killing a man by stuffing his throat with pebbles. The man happened to be the Director of the Religious Affairs Bureau.'

The *chandzoe* frowned. The abbot looked into his teacup.

'In the old days it was the traditional method for killing members of the imperial family,' Shan said. 'Even in battle they could only be taken and later suffocated.'

'Forgive me,' the *chandzoe* said. 'I do not understand your point.' He seemed to be expressing not confusion, but disappointment with Shan.

'Only that it was a very traditional sort of murder for a senior government official.'

'And as they said at trial,' the *chandzoe* said with a hint of impatience. 'Khartok is a very traditional gompa. You cannot execute Dilgo twice.' A murmur among the monks in the courtyard caught Shan's attention. He followed their stares towards Feng and Yeshe, in the shadow near the edge of the garden.

'If I were going to murder someone I would be sure not to use a method that would be associated with me or my beliefs.'

Suddenly the *chandzoe* stood. 'Yeshe?' he called out. 'Is it Yeshe Retang?'

Yeshe cowered a moment at the corner of the garden, then saw the enthusiasm in the *chandzoe*'s face and stepped closer. 'It is, Rinpoche. I am honoured you remember.'

The *chandzoe* threw out his arms again, in the expression Shan had seen when he first appeared on the stairs, and moved to pull Yeshe out of the shadow. Yeshe stood stiffly, glancing uneasily at Shan.

The *chandzoe* shifted his eyes from Shan to Yeshe, obviously confused.

'My detention has recently concluded, Rinpoche. I am on this assignment now. Temporarily.'

Yeshe cast a pleading glance at Shan, which the *chandzoe* seemed to follow with great interest. The *chandzoe* watched Shan now, waiting for Shan to speak. The Chinese in charge.

'His commitment to reform was exemplary,' Shan

heard himself say. 'He has unusual qualities of –' he searched for a word – 'dedication.'

The *chandzoe* nodded with satisfaction.

'I can get a job in Sichuan, I think,' Yeshe said uneasily.

'Why not return here?' the *chandzoe* asked.

'My record. I cannot be licensed.'

'Your re-education is completed. I could talk to Director Wen.' He spoke as though he were somehow obligated to Yeshe.

Yeshe's eyes grew round with surprise. 'But the quota.'

The *chandzoe* shrugged. 'Even if it's a problem, we have no quota on workers for the reconstruction.' He pulled Yeshe's hands open and squeezed one. 'Please come and see the new works,' he said, and pulled Yeshe towards the assembly hall. Slowly, with tiny steps that made it seem he was fighting an invisible force, Yeshe moved towards the hall. As he did so, Shan saw another monk on the steps, facing Yeshe. His hands formed a mudra that seemed aimed at Yeshe.

Yeshe looked to Shan in confusion. Shan nodded, and the two men went across the courtyard.

The abbot watched the *chandzoe* without expression, then sighed and turned to Shan. 'You assume that murderers lie,' he said, as if he had not noticed the interruption. 'Dilgo would not lie. It would violate his vows.'

'Did he do the killing, then?' Shan asked.

The abbot would not answer.

'Taking a life would have been a far more severe violation of his rules,' Shan pointed out.

The abbot finished his tea and dabbed his mouth with the sleeve of his robe. 'They are both prohibited by the 235 rules,' he said, referring to the rules of conduct prescribed for an ordained priest.

'I am confused,' Shan said. 'Those who break their vows are reincarnated as lower life forms. You have already said you believe him to have returned as a human.'

'I, too, am confused. What exactly do you want of us?'

'A simple question. Do you believe that Dilgo killed the Director of Religious Affairs?'

'The government exercised its authority. Dilgo did not protest. The case was closed.'

Why did it surprise him, Shan thought, to find that the head of a thriving gompa was also a politician? 'Did he do it?'

'Everyone has a different path to Buddhahood.'

'Did he do it?'

The abbot sighed and looked into a passing cloud. 'It would have been more likely for Mt Kailas to collapse into the earth from the weight of one bird than for Dilgo to commit such an act.'

Shan nodded heavily. 'Another such bird has been set into flight.'

The abbot looked with a new sadness into Shan's eyes.

'Do you ever think about it, about where the sin lies?' Shan asked.

'I do not understand.'

'It is easy for them, it is the way they stay in power. Danger is part of power, like shadow is part of light. Sometimes, if no one threatens it, it must invent threats. It is just as easy for you to justify what happened to Dilgo. You probably decided that it is as much the nature of things as the tidal wave of soldiers that washed over the gompas in 1959. It was his destiny, you can say, and besides, Dilgo is reincarnated in a better life. But it is not so easy for those in between.'

The abbot no longer looked into Shan's eyes.

'Did you expel Dilgo?'

'He was not expelled.'

'He was convicted of murder but you did not expel him. Instead you performed the rites of Bardo for him.'

The abbot looked into his hands.

Shan consulted his notebook. 'They found his rosary at the murder scene. A very special rosary. Beads carved like tiny pine cones, made out of pink coral, with lapis marker beads. Very old. Must have been brought from India. The file said it was unique, the only one of its kind.'

'It was his rosary,' the abbot confirmed. His voice grew very still. 'It was the proof against him.'

'Did he explain how it got there?'

'He could not explain it.'

'Had he lost it?'

'No. He did not miss it. In fact, he said he had it when he was arrested, when he was taken from his pallet, still sleeping. It was a miracle perhaps, that it could have been transported somewhere and returned that way. Dilgo said maybe it was a message.'

'Why did he not protest?' Shan said. 'Why did he not argue his defence? If you knew he was innocent, why did you not defend him?'

'We did everything we could.'

'Everything?' Shan slowly pulled the case file from the canvas bag he was carrying and dropped it on the bench between them. Shan had read the statement prepared for the abbot. The abbot had condemned the act of violence and apologized on behalf of the gompa and the church.

The abbot stared at the file, then looked up without blinking. 'Everything.'

He was wrong to expect any of them to feel guilty, Shan realized. Everyone in the drama of Dilgo, from the abbot to Prosecutor Jao, even to the accused, had played his role correctly.

The abbot rose and began to move back to his weeds.

'Then tell me this,' Shan said to his back. 'Have you heard that a Buddhist demon was at the site of the murder?'

The abbot turned with a frown. 'Traditions die hard.'

'So you did hear such a rumour?'

'Whenever a public figure dies there will be those who say it was this demon or that spirit who took revenge.'

'And there was such a report that night?'

'There was a full moon that night. A herder reported that he saw the horse-headed demon on a hill above the highway, doing something like a dance. The one called Tamdin. Among the pebbles that suffocated the Director of Religious Affairs was one bead, a rosary bead in the shape of a skull. The kind that Tamdin carries.' Shan had touched such a rosary. The rosary of a demon.

'A shrine was built by the local people, on the spot, to praise their protector.'

Doing a dance on a hill by the highway, Shan considered. Under a full moon. As though Tamdin wanted to be seen.

'Shrines were built after the other murders, too. People say a truck driver saw Tamdin when the Director of Mines was killed. As I said, there're always such rumours when an official dies. Tamdin is a favourite of the people. Very fierce, no mercy in defending the church. A very old demon, one of those they call a country god, from the old Tibetan shamans before the days of Buddhism. As the people evolved to Buddha they brought Tamdin with them.'

From the other side of the courtyard a sudden uproar of animals interrupted them. A gate had been opened and a huge pack of dogs was entering. Priests were feeding the dogs, more dogs than Shan had ever seen gathered in one place. He saw at least thirty and more were trotting through the gate.

Segeant Feng cursed and dropped onto the bench beside Shan, not taking his eyes off the animals. Three large black mastiffs, of the kind herdsmen used to patrol against wolves, lingered in the shadows, as though sensing that Feng and Shan were intruders. Feng's hand moved to his gun.

'Ai yi!' cried one of the monks. He rushed to stand in

front of the dogs. 'They are under our protection,' he said in a pleading tone. 'They are part of Khartok gompa. They come from all over Tibet to be with us.'

'Damned mongrels,' Feng growled. 'Where I come from they are raised for the pot.'

The monk could not hide his horror. 'They are part of us. The ones who remember. It is why they come here.'

'Remember?' asked Shan.

'Priests who failed,' the monk explained. 'The dogs are reincarnations of priests who broke their vows.'

As the monk spoke Yeshe appeared on the steps with the *chandzoe*. From the far side of the courtyard someone else shouted angrily towards Yeshe. The *chandzoe* put his hand on Yeshe's shoulder as though to calm him. The monk on the steps was still there, still aiming his mudra at Yeshe.

At last Shan recognized the mudra. It was to bestow forgiveness. A cold wave of realization swept through him as he looked back at Yeshe, as though for the first time. He had been so blind. He had asked Yeshe everything about himself except the most important question of all.

Two hours later they were at the top of the pass, so high that the stars on the far horizon were below them. Shan, in a drowsy haze, wanted the feeling of drifting through space to continue, until he floated into a world where governments did not lie, where jails were for criminals, where men were not killed with pebbles.

He became aware of a liquid rattle in the back seat. Yeshe had a rosary.

An hour later, as they moved into the crossroads at the head of Lhadrung valley, he put his hand on Feng's arm. 'Go left.'

'Lost your track, Comrade,' Feng grunted. 'The barracks are to the right. Sixty minutes more and we'll be in our bunks.'

'To the left, to the 404th worksite.'

'That's twenty miles out of the way,' Feng protested.

'That's where we are going.'

Feng pulled the truck to a stop as it passed the intersection. 'It will be past midnight by the time we get there. It's empty.'

'Improves the odds.'

'The odds?'

'Of meeting the ghost.'

Feng shuddered. 'The ghost?'

'I want to ask who killed him.'

Feng turned on the cab light and stared at Shan, as though hoping for evidence that it was a joke.

Shan returned the stare without expression. 'Scared of a ghost, Sergeant?'

'Damned right,' Feng shot back, too loudly. He slammed the truck into gear and turned around.

A half mile from the bridge Shan instructed Feng to turn off the lights. The 404th worksite was as empty as death. Feng climbed out and immediately produced his pistol. Shan said nothing but began walking towards the mountain. After thirty paces he looked back to see Feng circling the truck, as if on sentry duty.

Shan stood in the centre of Tan's bridge and gazed skyward, still in awe of the stars. He was afraid that if he reached out he would touch them. His knees were trembling.

He walked up the roadbed to the small cairn marking the site of Jao's murder and sat on a rock. There was no wind on the mountain. This was when the *jungpo* would prowl. This was when demon protectors would strike. He found his hand over his pocket which held the charm that called Tamdin. What were the words from Khorda's skull mantra? *Om padme te krid hum phat.*

A pebble moved behind him. His heart leapt into his throat as a shadow appeared beside him. It was Yeshe.

211

'It was a night like this,' Shan observed, trying to calm himself. 'Prosecutor Jao was driven to the bridge. Someone was here. Someone he knew.'

'I never understood. Why here?' Yeshe asked. 'It's so far from anywhere.'

'That's the reason. The road goes nowhere. No danger of being discovered by passers-by. Easy to escape.' But that was not all. The mountain still had not given up its secret.

'So they walked with Jao,' Yeshe said. 'To look at the stars?'

'To talk. In private. Someone stayed below.'

'The driver.'

'I am here with Jao,' Shan said, switching to the view of the murderer who had lured Jao to the mountain. 'I brought him up here to tell him a secret. But something happened to surprise him. A loose rock. The tingle of metal. He senses his attacker at the last minute, and turns to struggle with him, long enough for Jao to pull an ornament from the costume.' Shan stood with a rock in his hand, acting out the scene. 'Then I grab a rock and hit him from behind.' He threw the rock to the ground forcefully. 'I arrange him neatly after I empty his pockets of identity. Then Tamdin uses his blade.'

'So there're two killers.'

'I think so now. Jao didn't come here with someone in a demon costume. He came with a friend, who had the demon waiting.' Shan took a step away, back into character. 'I don't want to watch.' Shan walked towards the edge of the cliff. 'I don't want blood to spray on me. I come to the edge and throw away what I took from his pockets.' He picked up a stone and moved to the brink of the cliff. Extending his arm over the void, he released the stone.

'You told me why you were sent back from university,' he said after a moment, still facing the abyss. 'But you never said why you went to the university.' Investigations, meditations, careers, relationships were much the same, he mused. They failed because no one thought to ask the right question.

Shan sensed Yeshe moving towards him, and stepped to the very edge, until his toes hung out over the blackness.

'It was an honour to be invited to the university,' Yeshe said in a hollow voice.

A tiny shove, a mild gust of wind would be all it took. Yeshe could just slip and fall against Shan, and he would drop. On a night like this maybe you never hit the bottom. There would only be blackness, then a deeper blackness.

'But why would Yeshe Retang be invited? An unknown monk in a remote gompa?'

Yeshe moved beside him now, as if willing himself to take as much risk as Shan.

'They didn't start reconstruction at Khartok until after you left,' Shan pointed out. 'The *chandzoe*, he treated you like his hero. Like he owed you. As if Khartok received favours after you left.'

'I promised my mother I would be a monk,' Yeshe said to the stars. 'I was the oldest son. It was the tradition for Tibetan families, until Beijing came. The oldest son would have the honour of serving in a gompa. But I wasn't a good monk. The abbot said I had to reduce my ego. He gave me work in the villages, to see the suffering of the people. Twice a week I drove a truck to bring sick children to the gompa.'

A nighthawk called out on the slope behind them.

'He was just lying there, by the road. I thought I could save him. I thought I should push him over to get the pebbles out so he could breathe. I tried. But he was already dead.'

'You mean you discovered the body of the Director of Religious Affairs.'

'I never understood why he was up there, all alone,' Yeshe whispered.

'And Dilgo of your gompa was executed for it.' Shan remembered the missing sheets from the files. Witness statements.

'When I turned him over it was there. I recognized it immediately.'

'You mean the rosary belonging to Dilgo?'

Yeshe didn't respond.

'So you were a witness against him.'

'I told the truth. I found a dead Chinese. He had Dilgo's rosary under him.'

It was such a perfect parable. Antisocial cultist condemned by the testimony of a member of the new society, who happened to belong to his own gompa. Proof of how evil the old order was and how virtuous the new could be. 'They sent you to the university as your reward.'

'How could I refuse? How often does a monk get offered university? How often does a Tibetan get offered university? They said it wasn't a reward. They said my actions had simply demonstrated that I belonged in university, that I was a leader who should have been there all along.'

'Who gave it to you?'

'Prosecutor Jao. Religious Affairs. Public Security. They all signed the paper.'

It said nothing about who killed Jao, or who might be trying to manipulate Yeshe again. Granting such rewards was all in the course of business in administering Chinese justice. Someone might have used Yeshe, knowing he had a pattern of driving on the route. Or his involvement might have been entirely coincidental. What mattered was that Yeshe had proved himself susceptible, and someone else was seeking to influence him in the same manner now. Not Zhong. Warden Zhong was just a conduit, just co-operating to secure Yeshe's labour for a another year.

'I said it first,' Yeshe offered, as if it was an urgent afterthought.

'First?'

'I gave the statement long before they offered the university to me.'

'I know.'

'They said it was for being a good citizen.' He was whispering again. 'Only thing is,' he added forlornly. 'I don't know what it means any more – to be a good citizen now.'

As they watched the stars, the pain seemed to drift out of their silence.

'After we saw Religious Affairs, after Miss Taring said artefacts were still being discovered and put in the museums, I wondered. What if someone had found a second rosary like Dilgo's? What if I had lied and didn't know it?'

Shan put his hand on Yeshe's arm and eased him back from the edge of the cliff. 'Then you need to find out.'

'Why?'

'For Dilgo.'

They sat on a boulder and let the silence wash over them again.

'Do you think it's true what they say?' Yeshe asked.

'What is true?'

'That Jao's ghost is staying here, seeking vengeance.'

'I don't know.' Shan looked out into the night. 'If my soul were set adrift,' he said slowly, 'I'd never look back.'

They spoke no more. Shan had no idea how long they sat. It could have been ten minutes, or thirty. A shooting star arced across the sky. Then, just as abruptly, there was a loud sound, a wrenching, haunting half-moan, half-scream like he had never heard before. It came from below them, and seemed to pierce the skin around his spine. It was not the sound of a human.

Suddenly there were three gunshots, then dead silence.

Chapter Ten

The two soldiers came for him as in a dream, seizing him as he slept in the dark, dragging him out of bed and putting on manacles. They did not speak as they shoved him into the car. They did not answer his questions, except to slap him viciously after the third one. Shan willed his body upright, fighting the pain, reminding himself what to look for. They were not Public Security, but infantry. Soldiers had more rules to follow. He was in a staff car, not a truck. They would not shoot him in a car. They were going out into the valley, not into the mountains where disposals were made. He leaned against the window, letting the glass hold the weight of his head, and watched where they were taking him.

It was the crossroads below the Dragon Claws, where Colonel Tan stood silhouetted against a dull grey sky. The two escorts dragged him towards Tan, released his wrists and moved back to the car, where they stood and lit cigarettes. One man muttered something. The other laughed.

'He said you would do this,' Tan said. 'Zhong said you would mock me. Try to use me.'

'You'll have to be more specific,' Shan muttered through a cloud of pain. 'I only had three hours' sleep.'

'Stirring up the separatists. Conspiring to breach public security. Leading soldiers into ambush.'

Shan became aware of a dull rasping sound. Beyond Tan's car he saw a familiar grey truck. The rear hatch door was open, revealing the booted feet of a sleeping figure.

'Is that what Sergeant Feng told you?' Shan's jaw felt numb. 'That he was ambushed?' He touched his lip. His fingers came away smeared with blood.

'He had orders to call when he returned last night. Woke me up. Completely frantic. Asked for reinforcements. Says to give you to Public Security.' Tan glanced to the north. A column of trucks was approaching.

'Perhaps he didn't tell you how he shot one of the tyres,' Shan said. 'Or how he climbed onto the roof of the truck and wouldn't come down? Or that I had to drive back because he was too hysterical?'

The convoy overtook them. Shan recognized it at once, although there were twice as many trucks as usual. The extras were filled with knobs. He watched in despair. They would go to the South Claw. The knobs would set up their machine-guns. The prisoners would walk up the slope and sit, working their makeshift rosaries, waiting.

As the dust of the column settled Shan saw that two of the trucks had stopped. A dozen bone-hard commandos leapt from one truck and formed two lines at the rear of the second. A Tibetan prisoner was thrown out of the shadows and landed between the lines, groaning in pain. Others began to climb out. Shan realized Tan was not looking at the prisoners, but at him.

The prisoners, fifteen in all, were marched twenty feet into the heather and ordered to form a line. Two knob officers appeared from behind the truck with sub-machine guns and took up positions on the road, facing the monks.

'No!' Shan moaned. 'You can't –'

'I have the authority,' Tan said with a chill. 'Their strike is an act of treason.'

Shan stumbled forward. It was just another of his nightmares, he told himself. He would wake up any moment in his bunk. He fell to his knee. A piece of gravel painfully pierced his skin. He was awake. 'They did nothing,' he groaned.

'You will stop your masquerade. I will have a prosecutor's report on the murderer Sungpo. In one week.'

The prisoners began a mantra. They fixed their eyes over the heads of the executioners, staring towards the mountains.

Tan still did not move his gaze from Shan.

Shan's tongue seemed unable to move. He fought a rising nausea. 'I will not help to kill an innocent man,' he said in a cracking voice. He shook his head, hard, to clear the pain, and looked up at Tan with new strength. 'If that is what you want, I request to join these prisoners.'

Tan did not reply.

The officers cocked their weapons. Shan sprang forward. Someone grabbed him from behind and held him as they fired. The roar of the weapons echoed down the valley.

When the smoke cleared, three of the prisoners were on their knees, sobbing. The others were still staring into the distance, chanting their mantra.

The knobs had used blanks.

'You breached security at the South Claw!' Tan barked. 'Who authorized you to enter a restricted zone?'

Shan met Tan's gaze now. 'The murder scene is now off-limits to your murder investigator?'

'You said you were going to the monastery of Sungpo.' He narrowed his eyes. 'A prosecutor's report against the accused. Do you understand me?'

'Cruelty is never to be understood. It is to be endured.' Shan closed his eyes. He felt something new rising. Anger. 'Li Aidang would doubtless like my notes. I am going to tell one of these Public Security officers I need to speak to Li. Then I am going to climb into this truck' – he indicated the prisoners' vehicle – 'and return to my work unit.'

Tan lit one of his American cigarettes and moved silently around Feng's vehicle. He paused at the right rear, where the hubcap was missing and a mismatched tyre was on the wheel. 'Tell me about it,' he growled as he returned to Shan.

Shan watched the prisoners being loaded as he spoke. 'I was on the ridge, trying to understand what happened that night. Perhaps the hour was important, the hour he was killed. I wanted to know. There was a strange sound, like a large animal, then shots from the truck. I ran down. Sergeant Feng said there was a demon.'

'Your demon Tamdin,' Tan said tersely.

'He was hysterical. He said the demon was close, that he heard it speak. I was afraid for him. I asked for his gun.'

Tan sneered. 'And just like that, Sergeant Feng surrendered to you.'

'I returned it to him later, at the barracks.'

'I don't believe you.'

Shan fumbled in his pockets. 'I kept the remaining bullets, to be safe.' He dropped five cartridges into Tan's hand.

Tan stared at the bullets so long his cigarette burned to his fingers. He flinched and angrily threw the butt to the ground, then studied the dust of the convoy. 'Everything's going to hell,' he muttered, so low Shan was not certain he had heard correctly.

When he looked up there was something new in his eyes, something Shan had not seen before. The barest glimpse of uncertainty. 'It's all about the same thing, isn't it? The 404th and the trial of Sungpo. There's going to be a bloodbath and I am powerless to stop it.'

Shan looked at him in surprise. 'Do you want to stop it? Do you have the will to stop it?'

'What do you think I –' Tan began, but stopped as he looked down at the bullets. 'Feng was scared. He and I served together for many years. He came to Lhadrung because I was here. I never saw him scared.' Tan clenched his hand around the bullets and looked up. 'Jao understood. In criticism sessions he used to say my only mistake was to think the old causes would have the same old effects in Tibet.'

'Old causes have not done well here.'

Tan gazed at the line of prisoners and sighed. 'I am going to tell Zhong to allow them to be fed. To let the Buddhist charity in to feed them once a day.'

Shan looked at him in disbelief, then slowly nodded. 'It would be the right thing to do.'

'Americans are coming,' Tan said absently, then looked back at Shan. 'You're bleeding.'

Shan wiped the blood from his lip again. 'It's nothing.'

Tan extended a handkerchief.

Shan looked at it incredulously.

'I never told them to hit you.'

Shan accepted it and held it to his lip, watching as Sergeant Feng appeared at the rear of the truck, stretching and yawning. Catching sight of Tan, Feng leaned back as if to hide, then straightened and solemnly marched to the colonel.

He looked awkwardly from Shan to Tan. 'Request reassignment sir,' he said, dropping his eyes to his boots.

'On what grounds?' Tan asked gruffly.

'On the grounds that I'm an old fool. I failed to remain vigilant in my duty. Sir.'

'Comrade Shan,' Tan said, 'did Sergeant Feng lose vigilance at anytime last night?'

'No, Colonel,' Shan observed. 'His only fault perhaps was being too vigilant.'

Tan began to return the bullets to Feng, then reconsidered and handed the bullets to Shan, who handed them to Feng. 'Return to duty, Sergeant,' Tan ordered.

Sergeant Feng accepted the bullets sheepishly. 'Should've known,' he muttered. 'Can't shoot a demon.' He saluted the colonel and wheeled about.

Tan looked again at the dust of the convoy. 'There's too little time.'

'Then help me. There's too much to do. I have to try to

speak to Sungpo again. But I also have to find Jao's driver. Help me. He's the key to everything.'

'Not a bowl touched. Not a kernel,' the guard announced as Shan entered the cell block. There was a strange pride in his voice, as though his prisoner's starvation was a personal victory of some kind. 'Nothing but tea.'

Sungpo did not seem to have moved since Shan had seen him four days earlier. He sat erect and alert, wearing his thousand-mile stare.

'My assistant,' Shan said, looking around the cell house. 'I thought he would be here.'

'He's with the other one.'

'You have a new prisoner?'

The man shook his head. 'Climbed the fence. Lucky bastard. Ten minutes earlier, ten minutes later, the perimeter patrol would have shot him down.'

'An escapee?'

'No. That's the joke. He was trying to get in. Had to be taught that citizens may not freely enter military installations.'

Shan found Yeshe in the building next door. He was wringing out a towel in a basin of blood-tinged water. Shan watched for a moment, noticing something different in Yeshe's face. He looked calmer somehow. It wasn't peace of mind he had found, but maybe a new deliberation.

Shan followed Yeshe into the interrogation room. At first he did not recognize the figure on the table. One side of his face looked like a melon that had fallen off a speeding truck.

'Plenty hot good, eh?' the man said, raising one of his big pawlike hands in greeting. 'He sent for me. I found him.'

It was Jigme.

'What do you mean he sent for you?'

'You came, didn't you?'

'How could you be here so soon? You drove?'

His battered eyes somehow were able to twinkle. 'I fly through the air. Like the old ones. The spell of the arrow.'

'I've heard of it,' Shan said. 'I also remember seeing logging trucks on the road out of your valley.'

Jigme tried to laugh but the sound emerged as a hoarse, hacking cough.

Shan and Yeshe pulled him to his feet and, one at each shoulder, half dragged, half carried him out of the building. They were stopped on the stairs by a furious officer.

'These prisoners belong to Public Security!' the officer roared.

'This man is part of my investigation,' Shan said matter-of-factly and turned his back on the officer. Once inside the cell block, Jigme pulled himself away and straightened his clothing. He limped down the corridor alone and dropped to his knees with a cry of delight as he reached the last cell.

The guard at the cell door rose in protest. Shan cut him off with a gesture to open the cell.

Sungpo acknowledged Jigme with a nod which lit Jigme's bruised face. The gompa orphan closed the door behind him and surveyed the untouched bowls of rice. 'Everything okay now,' he said with a grateful smile to Shan.

'We need to speak with him.'

Jigme seemed to think Shan had made an excellent joke. 'Sure,' he grinned. 'Two years, one month, and eighteen days.'

'He doesn't have that long.'

Jigme soured and moved back to Sungpo with one of the bowls of rice. With small, affectionate strokes of his hand he began brushing the straw off Sungpo's robe.

'We have to speak with him,' Shan repeated.

'You think he's scared to throw off a face?' Jigme

222

shouted, suddenly defiant. 'You people from the north, you're a fly on his shoulder.' Shan saw a tear rolling down Jigme's cheek as he spoke. 'He's a great man. A living Buddha. He'll die easy, no bother. He'll throw off a face and laugh at all of us in the next life.'

They sat in an unused stall at the rear of the market and watched the sorcerer's shop. No one entered, no one exited. The market began to fill with vendors' carts piled high with spring greens, the early leaves of mustard and other plants that elsewhere on the planet would have been considered weeds.

Feng, still nervous from the night before, rubbed his palm over the handle of his pistol.

'I need fifty fen,' Shan said.

'Who doesn't?' Feng cracked.

'For food. You have expense money.'

'Not hungry.'

'We had no breakfast. You did.'

The announcement seemed to pain Feng, and Shan wondered if he was still stinging from the discovery of his nickname. Feng's eyes moved back and forth from Shan to Yeshe. 'One of you stays here.'

Yeshe, taking the cue, leaned back against the wall as though settling in.

Shan extended his hand and took the money.

Feng made a vague gesture towards the stalls in front of them. 'Five minutes.'

Shan lingered at a vendor selling writing supplies, then found a woman selling *momos*. He bought two for Yeshe, then moved to the first stall and quickly bought two sheets of rice paper, a writing brush, and a small ink stick.

'The first charm was requested a few days ago,' a voice from behind suddenly declared.

Shan began to turn. An elbow pushed into his back. 'Don't look,' the man said.

Shan recognized the voice. It was the *purba* with the scarred face. He saw tattered felt boots behind him. The man was dressed as a herder.

'They're always looking for a chance,' the *purba* said over Shan's shoulder. 'Witches like Khorda, he'll take their money. They have steady money. Business is always good for their kind.'

'I don't understand.'

'This one, she works in a bookshop. Asked for the Tamdin charms about a week ago. Yesterday she asked for one against dogbite.'

'She?'

'Daughter of a flesh monkey.'

'A *ragyapa*?'

'Green Bamboo Street,' came the reply.

Shan turned. The *purba* had disappeared.

Twenty minutes later Shan and Sergeant Feng watched from across the rutted gravel track on the north side of town as Yeshe ventured into the bookshop. A short, swarthy woman could be seen inside as he entered. As he spoke to her she pointed towards the rear of the store, then looked up and down the street before pulling the door shut.

Yeshe darted out of the store ten minutes later, a glimmer of triumph on his face. 'She's there,' he announced. 'That was her at the door. Says she's from Shigatse but she's not.' He said that he had asked for the owner, explaining he was conducting a quick audit of working papers. When the man had begun to question his authority, Yeshe had pointed out of the window. Seeing an official-looking vehicle and a soldier at the wheel, the man had quickly revealed his free enterprise licence and the girl's work papers. 'Showed she was from Shigatse nearly a year ago. But on the way out I asked if she liked climbing the walls of the old fortress at

Shigatse. She said she did, said she liked to take picnics there.'

'There's still a fortress there?' Shan asked.

'A fortress, in Tibet? Of course not, the Communists blew it up forty years ago!' He put his hands together as he spoke, then threw them apart, like an explosion. 'No more walls.'

'So she's not from Shigatse.'

'Impossible. She lives in the back, but the owner says she leaves almost every weekend. A store clerk would never make enough to travel two hundred miles to Shigatse so often.'

'Then her family is nearby,' Shan said. A family of fleshcutters. In the mountains. Where Tamdin the flesh-cutter lived. 'That's where she is going with the charms.' He looked expectantly at Yeshe.

Yeshe's face darkened. 'No,' he protested weakly.

'Her home shouldn't be hard to find,' Shan suggested. 'In Lhadrung there is an active market for death.'

Tan handed him several sheets of paper clipped with a pin at the top. 'I found Miss Lihua,' he said, with the exhilaration that progress brings. 'Prosecutor Jao's secretary. On leave in Hong Kong. The Ministry of Justice tracked her to her hotel. She went to the local Ministry office and used the fax. Reports that Assistant Prosecutor Li drove her to the airport, before Jao left for dinner with the American woman. I know her. Young, very dedicated. Great memory for details. Gave me Jao's schedule. His calls on the day of his murder. She faxed it all. No one called about a meeting.'

Miss Lihua was honoured to be able to assist the colonel, the first fax said. She was stricken with grief over the loss of Comrade Prosecutor Jao and felt she should return immediately. Tan had declined the offer, provided she would co-operate by fax.

'Did she know how to find the driver?' Shan asked.

'Told me where he lived. And said she was certain no one Jao knew had set up a meeting at the South Claw.'

'She wouldn't know,' Shan said. 'She wouldn't know if someone called.'

'Jao was a stiff bastard. Never took calls himself. And everything had to be planned in advance or it could not happen. Every hour was logged by Miss Lihua. He was in the office all that day, she said. He was loading the car for the airport when she left. Religious Affairs called about a committee meeting. The Justice office in Lhasa called about a late report. He had her call to confirm his flights. Nothing else that day except the dinner.'

'There are other places. Other ways to receive calls.'

'This isn't Shanghai. He didn't have a damned pocket phone. He didn't have a radio transmitter. He didn't go anywhere that day anyway. And he wouldn't have changed his plans,' Tan said, 'wouldn't have chanced missing the flight for his annual leave just for a message from some monk.'

'Exactly. Which is why it was someone he knew,' Shan replied.

'No. It is why he must have been ambushed on the way to the airport, then driven back to the Claw.'

'The road to the airport? It is a military road.'

'Of course.'

'So convoys drive down it into the valley. Do they travel at night?'

Tan nodded slowly. 'When supplies or personnel are picked up at the airport. Flights arrive in the late afternoon.'

'Then verify whether any military driver saw a limousine on his return drive. There aren't many limousines in Lhadrung. It would have been conspicuous.'

Shan studied the folder with the faxes as he spoke. Madame Ko had added Prosecutor Jao's itinerary, obtained directly from the airline. 'Why was he scheduled for a one-day layover in Beijing? Why not fly straight through?'

'Shopping. Family. Any number of reasons.'

Shan sat down and stared into his hands. 'I must go to Lhasa.'

Tan's face soured. 'There's no possible connection to Lhasa. If you think for a moment I'll drag in the outside authorities –'

'The prosecutor had planned an unaccounted-for day in Beijing. He received an unaccounted-for message from an unknown person who lured him to be killed by another unknown wearing an unaccounted-for costume.'

'There's more than one killer?' Tan said, with a tone of warning in his voice.

Shan ignored the question. 'We have to start answering questions, not raising more. In Lhasa,' Shan explained, 'there is the Museum of Cultural Antiquities. We need to account for all the costumes of Tamdin.'

'Impossible. I can't protect you in Lhasa. It would be my head if you were discovered.'

'Then you go. Check the museum records.'

'Wen Li verified it. Said there are none missing. And I can't leave the district with the 404th on strike. It would be a sign of weakness.' He looked up abruptly and cursed. 'Listen to me. As if I'm apologizing. Nobody makes me –' the words choked in his throat.

There were few better lenses to the soul, Shan mused, than anger.

The colonel moved back to the window and picked up the binoculars.

Shan could see with his naked eye that the worksite was empty. 'You are right, not to think of them as separate problems,' he said very quietly.

Tan slowly lowered the glasses and turned to him.

'The murder and the strike,' Shan said. 'They are about the same thing.'

'You mean the death of Jao.'

'No. Not the death of Jao. The thing that caused the death of Jao.'

As Tan stared at him the phone rang. He listened, uttered a single syllable of acknowledgement, and hung up. 'Li Aidang,' he announced with a frown, 'is out collecting your evidence again.'

Balti, the Ministry of Justice chauffeur, lived in a battered stucco and corrugated tin building that served as a government garage. Shan and the colonel followed voices up a steep stairway above the garage to a draughty, dim loft lined with shelves of auto parts. A long slab of plywood had been erected on cinder blocks to serve as a bed. On it were pieces of soiled canvas that appeared to have once served as drop cloths in the repair shop. On an upturned crate at the end of the bed was a butter lamp and a small ceramic Buddha, badly chipped.

Two men were at the end of the room, using hand lanterns to examine the shelves.

'We would not want the assistant prosecutor to surpass our own diligence,' Tan said under his breath. Shan half expected him to push him towards the shelves.

One of the men in the shadows approached. It was Li. He was wearing rubber gloves and had a *kiajiou* tied around his mouth. What was he afraid of? Buddhist contagion?

'Brilliant!' he said to Shan, lowering the mask. 'I never thought of it until Colonel Tan asked about the prosecutor's car.'

'Thought about what exactly?' asked Shan.

'The conspiracy. This *khampa*. He forced the prosecutor to the South Claw. Drove him there against his will. To be murdered by Sungpo. It explains how Sungpo travelled to the Claw and back. Why the car is missing. Why Balti is missing.' Li kept searching as he spoke. He examined a cardboard box near the bed. It held neatly folded clothing. He dumped it onto the floor and picked up each piece with an extended finger as if it might be infested with vermin. He knelt and looked under the bed, producing two shoes which he carelessly tossed behind him.

Shan bent and ran his hand under the bedding. Hidden underneath was a wrinkled, faded photograph of three men, two women, and a dog standing before a herd of yaks. His hand closed around something sharp and metallic. It was a circular piece of chrome. He held it at arm's length in confusion.

Tan took it from him and studied it. 'Jiefang,' he announced. 'Hood ornament.' Battered Jiefang trucks, sent to Tibet after a lifetime of work elsewhere, were fixtures on the region's roads.

Li grabbed the ornament and snapped an order to the man behind him, who produced a small clear plastic bag. Li ceremoniously dropped the chrome piece into the bag and looked at Shan with a gloating expression.

'You should watch American movies,' Li declared as he moved to the edge of the bed. 'Very instructive. Integrity of the evidence is the key.' Energized by the find, Li tore the bed clothing away. Finding nothing else, he overturned the plywood, then probed with his hand into the cavities of the cinder blocks. At the last one he looked up victoriously, producing a rosary of plastic beads.

'The limousine. It's obvious.' Li dangled the beads in front of Shan. 'He was given Prosecutor Jao's Red Flag limousine as his reward for abetting the murder.' He dropped the beads into another bag.

Yeshe awkwardly moved to the shelves of auto parts and began to absently move the cartons. A tattered postcard fell on the floor as he did so, an image of the Dalai Lama taken decades earlier.

'Excellent!' Li exclaimed, snatching the photo and patting Yeshe on the back. 'You are learning, Comrade.'

Yeshe stared blankly at Li. 'It is permitted to own such pictures now,' he said, 'as long as they are not displayed publicly.' Not quite an argument, but still there was objection in Yeshe's voice, a tone which surprised Shan and perhaps surprised Yeshe even more.

Li seemed not to notice. He waved the photo like a flag. 'No, but look how old it is. It *was* illegal when it was taken. *This* is how we build cases, Comrade.' An assistant held out another plastic bag, into which Li dropped the postcard.

Shan moved to the window at the other end of the room and rubbed his fingers through its grime. Outside he could see their vehicles. Someone was smoking a cigarette with Sergeant Feng. He rubbed the glass clean. It was Lieutenant Chang. Reflexively, Shan stepped backwards. Something brushed against his foot as he did so. It was one of the shoes. He picked it up and ran his finger around its edge. It was of cheap vinyl and covered with dust. It was new, probably never worn, but still covered with dust. He picked up the second shoe. It was not a match. Like the first it seemed unworn; and like the first it was for the left foot. Shan returned to the ruins of the bed and searched. There were no other shoes.

'And this was a man who had been cleared by Public Security.' Li was holding up the little Buddha.

'A little man with a fat belly is not illegal,' Tan observed icily.

Li gave Tan a condescending look. 'Comrade Colonel. You have little experience with the criminal mind.' He punctuated his comment with a satisfied smile, then extended his arm and dropped the Buddha into another bag held out by one of his assistants.

A small crowd had gathered outside the garage. They scurried like frightened animals when Tan appeared, vanishing down an alley. Only a child remained, a tiny figure of three or four wrapped in a black yak hair robe tied with twine. The child, whose sex was not obvious, stood looking at Tan with intense curiosity.

'I have to find Balti,' Shan said to Tan. 'If he has disappeared it is because of that night.'

'You heard Li. He is probably in Sichuan by now.'

'You saw his clothes upstairs. His entire wardrobe, in that box. He didn't pack it. He wasn't planning to leave. Besides, how far do you think the man who lived in that loft would get, without travel papers, in illegal possession of a government car?'

'So he sold the car.' Tan took a step towards the child.

'That is only one of the possibilities. He could have been part of the crime. Or he could have been killed. Or he could have fled in terror and is in hiding.'

The child looked at Tan and laughed.

'From fear of your demon?'

'Or fear of reprisal. From someone he recognized that night,' Shan said.

Tan paused, considering Shan's suggestion. 'Either way, he's gone. Nothing you can do.'

'I can talk to the neighbours. My guess is he lived here a long time. He was part of the neighbourhood.'

'Neighbourhood?' Tan looked around at the piles of empty oil barrels, heaps of scrap metal, and dilapidated sheds that surrounded the garage.

'People live here.'

'Fine. Let's interrogate them. I want to see my investigator at work.'

Someone called from the alleyway. The child did not respond.

Tan extended his hand towards the child. Suddenly three men appeared, square-built herdsmen holding poles in front of them as if to do battle. Instantly Sergeant Feng and Tan's driver were at the colonel's side, their hands on their weapons.

A short, stout woman ran between the men, crying out in alarm. She grabbed the child and shouted at the men, who slowly retreated.

A hardness settled over Tan's countenance. He lit a

cigarette in silence, studying the alleyway. 'All right. You do it. I'll send patrols back to the foot of the South Claw. Let's eliminate the most likely explanation first. We'll search for his body. They already looked below the cliff face when they searched for the head. But the driver's body could be anywhere. In the Dragon Throat gorge, maybe.'

As Tan sped off, Shan directed Sergeant Feng to move his truck into the shadow of the garage, then sat with Yeshe on rusty barrels in the repair yard.

'Did you tell Li I was coming here?' Shan asked Yeshe as the neighbourhood slowly returned to life. 'Someone did. Just like Jao's house.'

'I told you before, if they asked, how could I refuse the Ministry of Justice?'

'Did they ask?'

Yeshe did not reply.

'A marker was on the rock in Sungpo's cave where Jao's wallet was found. Someone planted it there so the arresting team would find it.'

Yeshe's face clouded. 'Why do you tell me this?'

'Because you have to decide what it is you want to be. Priests react to prison in many ways. Some will always be priests. Others will continue to be prisoners.'

Yeshe turned with a bitter glare. 'So you say I'm a non-believer if I answer questions from the Ministry of Justice.'

'Not at all. I am saying that for those with doubts, their actions begin to define their beliefs. I'm saying accept that you will always be a prisoner of men like Warden Zhong or decide not to accept it.'

Yeshe threw a pebble against the wall and took a step away from Shan.

An old woman appeared, cast them a spiteful glance, then opened a blanket at the edge of the street and began arranging the pile of matchboxes, chopsticks, and rolled candy which were her only wares. She pulled a worn photograph from inside her dress and held it to her forehead, then set it in front of her on the blanket. It was a photo of the Dalai Lama. Three boys began a game of tossing pebbles into a discarded tyre. A window in the tenement across from the garage opened and a bamboo pole bearing laundry appeared, hanging like a stick of prayer flags over the street.

Shan watched for five minutes, then bought a roll of candy from the woman, asking Yeshe to pay for it. 'I am sorry for the disturbance,' he said to her. 'The man who lived here is missing.'

'Damned fool of a boy,' she cackled.

'You know Balti?'

'Go for prayer, I told him. Remember who you are, I told him.'

'Was he in need of prayer?' Shan asked.

'Tell him,' she said, turning to Yeshe. 'Tell him only the dead don't need prayer. Except my dead husband,' she sighed. 'He was an informer, my husband. Pray for him. He became a rodent. He comes at night and I feed him bits of grain. The old fool.'

One of the herdsmen, still holding his staff, approached her and muttered under his breath.

'Be quiet, you!' the widow spat. 'When you're so rich none of us need work, you can tell me who to speak to.'

She produced five cigarettes wrapped in tissue paper and arranged them on her blanket, then studied Yeshe. 'Are you the one?'

'The one?' Yeshe asked awkwardly.

'I left a prayer in the temple. For the devils to be driven off. Someone will come. It can be done. There were priests in the old days who could do it. With one sound they could do it. If you make a groan that vibrates into the next world, you can fix everything.'

Yeshe looked in confusion at the woman. 'Why would you think it could be me?'

'Because you came. The only believer who came.'

Yeshe glanced uneasily at Shan. 'Do you know where the *khampa* is?' he asked the woman.

'He always said they would take him. He paid us to watch out. The nights when he brought it home, we would watch the stairs, my husband and me. Sleep all day so we could watch at night.'

'Brought what with him?' asked Yeshe.

'The case. The little suitcase. For papers. He would keep it some nights for his boss. Big secrets. First he's proud to have it. Later he's scared. Even with the place he made, he would be scared.'

'What kind of papers? Did you see them?' Yeshe asked.

'Of course not. I don't work for the government, do I? Dangerous secrets. Words of power. Government secrets.'

'He made a place, you said,' Shan interjected. 'You mean a hiding place?'

She paid him no attention. She seemed interested only in Yeshe now, as if she saw in him something no one else, including Yeshe himself, could see.

'Who would take him? What was he scared of?' Yeshe pressed on. 'Prosecutor Jao?'

'Not Jao. Jao was good to him. Gave him extra ration cards sometimes. Let him wear his clothes sometimes.'

'Then who?'

She wrinkled her brow and studied Yeshe. 'Your powers are not destroyed,' she said. 'You think they are. But they are just hidden.'

Yeshe retreated a step, as though frightened. 'Where is Balti?' he asked. A pleading tone had entered his voice.

'A boy like that, he goes up. Or he goes down.' She chuckled as she considered her words, and looked at the herdsman. 'Up or down,' she repeated to him with another laugh. She turned back to Yeshe. 'If they took him, he'll still come back. As a lion he'll come back. That's what happens to the meek ones. He will return as a lion and rip us all to shreds for failing him.'

Shan knelt in front of the woman. 'Show us the hiding place,' he whispered.

She did not seem to hear. 'Show us,' Yeshe asked. She fidgeted with her wares, confused.

'We need to see it,' Shan pressed. 'Balti needs us to see it.'

'He was so scared.'

'I think he was brave,' Shan said.

She acknowledged him at last. 'He cried at night.'

'Even a brave man can have reasons to cry.'

She kept her eyes from him. 'What if you are the ones he feared?'

'Look at us. Is that what you think? Would they come and talk to you this way?' He pressed her arm. She slowly looked up, as if it were painful to see Shan's eyes.

'Not him,' she said, nodding to Yeshe. 'He isn't one of them.'

'Then do it for him,' Shan said.

She moved quickly now, as if eager to be rid of them. The herdsman with the staff came also, following them into the garage. They moved into the shadows at the back of the structure, past their truck. Feng was snoring loudly.

A rough wooden rack had been built to hold large parts salvaged from vehicles. On the bottom was a row of long, narrow gas tanks removed from cars and trucks.

She put her hand on the third tank. 'He was small enough to go behind,' she said. Shan and Yeshe manhandled the tank from the rack. The rear had been neatly cut away, the edges bent so it could be pushed back into place. A ribbon of grease covered the seam. Shan found a screwdriver and pried it open.

Inside there was no briefcase, only a soiled envelope with several sheets of onionskin paper.

The woman helped them return the tank to the rack, then turned to Yeshe once more. 'Your powers are not destroyed,' she said again. 'They have only lost their focus.'

Yeshe seemed paralysed by the words. As Shan pulled him to the truck, calling for Feng to wake up, Yeshe was unable to take his eyes from the woman. He held his rosary as they drove to the opposite side of town. He did not count the beads, but only looked at it. 'In Sichuan,' he said suddenly, 'I could have my own apartment.'

Sitting behind Feng, Shan studied the papers from the tank. They had been ripped out of an investigation file, the file on the murder of Jin San, manager of Long Wall agricultural collective, the crime for which Dza Namkhai of the Lhadrung Five had been executed. At the bottom of the last sheet was a long series of Arabic numbers, five groups of five digits each.

'Powers,' Yeshe said in a haunted tone. 'What a woman. Great powers. The world bears witness to my great powers.'

Shan looked up. 'Don't be so quick to condemn yourself. The greatest power, I think, is the power to tell right from wrong.'

Yeshe considered Shan's words. 'But it never feels like right or wrong,' he said at last. 'It seems more like deciding which devil is least destructive.'

'What did she mean,' Shan asked, 'when she said a groan that could reach the next world?'

'Sound is like a thought with legs, some of the old gompas taught. If you can put the right focus in your thought you can see beyond this world. If you put the right focus in a sound you can actually reach and touch the other world.'

'Touch it?'

'It is supposed to create a rift between worlds. Like a lightning bolt. The rift has incredible energy. Some call it the thunder ritual. It can destroy things.'

Shan looked back at the papers. She had said someone would come for him, meaning someone other than Jao.

236

Balti had trusted Jao, as Jao had trusted him. An old file, a closed file, yet so secret Jao could not trust it in his own office. Or perhaps especially in his office.

'She said Balti would go up or go down,' Shan recalled distractedly. 'She thought it was a good line.'

Yeshe still spoke in his haunted voice. 'Go back to the Kham plateau, which is so high everywhere there is up compared to the rest of the world. Or stay and go down the chain of life forms.'

Shan nodded slowly, trying to connect the words to the file. The scent was so strong it felt almost tangible. Who ever wanted the file? Someone would come, Balti had said. It wasn't the *purbas*. They hadn't known who he was. Even if they did, they wouldn't terrify Balti. Who would? The knobs? A criminal gang? Soldiers? Criminal soldiers? Whoever it was would not fret over killing Balti. They would have taken him that night, and would have made him talk, made him sing out every last detail of every secret, every hiding place. If the tank still held at least some of its secrets, Shan suddenly realized, then Balti was alive, and free.

Chapter Eleven

The road to the *ragyapa* village had been deliberately built to terminate two hundred feet short of the village, culminating in a large clearing where flat rocks were arranged as unloading platforms. As Sergeant Feng edged into the clearing, a small flatbed truck pulled out with unnecessary speed. Shan glimpsed a woman at the window. She was weeping.

Along the path to the village a donkey pulled a cart with a long thick bundle wrapped in canvas.

Yeshe, to Shan's surprise, was the first out. From the back he pulled a burlap sack of old apples and with a look of sombre resolution began moving up the trail. As Shan stepped out, Feng took one look at the long bundle on the cart, then immediately locked the doors and raised the windows. As his last defence, he lit a cigarette and began filling the interior with smoke.

Shan was an alien to the *ragyapa*. They weren't accustomed to Han, dead or alive. They weren't accustomed to anyone but each other. Even other Tibetans seldom ventured near, except to leave the body of a loved one and a pouch of money or basket of goods in payment. In a cutter's village near Lhasa two soldiers had been killed for trying to film their work. Near Shigatse Japanese tourists had been beaten with leg bones when they got too close.

Shan quickly caught up and stayed one step behind Yeshe. 'You look like you have a plan,' he observed.

'Sure. To get out as quickly as possible,' Yeshe said in a low voice.

An unwashed boy with long ragged hair sat on the earth near the first hut, stacking pebbles. He looked up at the visitors and shouted, not a warning cry but a cry of abrupt pain, as though he had been kicked. The sound brought a woman from the inside of the hut. With one hand she carried a dented teapot and with the other balanced a baby on her hip. She glanced at Shan, not looking into his eyes, but slowly surveying his body, as though measuring him for something.

Beyond the hut was the central yard of the camp, around which several structures were arrayed. Some were makeshift huts of sticks, planks, even cardboard. Several, to his surprise, were small but substantial stone buildings. A knot of men worked in front of one, sharpening an assortment of axes and knives.

They had an apelike quality, short men with thick arms and small eyes. One of them detached himself and took a step towards Shan, brandishing a light axe. He had a disturbingly vacant stare, as if borrowed from the dead. Noticing the sack in Yeshe's arms, his face softened. Two other men stepped towards Yeshe, and solemnly extended their arms. As Yeshe handed the sack to them, they gave a nod of sympathy, then confusion appeared on their faces. One of the men looked inside the bag and laughed as he displayed an apple from inside. The others joined in the joke as he tossed the apple to the circle of men. It was not the kind of small burlap package the *ragyapa* usually received, Shan suddenly realized, not one of the small bundles of death that even the fleshcutters must hate to receive.

Yeshe's action broke the tension. More apples were thrown, and the men produced pocket knives – their longer blades being reserved for their sacred duties – and began distributing pieces of the fruit. Shan looked at the tools. Small knives whose blades ended with hooks. Long flaying knives. Rough handaxes that could have been forged two centuries earlier. Half the blades could easily have severed a man's head.

Children appeared, eager for the fruit. They stayed apart from Shan, but circled Yeshe, wide-eyed and happy.

'We came from the bookstore in town,' Shan announced.

The words had no effect on the children, but the men instantly sobered. Words were muttered among them, and one man split away and began running up the hill behind the village.

The children began to poke at Yeshe, and suddenly he seemed very interested in them. He knelt to tie one of their shoes, studying the youth's clothing, then they leapt on top of him, knocking him to the ground. Some of the older boys produced toy blades of wood and, laughing hysterically, made sawing motions over his joints.

Shan watched the mêlée for only a moment, then his gaze fixed on the running man. It quickly became clear that his destination was a rock outcropping at the top of the low ridge above the camp. Shan began walking up the trail, then stopped as he noticed the birds. Over a dozen, mostly vultures, were circling high in the sky. Others, birds of prey both large and small, sat perched along the path on stunted trees. They seemed strangely tame, as though the village belonged to them as much as the *ragyapa*. They watched the runner pass by with idle curiosity.

It was called sky burial. The quickest remove from the physical bounds of one's existence. In some parts of Tibet bodies were set adrift in rivers, which was why it was taboo to eat fish. Shan heard that in regions still closely tied to India immolation was practised. But for the devout Buddhist in most of Tibet there was only one way to dispose of the flesh left when an incarnation was extinguished. Tibetans couldn't live without the *ragyapa*. But they couldn't live with them.

Another man appeared at the top as the runner approached, holding a long handle like a staff with a wide blade at its end. He was middle-aged, and wore a winter military cap with its quilted side flaps hanging out at the sides like small wings. Shan, wary of the birds, sat on a boulder and waited.

The man evaluated Shan with suspicion as he neared the boulder. 'No tourists,' he barked in a high voice. 'You should go.'

'This girl in the bookstore. She is from this village,' Shan said abruptly.

The man stared at Shan with a grim countenance, then lowered his blade. He produced a cloth and began wiping off gobbets of wet, pink matter, watching Shan, not the blade, as he worked. 'She is my daughter,' he admitted. 'I am not ashamed.' It was a serious admission, and a brave one.

'There is no need for shame. But it was surprising, to find one of your people working in town.' He knew he did not need to mention the work papers. The realization that Shan had discovered the lie was, he expected, the only reason the man was talking to him.

The challenge in the man's eyes dissipated to a glint of stubborn resolve. 'My daughter is a good worker. She deserves a chance.'

'I am not here about your daughter. I am here about your family's business with the old sorcerer.'

'We don't need sorcerers.'

'Khorda has been supplying her with charms. I think she brings them here.'

The man pressed a fist against his temple, as though suddenly in pain. 'It is not illegal to ask for charms. Not any more.'

'But still, you are trying to hide it, by having your daughter buy them.'

The *ragyapa* considered this carefully. 'I help her out. One day she will have her own shop.'

'A shop can be very expensive.'

'Another five years. I have it worked out. *Ragyapa* have the steadiest job in Tibet.' It had the sound of an old joke.

'Has Tamdin been here? Is that why you need the charms?' Shan asked. Or does Tamdin live here, perhaps he should ask. Could it really be so simple? The bitter, forgotten *ragyapa* must hate the world, especially its officials. And who more qualified to conduct the butchery on Prosecutor Jao? Or to cut out the heart of Xong De of the Ministry of Geology?

The man sighed. 'The charms are not for here.'

'Then where? Who? You mean you are selling them to someone else?'

'These are not things to speak about.' The man wiped the blade again, as if in warning.

'Are you selling them?' Shan repeated. 'Is that how you will pay for her shop?'

The man looked up at the circling birds. A *ragyapa* village would be the perfect place for murder, Shan realized. Like shooting your own officer on a battlefield because you hated him. One body here would quickly become indistinguishable from the others.

The man did not respond. He looked down into the village and saw the men staring at him. He barked at them and they began working on the tools again. Yeshe, strangely, was still tumbling about with the children.

Shan looked at the man again. He was not only older than most of them, he was apparently the headman of the village. 'I just want to know who. Someone must be too embarrassed, or too scared, to ask for the charms directly. Is it someone in the government?' The man turned away from Shan. 'My questions may occur to someone else,' Shan said to his back. 'They would have other means of persuasion.'

'You mean Public Security,' the man whispered. Certainly the Bureau would be more interested than Shan in his daughter's work papers. His face seemed to crumble with the words. He stared into the dirt at his feet.

Shan told the man his name.

The headman looked up in surprise, unaccustomed to such a gesture. 'I am called Merak,' he said tentatively.

'You must be very proud of your daughter.'

Merak stopped and considered Shan. 'When I was a boy,' he said, 'I never understood it, why none of the others would let me near. I would go to the edge of town and hide, just to watch the others play. You know who my best friend was? A young vulture. I trained him to come to me when I called. It was the only thing that trusted me, that accepted me as I was. One day when I called an eagle was waiting. It killed my friend. Snatched him right out of the air, because he was watching me, not the sky.'

'It is hard to be trusted.'

'We're vultures too. That's what the world thinks of us. My father used to laugh about that. He'd say, "That's the advantage we have over everyone else. We know exactly who we are."'

'Someone has asked you to buy a charm. Someone who thinks they offended Tamdin.'

Merak swept his hand towards the buildings below. 'Why would we need them?'

'The *ragyapa* do not believe in demons?'

'The *ragyapa* believe in vultures.'

'You didn't answer my question.'

'First you tell me.'

'Tell you what?'

'You're from the world,' Merak said, nodding towards the valley. 'Tell me you don't believe in demons.'

The sound of scuffling arose further up the trail. Shan looked up, and instantly regretted it. Two vultures were engaged in a tug of war over a human hand.

Shan gazed down into his own hands a moment, his

fingers rubbing his calluses. 'I have lived too long to tell you that.'

Merak gave a knowing nod, then silently led Shan back to the village.

'The American mine,' Shan told Feng as he got into the truck. There was another *ragyapa*, he remembered, one who climbed the high ranges that were the home of Tamdin.

Yeshe, in the back seat, extended a child's sock towards Shan as if it were a trophy. 'Didn't you see?' he asked with a meaningful grin.

'See what?'

'The missing military supplies I had been categorizing for Warden Zhong. The hats, the shoes, the shirts. And everyone wore green socks.'

'I don't understand,' Shan confessed.

'The lost supplies. They're here. The *ragyapa* have them.'

'No,' Shan said as they turned from the highway onto the access road to Jade Spring. 'The American mine.'

'Right,' Sergeant Feng said. 'Just one stop. Not long.'

He pulled up next to the mess hall and, to Shan's surprise, opened Shan's door, waiting. 'Not long,' he repeated.

Shan followed, confused, then remembered. 'You were talking to Lieutenant Chang.'

Feng grunted non-committally.

'Has he been reassigned? He isn't spending much time at the 404th.'

'In a lockdown? With two hundred border commandos camped there? What's the point?'

'What did he want?'

'Just talking. Told me about a shortcut to the American mine.'

In the mess hall soldiers were gathered in small groups,

drinking tea. Feng surveyed the room, then led Shan towards three men playing mah-jongg near the rear.

'Meng Lau,' he called out. Two of the men jerked their heads up and stood. The third, his back to them, laughed and set down a tile. The others fell back as Feng put his hand on the man's shoulder.

Startled, the man cursed and turned. He was young, a mere boy, with greasy hair and hooded, lightless eyes. Headphones, turned upside down under his chin, covered his ears.

'Meng Lau,' Feng repeated.

The sneer on the man's face faded. He slowly lowered the headphones. Shan unbuttoned his pocket and showed him the paper provided by Director Hu. 'You signed this?'

Meng glanced towards Feng and slowly nodded. There was something wrong with his left eye. It drifted, unfocused, as if perhaps it were artificial.

'Did Director Hu ask for it?'

'The prosecutor came and wanted it,' Meng said nervously.

'The prosecutor?'

Meng nodded again. 'His name is Li.'

'So you signed one for Li and one for Hu?'

'I signed two.'

So it was true, Shan realized, Li Aidang was compiling a separate file. But why go through the trouble of providing Shan a duplicate statement? To ensure that he finished as quickly as possible? To deceive him? Or maybe to warn him that Li would always be one step ahead?

'They said the same thing?'

The soldier looked at Feng uncertainly before he answered. 'Of course.'

'But who put the words on the paper?' Shan asked.

'They are my words.' Meng took a step back.

'Did you see a monk that night?'

'The statement says so.'

The words seemed to deflate Feng for a moment. Then he grew angry. 'You damned pup!' he barked. 'Answer him straight!'

'Were you on duty that night, Private Meng?' Shan asked. 'You were not on the roster.'

The soldier began to fidget with his headphones. 'Sometimes we switch.'

Feng's hand came out of nowhere, slapping the soldier across the mouth. 'The inspector asked you a question.'

Shan looked at Feng in surprise. The inspector.

Meng looked at Feng vacantly, as if he were used to being hit.

'Did you see a monk that night?' Shan asked again.

'I think because I'm a witness for the trial I am not supposed to speak with anyone.'

Anger rose on Feng's face, then quickly faded, though not before the soldier had seen it, and stepped further back. 'It's political,' he muttered, and bolted away. Feng stared after him, looking no longer angry, but hurt.

The sergeant drove moodily, roaring through the gears, barely braking at the crossroads, until they began the long climb up the North Claw towards the American mine.

'Here,' he mumbled finally, pulling a cellophane bag from his pocket. 'Pumpkin seeds.' He handed the bag to Shan. 'Good ones, not the mouldy shit from the market. Salted. Get them at the commissary.'

They chewed the seeds slowly and silently, like two old men on a Beijing park bench. Before long Feng began leaning forward, watching the shoulder of the road.

'Chang said it would save an hour,' Feng offered as he swung onto a rutted track that seemed little more than a goat path. 'Back in time for evening mess this way.'

In five minutes they were following the track towards the crest of a sharp ridge. To the right, barely three feet

246

from their tyres, the path fell away over a nearly perpendicular cliff face, ending in a tumble of rocks several hundred feet below.

'How could this reach the Americans?' Yeshe asked nervously. 'We'd have to cross this chasm.'

'Take a nap,' Feng grumbled. 'Save your energy for all that work back at the 404th.'

'What do you mean?' Yeshe asked, alarm in his voice.

'Like you asked, I talked to the warden's secretary. She said no one is doing the computer work. Warden said just stack it up, someone's coming in two weeks.'

'It could be someone else,' Yeshe protested.

Feng shook his head. 'She asked one of the administrative officers. Said it was the warden's Tibetan pup who was coming back.'

There was a tiny moan from the back. Shan turned to find Yeshe nearly doubled over, his head in his hands. With pain, Shan turned away. He had already told Yeshe. It was time for him to decide who he was.

Suddenly Shan held up his hand. 'There –' he said as Sergeant Feng slowed down, pointing to a set of fresh tyre tracks that veered from the path and disappeared over the crest of the ridge.

'So we're not the only ones who use the shortcut,' Feng said with a tone of vindication.

Lots of people, Shan thought – like Americans searching for old shrines.

Shan opened the door and carefully eased around the truck, mindful of the sheer dropoff. He picked a stem of heather from the tyre tracks and handed it to Feng. 'Smell it. This was crushed not even an hour ago.'

'So?'

'So I'm going to follow this fresh trail. Your road curves around that rock formation to the crest. I'll meet you on the other side.'

Feng frowned but began to inch the truck forward.

Moving up the slope, Shan tried to piece together the

geography. The skull cave was less than a mile away. Was this the Americans' back door to the skull cave? Had Fowler and Kincaid been so foolish as to return to the shrine? As he neared the top he heard a peculiar sound. Like bells, he thought. No, drums. A few feet further he realized it was rock and roll music. As he reached the crest he crouched and dropped back. There was a truck, but it was not the Americans'. It was bright red.

Calming himself, he edged his head above the rocks. It was the big Land Rover that Hu had been driving, but the figure at the wheel, tapping in time to the music, was too tall to be Hu.

It made no sense to park there. There was no one else to be seen, no one to wait for. There was not even much landscape to survey, for the rock outcropping cut off much of the view down the ridge.

Slowly, unconsciously, Shan's curiosity forced him to rise. There were fresh mounds of dirt behind the rear wheels, and a huge five-foot boulder in front of the vehicle, balanced precariously close to the lip of a bank that dropped sharply down to the road. Suddenly the man inside straightened and looked intently at the track below. Their own truck was coming into view. The figure inside the Land Rover raised his fist as though in victory and gunned the motor.

'No!' Shan screamed, and ran towards the truck. Its wheels were spinning, throwing more dirt into the air. The boulder was beginning to move.

He launched himself through the cloud of dust, pounding violently on the driver's window. The man turned and stared dumbly. It was Lieutenant Chang.

Shan could see him reaching for the gear shift. The truck seemed to ease back as Chang fumbled with the controls, then lurched forward. In one violent heave the boulder and the truck both flew over the bank.

As if in slow motion Shan watched Feng stop, then

jump out of their truck with Yeshe just as the boulder hurled past them and disappeared over the edge. The Land Rover, airborne, struck the bank on its side and began to roll down the precipitous slope, glass popping, metal groaning, its wheels still whirling. It hit the road in the middle of a roll and landed on the driver's side in a cloud of dust, with the front half hanging over the chasm.

Shan, breathless, reached the road just as an arm rose through the shattered passenger's window. Chang, his forehead smeared with blood, appeared in the window and began to pull himself up. The music was still playing.

Lieutenant Chang stopped moving and shouted for Feng, who stood ten feet away. As he did so there was a groan of metal and something gave way. Chang screamed as the vehicle sank another foot over the edge and stopped.

Chang's face grew angry. 'Sergeant!' he bellowed. 'Get me –'

He never finished. The Land Rover abruptly tipped and disappeared from view. They could still hear the music as it fell.

Not a word was spoken as they backtracked down the ridge and onto the main road. Sergeant Feng's face was clouded with confusion. His hand shook on the wheel. Try as he might, Shan knew, in the end Sergeant Feng would not be able to avoid the truth. Chang had been trying to kill *him*, too.

As they finally cleared the ridge above the boron mine, Shan signalled for Feng to stop. There was a shrine he had not seen on their first visit, on a ledge three hundred feet above the valley floor. Prayer flags were fluttering around a cairn of rocks. Some were just bits of coloured cloth. Others were the huge banners painted with prayers that the Tibetans called horse flags.

'I want to know about that shrine,' he said to Yeshe and Feng as they parked the truck. 'Find a way up there.

See if you can tell who built it, and where they're coming from.'

Yeshe cocked his head towards the shrine with an intense interest and began moving towards it without looking back. Feng contemplated Shan with a sour look, then shrugged, checked the ammunition in his pistol, and jogged towards Yeshe.

The mine office was nearly empty as Shan entered. The woman who served tea was asleep on a stool, leaning against the wall. Two men in muddy work clothes huddled over the large table. One offered a nod of acknowledgment as Shan approached. It was Luntok, the *ragyapa* engineer. The red door at the rear was closed again. There were voices behind it, and the low whir of electronic equipment.

The two men were taking measurements on one of the colourful charts he had seen before. It had a blue rectangle in the centre, below rows of smaller blue-green rectangles. Suddenly Shan recognized the images.

'It's the ponds, isn't it? I have never seen such a map,' he marvelled. 'Do you make them here?'

Luntok looked up with a grin. 'Better than a map. A photograph. From the sky. From a satellite.'

Shan stared dumbly. It was not that satellite photography was beyond his imagination; it was just beyond his expectations. Tibet truly existed in many different centuries at once.

'We have to know about snow melt,' Luntok explained. 'About river flows. About avalanches above us. About road conditions when shipments go out. Without these we would need survey crews in the mountains every week.'

Luntok pointed out the mine's lakes, the buildings of the camp and a cluster of geometric shapes at the far right that was the outskirts of Lhadrung town. He outlined with his finger the big dyke at the head of the Dragon Throat, then picked up the map and pointed to a second, earlier photo. 'Here it is two weeks ago, just before construction was completed.' Shan saw the spots of colour that must have been pieces of equipment near the centre of the brown dyke.

'But how do you obtain these?'

'There is an American satellite and a French satellite. We have subscriptions. The surface of the earth is divided into sections, in a catalogue. We can order up a print by section number. It gets transmitted to our console,' he said, pointing his thumb towards the red door.

'But the army –' Shan began.

'There is a licence,' Luntok explained patiently. 'Everything is legal.'

A licence for a Western venture to operate equipment that could survey troop movements, air exercises, and army installations as easily as it could survey snow accumulations. The Americans had worked a miracle, to obtain such a permit in Tibet.

Shan found the road leading to the mine, visible as a tiny grey line that wandered in and out of the shadows cast by the peaks. He found the road from the north, to Saskya gompa, and finally the 404th worksite. The new bridge was a narrow hyphen that intersected the serpentine greyness of the Dragon's Throat.

Shan sat beside Luntok. 'I've been to the *ragyapa* village,' he announced. The second man tensed, and glanced at Luntok, who kept studying the maps without reacting. The man grabbed his hat and stepped out of the building.

'I spoke with Merak,' Shan said. 'Do you know Merak?'

'It is a small community,' Luntok observed tersely.

'It must be difficult.'

'There are quotas for us now. I was allowed to attend university. I have a good job.'

'I meant for them. Seeing the people here and in town, but knowing most will never break away.'

251

Luntok's eyes narrowed, but he did not look up from the photo map. 'The *ragyapa* are proud of their work. It is a sacred trust, the only religious practice that has been allowed to continue without restriction.'

'They seem well provided for. Happy children. Lots of warm clothes.'

As if Shan's comment were a cue he had been awaiting, Luntok picked up his own hat and rose. 'It is considered bad luck to underpay a *ragyapa*,' he said with a wary glance, then turned and left.

That the *ragyapa* had the ability to carry out Jao's murder Shan had no doubt. Had the military supplies been a reward? If so, someone else paid them to kill Jao. Someone with control over military supplies. Shan stepped back and studied the room. The woman was snoring now. No one else was present. Shan moved to the red door and opened it.

Computer terminals, four in all, dominated the room. A few bowls with noodles clinging to the rims, the remains of lunch, were on a large conference table. Two Chinese, dressed in Western clothes, one wearing a baseball cap pulled low over his head, sat studying glossy catalogues and sipping tea. From an expensive sound system came Western rock and roll. At a corner desk sat Tyler Kincaid, cleaning his camera.

'Comrade Shan,' said a familiar voice from the back of the room. Li Aidang rose from a sofa. 'If only I had known, I would have invited you to ride with me.' He gestured towards the table. 'We have a luncheon meeting twice a month. The supervisory committee.'

Shan moved slowly around the room. There was an empty cassette case on top of a speaker. The Grateful Dead, it said. Perhaps, Shan considered without remorse, it was what Chang had been listening to as he and his truck tumbled into the abyss. Li retrieved a Coca-Cola from a small refrigerator and extended it towards him.

There were photo maps on one wall. Photographs were

fastened with pins to another: more studies of Tibetan faces, taken with the same sensitivity as those Shan had seen in Kincaid's office. Li handed Shan the soft drink.

'I didn't realize the prosecutor's office had an interest in mining,' Shan said, and set the can on the table, unopened.

'We are the Ministry of Justice. The mine is the only foreign investment in the district. The people's government must be certain it succeeds. There are so many issues. Labour organization. Export permits. Foreign exchange permits. Work permits. Environmental permits. The Ministry must be consulted for such approvals.'

'I had no idea boron was such an important product.'

The assistant prosecutor smiled generously. 'We want our American friends to stay happy. One third of the royalties stay in the district. After three years of production we will be able to build a new school. After five, maybe a new clinic.'

Shan moved to one of the computer monitors, closer to Kincaid. Numbers were scrolling across the screen.

'You know our friend Comrade Hu,' Li said, pointing to the first of the two men at the table. Hu gave him the same mock salute he had left Shan with in Tan's office. Shan had not recognized him with the hat. He studied the Director of Geology closely. Was Hu surprised to see him?

'Comrade Inspector,' Hu acknowledged in a curt tone, his little beetle eyes fixing Shan for a moment, then turning back to the catalogue. The one he was reading had pictures of smiling blond couples standing in snow, wearing sweaters of brilliant colours.

'Still giving driving lessons, Comrade Director?' Shan asked, trying to look distracted by the console.

Hu laughed.

Li gestured towards the second man, a well-groomed, athletic figure who stood as though better to survey Shan. 'The major is from the border command.' Li looked meaningfully at Shan. 'His resources are sometimes useful for our project.' The major, nothing more. He was so polished that he could have been lifted from the pages of the catalogue, Shan thought at first. But then he turned his head towards Shan. A gutter of scar tissue ran across his left cheek; it could only have been made by a bullet. His lips curled up in greeting but his eyes remained lifeless. It was a familiar insolence. The major, Shan decided, belonged to the Public Security Bureau.

'A fascinating facility,' Shan said absently, continuing to wander about the room. 'Full of surprises.' He paused in front of the photographs.

'A triumph of socialism,' the major observed. His voice had a boyish tone belied by his countenance.

Tyler Kincaid gave a pregnant nod towards Shan but did not speak. Half his forearm was wrapped with a large piece of gauze taped over a recent injury. A shadow of dried blood could be seen through the gauze.

'Comrade Shan is investigating a murder,' Li announced to the major. 'Once he led anti-corruption campaigns in Beijing. The famous Hainan Island affair was his.' The Hainan Island case, in which Shan had discovered that provincial officials were purchasing shiploads of Japanese automobiles – for an island with only a hundred miles of roads – and diverting them to the black market on the mainland, had made Shan a celebrity for a few months. But that had been fifteen years earlier. Who had the assistant prosecutor been speaking to? The warden? Beijing?

Shan studied the major, who had no interest in Li's words. There had been no challenge in his eyes, no question in his voice despite Shan's abrupt intrusion. He already knew who Shan was.

'This is where your telephone system operates?' Shan asked Kincaid.

The American rose, and forced a smile. 'Over there,' he

said, indicating a speaker above a console on a small desk against the wall. 'Wanna order a pizza from New York?'

Hu and the major laughed hard.

'And the maps?'

'Maps? We have a whole reference library. Atlases. Engineering journals.'

'I mean the ones from the sky.'

'Amazing, aren't they?' Li interrupted. 'The first time we saw them, it seemed like a miracle. The world looks so different.' He moved towards Shan and leaned towards his ear. 'We must talk about our files, Comrade. The trial is only a few days away. No need for undue embarrassment.'

As Shan considered the assistant prosecutor's invitation, the door opened and Luntok appeared. He nodded to Kincaid and quickly left, leaving the door open. Kincaid stretched and made a gesture of invitation towards Shan. 'Afternoon climbing classes. How about some rappelling?'

'You're climbing with your injury?'

'This?' the American asked good-naturedly, raising his arm. 'Walking wounded. Came down on a jagged piece of quartz. Can't let it stop me. Always get back on the horse, you know.'

Li laughed again and moved back towards the sofa. Hu returned to his catalogues. The major lit a cigarette and glared at Shan until he left the room.

Outside he found Rebecca Fowler sitting on the hood of her truck, studying the valley.

He didn't think she had noticed him until she suddenly spoke. 'I can't imagine what it must be like for you,' she said.

He was uncomfortable with her sympathy. 'If I had never been sent to Tibet I would never have met Tibetans.'

She turned to him with a sad smile and reached into the deep pocket of her nylon vest. 'Here,' she said, producing two paperback books. 'Just a couple of novels, in English. I thought you might . . .'

Shan accepted them with a small bow of his head. 'You are kind. I miss reading in English.' The books indeed would be a treasure, except that they would be confiscated when he was returned to the 404th. He didn't have the heart to tell her.

He leaned back on the truck, gazing at the surrounding peaks. The snowcaps were glowing in the late afternoon sun. 'The soldiers are gone,' he observed.

Fowler followed his gaze over the ponds. 'Not one of my better ideas. Called away for some other emergency.'

'Emergency?'

'The major had something to do with it.'

Shan paced along the front of the truck, surveying the compound. Someone was sitting on one of the dykes, staring at the mountains. He squinted and saw that it was Yeshe. Sergeant Feng was sitting on the hood of their own truck. As his field of view extended behind the buildings, Shan froze. Behind the first one was a familiar vehicle. A red Land Rover. Another red Land Rover. 'Whose car is that?'

Fowler looked up. 'The red one? Must be Director Hu's.'

He resisted the urge to run to the vehicle and search it. The committee members could emerge at any moment.

'These Land Rovers. Do they all belong to the Ministry of Geology?'

'Don't know. I don't think so. I saw the major driving one.'

Shan nodded, as though he expected the answer. 'What do you know about this major?'

'One powerful son of a bitch, is all. He scares me.'

'Why is he on your committee?'

'Because we're so close to the border. It was a condition of our satellite licence.'

Somehow Shan felt he knew the man. With a wrench

256

of his gut he remembered Jigme's description of the man who had come for Sungpo. A man with a slice on his face, a deep scar. His name, Jigme had said, was Meh Jah.

'What if it wasn't Hu who wanted your licence suspended?' he asked abruptly.

'He signed the notice.'

'He would have to sign it, as Director of Mines, but it may be at the order of someone else. Or a political favour to someone.'

'What do you mean?' Fowler asked, suddenly interested.

'I don't know what I mean.' He shook his head despondently. 'I'm supposed to be finding answers, and all I find is more questions.' He gazed out over the pond complex.

Workers were moving along the dykes at a relaxed pace with shovels and pipe fittings. Yeshe and Feng were moving back down the slope, approaching the buildings.

'Did someone – did you have a ceremony? For your workers.'

She looked at him with a pained expression. 'I almost forgot – it was your idea, wasn't it?' The nervousness had not left her eyes.

'I never thought it would be so soon.'

The American woman jumped down and gestured for him to follow her along the line of buildings.

'Who was the priest who came?'

'There was no name,' Fowler said in a near whisper. 'I don't think we were suppposed to use his name. An old priest. Strange.'

'How old?'

'Not old in years. Middle-aged. But old like austere. Like timeless. Thin as a rail. An ascetic, I guess.'

'What do you mean strange?'

'Like from another century. His eyes. I don't know.

257

Sometimes it seemed like he didn't see anyone. Or he saw things we could not see. And his hands.'

'His hands?'

'He had no thumbs.'

On the side of the last building, facing the valley, was a patchwork charm, a square an arm's length on each side. It was filled with complex pictograms and writing. Two poles flanked it, draped with prayer flags.

Yeshe appeared behind him and muttered something under his breath. It had the tone of a prayer. 'Powerful magic,' he gasped. He held up his rosary as though for protection, and stepped back.

'What is it?' Shan asked. He remembered the building from his last visit. There had been a line of Tibetans outside, waiting for something.

'It's very old. Very secret,' Yeshe whispered.

'No,' Fowler said. 'Not old. Look at the paper. It has printing on the back.'

'I mean, the signs are old. I can't read them all. Even if I could I would not be permitted to recite them. Words of power.' Yeshe seemed genuinely frightened. 'Dangerous words. I don't know who – most of the lamas with the power to write such words are dead. I don't know of any in Lhadrung.'

'If he travelled far he must have been very fast,' she said, looking at Shan.

'The old ones,' Yeshe whispered, obviously still in awe of the charm. 'Those with this kind of power. They would say they used the arrow ritual to fly. They could jump between dimensions.'

No, Shan was tempted to say, the charm had not come far. But perhaps it had come between dimensions.

Fowler grinned uneasily. 'It's just words.'

Yeshe shook his head. 'Not just words. You cannot write such words unless you have the power. Not power, exactly. Vision. Access to certain forces. In the old schools they would say that if I tried to write this, or someone else without the training –' Yeshe hesitated.

'Yes?' Fowler asked.

'I would shatter into a thousand pieces.'

Shan stepped up and examined the paper.

'But what does it do?' Fowler asked.

'It is about death and Tamdin.'

She shuddered.

'No,' Yeshe corrected himself. 'Not exactly that. It is difficult to explain. It is like a signpost for Tamdin. It celebrates his deeds. His deeds are death. But good death.'

'Good death?'

'Protecting death. Transporting death. It offers the power of all souls here to help him open a path to enlightenment.'

'You said death.'

'Death and enlightenment. Sometimes the old priests use the same words. There're many kinds of death. Many kinds of enlightenment.' Yeshe turned back to Shan for a moment, as though he had just realized what he had said.

'All souls here?' Fowler asked. 'Us?'

'Especially us,' Shan said quietly, stepping closer to the charm.

'Nobody asked me if I wanted to offer my soul,' Rebecca Fowler said, trying to make a joke. But she did not smile.

Shan ran his finger over the patchwork. It was made of thirty or forty small sheets, stitched together with human hair. He didn't need to lift the edge to know that the sheets were from the guard tallies at the 404th. He had seen the charm being made.

'And this is all he did, this priest?' Shan asked.

'No. There was something else. He had them build the shrine on the mountain.' She pointed to the shrine Shan had seen earlier. 'I am supposed to go there tonight.'

'Why you? Why tonight?'

Fowler did not reply, but led them into the building, which was a dormitory for workers. The entrance chamber seemed to be a recreation area, but it was abandoned. Shelves were packed with jigsaw puzzles, books, and chess sets. Tables and chairs had been pushed to the sides, against the shelves. One small table stood in the centre. On it was a bundle, surrounded by flickering butter lamps. In an empty food tin incense was burning.

'Luntok found it near one of the ponds,' Fowler said. 'Where a vulture dropped it. At first we thought it was human.'

'Luntok?'

'He came from one of the old villages where they do – you know, sky burial. He has no fear of such things.'

'Does he know Director Hu?' Shan asked. 'Or the major? Does he ever speak with them?'

'I don't know,' the American woman said distractedly. 'I don't think so. He's like most of the workers, I think. Government officials scare them.'

Shan wanted to press, to ask how Luntok came to work for her, but suddenly she seemed incapable of hearing anything. She was staring desolately at the bundle. 'The workers say we have to give it back tonight.' Her voice cracked as she spoke. 'They say it is the job of the village headman. And that I am the headman here.'

Shan took a step forward and opened the bundle. It was a severed hand, a huge gnarled hand with long, grotesquely proportioned fingers that ended with claws covered in finely worked silver.

It was the hand of a demon.

Chapter Twelve

Kham was a vast and wild landscape, located not only on the top of the world but at what seemed the very end of it. It was a land that seemed to defy being tamed, or claimed, a land unlike any Shan had ever experienced. The wind blew constantly over the high lonely plateau, churning the sky into a mosaic of heavy clouds and brilliant patches of blue. When Sergeant Feng stopped, as he frequently did to consult his map, Shan heard fleeting, unidentifiable sounds, as if the wind carried fragments of voices and calls, strange broken noises like the distant cries of suffering. There were places, some of the old monks believed, that acted as filters for the world's woes, catching and holding the torments that drifted across the earth. Maybe here was such a place, Shan thought, where the screams and cries of the millions below collected to be beaten by the wind into snippets of sound, like pebbles in a river.

He waited until they had driven nearly six hours to call back to Tan from a battered, tin-roofed garage near the county border.

'Where are you?' Tan demanded.

'What do you know about Lieutenant Chang of the 404th?'

'Dammit, Shan, where did you go? They said you left before dawn again. Feng never called.'

'I asked him not to.'

'You asked him?'

In his mind's eye Shan could see Tan's lips curl in anger.

'Let me speak to him,' Tan demanded icily.

'Chang was an officer of the guard. I'd like to know his prior postings.'

'Don't mix my officers into –'

'He tried to kill us.'

He could *hear* Tan breathing. 'Tell me,' came his sharp reply.

Shan explained how they had followed Chang's short-cut, and how he had ambushed them.

'You're mistaken. He's an officer of the PLA. He has duties at the 404th, nothing to do with Prosecutor Jao. It wouldn't make any sense.'

'Fine. Try to locate him at the 404th. Then you might want to drive up his shortcut on the North Claw. It's an old trail to the north, two miles above the valley turnoff. From the top of the cliff you can see the wreckage. We told no one else. By now there will be vultures you can follow.'

'And you waited this long to tell me?'

'At first I wasn't sure. Like you said, he was in the army.'

'Weren't sure?'

'Whether you had arranged it.' Another silence from Tan. 'It might be tempting,' Shan suggested, 'if you had decided not to pursue a separate case.'

'What changed your mind?' Tan asked matter-of-factly, as if conceding the point.

'I thought about it all night. I don't believe you would kill Sergeant Feng.'

Shan heard a muffled conversation on the other end. Tan began barking instructions to Madame Ko. When he came back on he had an answer. 'Chang was off-duty yesterday. Acting on his own time.'

'He decided on his own to kill us? Just some idle amusement for his day off?'

Tan sighed. 'Where are you?'

'Every other lead is cold. I am going to find Jao's driver. I think he's alive.'

'Leave the county and you're an escapee.'

Shan explained the file found at the garage, and why it meant he had to look for Balti. 'If I had asked for permission, there would have been preparations. Word could have gone to the east. Any chance of finding Balti would have been lost.'

'You never told the Ministry of Justice either?'

'Not a word. It is my responsibility.'

'So Li doesn't know.'

'It occurred to me that we might benefit from speaking to Jao's driver without the assistant prosecutor's assistance.'

In the silence that indicated Tan's indecision, he decided to tell about the hand. It was a public phone, unlikely to be tapped. The demon's hand that had so frightened Rebecca Fowler's workers had been of exquisite manufacture. A casual observer could easily have been convinced it was nothing less than the shrivelled remains from a creature of flesh and blood. But Shan had shown Fowler how the ligaments had been meticulously crafted of leather sewn over copper strips. The pink palm had been made of faded red silk. When he had raised it the fingers had dangled limply, at odd angles.

'You're saying you found part of the Tamdin costume,' Tan observed tautly.

'The one Director Wen said was not missing.' Shan had already made a note in his pad: Check the audits done by Religious Affairs.

'There could have been one hidden away.'

'I don't think so. These were so rare, such treasures, that they all have been accounted for.'

'Meaning what?'

'Meaning someone is lying.'

There was a moment's silence. 'All right. Bring the driver back alive. Forty-eight hours. If you're not back in forty-eight hours I'll turn Public Security loose on you,' he growled, and hung up.

Patrols. If things went bad, Tan could still give up. Li would prosecute Sungpo, the case would be closed, and the 404th would receive its punishment. Tan could turn off his investigation by simply declaring Shan a fugitive. All a Public Security patrol would need to bring back was the tattoo on Shan's arm.

If he used two full days, moreover, Shan would have only four more until Sungpo was brought before his tribunal. Two days. Balti of the Dronma clan had had a week to lose himself in Kham. But Shan's task wasn't the impossible one of finding a solitary man in 150,000 square miles of the most arduous terrain north of Antarctica. It was simply the vastly unlikely one of finding Balti's clan. For a *khampa*, the safest place would always be the hearth of his family.

As they pushed on Shan turned towards Yeshe. 'You have my gratitude. For the *ragyapa*.'

'It wasn't hard to understand, once I saw all those army socks.'

'No. I mean thank you for not telling the warden. It would have made you look good, a victory in your record. It might have meant getting your travel papers.'

Yeshe gazed out over the seemingly endless plateau as it rolled by. 'They would have raided the place. All those children.' He shrugged. 'And maybe I'm wrong. Maybe they got the supplies legally. Maybe,' he said, turning to Shan, 'they got them in payment for the charms.'

Shan nodded slowly. 'Someone in the military who's scared of offending Tamdin?' he wondered out loud, then handed Yeshe the envelope of photos from the skull cave he had been given by Rebecca Fowler. 'Take a look.'

Yeshe opened the envelope. 'What am I looking for?'

'First, a pattern. I can't read the old Tibetan text. Are they just names?'

Yeshe frowned. 'That's simple. They're arranged by

264

date, in the traditional Tibetan calendar,' he said, referring to the system of sixty-year cycles that had started a thousand years earlier. 'The tablet in front of each skull shows the year and the name. The first –' Yeshe moved the photo into the direct sunlight by the window, '– the first is Earth Horse Year of the Tenth Cycle.'

'How long ago?'

'The Tenth started in the middle of the sixteenth century. Earth Horse Year is the fifty-second year of the cycle.' Yeshe paused and cast a meaningful glance at Shan. Shan remembered the empty shelves. The shrine must have been started far earlier than the sixteenth century.

Yeshe picked up the next few photos. 'The sequence continues. Tenth Cycle, Iron Ape Year, Wood Mouse Year, ten or twenty more skulls, then the Eleventh Cycle.'

'Then you may be able to find what happened to the one that was moved to make way for Jao.'

'Why wouldn't it just be discarded?'

'Probably was. I want to be certain.'

Feng slowed for a herd of sheep with two young boys, who tended their charges not with dogs but with slingshots. As he watched, Shan kept seeing the hand in his mind's eye. The damage to it had been more than would have been incurred by severing it, or even in the fall when the vulture dropped it. The delicate hinges comprising the knuckles had been smashed. The finger-tips had been crushed, ruining their fine filigree. Someone had smashed it deliberately, as if in a fight with Tamdin. Or as if in anger, to prevent further use of the costume. Had Balti fought with the thing, damaging the hand? Had Jao done it, when he struggled on the side of the mountain?

Feng stopped the solitary herdsman who sometimes walked along the road, asking for the clan listed in Balti's official record, the Dronma clan. Each herdsman replied warily, watching the gun on the sergeant's belt. Most of them reacted by pulling out their identity papers as soon as the truck slowed and waving their hands in front of their faces to indicate they spoke no Mandarin.

'It's there,' Yeshe gasped suddenly, as they pulled away from their fifth such stop.

Shan spun around. 'The skull?'

Yeshe nodded excitedly, holding up one of the photos. 'The skulls around the single empty shelf are from the late Fourteenth Cycle. Iron Ape Year on one side, then Wood Ox Year, the fifty-ninth year, on the other, say about one hundred and forty years ago. The last skull on the shelves in the sequence is eighty years old, Earth Sheep Year of the Fifteenth Cycle. Except the very last one, on the bottom. It's Fourteenth Cycle, Water Hog Year.'

Yeshe looked up with a satisfied gleam. 'Water Hog is the fifty-seventh year, between Iron Ape and Wood Ox!' He showed the photos to Shan, pointing out the Tibetan characters for the year. The missing skull, and its tablet and lamps, had been reverently arranged on the last shelf.

Their excitement quickly faded. Shan and Yeshe exchanged an uneasy glance. The movement of the skull was not the act of a looter, or a rabid killer. It was what a monk, a true believer would do.

Feng slowed down for an old man in the road. The man reacted to his enquiry by pulling out a tattered map of the region. It was contraband, for it depicted the traditional borders of Tibet, and Shan quickly moved to block it from Feng's view.

'Bo Zhai,' the old man said, pointing to a region about fifty miles eastward. 'Bo Zhai.' Shan thanked him by giving him a box of raisins from the supplies Feng had hastily packed. The man seemed surprised. He stared mutely at the box, then with a proud, defiant gesture swept his hand over the vast eastern half of the map.

'Kham,' he pronounced, and marched off the road onto a goat trail.

Most of the territory he had indicated had been partitioned by Beijing and given to neighbouring provinces. Thus it was that Gansu, Qinghai, Sichuan and Yunnan provinces contained sizeable Tibetan populations. Sichuan had Aba Tibetan Prefecture, Garze Tibetan Prefecture and Muli Tibetan County. It had been a subtle measure to erode the nomadic lifestyle of the Kham herders; residency permits could not be granted in more than one district at a time, and travel papers were seldom issued to such people. It had also been punishment for the emphatic antisocialist sentiments of the region. Kham guerrillas had fought longer and harder against the People's Liberation Army than any minority in China. Even in the 404th Shan had heard tales of resistance fighters still roaming the eastern ranges, sabotaging roads and attacking small patrols, then disappearing into the impenetrable mountains.

It was mid-afternoon before they arrived at the office of the Bo Zhai agricultural collective, an assembly of shabby buildings constructed of cinder blocks and corrugated tin surrounded by fields of barley. The woman in charge, clearly unaccustomed to unannounced visitors, eyed the three men uneasily. 'We have tours during harvest,' she offered, 'for the Ministry of Agriculture.'

'This is a criminal investigation,' Shan explained patiently, extending a paper with Balti's clan written on it.

'We are just ignorant herdsmen,' she said, too meekly. 'Once we had a hooligan from Lhasa hiding in the hills. The procedure was to use the local militia.' There was a faded poster on the wall behind her, with young proletarians extending their fists proudly. Demolish the Four Olds, it said at the bottom. It had been a campaign during the Cultural Revolution. The Four Olds were ideology, culture, habits, and customs. The Red Guard had invaded the homes of minorities and destroyed their traditional clothing – often heirlooms passed down for generations, burnt furniture, even cut the braids of the women.

'We have no time,' Yeshe said.

The woman eyed him stonily.

'You are correct, of course,' Shan confirmed. 'In our case the procedure would be to contact the Public Security Bureau to tell them we are waiting here. Bureau headquarters would contact the Ministry of Agriculture, who would arrange for a company of soldiers from the Bureau to assist. Perhaps I could use your phone.'

The challenge quickly left her face. 'No need to waste the people's resources,' she said with a sigh. She took the note from Shan's hand and produced a tattered ledger book. 'Not in our production unit. No Dronma clan,' she declared after a few minutes.

'How many units are there?'

'In this Prefecture, seventeen. Then you can start checking Sichuan, Gansu, and Qinghai provinces. And there're still the bad elements in the high ranges. They never registered.'

'No,' Yeshe said. 'He never would have been cleared for his job if his family weren't registered.'

'And his work papers,' Shan added, 'were not likely to be transferred from another province.'

'That's right,' Yeshe brightened. 'Doesn't someone have a master list, just for this prefecture?'

'Decentralization for maximum production.' The woman spoke now in a familiar antiseptic voice, the one for strangers, the one tuned to the safety of reciting only banners and anything heard over a loudspeaker.

'I've also heard that we should stop worrying about black cats or white cats,' Shan observed. 'And concentrate on catching mice.'

'We would have no authority to hold such a list,' the

woman said nervously. 'The Ministry's office is in Markam. They would have the master list.'

'How far?'

'Sixteen hours. If there's no mudslide. Or flood. Or military manoeuvres.' The woman knitted her brow and moved to a dusty shelf at the rear of the office. 'All I have is the names of those in the combined work units receiving production awards. At least, in the past five years.' She handed a stack of dusty spiral bound books to Yeshe.

'It's like searching for a single kernel of rice . . .' Yeshe began.

'No. Maybe not,' she said, for the first time warming to the task. 'Most of the old clans were concentrated in maybe six collectives. They were considered the greatest political risks, needed closer scrutiny. You're just looking for the one clan.'

'And if we find the right collective?'

'Then you start the real search. It's spring. The herds are moving.'

In thirty minutes they had identified three collectives with Dronma clan members. One was two hundred miles distant. The second, nearly a hundred miles away, answered its phone after twenty rings. The man recognized the name. 'Old clan. Not many left. Stays close to the herds. Gathering stock.' The man spoke with an urbane Shanghai accent that seemed out of place. 'Only half a dozen adult workers. Three over sixty. Another lost a leg in a riding accident.'

The third, only fifteen miles away, announced that their Dronma clan members were as plentiful as the sheep in the hills. Shan studied his map, marking the location of the three units. They had time for only one choice.

He wandered outside, as if the wind might bring an answer. He watched an old woman ride by on a pony, cradling a pig as if it were a child. Suddenly he halted and darted back inside. 'We're going here,' he announced and pointed to the second collective.

'But you heard them,' Yeshe protested. 'There're only half a dozen.'

'The shoes,' Shan said. 'I couldn't understand why Balti had two left shoes under his bed.'

Three hours later, as they approached the battered buildings that comprised the collective, Sergeant Feng slammed on the brakes and pointed. A helicopter bearing the insignia of the border commandos sat at its perimeter, guarded by a soldier with an automatic rifle.

'Congratulations,' Feng muttered. 'Your guess has been confirmed.'

Yeshe started to speak, but his words were lost in a sharp intake of breath. Shan followed Yeshe's gaze. Li Aidang was standing in the centre of the compound, arms akimbo, with the air of a military commander. Behind him, in the pilot's seat of the helicopter, Shan saw a familiar face in sunglasses. The major. He suddenly realized that for all his bravado Li, like so many others, might only be another pawn.

The assistant prosecutor greeted Shan with a condescending smile. 'If he's alive I'll have him in an interrogation cell by noon tomorrow,' he vowed smugly. Without waiting for a question, he explained. 'It's simple, really. I realized a security check would have been necessary for the chauffeur of an important official. Public Security computers had all the records of his past life.'

Shan had once participated in an audit of the billions spent by Beijing on central computers. Priority had gone to the Public Security applications. The 300 Million Project, they had called it. Shan had thought at first that it described the funding for the project, but in fact it was the number of citizens who had at one time fallen under scrutiny by the Bureau. He had begun to convince himself

270

that it was a welcome efficiency. Until he discovered his own name on the list.

'So he is here?'

'This is his family's collective. Though no one has seen him for a year, maybe two.'

'His family?'

'They're on the high plateau,' Li said, pointing to the north. 'Chasing yak and sheep.'

'Then he can be brought back here,' Shan suggested. 'Send someone from the collective who knows him.'

'Impossible,' Li shot back. 'He must be placed in our custody. He will be arrested and removed to Lhadrung.'

'There is no evidence against him, only conjecture.'

'No evidence? You saw what was in his tenement. Clear links to hooliganism.'

'A little Buddha and a plastic rosary?'

'He fled. You forgot he fled.'

'Why are you so sure that he's here? I thought you said he ran with the limousine to Sichuan. A limousine does him no good in Kham.'

'Strange question.'

'What do you mean?' Shan asked.

'Here you are, searching for him.'

Shan stared at the helicopter. 'If you go to arrest him he will bury himself in the mountains.'

'You forget that I know Balti. He will react better to a familiar face.'

Shan considered the assistant prosecutor. Balti, he knew, might not survive an arrest by Li and the major. *Khampas* seldom submitted peacefully. And if Balti died, Shan could never forgive himself, for he suspected that Li was only interested in Balti because of Shan's own interest. But who had told him?

With a chill he looked back and saw Yeshe speaking with the major beside the helicopter. The major became animated, almost violent, shaking a piece of paper at Yeshe, who looked as though he were about to cry. Then the major pointed a finger at Yeshe's chest. Yeshe recoiled, as if struck. Ripping the paper in half, the major spat a final curse and climbed back into the machine. Li, also watching now, uttered a disappointed sigh.

'Balti's interrogation will be completed by the time you return,' Li declared icily. 'We will take careful notes for your review.' He darted to the machine and climbed aboard.

They watched in silence as the helicopter disappeared over the mountains. 'You have destroyed him,' Yeshe accused.

'I wasn't the one who invited them,' Shan said bitterly.

'It wasn't me,' Yeshe said very quietly, still watching the horizon. 'The old woman at his loft, she expects me to help Balti.'

Shan wasn't sure he heard correctly. He was about to ask, when Yeshe turned to him with great pain in his eyes. 'He offered me a job,' Yeshe said in a hollow voice. 'Just now. The major had work papers filled out in my name, for a real job, as a clerk with the Public Security Bureau in Lhasa, maybe even Sichuan. The signatures were already on them.'

'You turned it down?'

Yeshe looked at the ground, the torment still on his face. 'I told him I was busy right now.'

'Shit, you said!' Feng gasped.

'He said it was now or forget it. He said maybe I could bring your case notes. I told him I was busy.' He searched Shan's eyes for something, but Shan did not know what to offer. Confirmation? Sympathy? Fear?

'Sometimes,' Yeshe continued, 'these past few days, I think maybe it is true, what you said. That innocent people will die if we don't do something.'

There was something unfamiliar in Sergeant Feng's eyes now as he gazed at Yeshe. For a moment Shan thought it might be pride. 'I knew that boy Balti,' Feng said suddenly. 'He never hurt anybody.'

Shan realized that both men were looking at him expectantly. 'Then we have to find him before they do,' he said, and opened the back of the truck to search through a pile of rags. He produced a tattered shirt and measured it against Feng's shoulders.

It was evening by the time they had climbed the long, increasingly high ridges that formed a fifty-mile stairway onto the high plateau, and located one of the nomad camps. They had sighted the three tents miles away as they drove onto the plateau, but had dismissed the low, grey shapes as rock outcroppings until they saw the long line of goats tied on a central tether nearby, their horns interlocked to keep them stable for milking. The squat, yak-hair tents were tied to the ground with stakes and leather straps, heightening the impression of crevassed boulders worn down by centuries of wind.

They stopped the truck fifty yards from the camp, and moments later were walking towards the tents, Sergeant Feng's uniform and gunbelt covered by the long shirt.

There were no humans to be seen. Prayer flags fluttered beyond the tents. Butter churns stood idle. Dried dung had been piled near the tents. Beyond the camp stood a small herd of yak, grazing on the spring grass. A goat with a ribbon tied on its ear grazed without fetters. It had been ransomed. By the entry to the largest tent the skull of a sheep hung over a willow rod frame in which yarn had been interwoven in geometric patterns. Shan had seen *khampas* make the same patterns with blanket thread at the 404th. It was a spirit trap.

A dog barked from the line of goats. A puppy on a tether lurched forward, upsetting a butter churn. From a bundle of fleece by the first tent a baby cried, and immediately the tent disgorged its inhabitants. Two men appeared first, one wearing a fleece vest, the other a heavy *chuba*, the thick sheepskin overcoat favoured by many Tibetan nomads. Behind them Shan could see several women clad in patchwork tunics; soot and grime muted the once vibrant colours of their clothing. A child, a boy of no more than three, wandered out, his chin and lips covered with yogurt.

The man in the vest, his leathery face lined with wrinkles, gave them a sour acknowledgment, then disappeared into the tent and emerged with a soiled envelope stuffed with papers. He extended it towards Shan.

'We are not birth inspectors,' Shan said, embarrassed.

'You are buying wool? It is too late. Last month was wool.' The man was missing half his teeth. With one hand he tightly gripped a silver *gau* which hung from his neck.

'We are not here for wool.'

From his jacket pocket Feng produced a piece of candy wrapped in cellophane and extended it towards the child. The boy approached cautiously, grabbed the candy and ran back to stand between the two men. The man in the *chuba* pulled the candy from the boy and smelled it, held it to his tongue, then returned it to the boy. The boy uttered a squeal of delight and ran inside. The man nodded, as though in gratitude, but the suspicion on his face did not disappear. He stepped aside and gestured for them to enter the tent.

It was surprisingly warm inside. Panels of yak-hair cloth, the same used for the tent itself, hung along one side to create a private dressing chamber. An ancient rug, once red and yellow but reduced to shades of soiled brown, served as the floor, bed, and chair for the tent's inhabitants. A three-legged iron brazier sat near the centre, holding a huge kettle over smouldering embers of a wood fire. A small wooden table made with pegs and hinges for disassembly when moving camp held two incense burners and a small bell. Their altar.

Ten *khampas* were huddled, wary as deer, on the far side of the altar, as though it might protect them. The six women and four men appearing to span four generations were dressed in thick, dirty woollens, skirts and aprons of faded red and brown stripes, heavy *chubas* that looked to have weathered many years of storms. A child of perhaps six wandered out of the group, clad in a length of yak felt draped around his body and tied at the waist with twine; a woman pulled the child into her skirt with a desperate look towards Shan. Necklaces of small silver coins, interspersed with red and blue beads, were the only adornment on the women. All their faces, male and female, were round, their cheekbones high, their eyes intelligent and scared, their skin smudged with smoke, their hands thick with calluses. One frail grey-haired woman leaned against a tent pole near the rear.

There was dead silence as everyone stared across the smokey chamber. The man in the vest, now holding the baby, still in its fleece cocoon, entered and uttered a single syllable. The knot of *khampas* slowly dispersed, the men sitting around the brazier, the women moving towards three heavy logs that held cooking utensils. The man, apparently a clan leader, gestured for his visitors to sit on the carpet.

The women chipped pieces from a large brick of black tea and dropped them into the kettle. Uncertain what to say, but compelled by their tradition of hospitality, the men talked of their herds. A ewe had birthed triplets. The poppies had been thick on the southern slopes, one of them said, which meant that this year's calves would be strong. Another asked if the visitors had any salt.

'I am looking for the Dronma clan,' Shan said as he accepted a bowl of buttered tea. On the table he noticed a framed photograph, face down, as though dropped in haste. As he leaned towards the table he noticed that the hanging panels at the back of the tent were moving.

'There are many clans in the mountains,' the old man said. He called for more tea, as though to distract Shan.

Shan picked up the photo. One of the women spoke urgently in the *khampa* dialect, and the younger men seemed to tense. The photo was sticking an inch out of the frame. It was Chairman Mao. Underneath he could see another image, the beads of a rosary and a red robe visible beneath Mao. It was a common practice in Tibet to keep a photo of the Dalai Lama in a conspicuous spot to bless the home, to be quickly covered by one of Mao when government callers arrived. Years earlier, mere possession of an image of the Dalai Lama had guaranteed imprisonment. As the woman noisily served tea to Feng, Shan pushed down the photo of Mao to finish covering the secret image, then stood it up on the table, facing away from them.

He sat on the rug, conspicuously crossing his legs under him in the lotus fashion favoured by the Tibetans. During the Demolish the Four Olds campaign Tibetans had been ordered not to sit cross-legged. 'This clan has a son named Balti,' Shan continued. 'He worked in Lhadrung.'

'Families stay together here,' the herder observed. 'We don't know much about the other clans.' The *khampas* looked down fretfully, watching the coals. Shan recognized the nervousness. No Chinese came who was not a wool buyer or a birth inspector. Shan stepped towards the hanging panel and pulled it aside.

Two young women were sitting behind it. They were pregnant.

'They are not inspectors,' said one of the girls as she boldly pushed past him. She couldn't have been more than eighteen. 'Not with a priest,' she said with a defiant smile towards Yeshe. She helped herself to some of the tea. 'I know the Dronma clan.'

One of the older women snapped out a complaint.

The girl ignored her. 'Doesn't matter. No one could tell where to find them. Too few for a full camp. All they can do is work the herder tents, in the high valleys.'

'Where?'

'Say a prayer for my baby,' she said to Yeshe, patting her stomach. 'My last baby died. Say a prayer.'

Yeshe looked at Shan uncomfortably. 'I am not qualified.'

'You have a priest's eyes. You are from a gompa, I can tell.'

'A long time ago.'

'Then you can say a prayer. My name is Pemu.' She cast a defiant glance around the chamber. 'They want me to say Pemee, to make it sound Chinese. Because of the Four Olds campaign. But I am Pemu.' As if to punctuate her statement she pulled a pin from her hair, releasing a long braid into which turquoise beads had been woven. 'I need a prayer. Please.'

Yeshe cast an awkward glance at Shan, then moved outside, as though to flee. The girl followed him. One of the women threw open the flap to watch. The girl called to Yeshe without response, then ran past him and knelt in front of him. As he tried to sidestep her, she grabbed his hand and put it on her head. The action seemed to paralyse him. Then slowly he withdrew the rosary from his pocket and began speaking to the girl.

The action pierced the tension in the tent. The clan began preparing dinner. One of the women began to mix *tsampa* with tea to make *pak*, a *khampa* staple. A pot was put on the fire with mutton stew. A woman pulled blackened loaves from the ashes. 'Three strikes bread,' she explained as she handed a piece to Shan. 'One, two, three,' she counted as she struck the loaf against a rock. On the third strike the outer shell of ashes and carbon fell away, revealing a golden crust. Shan was offered the first slice. He broke it in half and with a bow of his head solemnly placed one piece on the makeshift altar.

The herder in the vest cocked his head in curiosity at Shan. 'The Dronma,' he said, 'they follow the sheep. In the spring the yaks come down from the high land where they wintered. The sheep go up. Look for small tents.

Look for prayer flags.' He drew a map of likely locations, seven in all, in Shan's pad.

As he did so Shan became aware of a new sound, from another tent. It was one of the rituals he had learned at the 404th. Although the roads were already muddy, someone was praying fervently for rain.

Feng brought blankets from the truck and the three men slept with the children, rising when the goats began to bleat for the dawn milking. Shan folded one of the blankets and left it as a gift at the entrance of the camp.

Inside the truck, sleeping on the back seat, was Pemu. 'I will go with you,' she said, rubbing her eyes. 'My mother was Dronma clan. I will go and see my cousins.' She made room for Shan and offered him a piece of bread.

The distances were not that great. She did not need their truck to see her cousins. Perhaps, Shan considered, it was a test, a challenge. A Public Security squad would never accept a passenger.

They had covered three of the valleys by mid-morning and scanned the slopes with binoculars, to no avail. The skies began to darken. The herders had prayed for rain. Suddenly he understood why.

'Yesterday,' he said to the girl, who watched intently out of the window, 'your people saw a helicopter didn't they?'

'The helicopter is always bad,' she said, as if there was but one in existence. 'When I was young the helicopter came.'

Shan looked at her expectantly.

Pemu chewed her lip. 'It was a very bad day. At first we thought the Chinese had a new machine to make thunder. But it wasn't thunder. They came to earth by the camp. I was only four.' She looked out of the window again. 'It was a very bad day,' she repeated with a distant, vacant stare.

Pemu moved to the edge of the seat as they approached

an outcropping along the path. When the track moved into a small, rugged canyon she asked to get out. 'To clear rocks,' she said. 'I will walk in front.'

But Shan saw no rocks. Feng's hand instinctively moved to his pistol and suddenly Shan realized that she had come to protect them, to use herself as a shield. After a moment, Feng, too, seemed to understand. His hand moved away from his holster, and he concentrated on keeping the vehicle as close to the girl as possible. They moved slowly, in brittle silence.

Shan thought he saw a glimmer of metal ahead. The girl began singing, loudly. The glimmer was gone. It could have been a gun. It could have been a particle of crystal catching the sun.

As they left the canyon she returned to the truck, with a new, haggard look. She began rubbing her belly. She started singing again, to her baby now.

'My uncle is in India,' she said suddenly. 'In Dharamsala, with the Dalai Lama. He writes me letters. He says the Dalai Lama tells us to follow the ways of peace.'

They almost missed the small black tent in the fifth valley, in the shelter of a ledge. It took nearly an hour for Pemu to lead Shan and Yeshe up the steep switchbacks that led to the camp. Three sheep were tethered to a stake near the tent. Red ribbons were tied to their ears. A huge long-haired dog, a herder's mastiff, sat across the entrance to the tent. It reacted only with its eyes, watching them intently, then bared its teeth when they reached the smouldering campfire.

'Aro! Aro!' Pemu called out, taking a tentative step towards the hearth.

'Who would it be then?' a ragged voice called from inside. A small swarthy face appeared just above the dog. 'You're right, Pok,' the man said to the animal. 'They don't look so fearsome.' He laughed and disappeared for a moment.

He came out on a crutch. His left leg was gone below

the knee. 'Pemu?' he said, squinting at the girl. 'Is it you, cousin?' He seemed choked with emotion.

The girl produced a loaf of bread from a bag around her waist and handed it to him. 'This is Harkog,' she said, introducing him to Shan. 'Harkog and Pok are responsible for this range. We're not sure which is in charge.'

Harkog's mouth opened in a crooked smile that showed only three teeth. 'Sugar?' he asked Shan abruptly. 'Got sugar?'

Shan explored the bag Yeshe had brought from the truck and found an apple, brown with age. The man accepted it with a frown, then brightened for a moment. 'Tourists? Big power place on the mountain. I can take you. Secret trail. Go there, say prayers. When you go home you will make babies. Always works. Ask Pemu,' he added with a hoarse laugh.

'We're looking for your brother. We want to help him.'

The man's carefree expression disappeared. 'Got no brother. My brother's gone from this world. Too late to help Balti.'

Shan's heart sank. 'Balti has died?'

'No more Balti,' Harkog said, and began tapping his forehead with his fist, as if in pain.

Pemu pulled the tent flap open. Inside there was a vague human shape, a shell of a man with a gaunt face and eyes like the sockets of a skull. 'Just his body is here. Not much left. For days now. He stays awake. Night and day, with his mantras.' He studied the rosary hanging from Yeshe's belt. 'Holy man?' he said with new interest.

Yeshe did not reply, but stepped closer. 'Balti Dronma. We must speak with you.'

The brother did not protest as Shan and Yeshe entered the tent and sat down.

Pemu stepped in behind them. 'He's more dead than alive,' she whispered in horror.

'We have questions,' Shan said quietly. 'About that night.'

'No,' Harkog protested. 'He's with me. All those nights.'

'What nights?' Shan asked.

'Whatever nights you ask about.'

'No,' Shan said patiently. 'That last night in Lhadrung he was with Prosecutor Jao. When Jao was murdered.'

'Don't know nothing about murder,' Harkog muttered.

'The prosecutor. Jao. He was murdered.'

Harkog seemed not to hear. He was staring at his brother. 'He ran. He ran and ran. Like a jackal he ran. For days he ran. Then one morning I see an animal under a rock. Smells like a dying goat, the dog said. I reached under and pulled him out.'

'We came from Lhadrung to understand what he saw that night.'

'You do mantra,' Harkog said suddenly to Yeshe. 'Protect against demons while he sleep. Call back his soul so he can rest. Afterwards maybe he talk.'

Yeshe did not reply, but awkwardly sat next to Balti. Satisfied, Harkog left the tent.

'Like you blessed my baby,' Pemu said to Yeshe.

Yeshe looked beseechingly to Shan. 'I'm sorry,' he said twice, once to Shan, and once to the woman. 'I am not able to do this thing.'

'I remember what the woman said at the garage,' Shan reminded him. 'Your powers aren't lost, they have only lost their focus.'

Pemu pressed the back of his hand against her forehead.

Yeshe emitted a little groan. 'Why?'

'Because he is dying.'

'And I am supposed to work a miracle?'

'The medicine he needs can't be provided by a doctor,' Shan said.

Pemu still held Yeshe's hand. He looked at her with a new serenity. Perhaps, Shan considered, a miracle was already underway.

Shan sat with the herdsman outside as Pemu stoked the fire and fixed tea. A clap of thunder shook the air about them. A curtain of rain began moving up the valley. As Harkog fixed a sheltering canvas over the fire circle, a chant began inside.

Shan listened to the drone of Yeshe's chant for an hour, then went to bring back Feng and the food in the truck. The sergeant paused just as they were leaving the vehicle, and ran back. 'Have to hide the truck,' he said over his shoulder. He did not say from whom. By the time they returned the rain had stopped and Yeshe was exactly as Shan had left him, seated in front of Balti's pallet, repeating his mantra of protection. There would be no stopping now until it was done. And no one, not even Yeshe, knew when that would be.

They gathered firewood and cooked a stew as the sun set, then ate in silence as the heavens cleared and Yeshe droned on inside the tent. Shan sat with Pemu and watched the new moon climb across the eastern sky. A solitary nighthawk called from the distance. Wisps of mist wandered down the slope. Feng lay down with a blanket and in a moment was snoring. Yeshe droned on. Pemu found a fleece and curled up in it, staring at the fire. At the edge of the flickering circle of light Harkog sat with Pok, the dog, facing the darkness. Yeshe was in his sixth hour of chanting.

Everything felt so distant to Shan. The evil that lurked in Lhadrung. The gulag he would return to. Even the ever-present tentacles of Minister Qin and Beijing seemed part of a different world for the moment.

From his bag Shan pulled the rice paper and inkstick he had purchased from the market. It had been a very long time. So many festivals had been missed. He rubbed the stick and with a few drops of water made ink in a curved piece of bark. He practised, making small strokes in the air with the brush, composing the words in his mind before laying out the sheet and beginning to draw. He used the elegant old-style ideograms he had learned when he was a boy.

Dear father, he began, *forgive me for not writing these many years. I embarked on a long journey since my last letter. Famine raged in my soul. Then I met a wise man who fed it.* The strokes had to be bold yet fluid, or his father the scholar would be disappointed. Written properly, his father would say, a word should look like wind over bamboo. *When I set out I was sad and afraid. Now I have no sadness left. And my only fear is of myself.* He used to write letters often, alone in his tenement in Beijing. He read the ideograms over, unsatisfied. *I sit on a nameless mountain, honoured by mist and your memory*, he added, and signed it as his father would call him: *Xiao Shan*.

Folding the second sheet into an envelope for the first, he pulled a smouldering stick from the fire and stepped into the darkness. He walked in the moonlight until he reached a small ledge that overlooked the valley, then made a small mound of dried grass between two stones and laid the letter on top. He studied the stars, bowed towards the mound and ignited it with the stick. As the ashes rose towards heaven, he watched reverently, hoping to see them cross the moon.

He lingered, covered in stars. He smelled ginger and listened to his father, certain now that he could remember joy.

Halfway back to the camp his heart leapt to his throat as a black creature appeared on the path in front of him. It was Pok. The huge dog sat and blocked his way.

'They say it was a riding accident but it wasn't,' a voice rang out from the shadows beside the trail. It was Harkog. He had a strange new determination in his voice. 'It was a land mine. Running from the PLA.

Suddenly I was in the air. Never heard the explosion. My leg flew past me while I was still in the air. But the soldiers stopped. The bastards stopped.' He stepped from the shadows and looked up into the sky, just as Shan had been doing.

'You still stopped them?'

'Three of them came charging after me, to finish me. I shouted a curse and threw my leg at them. They fled like puppies.'

'I am sorry about your leg.'

'My fault. I should not have run.'

They walked back together, slowly, silently, Pok leading the way.

'We could take you both back if you want,' Shan offered.

'No,' the man said in a slow, wise voice. 'Just take his Chinese clothes. Everything else from Lhadrung. Balti must wear a fleece vest again. This has happened to him because he tried to be someone he is not. I got a truck ride there once. To Lhadrung. Good shoes. But that Jao, he was bad joss.'

'You knew Jao?'

'I rode in the black car with Balti once. That Jao, he had the smell of death.'

'You mean you knew Jao was going to die?'

'No. I mean people around him died. He had power, like a sorcerer. He knew powerful words that could be put on paper to kill people.'

They were close enough to see the glow of the campfire when Pok growled. There was a shadow against the rock, waiting. Harkog muttered an order to the dog and the two had already moved on towards the camp before Shan recognized Sergeant Feng.

'I know what you were doing,' Feng said. 'Sending a message.'

Shan clenched his jaw. 'Just walking.'

'My father tried to teach me when I was young,' Feng

284

said, in a voice that seemed to ache. Shan realized he had misread Feng. 'To speak to my grandfather. But I lost it. Up here, so far away. It makes you think about things. Maybe –' he was struggling. 'Maybe you could show me how again.'

Trinle had once told Shan that people had day souls and night souls, and the most important task in life was to introduce your night soul to your day soul. Shan remembered the talk of Feng's father on the road to Sungpo's gompa. Feng was discovering his night soul.

They moved back to the ledge where Shan had sent his letter. Feng lit a small fire and produced a pencil stub and several of the blank tally sheets from the 404th. 'I don't know what to say.' His voice was very small. 'We were never supposed to go back to family if they were bad elements. But sometimes I want to go back. It's more than thirty years.'

'Who are you writing to?'

'My grandfather, like my father asked.'

'What do you remember about him?'

'Not much. He was very strong and he laughed. He used to carry me on his back, on top of a load of wood.'

'Then just say that.'

Feng thought a long time, then slowly wrote on one of the sheets. 'I don't know words,' he apologized and handed it to Shan.

Grandfather, you are strong, it read. *Carry me on your back.*

'I think your words are very good,' Shan said, and helped him fashion an envelope from the other sheets. 'To send it you should be alone,' he suggested. 'I will wait down the trail.'

'I don't know how to send it. I thought there were words.'

'Just put him in your heart as you do it and the letter will reach him.'

When they returned to camp, Harkog, Yeshe and Balti were sitting at the fire. Pemu, speaking in the low comforting tones that might be used with an infant, was feeding Balti spoonfuls of stew. The gauntness seemed to have been lifted from Balti and transferred to Yeshe, who studied the flames with a drained, confused expression.

'We visited your house,' Shan began. 'The old woman married to the rat showed us the hiding place. It was made for a briefcase.'

Balti gave no sign of having heard.

'What was in there that was so dangerous?'

'Big things. Like a bomb, Jao says.' Balti's voice was thin and high-pitched.

'Did you ever see these things?'

'Sure. Files. Envelopes. Not real things. Papers.'

Shan shut his eyes in frustration as he realized why Jao had trusted him with the papers. 'You can't read, can you?'

'Road signs. They taught me road signs.'

'That night,' Shan said. 'Where were you driving?'

'The airport. Gonggar. The airport for Lhasa. Mr Jao trusts me. I'm a safe driver. Five years no accidents.'

'But you took a detour. Before the airport.'

'Sure. Supposed to go to airport. After dinner he told me different. All excited. Go to the South Claw bridge. The new one over the Dragon Throat built by Tan's engineers. Big meeting. Short meeting. Won't miss the plane, he said.'

'Who did he meet?'

'Balti just the driver. Number one driver. That's all.'

'Did he take his briefcase?'

Balti thought a moment. 'No. In the back seat. I got out when he got out of the car. It was cold. I found a jacket in the back. Prosecutor Jao gives me clothes sometimes. We're same size.'

'So what happened when Jao got out of the car?'

'Someone called out to him from the shadows. He

286

walked away. So I sat and smoked. On the bonnet of the car I smoked. Half a pack almost. We're going to be late. I honk the horn. Then he comes out. He's plenty mad. He's going to eat me like a pack of wolves. I never meant it. Maybe it was the horn. He was plenty angry.'

They weren't talking about the prosecutor any more, Shan realized.

'You saw him?'

'Sure I saw him. Like a yak stampede I saw him.'

'How close?'

'At first I thought it was Comrade Jao. Just a shadow. Then the moon came out of the cloud. He was golden. Beautiful. At first that's all I could think, like a trance. So beautiful, and big like two men. Then I see he is angry. Holding his axe. Snorting like a bull. My heart stops. He did that. He stopped my heart. I kept telling it to beat but it wouldn't. Then I'm down in the heather. Running. I'm wetting myself, I'm crying. In the morning I found the eastern road again. Truck drivers stop for me. Between rides I run, always running.'

'Tamdin,' Shan said. 'Did he chase you?'

'One angry son of a bitch, Tamdin. He wants me. I hear him in the night. If I stop the mantras he will have me. He will bite my head off like a sweet apple.'

'What was in the car?'

'Nothing. Suitcase. Briefcase.'

'Where's the car now?'

'Who knows? No driver, no more. Never again.'

'It wasn't found at the bridge.'

'That Tamdin,' Balti croaked, 'he probably picked it up and threw it over two mountains.'

When they left at dawn Balti was back in the tent, casting fearful glances outside, rocking back and forth with a new chant. Tears streaked his face. A bundle of clothing had appeared on Shan's blanket.

'Move your camp,' Shan said quietly to Harkog after

Pemu had led Sergeant Feng down the slope towards the truck. 'So it cannot be seen from the road. In shadows where it can't be seen from the air.'

As Harkog nodded grimly, Yeshe extended a slip of paper. 'Here. A charm,' he said, 'to be fastened to the tent. Let him chant. But he must follow my prescription. All day today. Half a day tomorrow. And only one hour a day afterwards. For the next month. After tomorrow he must come out. He must walk the hills. The ghost is gone from him. He must become what he is.'

Harkog replied with a big three-toothed grin. 'We'll be *khampa*.'

Back in the truck, Shan examined the clothing. They were caked with mud. Cheap work clothes, barely better than those issued to prisoners. But the battered shoes were wrapped in a jacket, a suit jacket. It was torn and soiled but of a very different quality, the product of a tailor's shop. In one pocket was a handkerchief and a bundle of business cards in a rubber band. *Jao Xengding*, they said, *Prosecutor for Lhadrung County*. Balti had been wearing Jao's jacket. It was cold that night, he said. He had put on Jao's jacket and sat on the bonnet of the car.

In the second pocket were folded slips of paper in a clip. Shan unfolded the papers. Several were receipts, the top one from the Mongolian restaurant with 'American mine' scrawled across the top. Beneath it was a small square of paper on which was written two words. *Bamboo Bridge*. A square of yellow paper said *You don't need the X-ray machine*. Below the words was a symbol like an inverted Y with two bars across the stem. It could have been the ideogram for sky, or heaven. It could have been careless doodling. Another slip listed cities. *Lhadrung, Lhasa, Beijing, and Hong Kong* it said, followed by the words *Bei Da Union*. Where had he heard that? The lama at Khartok, he remembered, the one who was the business manager, had said they were rebuilding with the help of the Bei Da Union. Bei Da was Beijing University.

A fourth note may have been a shopping list. *Scarf, incense, and gold*, it said. One of the notes, he realized, was probably the one that lured Jao to his death.

Shan was still trying to make sense of the references as they drove through the narrow pass that took them out of the plateau. They had left Pemu near her herds after she had placed Yeshe's hand on her head and uttered a prayer of gratitude. A bolt of lightning erupted in front of them, igniting a bush on the side of the road. The bush roared into flame. No one spoke. They waited until the bush crumbled into ashes, then drove on.

Chapter Thirteen

The front gate at Jade Spring barracks had been attacked.
Boards were split, wire hanging loose. The heather was
crushed for twenty yards on either side of the gate. In the
light from the guard's shed Shan saw shreds of clothing
hanging from the barbed wire. A sombre, angry-looking
squad was replacing the hinges on one of the two huge
gates. Shan stared, blinking with exhaustion. He and
Sergeant Feng had shared the driving for sixteen gruelling
hours. During his turn for rest he had been unable to
close his eyes for more than a few minutes before being
haunted by the vision of Balti as they had left him,
rocking back and forth in the darkness of his tent.

Shan stumbled out of the truck in confusion, his eyes
reflexively searching for stains of blood on the soil.

As he approached the guard's shed, floodlights were
switched on, blinding him momentarily.

When his vision cleared a PLA officer was standing
beside him. 'We missed you,' the officer said with icy
sarcasm. 'They paid us a visit. You could have been guest
of honour.'

'They?'

The officer snarled out orders to the squad as he
explained. 'The cultists.' There had been a riot. Or nearly
one. 'Just after dawn. A logging truck stopped. Dropped
off an old man, wearing a robe. He just sat down. Not a
word. We let him do his beads. A peasant rode by on a
bicycle and stopped. We should have kicked them both
down the road. But Colonel Tan, he said no trouble. No
incidents. Beijing is about to arrive. Americans are about

290

to arrive. Just keep it quiet.' The officer opened the driver's door and glared at Sergeant Feng, as if he somehow shared responsibility for the incident.

He signalled for the gate to open, then turned back to Shan. 'In another hour there were six of them. Then ten. By noon maybe forty. The man in the robe was something special to them, I guess.' Shan looked at the rags more closely. They weren't remnants of clothing from people thrown against the wire. They were tied to the wire. They were prayer flags.

'So I go out to talk. Mediate. Discuss the socialist imperative of coexistence. You must move, I said. There's an army convoy coming soon. Heavy equipment. Someone could get hurt. But they say they want your man Sungpo released. They say he's no criminal.' The officer's eyes flared. 'Big secret. Everyone was ordered to strict secrecy. No one to know your monk is locked up here. I know no one here talked,' he said with an accusing stare.

'When I leave they move to the fence, begin chanting and rocking it. The poles begin to loosen. So I call out a riot squad. No guns. But they turn around and tie their hands together. Like a chain. With socks, shoelaces, whatever. They all get tied together. They're just showing their backs. Ignoring us. Chanting. What can we do? We have tourists coming. I'll be carrying night soil for recruits if some round-eye comes by and photographs us pounding on their backs.'

'The old man,' Shan said. 'He came from the north?'

'Right. Ancient. As if he's going to collapse into dust.'

Shan, suddenly alert, looked up. 'Where is he now?'

'We finally let him through an hour ago. Only way to get them to leave. When the hell are you going to –'

Shan did not stay for the rest of the irate question. He darted through the gate and ran to the guardhouse.

Inside, the only lights were at the end of the corridor. Jigme sat at the cell door, watching Sungpo, exactly as

Shan had left him three days earlier. Beside him was Je Rinpoche.

The old man did not acknowledge Shan. He was facing Sungpo, who sat in the middle of the cell. They were not talking, but their eyes seemed to be focused on the same invisible point in the distance.

As Shan opened the cell door, Yeshe placed a restraining hand on his arm. 'You cannot interfere. We must wait for their return.'

'No,' Shan insisted. 'It is too late for not interfering.' He stepped inside and touched Sungpo on the shoulder. Something seemed to surge through his fingers as he did so, like electricity without the shock. He told himself it was his imagination. Sungpo moved his head from side to side, as though shaking off a deep slumber, then looked up and acknowledged Shan with a negligible blink of his eyes.

Je Rinpoche gave a deep exhalation and his head slowly slumped onto his chest. Yeshe glared at Shan with an unfamiliar vehemence.

'Does anybody understand what is happening here?' Shan asked, his voice breaking with emotion. No one replied.

Shan measured the look in Yeshe's eyes. 'I need to speak to Dr Sung. Go now. Call her. Tell her I must see her.'

'This old lama is meditating,' Yeshe warned. 'You cannot interrupt him.'

'Tell her I need to speak to her about the group called the Bei Da Union.'

Yeshe registered his disapproval with a frown, then spun about and left the building.

Shan dropped to his knees between the two monks. 'Do you understand what is happening?' he said again, more loudly, at a loss to find a way to stir the lama without such shameful rudeness.

'A man was killed,' Je Rinpoche said suddenly, his head lifting. 'The government considered him important.'

Shan watched Sungpo. His eyes blinked.

'They will enforce their equation,' the old lama said matter-of-factly.

'Equation?' Shan asked.

'They will take one of us.'

'Is that what you want?'

'Want?' Je asked.

'What about justice?'

'Justice?'

Shan had used the Chinese word *yi*, the ideogram for which was a large human standing with a protecting sword over a smaller human. It was not a symbol favoured by Tibetans.

'Do we believe in Beijing's justice?' Je asked in the same serene tone he had used to speak to the mysterious raven at Saskya. He was speaking to Sungpo.

Suddenly Sungpo spoke. He looked at Je, and only Je. 'We believe in harmony,' Sungpo said, in a voice that was barely audible. 'We believe in peace.'

Je turned to Shan. 'We believe in harmony,' he repeated. 'We believe in peace.'

'I was sent to a commune for re-education,' Shan said, looking at Je. 'During the dark years.' Everyone had their own name for the period of torment Mao had called the Cultural Revolution. 'The first week we stood in a rice paddy. In the mud. In rows. They called us seedlings. No talking was allowed. The political officer said she had to have peace in the fields. If anyone spoke or laughed or cried they were beaten. We were quiet for a long time. But it never felt like peace.'

Je only grinned in reply.

Sungpo seemed to be drifting off, back into his meditation.

'I have questions,' Shan said urgently. 'Ask about the

arrest. What did they say? When did he last see Prosecutor Jao?'

Je leaned forward and spoke in a whisper to Sungpo.

'He was away,' Je explained, referring to Sungpo's meditation. 'A long distance. He knew nothing until he returned. He found himself in a car, with manacles on. There were two cars, filled with uniforms.'

'Why did they find Prosecutor Jao's wallet there?'

Je conferred with Sungpo. 'That is a curious thing,' he announced with wonder in his eyes. 'Sungpo did not have the wallet. He did not know they found it there. Something could have come. Something could have put it there.'

'Someone or something?'

When the old man sighed his throat made a wet, wheezing sound. 'Sometimes when lightning strikes it leaves things. It was meant to be there. It does not seem important how it came to be there.'

'Lightning made a wallet materialize in Sungpo's cave?' Shan asked slowly, his spirits sinking.

'Lightning. Spirits. They work in inscrutable ways. Perhaps it is their way of calling him.'

'And if the true killer is not found, if the death cannot be resolved, the 404th will continue their strike. They will be found guilty of mass treason.'

'Perhaps that, too, is the destined path to their next incarnation.'

Shan closed his eyes and breathed deeply. 'Did Sungpo know Prosecutor Jao?'

Je conferred for a moment with Sungpo. 'He remembers the name from some trial.'

'Did he kill Jao?'

Je looked at Shan wearily. 'He has no weight on his soul. Only the width of a hair separates him from the gates of Buddhahood.'

'That is not a legal defence.'

Je sighed. 'To kill anyone would be a violation of his

294

vows. He is a true believer. He would have told me immediately. He would have stripped off his robe. His cycle would have been broken.'

'But he still will not say that he did not do it.'

'It would be an act of ego. We are taught to avoid such acts.'

'So the reason he is not protesting his innocence is because he is not guilty.'

'Exactly.' Je smiled. He seemed very pleased with Shan's logic.

'The head of the Religious Affairs Bureau visited the gompa recently. Did Sungpo see him?'

'Sungpo is a hermit. If he were in meditation he would not have seen such a visitor even if he walked in and kicked Sungpo.'

Shan turned to Jigme. 'Is there any other route to your hut, other than the trail we climbed?'

'Old game trails. Or up the rocks.'

Sungpo drifted off. He seemed unable to hear any of them, even old Je. 'To know that he dies for another's crime, isn't that a form of a lie?' Shan asked the old lama, fighting the desperation in his voice.

'No. To confess falsely, that would be the lie.'

'The Bureau has been kept away for now. But before the trial, they will seek a confession. They seldom fail.' He had seen a directive once in Beijing. 'It is considered mismanagement of judicial resources, and an abuse of the socialist order, to proceed to trial without a confession. If he does not participate, one will be read for him.'

'But that would be inconsistent,' Je observed, still in his serene voice.

Shan envied his naivety. 'The trial is conducted for the people, to instruct them.' Or perhaps, he reflected, remembering Beijing stadiums packed with twenty thousand citizens to witness an execution, to entertain them.

'Ah. You mean like a parable.'

'Yes,' Shan said in a hollow voice. A vision streaked

through his mind. The old woman with the mop and bucket, moving up the stairs behind Sungpo. 'Except it is more absolute than a parable.'

Yeshe was sitting on the steps to their quarters when Shan went to gather blankets for Je, who was insisting on staying in the cell block. 'I am going to request a return to duties at the 404th. I'll take another year with Zhong if I have to,' Yeshe announced as he followed Shan through the door. 'I do not wish to be a part of this. It is too confusing. What if Jigme is right when he says Sungpo can easily throw off a face?'

'Meaning we should accept his sacrifice?'

'It is not just Sungpo. You said it yourself. It will not be enough to prove Sungpo innocent. We will have to provide them with an alternative. They could arrest four or five more monks. Even ten or twenty. Call it a conspiracy of the *purbas*. They would all be deemed equally guilty. And maybe they would not stop at just the *purbas*. There are many forms of resisters.'

'You're saying the choice is to sacrifice Sungpo or sacrifice the resistance?'

'The resistance in Lhadrung County, yes.'

'You speak for the resistance now?'

'You saw my gompa. I could not be a *purba* without breaking my vows. I would be expelled for ever. There would be no hope of returning.'

'Is that your hope?' Shan asked.

'No,' Yeshe said, in a voice filled with emotion. 'I don't know. Two weeks ago I would have said no. Now all I know is how painful a return could be.'

Shan remembered the dogs at Yeshe's gompa. The spirits of fallen priests, they said.

There was a shout from outside, and a hammering of boots on the parade ground. Jigme was struggling with the knobs, being dragged away from the brig. Shan looked back at Yeshe. 'I need your help. More than ever.'

By the time Shan reached him Jigme had been deposited a hundred yards from Sungpo's cell.

'Only one visitor allowed to stay with the prisoner,' the closest knob snapped, and marched away.

'Not much you can do for him here,' Shan observed as he sat beside Jigme.

'If he would eat, then I could fix his meals.'

'There may be other ways,' Shan suggested. 'Depending on who it is you want to help.'

'Sungpo.'

'Sungpo the holy man? Or Sungpo the mortal?'

Jigme took a moment to answer. 'It is confusing sometimes. I am supposed to say it is the same.'

'You and I have Chinese blood. It is said that one of our curses is that we always compromise. Maybe it would take years to find the answer to that question. But after five more days it will not matter.'

They sat in silence. Jigme began idly drawing in the dirt with his finger.

'I want you to do something,' Shan said. 'Go to a place in the mountains. The Dragon Claws. We can get you food and water. There are blankets in the truck. Sergeant Feng can drive you there. He will check on you each day. But once you are out I do not know if the guards will let you through the gate again.'

Jigme thought a long time. 'They say there is a demon up there.'

Shan nodded sympathetically. 'I want you to find where the demon lives.'

Jigme did not shrink back, but his face drained of colour.

'He will not harm you.'

'Why not?' Jigme asked in a forlorn voice.

'Because you are one of the few who are pure of heart.'

Dr Sung would not stand still when Shan arrived. 'Get out,' she said. 'You spread danger like infection.' He followed her as she moved down the corridor of the clinic.

'What is the Bei Da Union?' he asked, nearly running to match her pace.

'Bei Da is the university. A union is a union,' she snapped.

'Are you a member?'

'I am a doctor employed by the people's government. The only doctor here, if you haven't noticed. I have work to do.'

'Who was it, doctor?'

She stopped and looked at him quizzically.

'Who got to you?'

Her face flushed. At first Shan thought it was anger, but then he saw it could be shame. 'They say it's a club for graduates of Beijing University,' she said. 'Of course, there're only a handful of graduates in all of Lhadrung. They asked me to a meeting once. Dinner at an old gompa outside the town. I thought perhaps they were going to ask me to join.'

'But they didn't.'

'Except for Beijing there's little we have in common.'

'Who are they?' An orderly was mopping the floor, a Tibetan. He pushed the bucket towards them. Shan motioned for the doctor to move out of earshot.

'The rising stars. The young elite. You know. Back-door blue jeans. Sunglasses that cost an average family's monthly wage.'

'You don't like blue jeans and sunglasses?'

Dr Sung seemed surprised by the question. She gazed down the corridor before answering. 'I don't know. I remember I once did.'

'How about Prosecutor Jao? Was he a member?' Shan said.

'No. Not Jao. A graduate, but too old I guess. Li's a member. Wen of Religious Affairs. The Director for Mines. Some soldiers.'

'Soldiers? A major in the Bureau?'

The reference to the Bureau seemed to disturb Sung. She considered the question a moment. 'Don't know. There was one. He was slick. Arrogant. A bullet scar on one cheek.'

'Have you ever treated any of them?'

'Healthy as yaks, every one.'

'Not even for a dogbite?'

'Dogbite?'

'Never mind.' Shan had not forgotten that the secret charms being bought by the *ragyapa* had included charms against dogbite. There was no logic to it, but something about it continued to gnaw away at him. Someone wanted to be forgiven by Tamdin but protected from dogs.

'Did Jao ever tell you he expected to be moving away? A reassignment?'

'He dropped hints. About how good it would be, back in the real China.'

'His words or yours?'

She flushed again. 'He talked about going back. Everyone does. He said he would buy a colour television when he got home. Said in Beijing they get stations from Hong Kong now. I guess he finally made it,' she added, as an afterthought.

'He made it?'

'To Beijing. Miss Lihua sent a fax from Hong Kong. Requesting his body and effects be sent back.'

Shan stared in disbelief. 'Impossible. Not until the investigation is over.'

Sung turned with a victorious glare. 'A Public Security truck came this morning. Took it all. Had a coffin ready. Left on a military flight out of Gonggar.'

Shan stared in disbelief. 'Obstruction of judicial process is a serious charge.'

'Not when Public Security requests it. I asked for it in writing.'

'Didn't it strike you as odd? Didn't you remember that this investigation is under the direct authority of Colonel Tan?'

Sung looked at him with alarm. 'Prosecutor Li forwarded the order,' she explained in a worried tone.

'Prosecutor? There is no new prosecutor. Not yet.'

'What was I supposed to do? Wire the chairman's office for confirmation?'

'Who signed it?'

'The major.'

Shan wrung his hands in frustration. 'Doesn't this major have a name? Doesn't anyone ever ask him why?'

'Comrade, the one thing you never do with Public Security is ask questions.'

Shan took a step towards the door and turned. 'I need to borrow a phone,' he said. 'Long distance lines.'

She asked no questions, but escorted him to an empty office in the rear of the building. As she left a figure appeared at the door. Yeshe's anguish was still evident, but there was a glint of determination in his eyes.

'When they sent me back from university,' he announced as he stepped into the room, 'I knew who put the Dalai Lama's photo on the wall. It wasn't even a Tibetan, it was a Chinese friend of mine who did it. For a joke.' He dropped into a chair. 'They sent me back to labour camp because I was supposed to have been capable of it. But I wasn't. Never would I have had the courage.'

Shan put his hand on Yeshe's shoulder. 'It is a mistake to think of courage as something you show to others. True courage is only something you show to yourself.'

'You have to know who you are to be able to recognize that kind of courage,' Yeshe said into his hands.

'I think you know.'

'I don't.'

'I think the man who stood up to the major and saved Balti's life knew who he was.'

'Now, back here, it feels like I was just performing. I don't know if it was me.'

'Performing for whom?'

'I don't know.' Yeshe looked up and met Shan's eyes. 'Maybe for you,' he said quietly.

Shan shut his eyes. Strangely, the words made him think of his son, the son who was so remote that he was never an image in Shan's mind, only a concept. The son who probably assumed Shan was dead. The son who would always despise him, dead or alive, as a failure. The son who would never utter such words to him.

'No,' he said, returning Yeshe's stare. Not me, he wanted to say. There is no room on my back for another burden. 'You did it because you want to find the truth. You did it because you want to become a Tibetan again.'

Yeshe's gaze did not flicker. He gave no sign of having heard Shan's words.

Shan transcribed the numbers from Jao's secret file. 'If these are phone numbers I need to know where,' he said and extended the slip.

Yeshe sighed, and studied the paper. 'We could do this at the 404th. Or the barracks.'

'No, we couldn't,' Shan said curtly. The Bureau would not be listening to the lines from some forgotten office of a forgotten clinic. 'As far as the operator knows, you're just a clerk in the clinic. Trying to track someone due to a sudden death. Try Lhasa. Try Shigatse, Beijing, Shanghai, Guangzhou. New York. Just find out.' He pulled out the American business card found with Jao's body. 'Then find out about this.'

As Yeshe raised the receiver Shan left the room and moved to a window in the corridor. He could see Sergeant Feng in the truck outside, sleeping. He turned. The Tibetan orderly was nearby again, at an open door now, watching Shan as he mopped. Another orderly appeared at the opposite end of the corridor, pushing a wheelchair. The first one stopped and caught Shan's eye, then motioned urgently towards the open door. As Shan moved hesitantly towards him, he heard a metallic rattle behind him. The second orderly was approaching at a trot.

'Inside,' the first orderly instructed.

It was a darkened closet. In the dim light he saw a broom and cleaning supplies. An arm suddenly wrapped around Shan's chest and a cloth stinking of a strong chemical was clamped over his mouth. Something hard struck him behind the knees. The wheelchair. The last thing he remembered was the sound of bells.

He woke on the floor of a cavern, a bitter taste in his mouth. Chloroform. The cavern was crammed with small gold and bronze statues of Buddha and hundreds of manuscripts stacked on shelves. By the dim light of butter lamps he saw two figures with hair cropped to the scalp. One of them stooped and began wiping Shan's face with a damp cloth. It was one of the orderlies. On his wrist hung a rosary with tiny bells tied to it. A match flared. The cave brightened as he straightened and the other one uncovered a kerosene lantern.

There was a low rumble, as of thunder. In the rising light Shan saw a door in a wooden frame. It wasn't a cave. It was a room carved out of the living rock, and the thunder was the sound of traffic passing overhead.

'Why are you so concerned about the costume of Tamdin?' the figure with the lantern asked abruptly. It was the illegal monk from the marketplace, the *purba* with the scarred face. 'You asked Director Wen of the Religious Affairs Bureau about the costumes in the museum.'

'Because the murderer wanted to be seen as Tamdin,' Shan said, rubbing away a pain in his temple. 'Maybe he felt he was carrying out the wishes of Tamdin.'

302

The man frowned. 'And you think that someone has the costume?'

'I know someone has it.'

'Or did someone plant artefacts to make you think that?'

Shan weighed the possibility. 'No, he has been seen. Someone wearing the costume was seen by Prosecutor Jao's driver. He wasn't lying. And not just at Jao's murder. At some of the other murders, too. Maybe all of them.'

The *purba* held the light near Shan's face. 'Are you saying there has been only one murderer all along?'

Shan nodded. 'Two, I think, but acting together.'

'But showing that one of them was dressed up in a religious costume will just make them think it was Buddhists.'

'Unless we prove otherwise.'

The *purba* gave an incredulous grunt. 'Every minute the Knobs could open fire on the 404th, and you spend your time on demons.'

'If you know of a better way to save them, please tell me.'

'If it continues, Lhadrung will be lost. It will become a militarized zone.'

Shan's mouth went dry. 'What are you going to do?'

'Maybe,' the *purba* suggested, 'we give them the fifth one.'

'The fifth one?'

'The last of the Lhadrung Five. Put him in prison again. Maybe then their conspiracy has to be over. There will be no one else to blame.'

It was a very Tibetan solution. Shan saw something new in the *purba*'s eyes. Sadness. 'Just like that,' Shan said, 'the last of the Five asks to go to prison.'

'I've been thinking. He could go to the mountain and conduct Bardo rites, get rid of the *jungpo*. The 404th could stop its strike and return to work.'

'And Public Security would be furious,' Shan acknowledged. 'Whoever conducted the rites would be sentenced to the 404th.'

'Exactly.' The *purba* shrugged. 'There are other solutions. The people are angry.'

The words frightened Shan. 'Choje, at the 404th, he said once that those who try too hard to commit perfect goodness are in the greatest danger of creating perfect badness.'

'I don't know what that means.'

'It means that much evil can be done in the name of virtue. Because to many virtue is a relative thing.'

The *purba* looked into the flame of the lantern. 'I don't believe virtue is a relative thing.'

'No. I don't suppose you do.'

The man sighed. 'I didn't say we would use violence. I said the people are angry.' He picked up one of the small bronze Buddhas and pressed his hands around it. 'The night the prosecutor died,' he announced, 'a messenger came to the restaurant where he ate. A young man. Well-dressed. Chinese. Wearing a hat. He had a piece of paper for Jao. One of the waiters spoke to the prosecutor, who immediately rose and spoke with this man. And the man gave something to Jao. A flower. An old red flower, all dried up. Jao became very excited. He took the paper and flower, then gave money to the man. The man left. The prosecutor talked with his driver then returned to dinner with the American.'

'How do you know this?'

'You said you needed to know about what Prosecutor Jao did that night. Workers in the restaurant remembered.'

Shan recalled the Tibetan staff at the restaurant, cowering in the corner, afraid of him. 'I must know who sent the message.'

'We do not know. But there was something about the messenger's eyes. One of them wasn't straight. One of the waiters recognized the man. He was a witness at the murder trial of the monk Dilgo.'

'Dilgo of the Lhadrung Five?'

The scar-faced man nodded.

'Would he recognize him again?'

'Certainly. But perhaps we could just give you his name.'

Shan's head jerked up. 'You know his name?'

'As soon as I heard the description I knew. I was at the trial. It was a man named Meng Lau. A soldier.'

'The same man who now claims to have seen Sungpo,' Shan gasped. He stood excitedly, as if to go. The *purba* moved back to reveal a new figure in the shadows, who stepped in front of him to block his exit. 'Not yet please,' the figure said. It was a woman. A nun.

'You don't understand. If I am not back –'

The nun just smiled, then took his hand and led him down a short corridor to a second chamber. It must have been a gompa, Shan realized, the subterranean shrine of an ancient, forgotten gompa. It made sense. Once every Tibetan town had been built around a central gompa. The second room was brightly lit with four lanterns hanging from beams.

A small man was bent over a rough-hewn table, writing in a large book. He looked up, removed a pair of frail wire-rimmed glasses, and blinked several times. 'My friend!' he squealed with delight, leaping off his stool to embrace Shan.

'Lokesh? Is it you?' Shan's heart leapt as he held the man at arm's length and studied him.

'My spirit soared when they said you might come,' the old man said with a huge smile.

Shan had never seen Lokesh in anything but prison garb. He gazed at him with a flood of emotion. It was like finding a long-lost uncle. 'You've put on weight.'

The old man laughed and embraced Shan again. '*Tsampa*,' he said. 'All the *tsampa* I want.' Shan saw a familiar tin mug on the table, half-filled with roasted barley. It was one of the mugs used at the 404th. Old habits died hard.

'But your wife. I thought you went to Shigatse with her.'

The old man smiled. 'I did. Funny thing, two days after I got home, my wife's time came.'

Shan stared at him in disbelief. 'I am –' I am what? he considered. Heartbroken? Furious? Paralysed by the helplessness of it all? 'I am sorry,' he said.

Lokesh shrugged. 'A priest told me that when a soul gets ripe, it will just pop off the tree like an apple. I was able to be with her at her time. Thanks to you.' He put his arms around Shan again, stepped back and pulled a small ornamental box from around his neck. It was an old *gau*, the container for Lokesh's charms. He placed its strap over Shan's head.

'I can't.'

Lokesh put his finger to his lips. 'Of course you can.' He looked at the nun. 'There is no time to argue.'

The nun was looking back into the shadows, where they had left the scar-faced *purba*. Her eyes were wet when she turned to Shan. 'You have to help, you have to stop him.'

Shan was confused. 'He said he would not commit violence.'

The nun bit her lip. 'Only on himself.'

'Himself?'

'He wants to go to the mountain, to do the prohibited rites.' Her hand clamped around his arm as he stared back into the shadows of the underground labyrinth, comprehending at last. The scar-faced *purba* was the fifth, the last of the Lhadrung Five, and the next to be accused of murder if the conspiracy continued.

Lokesh gently pulled the nun's hand away and moved Shan towards the table. 'The 404th is troubled again. We need your wisdom once more, Xiao Shan.'

Shan followed Lokesh's gaze to the book on the table. It had the dimensions of an oversized dictionary, and was bound with wood and cloth. It was a manuscript, with entries in several hands, even several languages. Tibetan mostly, but also Mandarin, English, and French.

The nun looked up with deep, sad eyes. 'There are eleven copies of this in Tibet,' she said quietly. 'Several more in Nepal and India. Even one in Beijing.' She moved to the side and gestured for Shan to sit at the table. 'It is called the *Lotus Book*.'

'Here, my friend,' Lokesh said excitedly as he turned to the front pages of the book. 'It was such a wonderful time to be alive in those days. I have read these pages fifty times and still sometimes I weep with joy at the memories they preserve.'

The pages were not uniform. Some were lists, some were like encyclopedia entries. The very first word in the book was a date. 1949, the year before the Communists began to liberate Tibet.

'It is a catalogue of what was here before the destruction,' Shan spoke in awe. It wasn't just lists of gompas and other holy places, it also held descriptions of the numbers and names of monks and nuns, even the dimensions of buildings. For many sites, first-hand narratives by survivors had been transcribed, telling of life at the place. Lokesh had been writing when Shan entered the room.

'The first half, yes,' the nun said, then opened the pages to a silk marker where another list began.

It was an inventory of people, a list of individual names. Shan felt a choking sensation as he read. 'These are all Chinese names.'

'Yes,' Lokesh said, suddenly more sober. 'Chinese,' he whispered, then his arms slackened and he fell still as if he had suddenly lost his strength.

The nun bent over the book and turned to the back, where the most recent transcriptions had been made. One by one, she pointed out names to Shan as he stared in a mixture of horror and disbelief. Lin Ziang was there, the murdered director of Religious Affairs, as was Xong De, the deceased Director of Mines, and Jin San, the former head of the Long Wall Collective. All victims of the Lhadrung Five.

Forty minutes later they returned him in the wheel-chair, blindfolded, creaking down corridors hewn from the stone, then onto the smooth floors of the clinic, turning so many times he could not possibly have retraced the route. Suddenly, with the sound of the bells again, the scarf that had covered his eyes was untied and he was in the front corridor, alone.

Yeshe was still on the phone, arguing with someone. He hung up when he saw Shan. 'I've tried every combination. Nothing seems to work.' He handed the paper back to Shan. 'I wrote down other possibilities. Page numbers. Coordinates. Specimen numbers. Product numbers. Then I thought to call about his travel plans. There's a travel office for government officials in Lhasa. I call to confirm what they said about his trip.'

'And?'

'He was going to Dalian all right, with a one-day stopover in Beijing first. But no other arrangements for Beijing. No Ministry of Justice car to pick him up.'

Shan gave a slow nod of approval.

'When you didn't return I went on to other things. I called that woman at Religious Affairs. Miss Taring. She told me she would check the audits of artefacts herself and to call back. When I did, she said one was missing.'

'A missing audit report?'

Yeshe nodded meaningfully. 'For the audit done at Saskya gompa fourteen months ago. Shipment records show everything went to the museum in Lhasa. But there was no accounting in her records for what was actually found. A breakdown in procedures.'

'I wonder.'

Yeshe looked puzzled by Shan's reaction, then offered more news. 'And I tried that Shanghai office.'

'The American firm?'

'Right. They didn't know Prosecutor Jao. But when I mentioned Lhadrung they remembered a request from the clinic here. Said there was some correspondence.'

'And?'

'Lots of static, then the line went dead.' He paused and pulled a sheet of paper from under the blotter. 'So I went to the office here. Said I had to check their chronological files. Found this, from six weeks ago.' He handed Shan the paper.

It was a letter from Dr Sung to the Shanghai office, asking if the firm would provide a portable X-ray unit on approval, to be returned in thirty days if found not to be compatible with the clinic's needs.

Shan folded the paper into his notebook. He moved towards the exit, and broke into a trot.

Madame Ko led them to a restaurant beside the county office building. 'Best to wait,' she said, gesturing to an empty table near the rear, beside a door guarded by a waiter holding a tray in arms folded across his chest.

Sergeant Feng ordered noodles; Yeshe, cabbage soup. Shan sipped tea impatiently, then after ten minutes stood and moved to the door. Madame Ko intercepted him, pulling him back. 'No interruptions,' she scolded, then saw the determination in his eyes. 'Let me,' she sighed, and slipped behind the door. Moments later half a dozen army officers began to file out, and she opened the door for Shan.

The room stank of cigarettes, onions, and fried meat. Tan sat alone at a round table, smoking as the staff cleared away dishes. 'Perfect,' he said, exhaling sharply through his nostrils. 'You know how I spent the morning? Being lectured by Public Security. They may decide to report a breakdown in civil discipline. They note my abuse of investigation procedures. They have recorded that security at Jade Spring Camp has been breached twice in the last fifteen years. Both times this week. They say one of my cell blocks has been turned into a damned gompa. They hinted about an espionage investigation. What do you know about that?' He drew on the cigarette again and exhaled slowly, watching Shan through the cloud of smoke. 'They say their units at the 404th will begin final procedures tomorrow.'

Shan tried to conceal the shudder that moved down his spine. 'Prosecutor Jao was killed by someone he knew,' he announced. 'A colleague. A friend.'

Tan lit another cigarette from the butt of the first and stared silently at Shan. 'You have proof finally?'

'A messenger came that night with a paper.' Shan explained what had happened at the restaurant, without disclosing the messenger's identity. Tan would never accept the word of a *purba* against that of a soldier.

'It proves nothing.'

'Why wouldn't the messenger give the paper to Jao's driver? Everyone knew Balti. Everyone gives messages to drivers. It is the custom. Balti was right outside with the car. They were going to the airport.'

'Perhaps this messenger didn't know Balti.'

'I don't believe that.'

'Then by all means we'll release Sungpo,' Tan said acidly.

'Even if he didn't know Balti, the waiters would have sent him to the car. The waiter intercepted him assuming that was what Jao would want. But instead, Jao expected something, or recognized something, something that required his instant attention. So he spoke to the messenger. Away from the waiter. Away from his table where the American sat. Away from Balti. And he heard something so urgent that despite his orderly nature he broke his schedule.'

'He knew Sungpo. Sungpo could have sent the message,' Tan said.

'Sungpo was in his cave.'

'No. Sungpo was on the Southern Claw, waiting to kill.'

'Witnesses would say that Sungpo never left his cave.'

'Witnesses?'

'This man named Jigme. The monk Je. Both have made statements.'

'I read them. A gompa orphan and a senile old man.'

'Suppose it was Sungpo who sent the message,' Shan offered. 'Prosecutor Jao wouldn't go to some remote location alone, unprotected, to meet a man he had imprisoned. There was nothing any monk could say to get Jao to act that way. He was anxious to get to Beijing.'

'So someone helped Sungpo. Someone lied.'

Shan stared at the colonel with a grin of victory.

'Shit,' Tan muttered under his breath.

'Right. Someone he trusted lured Jao with news he could use on his trip. Information that would help him in his secret investigation. Something he might use in Beijing. We have to find out about it.'

'He had no business in Beijing. You saw the fax from Miss Lihua. He was just passing through to Dalian.' Tan watched the ashes of his cigarette build a small hill on the tablecloth.

'Then why would he arrange to stop for a day there?'

'I told you. A shopping trip. Family.'

'Or something about a Bamboo Bridge.'

'Bamboo Bridge?'

'It was on a note in his jacket.'

'What jacket?'

'I found his jacket.'

Tan's head snapped up with a flash of excitement. 'You found the *khampa*, didn't you? You told the assistant prosecutor you didn't, but you did.'

311

'I went to Kham. I found the prosecutor's jacket. That was the best we could do. Balti was not involved.'

Tan offered an approving smile. 'Quite an accomplishment, tracking a jacket into the wilderness.' He snuffed out his cigarette and looked up with a more sombre expression. 'We asked about your Lieutenant Chang.'

'Did someone recover his body?'

'Not my problem.'

Another sky burial, Shan thought. 'But he was army. One of yours.'

'That's the point. He wasn't PLA. Not really.'

'But he was in the 404th.'

Tan silenced him with a raised palm. 'Fifteen years in the Public Security Bureau. Transferred to the PLA rolls just a year ago.'

'That doesn't make sense,' Shan said. No one left the elite ranks of the knobs to join the army.

Tan shrugged. 'With the right patron it could.'

'But you knew nothing about it?'

Tan shrugged. 'The transfer was entered on the army books two days before he arrived here.'

'It could be something else,' Shan suggested. 'He could have still been working for someone in the Bureau.'

'Nonsense. Without me knowing?'

Shan just stared in reply.

Tan clenched his jaw and let the words sink in. 'The bastards,' he snarled.

'Where did Lieutenant Chang serve before?'

'South of here. Border security zone. Under Major Yang.'

So he had a name after all, Shan thought. 'What do you know about this Major Yang?'

Tan shrugged. 'Hard as a rock. Famous for stopping smugglers. Takes no prisoners. Be a general some day.'

'Why, Colonel, would such an esteemed officer bother to personally make the arrest of Sungpo?'

Tan's brows furrowed. 'You know this?'

Shan nodded.

'A man like that goes anywhere he wants,' Tan said, sounding unconvinced. 'He doesn't report to me, he's Public Security. If he wants to help the Ministry of Justice, I can't stop it.'

'If I were conducting a Bureau investigation I don't think I would parade around the county in a brilliant red truck or buzz the countryside in a helicopter.'

'Maybe you're just bitter. I seem to recall that your warrant for imprisonment was signed by Bureau head-quarters. Qin ordered it, but the Bureau made it happen.'

'Maybe,' Shan admitted. 'But still, Lieutenant Chang tried to kill us. And Chang was probably working for the major.'

Tan shook his head in uncertainty. 'Chang's dead, and you still have a job to get done.' He rose as though to leave.

'Have you heard of the *Lotus Book*?' Shan asked, stopping Tan at the door. 'It's a work of the Buddhists.'

'The luxury of religious studies is not available to me,' Tan said impatiently.

'It is more of a catalogue,' Shan said in a hollow tone. 'They started writing it twenty years ago. A catalogue of names. With places and . . .' – he searched for a word – 'events.'

'Events?'

'In one section the names are nearly all Han Chinese. Under each name is a description. Of his or her role in destroying a gompa. Of participating in executions. Or looting shrines. Rapes. Murders. Torture. It is very explicit. As it is circulated it is expanded and updated. It has become something of a badge of honour, to add your name to its list of authors.'

Tan had stiffened. 'Impossible!' he flared. 'It would be an act against the state. Treason.'

'Prosecutor Jao was in the book. For directing the destruction of the five biggest gompas in Lhadrung

313

County. Three hundred and twenty monks disappeared. Another two hundred were shipped to prisons.'

Tan slipped into a chair, a new excitement on his face. 'But that would be proof. Proof that he was targeted by the radicals.'

'Lin Ziang of the Religious Bureau is in the book,' Shan continued. 'Twenty-five gompas and chortens destroyed at his command in western Tibet. Directed the transportation of an estimated $10 million worth of antiquities to Beijing where they were melted down for gold. Came up with the idea of allotting nuns to military installations for entertainment. Xong De of the Ministry of Geology was in there. Commanded a prison when he was younger. He had a predilection for thumbs.'

'I want it!' Tan bellowed. 'I want those who wrote it.'

'It does not exist in one volume. It is passed along. Copies are transcribed by hand. It is all over the country. Even outside.'

'I want those who wrote it,' Tan repeated, more calmly. 'What it says is unimportant. Just history. But the act of writing it –'

'I would have thought,' Shan interrupted, 'that just the one investigation was more than we could handle.'

Tan pulled out a cigarette and tapped it nervously on the table, as if conceding the point.

'I know prisoners in the 404th,' Shan continued, 'who can recite the details of atrocities committed in the sixteenth century by the pagan armies which attacked Buddhism, as if it happened yesterday. It is a way of keeping the honour of those who suffered, and keeping the shame of those who committed the acts.'

Tan's anger began to burn away. He did not, Shan suspected, have the strength for more than one battle at a time. 'This is your proof that the killings were connected,' he observed.

'I have no doubt of it.'

314

'But it just proves my point about the destabilizing force of the minority hooligans.'

'No. The *purbas* wanted me to know about it to protect themselves.'

'What do you mean?'

'They want us to solve the murders, too. They realized that if the Bureau found out about the book and thought it was connected to the killings, it would be used to destroy them. There's still one more of the Lhadrung Five left. One more murder to frame him for. And if someone in the top rank is assassinated, the knobs will move in permanently. Martial law. It would set Lhadrung back thirty years.'

'Top rank?'

'There was another name in the book,' Shan said. 'Listed for elimination of eighty gompas. Destruction of ten chortens to construct a missile base. Responsible for the disappearance of a truckload of *khampa* rebels being transported to *lao gai*. In April 1963.

'It's the only other *Lotus Book* name in Lhadrung. The only one still alive. A man who supervised the burning of another fifteen gompas. Two hundred monks died inside as the buildings burned,' Shan reported with a chill. He tore the entry he had transcribed from his notebook and dropped it onto the table in front of Tan. 'It's your name.'

Chapter Fourteen

Outside, Sergeant Feng stood uneasily between two knobs.

'Comrade Shan!' Li Aidang called from a dark grey sedan parked just across from the restaurant. The assistant prosecutor opened the door and gestured for Shan to climb inside. 'I thought we might chat. You know. Colleagues on the same case.'

'So you returned safely. Kham is such an unpredictable place,' Shan said dryly. He hesitated, seeing the uncertainty in Feng's eyes, then slid into the back seat beside Li.

'We found him, you know,' Li announced.

Shan willed himself not to take the bait.

'That is to say, we persuaded a clan in the valley to tell us where his camp was.'

'Persuaded?'

'Doesn't take much,' the assistant prosecutor said smugly. 'A helicopter, a uniform. Some of the old ones just whimpered. We found out where to look, but when we arrived they had gone. Fire ashes still warm. Not a trace.' Li studied Shan. 'As if they had been warned.'

Shan shrugged. 'Something I've noticed about nomads. They tend to move about.'

The door was slammed shut by one of the knobs, who climbed behind the wheel and started the engine. As they drove away Shan turned to see the remaining soldier step in front of the driver's door of their own truck, blocking Sergeant Feng's way.

A shadowy figure in the front seat turned and looked at Shan without speaking.

'You remember the major,' Li said.

'Major Yang, I believe,' Shan observed. 'Minder of Public Security.'

'Exactly,' Li confirmed tersely.

One side of the officer's face curled up in acknowledgment of Shan, then he turned away.

They moved out of town quickly, the horn blaring intermittently to scatter pedestrians and any vehicles that dared to get close.

Ten minutes later they entered an evergreen forest, in a small valley three miles or so from the main road. As they passed through the ruins of an ancient *mani* wall, a shrine wall carved with mantras, the trees began to assume an orderly appearance. They had been groomed. Spring flowers bloomed along the road, beside raked gravel.

They passed another wall, taller than the first, and entered the courtyard of a very old gompa. It had one tower of stone and grey brick and a small chorten, twice the height of a man, on the opposite side of the courtyard. Newly laid flagstones lined the courtyard. The walls had been replastered and were being painted. Along the far wall was a collection of statues of Buddha and other religious figures, several plated with gold. They were in a disorganized row, some facing the wall, some listing sharply, some propped against each other. Shan had the sense of visiting a wealthy, neglected villa. A faint aroma of peonies wafted through the courtyard.

The major disappeared behind a large gate. Li led Shan into the anteroom of the assembly hall, switched on a lightbulb and gestured towards a rough wooden table surrounded by stools. Shan studied the wiring, which was new. Few of the remote gompas were wired for electricity.

Li made a gesture that swept the room. 'We have done

what we can to preserve it,' he said with affected humility. 'It is always a struggle, you know.'

The floor was of the original wood planking, hand-cut centuries earlier. It was pockmarked with cigarette burns.

'There are no monks here.'

'There will be.' Li roamed about the room with the eye of an owner inspecting his premises. On pegs along the interior wall, robes had been arranged to give the effect of a lived-in gompa. 'Director Wen is arranging everything. A stop for the Americans. A few re-enactments. Let the Americans light some butter lamps and incense.'

'Re-enactments?'

'Ceremonies. For atmosphere.' Li selected one of the robes, an antique ceremonial robe with gold brocade and silk panels depicting clouds and stars. He slipped off his suit jacket and with a grin tried on the robe, stroking the sleeves with satisfaction as he continued speaking. 'We're finalizing things. Just a few more days before they arrive.' He strolled the room like a proud cockbird, trying to catch a reflection of himself in the small window panes. 'For a few dollars extra we'll let the Americans put on robes and spin prayer wheels. Soundtracks of mantras will play in the background. For a few more dollars we'll offer a one-hour course on how to meditate like a Buddhist.'

'Sort of a Buddhist amusement park?'

'Precisely! We think so much alike!' Li exclaimed, then sobered. 'Which is why I had to speak to you, Comrade. I have a confession to make. I have not been totally open with you. But now I must be, to make you understand something. I have a concurrent investigation, separate from Prosecutor Jao's murder. More important. But what you are doing, you have no idea of how damaging it could be. You make it very difficult.'

'Difficult?'

'Difficult for us to do the right thing. You are out of your element. You are being used.'

'I'm confused,' Shan said, studying a shelf of trinkets behind a table. 'Exactly which right thing are you speaking of?' There were small ceramic figures of yaks and snow leopards, and an entire row of muscular Buddhas carrying Chinese flags.

Li moved to a stool beside Shan, oblivious to the sound of popping threads in the shoulders of the old robe as he sat. 'Tan can pretend all he wants. It is a luxury of office. But you. You cannot pretend. I am sorry. We must be frank. You are a prisoner. You were a prisoner. You will be a prisoner. Neither you nor I can do anything to change that.'

'Assistant Prosecutor Li. I lost the capacity to pretend many years ago.'

Li laughed, and lit a cigarette. 'Go back to the 404th,' he said abruptly.

'It is not within my power.'

'Join the strike. We can let you resolve it. Big hero. Notation in your file. Maybe save a lot of lives.'

'What exactly are you offering?'

'We can reassign the troops.'

'You're saying you will recall the knobs if I stop investigating?'

Li walked over to the shelf of ceramic novelties. He picked up one of the Buddhas and blew into the bottom. Smoke came out of the eyes. 'It would solve a lot of problems.'

'You haven't said why.'

'Obviously there are things I am not permitted to tell you.'

'So you brought me here to tell me that you would not be telling me anything.'

Li stepped back to his side and patted Shan on the back. 'I like your sense of humour. I can tell you're from Beijing. Someday, who knows? You could fit well with us.' He paced around Shan. 'I brought you here to save you. The major and I are trying to find a way to be

319

generous. There've been too many victims. There's no need for you to be hurt further. If Minister Qin in Beijing wants you in *lao gai*, that's between you and him. But Minister Qin is very old. Someday you may have another chance. I can see you are an intelligent man. A sensitive man. You will be of use to the people again one day. But not with Colonel Tan. He is very dangerous.'

'I am no danger to him.'

Li studied his cigarette. 'I don't mean it that way. He manipulates you. He thinks he can ignore state procedures. Have you considered why he avoids the prosecutor's office?'

Shan did not answer.

'Or why he makes you work with unreliables?'

'Unreliables?'

'Discredited sources. Like Dr Sung.'

'I respect Dr Sung's medical expertise.'

Li shrugged. 'Precisely my point. You weren't told about her problems. Her prejudices. How she was refused her normal rotation home for neglect of duty. Went off for a week on her own decision to work on unauthorized patients.'

'Unauthorized patients?'

'A high mountain school. Very remote. Forgotten by anyone in Lhasa. Kids dying of something. They get things up there, diseases that have disappeared in the rest of the world.'

'So the doctor was punished for helping children who were dying?'

'That's not the point. The stated procedure is for such parents to bring their children to the clinic. She left a number of important patients at the clinic. Some were Party members. She won't be going home. Not for a very long time.'

'And no opportunity if she stays.' Shan was tempted to ask when the doctor's indiscretion happened. She had been invited to dinner but later denied membership in the

320

Bei Da Union. He remembered the nervous way she had recited to him party dogma on the inferiorities of the Tibetan minorities and policy on treating unproductive patients in the mountains. She must have been the subject of a *tamzing*.

'You understand,' Li said with affected gratitude. 'You put me in a very awkward position, Comrade Shan. What you are saying is that you want me to trust you, aren't you?'

Shan did not reply.

'This is most unorthodox. The prosecutor's office confiding in a convicted criminal.'

'I never had a trial, if that helps.'

Li raised his brows and slowly nodded. 'Yes, Comrade, good point. Not a convict, just a detainee.' He lit a second cigarette from the butt of the first. 'All right. You need to know. There is a corruption investigation. The biggest ever in Tibet. We were almost done. Jao was about to announce his conclusions. We can move soon. But you will make them flee.'

'So Jao was killed by a suspect in his corruption investigation?' Shan asked. It would be a very balanced solution. The kind of ending that would please the Ministry of Justice.

'Not exactly. It's just that this hooligan monk Sungpo, he had no idea of the effects of his murder. With Jao gone, the corruption case is in ruins. We've had to piece it together. We owe it to Jao to finish. We owe it to the people. But you are stirring up too much dust. You are beginning to frighten our suspects. You will ruin it.'

'If you're saying that Prosecutor Jao was going to arrest Colonel Tan, then Tan had more reason than anyone to kill Jao. Accuse him of the murder and Sungpo can be released. The knobs can stand down at the 404th. That's a solution.'

'Give me some evidence.'

'Against Colonel Tan?' Shan asked. 'I thought you meant you already had evidence.'

'One might surmise you could have reason to celebrate the passing of the old guard.'

'I have a preference,' Shan said contemplatively, 'for natural causes.'

'You can't possibly think Tan would protect you.'

'I have been relieved of the need to worry about protection. I have been entrusted to the custody of the state.'

A sneer built on Li's face. 'You are his fallback. His safety net. If you fail to build a case, he will create one. He will have his own case file even if you do not finish yours. All your actions can be construed as an effort to protect the radicals. Obstruction of justice is a *lao gai* charge in itself. I told you. I made inquiries about you. You weren't picked by Tan simply because you were an investigator. You were selected because by definition you are guilty. And expendable.'

It was the only thing Li had said that Shan believed. Shan watched his own fingers move, seemingly of their own volition. They made a *mudra*. Diamond of the Mind.

'No one will defend you. No one will say Shan is a model prisoner, a worker hero. Tan can't even put your name on the report. You don't exist. There is no need for you to be a victim also.'

It was the closest Li had come to putting his threat into words.

Shan studied his *mudra*. 'This place,' he said suddenly as he surveyed the room again. 'It is the Bei Da Union.'

Behind him, Shan sensed an abrupt movement by Li, as if his head had snapped up. 'It is an old gompa. It has many uses.'

'I saw a list of gompas licensed for reconstruction. This wasn't on it.'

'Comrade. I fear for you. You don't want to listen to those who want to help you.'

'Does it have a licence?'

Li sighed as he eased off the ceremonial robe and tossed it on a stool. 'It has been classified as an exhibition facility by Religious Affairs. It does not need a licence.'

Shan raised his palms in a gesture of frustration. 'I admire your ability to reconcile it all. For me, it is so confusing. If a group paid by Beijing meets to discuss educating the people it is socialism at work. But if people wearing red robes do so it is an unlicensed cultural activity.'

Li was studying Shan closely now. They were both aware of how dangerous the game was becoming. 'You have been out of touch, Comrade. Much progress has been made in defining the socialist discipline for ethnic relations.'

'I do not have the benefit of your training,' Shan admitted. He rose and moved to the door.

'Where are you going?' Li asked, annoyed.

'The sun is coming through the clouds.' Before Li could protest Shan was moving into the courtyard.

A van had arrived with markings for the Bureau of Religious Affairs. Workers were arranging benches at the side of the courtyard, as if for a lecture. Directing them was the young woman Shan had met at Director Wen's office – Miss Taring, the archivist.

The moment he saw her Shan understood. In their underground refuge the *purbas* had said they knew about Shan's discussion of the costume with Director Wen. There was only one person who could have told them. He studied Miss Taring as though for the first time. Her hair was tied in a tight bun at the back, and she wore a white blouse with a long dark skirt that gave her the gleam of professionalism, the model worker. She stopped, nodded casually and started to turn when she caught his gaze. She slowly turned away to issue orders to the workers, her hands behind her back. Shan was about to turn too when he saw her fingers moving. Her knuckles clenched together in fists, the thumbs facing each other at forty-five degree angles, the hands almost touching. He had seen it before, an offering *mudra*. *Aloke*, the lamps to light the world.

She held the *mudra* only a moment, then slowly turned her head towards the rear of the courtyard. She then walked to the far wall and stood beside one of the large Buddha heads, turning at an angle towards something Shan could not see.

He watched, perplexed, then walked towards the woman. She moved away before he reached the wall, not acknowledging him. He stood where she had stood, trying to understand. There was a gap between the buildings that was being blocked with brickwork. The job was not yet completed. He could see over the unfinished wall into an elegant courtyard. There was a man in the attire of a waiter carrying a tray with tall drinking glasses. A large wooden tub with steaming water was partially set in the ground. Two sleek young women in bikini swimsuits were stepping into it.

He slowly turned, confused, and found himself facing the opposite direction. He stared for a moment in shock. There was a low building, a stable converted to a garage. Inside it were two red Land Rovers.

Through the corner of his eye Shan saw Li approaching. He turned and slowly moved along the statue heads, letting Li catch up.

'Is Lieutenant Chang of the 404th part of your Bei Da Union?' he asked.

Li frowned. 'I believe he qualified for membership,' he said cryptically.

'How about a soldier named Meng Lau?'

Li ignored the question, and moved closer. 'Listen, you should become a witness,' Li offered. 'Surely having the lead in an investigation must be overwhelming for one in your position. Become a co-operative witness instead.'

'A witness from the 404th?'

'A witness recently transferred to trusty duties at the 404th, let's say. A model prisoner. I will vouch for you. You are always diligent, you have never been accused of lying, that kind of thing. Your problems have been of a different nature, in Beijing. The tribunal need not know of them.'

'But I have nothing to say.' Shan kept walking. There was a pool in one corner of the courtyard. It was made of stone blocks, elegantly carved centuries before, and was populated with small silver fish. Lotus blossoms floated in it, and an empty beer bottle.

'You might be surprised at what you could say,' Li said from behind.

Shan walked to the edge of the pool and turned. 'You haven't described the nature of your corruption investigation.' From his perspective he could see a small knoll just beyond the compound. On it was a magnificent seated Buddha, at least twenty feet high. It had an unfamiliar headdress. Shan recognized it with a start. Someone had bolted a satellite dish to the head of the Buddha.

Li moved to his side and bent towards his ear. 'Irregularities in the prison accounts. Unexplained withdrawals from state accounts. Missing military assets.'

'Are you saying that Tan and the warden are conspirators? You're implicating the warden?'

'Would you like him to be implicated?'

Shan stared, wondering if he had heard correctly. 'I would need to see your files.'

'Impossible.'

'Let me speak to Miss Lihau.'

'Jao's secretary? Why?'

'Let her confirm Jao's corruption investigation. She would know.'

'You know she is on vacation.' Li shrugged as he saw

the frustration on Shan's face. 'All right. You can send a fax.'

'I don't trust faxes.'

'Okay, okay, as soon as she returns.' He glanced at his watch. 'The car will return you to town.'

Shan climbed into the car without looking back. He knew Li was lying when he said he didn't want Shan to be a victim. But was he lying because he was worried about the investigation or just for all the usual reasons?

Li leaned into the window. The sneer was gone from his face. 'Damn you, Shan. I don't know why I'm telling you this. It's worse than you could ever imagine. Heads are going to roll and no one will be there to protect yours. You have to go back to the 404th and I have to get my case done before the madness starts.'

'The madness?'

'They're opening an espionage case. Someone in Lhadrung has stolen computer disks containing secrets of the Public Security border defences.'

Shan watched Dr Sung march past Yeshe sitting on the bench in the corridor and into her dimly lit office. She threw her clipboard on a chair, switched on a small desk lamp, and pushed aside a plate of old, half-eaten vegetables. She hit a button on a small cassette player and turned to a chessboard. It was in the middle of a game. Opera music began to play. She moved a pawn, then spun the board about. She was playing against herself.

After two moves she stopped and looked out at the bench. Muttering angrily, she twisted the lamp upward, illuminating Shan's chair in the corner.

'The most fascinating thing about investigations,' Shan observed with great fatigue, 'is discovering how subjective truth really is. It has so many dimensions. Political. Professional. But those are easy to discern. What is hardest is understanding the personal dimension. We find so many ways to believe in the lies and ignore the reality.'

326

The doctor switched off the music and stared absently at the chessboard. 'The Buddhists would say we each have our own ways of honouring our inner god,' she observed, with a choke in her voice.

The words shook Shan. Suddenly he did not know what to say. He wanted most of all to let her go, to leave the woman to her peculiar misery, but he could not. 'When did you stop honouring yours?'

He yearned for one of her sharp, angry comebacks, but all he got was silence.

Unfolding Sung's letter to the American firm, he dropped it in front of her. 'Did you feel you were lying to me when you pretended to know nothing about Jao's interest in an X-ray machine? Or did you really believe yourself because only your name was on the official record?'

'All I said was that it was too expensive.'

'Good. So you didn't mean to lie.'

Sung absently moved a castle. 'Jao asked me to write a letter. No one would suspect such a request from a clinic.'

'Why would he need to hide it? Why not just ask himself?'

She picked up a knight and stared at it. 'An investigation.'

'He would have wanted your help to operate it. He didn't say where he would need it?'

She still stared at the chess piece. 'Sometimes he would come, not very often, and we would sit here and play chess. Talk about things at home. Drink tea. It felt like, I don't know. Civilized.' She put both hands on the knight and twisted it as though to break it.

'So you wrote the letter to help in an investigation. To find something that was hidden.'

'It would be so easy, to be like you, Comrade Shan, just to ask questions. But I told you before, there are questions that may not be asked. All you have to do is ask about other people's truth. Some of us have to live it.'

'Did Jao mention a murder investigation?' Shan pressed. 'Corruption? Espionage?'

Sung laughed weakly. 'Espionage in Lhadrung? I don't think so.'

'What was he going to use the machine for?'

Sung shook her head slowly. 'He wanted to know if it would fit in one of his four-wheel-drive trucks. He wanted to know the power source it would require. That's all I know.'

'Why wouldn't you ask? He was your chess partner.'

'That's why.' Sung opened her hand and stared forlornly at the knight. 'I assumed he wanted it to open one of their tombs. And if I knew that I could not let him sit here again.'

The 404th was like a cemetery. The faces of prisoners, gaunt and expressionless, peered out of the barracks. The patrols which kept them confined to quarters marched stiffly through the compound. The soldiers kept looking over their shoulders.

The stable was in use. Shan could tell – not because there were screams. There were never screams from the Tibetans. Nor because of greater activity in the infirmary. He could tell because an officer who walked by was carrying rubber gloves.

A cloud seemed to have settled over Sergeant Feng as he moved through the gates with Shan. He did not speak to the knobs on guard at the dead zone but looked straight ahead until they reached the hut, then opened the door for Shan and stood to the side, gesturing him awkwardly inside.

The scene was much as it had been when he left the hut four days earlier. Trinle lay in bed, prostrated by fatigue, a blanket covering his head and most of his body. The others sat on the floor in a circle, taking instruction from one of the older monks.

Choje Rinpoche had braced his knees and back with a *gomthag* strap torn from his blanket, so he would not fall while meditating. One of the novices held a rag to the back of Rinpoche's skull. It came away pink with blood.

It took several minutes for him to acknowledge Shan's inquiries. His eyes fluttered, then opened wide and brightened. He surveyed the hut with an intense, curious gaze, as though to confirm which world he was in. 'You are still with us,' he said, not as a question but as a declaration of welcome.

'I need to know something about Tamdin,' Shan said, fighting the knot that was tying in his gut. It seemed he felt the lama's pain more than Rinpoche himself. 'Rinpoche,' he asked, 'what if Tamdin had to choose between protecting the truth and protecting the old ways?'

Of all the paradoxes that riddled his case, the one that troubled him most was that of the killer's motives. Tamdin was protector of the faith, and his victims defiled the faith. But how could such a killer then let innocent monks die for his crimes? That was defiling the faith too.

'I don't think Tamdin chooses. Tamdin acts. He is conscience with legs.'

And a flaying knife, thought Shan.

'Like conscience with legs,' the lama repeated.

Shan considered the words in silence.

'When I was young,' Choje offered, 'they said there was a man in a nearby village who prayed for Tamdin's help and never received it. He renounced Tamdin. He said Tamdin was a fiction created for the dancers in the festival.'

'I haven't met many recently who would call Tamdin a fiction.'

'No. Fiction is not the word to describe him.' Choje held his clenched fingers before Shan's face. 'This is my fist,' he said, then threw his fingers out. 'Now my fist does not exist. Does that make it a fiction?'

'You're saying in certain moments anyone can become Tamdin?'

'Not anyone. I'm saying the essence of Tamdin may exist in something that is not always Tamdin.'

Shan recalled the last time they had spoken about the demon protector. Just as some are destined to achieve Buddhahood, Choje had said, perhaps some are destined to achieve Tamdinhood.

'Like the mountain,' Shan said quietly.

'The mountain?'

'The South Claw. It is a mountain but it hides something else. A holy place.'

'It is such a small piece of the world we have,' Choje said, speaking so low Shan was forced to lean towards his mouth.

'There are other mountains, Rinpoche.'

'No. It's not that. This –' he said, gesturing around the hut. 'The world does not take notice of us. There is so much time before, and after. So many places. We are a mote of dust. No one outside should care about us. Only we should care about us. Our particular being occupies this place for now. That is all. It is not much, really.'

The words chilled Shan. Something terrible was going to happen. 'You're never going back to the mountain, are you?' He looked up with dread in his face. 'No matter what happens. You can't have the road built. That is what it's all about.' Why was it so important? Is that where he had gone wrong, not paying enough attention to the secret of the mountain?

'Waking up every day for fifty years, for a hundred years is no great accomplishment, after all,' Choje said with a serene smile. 'It is like arguing that your mote of dust is bigger than my mote of dust. They are the arguments of an incomplete soul.'

They would bring others to build the road, Shan wanted to say. But he did not have the courage.

'We have talked. All of us. Everyone has agreed. Except for a few. Some with families. Some who have another path to follow.'

Shan looked around. The *khampa* was gone.

'They have received our blessings. They were accepted across the line this morning. Those of us who are left . . .' Choje said with his peaceful smile. He shrugged. 'Well, we are the ones who are left. One hundred and eighty-one,' he repeated, still smiling.

The whistle for exercise blew, then another, and another, in relays through the camp. The men began to stir, without talking, towards the door.

'It is time, Trinle,' Choje called with new strength, and the figure in the blanket rose. Not taking his eyes off Choje, Shan sensed Trinle struggling to his feet. With a shudder he realized that Trinle must have been in the stable. From the corner of his eye he saw the stooped figure wrap the blanket around his makeshift robe and over his head like a hood, then shuffle to the door.

Only Shan and Choje remained in the hut. They sat in silence amid the brilliant shafts of light that leaked through the loose boards of the walls and roof.

'What happened to that man? The one who didn't believe?'

'One day part of the mountain above him collapsed. It destroyed everything. The man, his children, his wife, his sheep. And worse.'

'Worse?'

'It was strange. Afterwards, no one could remember his name.'

Suddenly there was a peculiar swelling of sound from outside – not a shout, but a rapidly rising murmur that carried through the camp. Shan helped Choje to his feet.

They found the prisoners in the small yard behind the

hut, or rather around the small yard, packed two and three deep around an empty space twenty feet in diameter.

'He's gone!' exclaimed one of the monks as they approached. 'The magic . . .' he began, but seemed unable to complete the sentence.

'Like the arrow! I saw it. Like a blur!' someone shouted.

The line parted to let Choje through, Shan at his side.

'Trinle!' one of the young monks whispered. 'He's done it!'

There was nothing in the clearing but Trinle's shoes, sitting side by side as if he had just stepped out of them.

No one breathed. Shan stared, stunned. It had the quality of a strange, poorly timed joke at first. He looked up with alarm as it sank in. Trinle was gone. Trinle had escaped. He had spirited himself away, after all the years of trying.

The monks stared reverently at the shoes. Some dropped to their knees and offered prayers of gratitude.

But the spell did not last long. From somewhere the whistle began to blow, signalling the end of the exercise period. From the back a man with a deep baritone voice began to chant. *Om mani padme hum*. He continued, solo, for perhaps thirty seconds, then was joined by another, and another, until soon the entire group joined in, drowning out the angry whistles.

The prisoners began to move into the central yard, celebrating the miracle with their mantra. Shan found himself moving with them, beginning the chant. Suddenly a hand seized his elbow and pulled him to the side. Sergeant Feng.

They stayed there, watching, as the prisoners arranged themselves in a large square and sat, still chanting loudly.

Instantly the knobs were among them. Shan could see the soldiers shouting, but their voices were lost in the reverberating mantra. He tried to pull away but Feng held him with an iron grip. The batons were raised and the knobs began slowly, methodically, to beat the prisoners on their shoulders and backs, swinging their batons up and down as if cutting wheat with sickles.

The batons had no effect.

A Public Security officer appeared, his face a mask of fury. He screamed into a bullhorn, but was ignored. He grabbed a baton from one of his men and broke it over the head of the nearest monk. The man slumped forward, unconscious, but the chanting continued.

He threw the stump of the baton to the ground and moved along the ranks. The scene unfolded as if in slow motion.

'No!' Shan shouted and twisted in vain against Feng's grip. 'Rinpoche!'

The officer paced around the entire square, then ordered two knobs to drag a monk to the centre. It was one of the younger men, from another hut. The monk had shaved his head and wore a red band on his arm. He continued chanting, still kneeling, seeming not to notice the knobs. The officer stepped behind him, drew his pistol, and fired a bullet through his skull.

Chapter Fifteen

Sergeant Feng had stopped speaking. As they drove out of the base onto the Dragon's Claw he gripped the wheel with both hands, a distant, desolate look on his face. He only grunted when they pulled into the turnout above the ancient suspension bridge. He did not argue this time, nor did he try to follow as Shan and Yeshe crossed over the span, each carrying small drawstring bags with a day's provisions.

The air was unusually still, without the wind that almost always rose with the sun. Shan surveyed the slope ahead with the binoculars. He still was not certain what to look for or where to go, only that the mountain held a vital secret. There was no sign of the sheep that might have led him to the enigmatic young herdsman. Perhaps he needed to return to the ledge with the chalk symbols. Then, at the southern end of the ridge, he spotted a patch of red among the early morning shadows. Once he had the pilgrim in the lenses, he could see the man was moving along the track at a remarkably fast pace, rising, standing, kneeling, and dropping in the act of *kjangchag*, the prostration of the pilgrim, as though the movements were callisthenics.

'I still don't know what it is we seek,' Yeshe said at his side.

'I don't either. Something out of the ordinary. The pilgrim, maybe.'

Yeshe shrugged. 'Each time we've been here we've seen a pilgrim. In Tibet it's ordinary as rain.'

'Which makes it a perfect camouflage.' Shan suddenly

saw what had been eluding him. 'Let's go,' he called out, still not certain of anything except that he wanted to know where the pilgrim was going.

They moved at a half trot along the ridge, keeping the pilgrim in sight. After an hour they had nearly caught up, and rested as they watched the figure begin its descent of the ridge towards the valley beyond.

The red robe arrived at the bottom of the ridge and disappeared behind a long formation of rocks. Shan and Yeshe shared a bottle of water and waited for the pilgrim to reappear on the other side of the rocks.

'My mother made a pilgrimage,' Yeshe said. 'After my sister died. I was away at the monastery already. She went to Mt Kalais,' he continued, referring to the most sacred mountain in Tibet. 'It was a bad time. Late blizzards in the mountains. Troop movements because of the uprising.'

'Such challenges add to the accomplishment.'

'We never saw her again. Someone said she became a nun, others that she tried to cross the border. I think it was probably simpler.'

'Simpler?'

'I think she just died.'

Shan didn't know what to say. He offered Yeshe the bottle and picked up the glasses. 'He hasn't come out,' he observed. Feng had loaned him his wristwatch for the day, and Shan stared at it in confusion. 'How long since he went behind that rock?'

'Ten, fifteen minutes.'

Shan leapt up and began trotting down the slope, leaving Yeshe still holding the bottle in his outstretched hand.

He intercepted the pilgrimage trail, worn by centuries of use, as it wound its way through the boulders and emerged into the rolling heather of the high valley. By the time Yeshe caught up, Shan had scouted past the rocks and retraced the pilgrim's route looking for a second trail, a cutoff, to no avail.

Minutes later Yeshe called out and pointed to a small hole, a low, six-foot-long tunnel created by a slab that had collapsed between two sheer rock walls. It was barely wide enough to crawl into. But by the time Shan arrived and bent to look into it, Yeshe had disappeared.

The hole, he discovered, did not end in six feet, but jogged at a sharp right angle to the left. Shan squeezed inside, following Yeshe's dim shape for fifty feet before the roof rose, then disappeared entirely. They were in a narrow, twisting passage between the rock walls, which they followed into a small canyon.

'We are not supposed to be here,' Yeshe whispered nervously. 'It is a holy place. A very secret place. It is protected . . .'

His words drifted away, his tongue silenced by the power of the scene before him. A sheer rock face, five hundred feet high, rose opposite them, a stone's throw away. Diamond-bright blades of sunlight cut through the canyon shadows, heightening the sense of elevation. A hundred feet up the wall were five large rectangular holes, windows, carved out of the rock. Three other smaller openings, obviously manmade, were arrayed above the five, leading to a final smaller opening nearly three hundred feet above them. Brilliantly coloured horse-flag banners, thirty feet long and emblazoned with sacred symbols, hung from poles below the five windows, flapping in the wind.

The Dragon Claws, Shan realized, were about to give up their secret.

'Into the shadows!' Yeshe cautioned, stepping behind a rock as though to hide. 'There is someone at the water.'

Shan peered towards the end of the canyon, where a shimmering pool of water reflected the images of the flags. Under a solitary willow tree at the end of the pool sat a lone figure, his back to them.

'We are not supposed to find this place,' Yeshe warned again. 'We should go. We can ask permission from the old –'

'There is no time for permission,' Shan said, and moved towards the pool. There were small irises growing among the rocks, and a flock of birds at the water's edge.

'Not everyone is glad that you came,' the figure said when Shan was ten feet from its back. It did not turn. The water and the rock gave a strange resonance to what was the voice of a child. 'But I had hoped we would meet again. They say things about you I do not understand. Now we can speak once more.'

'Your sheep have lost you again, I see,' replied Shan.

The youth turned about slowly, wearing a grin. 'Welcome to Yerpa.'

Shan gestured to Yeshe, who stood behind him. 'This is –'

'Yes. I have been told. Yeshe Retang. You may call me Tsomo.'

He rose and silently led them back towards the passage they had just left, then veered to the canyon wall where he entered a narrow cleft obscured by the shadows. Tsomo led them for twenty paces through the darkness, until they reached a dim butter lamp at the bottom of a winding stairway carved out of the living rock.

They climbed the steps until Shan's feet ached; then rested, then climbed further. Along the corridor were several low doors leading to darkened chambers. From one came the sound of a solitary prayer, from another a foetid smell and an abject groan. At last they reached a large chamber lit by a single long window and dozens of candles.

The walls were covered with murals, paintings of guardian deities and the past and future Buddhas. It was not the chapel Shan had expected. It was far smaller, and he began to understand that he was not in a gompa at all, but in another type of holy place he did not recognize. A

337

solitary man in the robe of a monk was on the floor, tapping a tapered metal tube from which vermilion sand fell. He sat at the edge of a six-foot wide circle, most of which had been filled with intricate shapes and geometric designs composed of coloured sands. The unfinished portion where he sat was inscribed with chalk.

'This is the Kalachakra mandala,' Tsomo explained. 'A very old style.'

The sand painting was in concentric rings which led to square lines depicting the walls of three palaces, one inside the other. Inhabiting the palaces were scores of deities presented in minute detail.

'It is about the evolution of time,' Tsomo continued, 'the folding of time, because Buddha cannot bear to abandon a single soul, so that time continues in a great circle until all beings are enlightened.'

Shan knelt reverently at the edge of the sand. The monk bowed his head towards him and continued working, building the mandala one particle at a time.

'Seven hundred and twenty-two deities,' Yeshe said behind him in a hushed tone. 'They used to do this in Lhasa every year, for the Dalai Lama.'

'Exactly,' Tsomo said enthusiastically, pulling Yeshe forward for a closer look. 'Dubhe trained with an old lama from the Potola. When it is completed it will have all the traditional deities, each one different, each in the prescribed position. Dubhe has worked on it for three years now. In four or five months he will finish. We will consecrate it, and celebrate its beauty. Then he will destroy it and start again with fresh sand.' Tsomo gestured to shelves of rough-hewn timbers that lined the lower walls. They held scores of small clay jars. 'Some of the sand from each mandala ever made here has been kept. It is very sacred, very powerful.'

They continued along a corridor to a bigger room lit by five windows, the rectangular openings they had seen from below. The chamber held wide, sloping tables of rough wood along its perimeter, most of which were empty. Three monks and a nun were at work, each surrounded by butter lamps and containers of brushes and ink stones.

Shan saw the look of deference from those at the tables as Tsomo approached, and the nervous way they studied Shan and Yeshe. They had been prepared to receive strangers, but clearly were uncertain how to react. They chose silence, letting Tsomo explain the elegant manuscripts they were transcribing, writing from ancient bamboo tiles and tattered prayer books onto long narrow pages that, in the traditional style, would not be bound but covered with silk wrappers. Above the tables were shelves holding scores of similar silk packages. They were called *potis*, Trinle had told Shan once, books wrapped in robes. At one table a monk sat not with brushes but with long chisels and gouges. He was carving the long boards between which the *potis* were tied. Shan paused at the table, surprised not by the intricate detail of the birds and flowers the monk was carving, but because the man could create such beauty despite the fact that one of his thumbs was missing.

The nun rose and wandered towards them. 'The history of every gompa in Tibet,' she said, gesturing to the far wall. Her voice was rough, as though from lack of use. 'There are letters from the Great Fifth to the *kenpos* announcing funds for new chapels. There are the original plans for the rope bridge across the Dragon Throat.'

Tsomo pulled Shan by the arm as the nun led an awestruck Yeshe along the manuscripts, away from the door. They moved up more steps to an inner chamber deep inside the mountain. It had the air of a classroom. There were only two lamps in the room, both on a small altar. At the far end were shelves of pottery, most of which was broken; above the pottery were symbols painted on the wall. There was a carpet on the floor, and seat cushions on which two monks sat.

One of the monks was facing away from them towards the altar. The other, an older, austere man with twinkling eyes, greeted them with a slight bow from his waist. 'You are most persistent, Xiao Shan,' the monk said in Mandarin. There was the sound of bare feet scampering behind him. Three boys in the robes of students moved inside and sat behind the monk who spoke. They looked at Shan with round, bewildered expressions.

'You have presented us with quite a dilemma, you know,' the old lama continued.

'I am only investigating a murder.' Shan's eyes moved back to the symbols above the pottery. With a start he realized he had seen them before, made in chalk at the ledge above the Dragon Throat Bridge.

'Yes. We know. The prosecutor was killed not far from here. Sungpo the hermit is detained. The 404th is on strike. Seventeen priests have been tortured. A prisoner has been executed. The Public Security Bureau is poised for another atrocity.'

'You know more about the 404th than I do,' Shan said in awe. 'Are you the abbot of this place?'

The man's smile seemed to cover his entire face. 'There is no abbot here. My name is Gendun. I am just a simple monk.' As he spoke his fingers worked rosary beads carved of dark reddish wood. 'Will they send you back there, when it is done?'

Shan paused, considering the man, not the question. 'Unless they choose a worse place.'

Another boy appeared with a pot of buttered tea and filled bowls in silence. From somewhere came the sound of *tsingha*, the tiny, chimelike cymbals of Buddhist worship.

'You said I was a dilemma,' Shan said as he accepted one of the bowls.

'Yerpa is the secret room of a house never seen, built in a land of shadow. Three hundred years ago one of our scholars wrote that in a book.' Gendun paused and smiled at Shan. 'We write books for each other some-times, since no one else can see them. He said we were between worlds here. A stopping-over place. Not of the earth, not of the beyond. He called it the mountain of dreams.'

'The eye of the raven,' the other priest said, still with his back to them. Something in his voice sounded familiar.

Tsomo smiled. 'In the library there is a poem, about the dead of winter. Among a hundred snowy mountains, it says, the only thing moving is the eye of the raven.'

Shan realized that Gendun was looking at Feng's wristwatch. Shan extended his arm.

'What do you call this?' the monk asked.

'A watch. A small clock.' Shan removed it and handed it to him.

Gendun looked at it with wonder in his eyes and held it to his ear. He smiled and shook his head. 'You Chinese.' He grinned, and handed it back.

Tsomo left his side with a small reverent bow, and knelt beside the second monk, who still faced the altar.

'Even before the armies came from the north this place was known only to the few who needed to know,' the old monk continued. 'The Dalai Lama. The Panchen Lama. The Regent. It is said to be one of the caves of the great Guru Rinpoche,' he said. 'It is a world in itself. Usually those who come never leave. It was as you see it five hundred years ago. It will be like this five hundred years from now,' he said with absolute confidence.

'I am sorry. But if we do not go back soldiers will come. We mean no harm.'

'The tunnel can be sealed against searchers. It has been done in the past. For years at a time when necessary.'

'He could teach us the way of the Tao,' Tsomo interjected. 'We could better understand the books of Lao Tze.'

'Yes, Rinpoche. It would be wonderful to have such a

teacher.' Gendun turned to Shan. 'Are you able to teach these things?'

Shan did not hear until he was asked the second time. The monk had called the boy Rinpoche, the term for a venerated lama, a reincarnated teacher. 'An old abbot once said to me, I can recite the books. I can show you the ceremonies. But whether you learn them is up to you.'

Tsomo gave a small laugh of victory, then rose and poured Shan more tea. 'They say in parts of China it is impossible to separate the Tao from Buddha's way.'

'When I lived in Beijing I visited a secret temple every day. On one side of the altar sat a figure of Lao Tze. On the other sat Buddha.'

Tsomo's eyes grew round again. 'Things always seem so far away from the top of a mountain. We have much to learn.'

The moment was magical. No one spoke. The sound of the *tsingha* grew closer. A boy appeared, the small cymbals dangling in front of him. Behind him came two women, nuns, one carrying a tray with two covered bowls and the second a large pot of tea. They set the objects before the altar and the monk who knelt there, his back still to Shan, began a ritual of blessing.

Shan knew he had heard the voice before, but there were so few monks he knew outside the 404th. Had he seen this man at Saskya? At Khartok, perhaps? He strained to see the man through the dim light as the nuns and monks spoke in turns, ceremonial words that Shan did not understand. When it was over the monk at the altar stood and straightened, then turned to face Shan.

'Are you ready?' he asked. It was Trinle.

They studied each other in silence. Shan felt strangely overwhelmed. For some reason he felt unable to ask how Trinle had spirited himself out of the camp, or why he had laboriously masqueraded as a pilgrim to reach Yerpa. Instead he followed them, Trinle and Tsomo and the two nuns, as they began climbing still another set of steep stairs, a narrow twisting passage worn, like the others, from centuries of use. After a minute's hard climb they reached a landing. The stairs continued ahead, but a dimly lit passage led to the left, towards the heart of the mountain. Along its sides several heavy wooden doors could be seen before the passage curved out of sight.

The group continued up the stairs, climbing in silence for at least five minutes. Twice Shan had to stop and lean against the wall, not from fatigue but from a strange overwhelming sense of passing through something, of straining against a barrier. He seemed to be hearing something but there were no sounds. He seemed to be seeing swarms of shadows shifting on the wall but there was only one steady lamp, carried far ahead. It was as though each step took them not towards another part of the mountain but towards another world. Each time he paused, Trinle was waiting with his serene smile.

They reached a landing with a thick wooden door, intricately carved with faces of protective demons and fastened with a heavy wrought-iron latch. Tsomo waited for them to gather on the landing and form a single file procession, then opened the door, and led the way into the chamber with a low prayer.

There was no one inside. It was a sparse, square room, perhaps thirty feet to a side, furnished with one rough-hewn table and two chairs, a large iron brazier for holding coals, and several shelves of manuscripts. One wall was covered with an intricate mural of the life of Buddha. The opposite wall was of cedar planks with a central wooden panel that seemed to match the door but it had no hinges or latches. It was held fast with huge hand-wrought bolts, fastened with nuts nearly the size of Shan's fist. On the floor beside it was one of the illuminated manuscripts, just below a black rectangular panel, perhaps ten inches high and twenty inches long.

Trinle silently lit more butter lamps and turned to Shan 'Do you know the term *gomchen*?' he asked, as casually as if they were together in their hut at the 404th. 'It is little used these days.'

Shan shook his head.

'A hermit of hermits. A living Buddha, on a lifetime hermitage,' Trinle said.

'It was the Second who decided the *gomchen* had to be protected,' Tsomo continued. 'A sacred trust. A small remote gompa had to be selected, to shelter him so deeply that the secret would always be kept.'

'The Second?' Shan asked in confusion.

'The Second Dalai Lama.'

'But that was nearly five hundred years ago.'

'Yes. There have been fourteen Dalai Lamas. But only nine of our *gomchen*.' Trinle's voice, almost a whisper, was filled with uncharacteristic pride.

Tsomo was at the manuscript now. He opened it to a page marked with a strip of silk. The serene smile returned to his face as he read.

The nuns uncovered the tray and set bowls of *tsampa* and tea where the manuscript had been. It wasn't a black panel on the wall, Shan realized. It was a hole in the wall, an access to a room beyond. He remembered the small solitary window high in the face of the cliff.

'You care for a hermit here,' he said in a whisper.

Trinle put his finger to his lips. 'Not a hermit. The *gomchen*,' he said, and silently watched as Tsomo and the nuns prepared the food. When they were done, Trinle joined them in kneeling on the floor and prostrating themselves towards the cell, chanting as they did so.

No one spoke until they had climbed down the long flight of stairs and re-entered the small chapel where Shan had discovered Trinle.

'It is hard to explain,' Trinle said. 'The Great Fifth, he said the *gomchen* was like one brilliant diamond buried in a vast mountain. Our abbot, when I was young, said the *gomchen* was all that was trying to be inside us, without the burden of wanting.'

'You said there was a trust. A gompa that protects the *gomchen*.'

'It has always been our great honour.'

Shan looked up, confused. 'But this place. It is not exactly a gompa.'

'No. Not Yerpa. Nambe gompa.'

Shan stared. 'But Nambe gompa is gone.' Choje had been the abbot of Nambe gompa. 'Destroyed by army planes.'

'Ah, yes,' Trinle said with his serene smile. 'The stone walls were destroyed. But Nambe is not those old walls. We still exist. We still have our sacred duty to Yerpa.'

Shan, numbed by Trinle's announcement, thought of Choje back at the 404th, performing his own sacred duty to protect Yerpa. He became aware that Tsomo was sitting beside him. 'He writes very beautifully, when he is not meditating,' Tsomo said. 'About the evolution of the soul.'

Shan remembered the manuscript in the ante-chamber. The *gomchen* communicated with them by writing religious tracts in the manuscript. 'How long has it been,' Shan asked, still awed, 'since the bolts were tightened?'

Trinle seemed hard-pressed to answer. 'Time is not one of his dimensions,' he said. 'Last year he recorded a conversation with the Second Dali Lama. As if he were there, as if it had just taken place.'

'But in years,' Shan persisted. 'When did he –'

'Sixty-one years ago,' Tsomo said. A flash of joy lit his eyes.

'It was a very different world,' Shan observed reverently.

'It still is. For him. He does not know. It is one of the rules. Outside is irrelevant. He only considers Buddhahood.'

'At night,' Tsomo said with a strangely longing tone. 'He can watch the stars.'

'You mean he doesn't know about . . .' Shan struggled to find the words.

'The troubles of the secular world?' Trinle offered. 'No. They come and go. There has always been suffering. There have always been invaders. The Mongolians. The Chinese, several times. Even the British. Invasions pass. They do not affect our good fortune.'

'Good fortune?' Shan asked, his voice breaking with emotion.

Trinle seemed genuinely surprised at Shan's question. 'To have been able to pass the current incarnation in this holy land.' He studied Shan. 'The suffering of our people is unimportant to the work of the *gomchen*,' Trinle said with new concern in his voice as he studied Shan. It was as though he felt a need to calm his visitor. 'He must not be burdened with the world. That is why there was so much concern, the first time you met Tsomo.'

'When I met Tsomo?'

'Consultations were made. Had he been contaminated? we asked.'

'If it is unimportant inside, it must be kept unimportant outside, I told them,' Tsomo offered.

Suddenly, with painful clarity, Shan understood. 'He could die soon, the *gomchen*.'

'At night we can hear him coughing,' Trinle said heavily. 'There is blood sometimes in his basin. We offer more blankets. He will not use them. We must be ready. Tsomo is the Tenth.'

The announcement sent a shiver down Shan's spine. He stared, speechless, at the vibrant, wise youth who would soon be locked into the stone for ever. Tsomo returned his stare with a broad smile.

They walked Shan back to the library where Yeshe was still poring over the manuscripts. As Trinle and Tsomo joined Yeshe, Gendun appeared at the door.

'I believe Prosecutor Jao was killed to protect your

gompa.' Shan spoke abruptly, before they entered the room.

'The prosecutor had many enemies,' the old monk observed.

'I mean, I believe his murder was committed on the Dragon's Claw to protect the *gomchen*.'

Gendun shook his head slowly. 'Every morning we have a prayer. A blessing of the wind, to be gentle on the birds. A blessing of our shoes, to keep them from treading on insects.'

'What if there were other Tibetans who wanted to protect you, who cared less than you about killing insects?'

The old man looked very sad. 'Then the trust imposed on us by the Second would have been broken. We could not accept being protected by a violation of a holy vow.'

Shan moved around the room and paused at the row of windows. Gendun joined him a moment later. The small pool was lit by the sun now. Near the water, lying in the sunlight, were four figures on blankets. They were not meditating, but lay as though debilitated, without the strength even to sit.

'You have sickness here?' he asked the monk.

'It is the price we pay. In recent years there have been new diseases which our herbs cannot cure. Sometimes we get pockmarked faces and fevers. We sometimes move to the next life at an early age.'

'Smallpox,' Shan said in alarm.

'I have heard that name, from the valley,' Gendun nodded. 'We call it rotting cheek.'

Shan studied the frail forms below him with a sense of helpless horror. What was it Li had said when he mocked Dr Sung? Sometimes in the mountains they contract diseases that had disappeared in the rest of the world. He had a sudden, waking nightmare, in which all the monks had died of disease, and left the *gomchen* sealed in his chamber. He blinked away the vision and turned back to the room. Gendun had stepped to the table beside Yeshe. Shan was unattended for the moment. The monks were all with Yeshe now, who was firing a barrage of excited questions at them as he studied another ancient manuscript. Shan quietly moved out of the room.

The hallway was clear. He ran up the first flight of stairs to the landing and stepped into the dimly lit passage. He pulled one of the butter lamps from its niche in the wall and opened the first door.

It was a small room, not much more than a closet. Its shelves were filled with folded tapestries. A huge cedar trunk held nothing but four pairs of worn sandals.

The next room was bigger, but its only contents were clay jars of herbs and boxes of ink brushes.

The third contained huge ceramic jars of barley and, on a central table, a four-foot-long wrought-iron wrench. He stopped in frustration. There should be costumes. He had been certain there would be costumes. Someone had broken the trust and used a costume from Yerpa to kill Jao. He followed the curve of the passage at a jog, passing four more doors until he reached the end, where a large tapestry of the lives of Buddha was hung. He pushed it aside. It concealed a door.

The room was larger than the others, mustier, heavy with the scent of incense. He held up the lamp with a sigh of satisfaction. Gold brocade flickered in the light. The costumes were there, eight in all, laid out on deep shelves along each wall. His hand closed around the *gau* on his neck and he stepped forward. The skeletal leatherbound arms of the creatures hung out of the sleeves. He stepped to the nearest, raised the lamp to the head and groaned in horror.

He fell to his knees. A dry heave wracked his belly.

'It is a very special place,' someone said behind him. It was Tsomo.

Shan slowly looked up, filled with self-revulsion. 'I

didn't –' he croaked. 'I had to know. If there were costumes. For demon dancers.'

Tsomo nodded, forgiveness already in his eyes. 'It is understandable. But this is a poor hermitage. We do not celebrate many festivals. We have no such costumes.'

Shan stood and lifted his eyes. 'I was afraid you had Tamdin here. I had to . . .' He did not finish the sentence.

'Not here. Here –' Tsomo extended his hand reverently towards the silent forms on the shelves. 'Here it is just a few old men asleep in their mountain.'

Shan began backing out, the scene of the mummified hermits of Yerpa forever seared into his brain.

As he closed the door, Tsomo smiled serenely. 'Sometimes I visit them, to meditate. I am very peaceful when I am with them.'

When they met Yeshe at the door to the mandala room, Gendun handed Yeshe and Shan each one of the small jars from the shelves.

'A hundred years ago there was a very great mandala, done by a monk who was soon to become our *gomchen*. These are the last of his sands.'

Yeshe gasped and pushed the jar back. 'I cannot take such a gift.'

Gendun smiled. 'It is not a gift. It is an empowerment.'

Shan saw that Yeshe understood. The gift was their trust. The old monk put his hand on the back of Yeshe's head and uttered a small prayer of farewell.

They spoke no more until they were at the rock maze that led out of Yerpa. Yeshe had already disappeared into the rocks when Tsomo put a hand on Shan's shoulder.

'Why do you do this?' Shan asked. 'Why endanger your secrets with me?'

'I would be saddened if you thought them a burden.'

'Not a burden. An honour. A responsibility.'

'Trinle and Choje, they decided it was no longer honourable not to let you know.'

'But will it help me find the murderer?' Shan said in a

near whisper, his hand clasped around the jar of sand in his pocket. They had given him empowerment. Could the secrets of Yerpa empower him to save Sungpo?

Tsomo shrugged. 'Perhaps it will just make it easier when you do not find him. You must remember what you told me that first day. From Lao Tze. To know that you do not know, that is best.' The youth gave a small smile that seemed almost mischievous.

'There is something that puzzles me about you,' Shan said. 'The *gomchen* knows nothing about the world outside. But you are the future *gomchen*. You know about it. Invaders. Murder. Massacre.'

Tsomo shook his head. 'I do not know those things. I am trained not to look beyond the mountains. I have heard of such possibilities. Like our Ninth heard of the Great War and that the Emperor Pu Yi had been dethroned in Beijing. But they are only words. Like hearing of the atmosphere of a distant planet. Like fables. Not one of my realities. I have not encountered them.' He studied Shan in silence for a moment. 'I have encountered you. You are the most outside I have ever been.'

Shan didn't know whether to laugh or cry. 'I'm not much to judge the world by.'

'There is no need to judge. I only celebrate what the great river of life pushes towards us. One day in his book, our *gomchen* drew a picture of a Buddha with long flat wings. It is what he saw when an aeroplane flew over.'

Shan looked up at the high, tiny window, barely visible in the afternoon shadows. 'I am envious,' he said.

'Of the *gomchen*?'

Shan nodded. 'I think it is best,' he said heavily, 'to know of not knowing.'

Chapter Sixteen

Rebecca Fowler was at her desk, her head propped up on one arm, a haggard expression on her face.

'You look like hell,' she said, as Shan walked in.

'I have been on the South Claw,' Shan replied, trying to fight the exhaustion of his day. 'Exploring.' Sergeant Feng was sharing cigarettes with workers outside. Yeshe was asleep in the truck. 'I need to ask you something.'

'Just like that,' she said, the bitterness returning. 'Something came up while you were strolling over the Dragon Claws.' She ran her fingers through her mop of auburn hair and looked up, not waiting for an answer. 'I took his hand up there. Your demon's hand. They wanted me to recite mantras with them. Something began howling up on the mountain.'

'Something?'

She didn't seem to hear him. 'The sun went down,' she recounted with a haunted expression. 'They lit torches and continued the mantra. The moon came out. The howling began. An animal. Not an animal. I don't know.' She put her head in her hands. 'I haven't slept much since. It was all so – I don't know. So real.' She looked up apologetically. 'I'm sorry. I can't describe it.'

'There was a man from Shanghai in my hut last year,' Shan said quietly. 'He scoffed at the monks at first. But later he said sometimes at night when he heard the mantras he held his hand over his mouth for fear his soul would pop out.'

The American responded with a small, grateful smile. 'I need to see maps. Satellite maps.'

She winced. 'When Public Security approved my satellite licence they made us agree to a protocol for access. Only eight authorized people. Software generates a log for every printout. The major was quite insistent. So they can be sure we're not looking at something we're not supposed to see.' She was growing distant, suddenly wary of Shan. His request seemed to have scared her.

'That's why I came to you.'

She sighed but did not reply.

'I'll need the sections that cover the South Claw. More than one date. But including the date of Jao's murder and one month before.'

'I was supposed to be at the back ponds an hour ago.'

'I need your help.'

'The tourists arrive in Lhadrung in three days. My monthly report is already a week overdue. Faxes came from California, demanding to know if I resolved the permit suspension. I have a job to do. My shareholders expect me to do it. The Ministry of Geology expects me to do it. Beijing expects me to do it. The ninety families that depend on this mine for survival expect me to do it.' She stood and lifted the hard hat that sat on her desk. 'You, Mr Shan, are the only one who doesn't expect me to do it.'

'I thought it was a simple request.'

'It's not. I just told you. Somehow I think you never make simple requests.'

'I think Jao was taken to the South Claw to be killed because of something seen on one of your maps.'

'Seen by Jao?'

'Maybe. Or by the murderer. Or both.'

'Ridiculous. We're the only ones who see the maps.'

'You said eight people. With eight people secrets can be difficult to keep.'

'If you think I'm going to invite half the Bureau to climb all over us for some security violation, you're crazy.' She took a step towards the door. 'I thought you and I, we were –' she shook her head and sighed. 'When we first got the satellite licence Kincaid said Colonel Tan might try to trick us into giving up the maps.'

'Why would Colonel Tan do that?'

'To catch us in a security violation, then use it against us.'

'Do you think I am trying to trick you?'

Fowler sighed. 'Not you. But what if you are being used?' She took another step towards the door. 'Get someone to put it in writing.'

'No.'

She looked back over her shoulder.

'Because then you *would* be caught in a security violation,' he observed.

She shook her head slowly and moved towards the door again.

'I knew a priest once. When I lived in Beijing. He used to help me.' Shan spoke to her back. 'Once I had a similar dilemma. About whether to seek justice or to just do what the bureaucrats wanted. Do you know what he said? He told me that our life is the instrument we use to experiment with the truth.'

Fowler stopped and slowly turned again. She looked at him in silence, then tore herself away to pour a cup of tepid tea from a thermos. She sat and studied the cup. 'Damn you,' she said. 'Who the hell are you? Every time things are calming down, you . . .' she didn't finish the sentence.

'We want the same thing. An answer.'

She rose, threw the tea in the sink, and stepped into the computer room. Unlocking a large cabinet with long narrow drawers, she quickly sifted through the top drawer and laid a sheet on the table. 'We only print them once a week, sometimes only twice a month. This is two weeks ago. Twenty-mile grid. Best for our purposes. We also have a hundred miles and five miles.'

'I need more detail. Perhaps the five-mile grid.'

She searched through the drawer and looked up, confused, then opened a second drawer. 'It's not there. None of them for the South Claw.' She gazed at the empty drawer.

'But you can print more,' Shan suggested.

'Kincaid would be furious. It comes out of his budget. He's responsible for the mapping system.'

'You said you wanted this thing over.'

'At this point I'd be satisfied just to know what *over* means,' Fowler said, then stepped to the console and began typing instructions. Five minutes later the printer came to life.

As she laid the photo on the table she handed Shan a magnifying lens. He followed the slope of the ridge towards the bottom of the map. At its end, where the small valley to the south began, was a V-shaped blackness. 'Are they all taken at the same time of day?' he asked. There was an hour written on the margin. 1630 hours. 'Can we obtain something from earlier in the day? Noon, perhaps.'

She printed one, dated two months earlier, taken at 1130 hours. The shadow at the south end of the ridge was gone. He could see them now, in the remote gorge, a smudge of brilliant colour where none had been before. The big horse flags of Yerpa were visible to the satellite.

'That night with Jao,' Rebecca Fowler said abruptly. She had been watching him, from across the table. 'There was something else. I didn't tell you. It wasn't just because of the wager that we met. We could have done that later. I think he wanted to meet because he had asked some questions. He pressed for answers that night.'

'Questions for you?'

'We talked about it. Kincaid and I. We didn't want to obstruct anything. But with all of our production problems we didn't need to become part of some investigation.'

'But you changed your mind later.'

'When the ponds were being laid out, before I arrived, the mine got its water permits. Rights to take water for the ponds and processing unit as needed. You have to be registered, so irrigation in the valley can be planned. When I got here I saw there was a mistake. The permit covered a stream that doesn't flow here. It's on the other side of the mountain, the far end of the North Claw and beyond, a different watershed. I told Director Hu. He said he would take care of it, that we wouldn't have to pay for the water. We didn't pay. But the permit was never changed.'

'What does it mean, having the permit for that watershed?'

'Not much. Just keeps anyone else from using the water, I guess.'

'So it was a bureaucratic oversight.'

'It's what I assumed. But Jao, as soon as he sat down to dinner, wanted to know about it. He had found out about it somehow, and he was excited. He asked who issued the permit. How much water was available in that area. I couldn't tell him. He asked if I had a copy of the permit somewhere, with an official signature. When I said I did, he was very pleased. It seemed like he wanted to laugh. He said he would call from Beijing with a fax number, so I could send it to him. Then he dropped the subject. Ordered some wine.'

Voices rose from outside. Workers were approaching the building. Fowler sprang up to close the red door. She leaned against it, as though bracing for intruders. 'I forgot about it. Then Li came into my office. Trolling for information about the permit.'

'Trolling?'

'He knew about it. He had questions but didn't seem sure of what he wanted to know. He asked me to explain what Jao had asked for.'

'He's the assistant prosecutor,' Shan said. 'Probably

Jao's replacement. There may have been a file he needed to follow up on.'

'I don't know,' Fowler said. She looked at the floor as she spoke. 'What if they had to do with Jao's being killed? The water rights. That's not something a Tibetan would kill for. Why would that monk care?'

'I told you before, Sungpo did not kill him.'

She fixed him with a forlorn stare. 'Sometimes I wonder. If it got Jao killed, then what about me? That dinner. We talked a long time. Maybe the killer thinks I know what Jao knew. Someone may want to kill me and I don't even know why. Nothing makes sense. If it wasn't this monk Sungpo, then who is trying to frame him? Colonel Tan? Assistant Prosecutor Li? The major? They all seem in such a rush to get him to trial.'

'They say they're just eager to get the file closed, because of all the visitors.'

'Someone may be lying for personal reasons, not just political ones.'

Shan offered a nod of respect. 'You've learned fast, Miss Fowler.'

'It scares me.'

'Then help me.'

'How?'

'I need more maps. The skull cave, perhaps.'

'We don't have them. We only have maps of our watershed.'

'But the computer can give you access.'

'We have a contract for this area. Outside that, it's expensive. Fifty dollars an order. U.S. We type in the grid reference. Some computer back home processes the order, verifies our account number, processes it for download, and invoices us.'

'A grid reference?'

'There's a catalogue with map grids, identified by a code for the grid number.'

Shan reached into his pocket and pulled out the

numbers transcribed from Jao's secret file. 'The catalogue,' Shan asked with new urgency. 'Is it here?'

The numbers fitted the format perfectly. It took less than five minutes to find the reference. It was for the North Claw and farmland beyond. Jao had seen photos of the area where Fowler had mistakenly received water rights.

'But he didn't get these from us,' Fowler protested. 'They're unrelated to our operations. We would never order maps outside our operations area.'

'Are you sure? Is there a record?'

'The invoices show all the orders. I'm about three months behind in checking the details.' They moved into her office. Five minutes later she located the entries. Someone had ordered a three-month sequence of photos of the northern site two weeks before the prosecutor had been killed.

Shan put the invoice in his notebook. 'Can you print them out, the same ones Jao saw?'

Fowler nodded weakly.

Shan stood in the doorway to verify that no one was in earshot. 'Bring them to me tomorrow at Jade Spring. And I need to take the disks. The ones you took from the cave.'

Fowler hesitated. 'I need them, too.'

'Have you looked at them?'

'Sure. Mostly files in Chinese that Kincaid and I can't read. Some in English, listing contents of the shrine. They sent the altar to a new restaurant in Lhasa. Jansen will want to know.'

'Why would they put them in English?'

Fowler cocked her head at Shan. 'I hadn't thought about it.'

'Because,' Shan suggested, 'it is a trap.'

She sat down heavily at her desk. 'For us?'

'For you. For me. For Kincaid. Whoever might take them. I think the major put them there.'

'I want to give them to the United Nations office.'

'No.'

'Why the major?'

Shan dropped into a chair by the wall. 'Sort of an insurance policy.' He leaned over, placing his head in his hands for a moment. He had an overwhelming temptation just to curl up on the floor and sleep. He looked up. 'If you were forced out as manager, who would replace you?'

Fowler grimaced. 'You're talking about the permit suspension,' she said with a sigh. 'There's a procedure in the contract. The company appoints the first manager. After that, the committee would have the choice.'

'An American?'

'Not necessarily. Kincaid, maybe. But it could be Hu.'

'If you want to keep your job, Miss Fowler, I need those disks.'

She considered Shan for a moment, then with a quick, urgent movement pulled some books from a top shelf. Reaching behind the other volumes, she produced a thick envelope and dropped it into his hand.

'I need something else,' Shan said apologetically. 'I need you to take me to Lhasa.'

Colonel Tan was waiting in their room at Jade Spring, sitting in the dark, smoking. Feng and Yeshe hesitated as they saw Tan's expression, then moved out to the front step as Shan turned on the light and sat across from him. Five cigarette butts stood end up in a row beside a folder on the table.

Tan's face was drawn and tense. He seemed worn out, as though he'd just returned from extended manoeuvres. 'You believed them, didn't you?' He spoke to the cigarette. 'That I did those things in the *Lotus Book*.'

'I only repeated what I read,' Shan said. The air was so brittle it seemed about to shatter. 'Is it so important what I believe?'

'Hell no,' Tan snapped back.

'Then why should you be so offended by what is in the *Lotus Book*?'

'Because it is a lie.'

'You mean because it is a lie about you.'

'Sergeant Feng!' Tan bellowed.

Feng's head appeared at the door.

'Where was I in 1963?'

'We were at Border Security Camp 208. Inner Mongolia. Sir.'

Tan pushed the folder towards Shan. 'My service record. Everything. Postings. Commendations. Reprimands. Assignment orders. I didn't come to Tibet until 1985. If you want, talk to Madame Ko. I want the lies stopped.'

'Do you want Sungpo executed or do you want the lies stopped?'

Tan glared across the table. In the dim light, as he exhaled the smoke through his nostrils, his bony face seemed to hover, disembodied, above the table. 'I want the lies stopped,' Tan repeated.

'That's not going to help the monk who was executed at the 404th.'

'That's the knobs. They didn't consult me.'

'Somehow I find it hard to believe, Colonel, that you couldn't stop the knobs if you wanted to.'

There was a low, surprised curse by the door, and Shan caught a glimpse of Sergeant Feng as he retreated towards the parade ground. He did not want to be caught in the imminent explosion.

Tan's glare continued, hot and silent.

'I had an offer from Assistant Prosecutor Li. A way to resolve it all,' Shan announced.

'An offer?' Tan repeated ominously.

'To tie it all up in a neat package. He said Prosecutor Jao was engaged in a corruption investigation against you. So you had him killed. Said if I testified against you, he could make me a hero.'

Tan's eyes narrowed to two dangerous slits. His hand wrapped around the cigarette package on the table and began to slowly squeeze its contents. 'And your intentions, Comrade?' Shreds of tobacco fell from the package.

Shan's gaze stayed steady. 'Colonel, I could say you are insensitive, stubborn, short-tempered, manipulative, and quite dangerous.'

Tan shifted in his seat. He seemed on the verge of leaping for Shan's throat.

'But you're not corrupt.'

Tan gazed down at the ruined package of cigarettes. 'So you didn't believe him.'

Shan shook his head slowly. 'You never trusted Li. That's why you found me. You thought he might try something like this. Why?'

'He's a snivelling Party pissant, that's why.'

Shan considered the words and sighed. 'No more lies, you said.'

With an angry sweep of his hand Tan batted the mess he had made off the table. 'Miss Lihua caught him a few months ago, about to send a secret report to Party headquarters in Lhasa. Complaining that Jao and I were incompetent, not in touch with modern governmental technique, petitioning for our forced retirement.'

'You could have told me.'

'It's hardly evidence for a murder case.'

Shan clasped his hands and looked into them. 'Li is in it, I know it. There is no direct evidence. But everything he says, everything he does, the smell is all over him.'

'Smell?'

'Like why he went to Kham.'

'He went because you went.'

'Not because he was following me, but because he sensed I was getting too close, because Li realized that if I

360

thought there might be a witness I would go in search of him. Back in Balti's tenement, Li tried to make us believe that Balti had stolen the car and left for a city to sell it. But Li knew differently. If I was getting close, then Li had to get to Kham urgently, because he knew for certain that Balti was still alive. Which meant he saw him running away that night. Or the murderer told him.'

The colonel breathed heavily. 'You're saying it's not only Li.' He searched the crushed pack for an intact cigarette, then threw it down in disgust.

'There was something else, something he said when he made me the offer. That if I co-operated he would have the knobs pulled out of the 404th.'

'Impossible. Li does not control the Public Security Bureau.'

'Exactly.' Shan let the words sink in. 'But all he would need is the co-operation of a senior officer in the regional command. Maybe the same officer who brought Lieutenant Chang up from the border.'

A different kind of fire began to burn in Tan's eyes. 'What do you want me to do?'

'Send for Miss Lihua. We need her here, to interview face to face.'

'Done. What else?'

'One of the gold skulls from the cave. I want one, a sample, as evidence.'

Tan nodded.

'And the prosecutor had an important meeting in Beijing. Something to do with water rights. Something about a Bamboo Bridge. We need to find out everything about it. It is not something I can do, and not something you can do. But you have someone who can.'

There was movement at the door. Feng had drifted back. Yeshe was standing in the shadows just outside the entrance.

'One more thing, Colonel. I need to know. In the

Lhadrung uprising, did you have the thumbs of monks cut off?'

'No!' Tan spat. He stood up so fast his bench toppled over. He looked at Feng and back to Shan. The fire in his face did not stop Shan's steadfast stare. Slowly, the defiance in his eyes faded and Tan seemed to swallow something hard. 'The damned Buddhists,' he said in a beseeching tone. 'Why can't they give up?'

Because they're better people than you or I, Colonel, Shan almost said.

Tan dropped his eyes to the table. 'Yes,' Tan said in a much lower voice. 'I knew the Bureau was cutting thumbs and I could have stopped them.' He grimaced, straightened his tunic, and marched out of the barracks.

There was a heavy silence as Sergeant Feng and Yeshe stepped in. Feng righted the bench and began to sweep up the tobacco.

'How about you, Sergeant?' Shan asked. 'Do you want it to stop this time?'

The sullen expression had not left Feng's face all day. 'I don't understand anything any more.' He wrung his fingers together. 'They shouldn't be killing my prisoners.'

'Then help me.'

'I am. It is my job.'

'No. Help me.' Shan glanced at Yeshe, who had moved to a bed. 'Sungpo will be executed in four days. If he is, we will never know who the murderer is. And the 404th will be sacrificed.'

'You're one crazy son of a bitch, thinking you can stop them,' Feng muttered.

'Not just me. All of us.' He gazed at his two exhausted companions. 'In the morning, early, the Americans will come with maps. Photo maps. Yeshe will need to study them, and examine these disks.' Shan pulled the envelope from his pocket and handed it to Yeshe. 'It will take several hours.'

He turned to Feng. 'I want you to join Jigme in the

mountains. Four eyes are better than two. I want you to stay until you find where the demon lives.'

The sergeant seemed to shrink. Then his eyes turned up, sad but determined. 'How?'

'Go to the shrine by the Americans. See if the hand of Tamdin is still there. If it is, follow it when it leaves. If it's gone, find who has been leaving prayers for protection against dogbite. And follow them.'

Feng dropped onto the bench. 'You mean leave you? It's not in my orders.' The words were spoken not in protest, but as a chagrined declaration. 'I don't know how to read prayers,' he muttered. 'That Jigme, he won't either.'

'No. You will take someone with you who does know. An old man. I will arrange for you to meet him in the market.'

'How will I recognize him?'

'You already know him. His name is Lokesh.'

Tyler Kincaid seemed highly amused. As they cleared the security checkpoint at the county border, he accelerated the truck and made a whooping sound, the kind Shan had only heard before from cowboys in American movies. Rebecca Fowler turned and pulled away the blanket that covered Shan. He climbed up from the floor and sat on the backseat.

'They never check,' she said in a taut voice. 'Just a wave.'

'Like some big MFC,' Kincaid cracked. He tried to look at Shan, who was rubbing the circulation back into his legs. He had been lying on the floor for nearly two hours, since they had left Yeshe with a stack of photo maps at Jade Spring. 'Someone said you were a big man in the Party once. Said you took on the chairman and lost.'

'Nothing so dramatic.'

'But that's why you're here, isn't it? You took on the

MFCs. They're the ones who put you in prison, right?' Kincaid asked, in the same light-hearted tone.

'Someone must be living a very unfulfilled life, to waste time talking about me.'

Fowler glanced back with a grin.

'And you, Mr Kincaid, is your injury healing?'

The American held up his arm, still covered with a long bandage. 'Sure. Good as new soon. High-altitude healing, it's great conditioning for the climb up Chomolungma.'

'We should do Gonggar first,' Fowler suggested. They were going to drop off brine samples at the airport for shipment to Hong Kong. Behind Shan sat two large square wooden crates, each holding twelve stainless-steel cylinders. The crates were their cover.

'There's a jacket,' she explained. 'With a mine logo. Put it on. At the airport just help with the crates like you work for us.'

'But afterwards,' Shan asked, 'do you have authority to go to Lhasa? I could find a ride with a truck driver.'

'And how do you get back? How many truck drivers are going to risk hiding a stranger without papers at the checkpoint? We'll just go see Jansen at the UN office. I want to talk to him about the skull shrine.'

'It's just that you shouldn't be involved, shouldn't be at further risk,' Shan said. 'You're risking too much already.'

'I want this thing over,' Fowler said with a new tone, almost pleading. 'If you get caught it may never be over.' She turned towards the backseat. The haunted look Shan had seen after she returned the demon's hand was there again. 'They came last night. I guess that's what you were trying to warn me about.'

'Who came?'

'Public Security. Not the major. Tyler called the major to complain. It was a squad of technicians, seemed like.

All they did was search the computers. Looked at every hard drive and disk.'

'Big MFC show,' Kincaid observed with a small, sour smile. 'Just to keep us scared. Routine. They know we help Jansen. We know they know. We know they want it to stop. They know if they push too hard the UN could get really interested, call out the watchdogs.'

'The UN has watchdogs?'

'Human rights investigators.'

Shan stumbled on the words. Human rights investigators, he repeated to himself. The Americans used the words so casually. They didn't come from another part of his world. Surely they came from a whole different planet? He looked out of the window and sighed. 'What did the major say when you called?' he asked.

'Couldn't get through,' Kincaid replied. 'Busy with preparations for the American tourists.'

'One of them talked a lot,' Fowler continued nervously. 'He kept going at me, taunting me like he hated Americans. Asked if I knew the penalty for espionage. Said it was death, no matter who you were.' She looked at Kincaid. 'No one would stand up for us then. Not the UN. Nobody.'

Kincaid felt her gaze and turned to her, strangely affected by her tone. 'It's all right,' he said uncertainly. 'We'll be okay. You know there's no damned spies. Just their damned games.' His hand moved across the console and rested on her leg.

'I don't know,' she said, speaking to the window. 'I've been so jumpy. I get scared for no reason. Premonitions.'

'About what?' Kincaid asked.

'Nothing. I mean, nothing, exactly. Like smelling something rotten for a second, then it's gone, something in the wind.' She pushed his hand away.

'Everyone's jumpy,' Kincaid said. 'Ever since the knobs arrived. They killed a man at the prison.' Shan noticed that the American was wearing a piece of heather in his pocket.

'They can't do that, can they?' Fowler asked. There was a small tremble in her voice. 'At the prison. Luntok said they're on strike, and the knobs have machine guns. He says it's like the old days. He's scared. Is that where you –?'

Why was it so hard for him to talk with Fowler about the 404th? He broke away from her green eyes and looked out of the window. They were following a wide river lined with willows. 'I'm scared too,' he said. Kincaid was right. Everyone was jumpy.

They passed fields lush with barley. Near the river there was enough water for irrigation. 'Why do you do it?' Shan asked. 'Why did you start helping them, looking for the artefacts? Just running the mine, wouldn't that be enough?'

'Because it has to be done,' Fowler said without hesitation.

'There're others who could do it.'

'But we're the ones who are here.'

'It scares me,' Shan said quietly. 'I fear you don't understand the danger.'

Fowler took offence. 'You think we do it for a lark?' Her voice grew louder than Shan had ever heard it. 'What, so we can brag about it when we get home? That's not it, dammit!' She looked down, as though taken aback by her own outburst. 'I'm sorry,' she said quietly. 'It's just that Tibet gets inside you. It's real here. More real than anything back home.'

She had used the word before, Shan remembered, to describe the moment when she had returned Tamdin's hand and the beast had howled. Real.

'It's important here,' Fowler concluded.

'Important?' asked Shan.

She twisted in her seat and looked back at him, her

eyes moving as though searching for the right words, but she did not speak.

'We make a difference here,' Kincaid continued, as if he and Fowler had discussed the topic many times before. 'Back home the world sits and watches MTV. Buys cars. Buys houses. Has one-point-eight kids.'

'MTV?' Shan asked.

'Never mind. Life is wasted back there. There, they just live *on* the world. Here, you can live *in* the world. The Buddhists, they have eight hot and eight cold hells. But there's a whole new level in America. The worst one. The one where everyone's tricked into ignoring their souls by being told they're already in heaven.'

'But you must have important things at home. Family.'

'Not much,' Kincaid quipped brightly, as though he were proud of it.

Not much, Shan considered. What was it Fowler had told him? That Kincaid would be running the company, that he would become one of the wealthiest men in America.

'My parents and I don't speak much.'

'No brothers or sisters?'

'Had a dog,' Kincaid said whimsically. Shan envied the American his ability to be so carefree. 'The dog died,' Kincaid concluded with a wide grin.

'But you're rich at home,' Shan offered clumsily.

Kincaid shot Fowler an exaggerated frown, as though to chastise her for talking too much. 'Not any more. Gave it up. My father's rich. Guess I'll be rich again. I try not to let it upset me. Rich doesn't make a home. Rich doesn't give you peace of mind.' He cast a sideways, hopeful glance towards Rebecca Fowler. 'Hell, in Lha-drung, I feel more at home than I ever did in the United States.'

Fowler gave him a weak smile. 'The poor lost soul finally finds a roost.'

'Don't make it sound like I'm the only one,' Kincaid chided, still grinning.

Shan saw Fowler stiffen, then hesitantly turn towards him, as though she owed Shan an explanation. 'My parents divorced fifteen years ago. I lived with my mother, who now has Alzheimer's disease. Destroys the memory. She hasn't recognized me for over four years. And I haven't seen or heard from my father in eight years.'

It didn't explain anything for Shan. It just made him sad. Maybe in the spirit realm Lhadrung was another kind of catching place, where lost souls collected and were battered about until, worn and hard as old stones, they were safe in the world again.

Shan closed his eyes, reviewing what he had seen in Colonel Tan's service record. Service in Manchuria, Inner Mongolia, and Fujian. But nothing in Tibet before 1985. He stared out of the window at the desolate landscape. Everything was wrong. Everything he had assumed had been mistaken. He had thought the key had been Director Hu, but he had been wrong. He had thought it had been about the skull cave, but then he found Yerpa. He had hoped it had merely been a battle between looters, but a looter didn't kill over one shrine to protect another. He had thought perhaps it had been only Li, then Li and the major, but neither had any connection to Tamdin. He had thought it could never be Sungpo, yet who but a monk would have reverently arranged the dislocated skull in the cave? He had thought the *Lotus Book* provided the answers, the motives, but the *Lotus Book* was wrong – about Tan, anyway. They were all pieces of the puzzle, but the shape of the puzzle eluded him, and he had no idea how many more pieces he needed before they began to make sense.

To know of not knowing is best, Tsomo had reminded him. He had to begin again, erasing it all, assuming he knew only of not knowing. There was so much he did not know. He did not know who had the Tamdin costume. He did not know who had given the *ragyapa* the stolen military supplies. He did not know why the *purbas* would have recorded lies in the *Lotus Book*. He did not know why Jao was interested in water rights on a remote mountainside. He felt no closer to an answer than he had the day they found Jao's head. If he did not find answers in Lhasa, he would have no hope of finding the true killer, no hope of saving Sungpo. No hope of saving himself, or the 404th, when he refused to write the report condemning an innocent monk.

They drove to a warehouse at the far end of the airport, where a sleepy customs officer waved them through and two freight handlers waited for Fowler to hand them each a ten renminbi note before unloading the crates and wheeling a dolly bearing a rack of empty canisters to the truck. In less than fifteen minutes they were on the road to Lhasa.

An hour later they passed the familiar blocks of low, slate-coloured barracks that Beijing built for urban workers all over China. The paths along the highway began to fill with figures in grey and brown clothing. Carts pulled by haggard ponies hauled plastic barrels of night soil out of the city. Farmers carried cabbages and onions in huge net bags. Chickens and small pigs were trussed on sticks balanced on bicycles. Grandparents walked to market with children. The streets seemed more Chinese than Tibetan, and with a pang of sorrow as sharp as a blade Shan remembered why. Beijing had 'naturalized' the city by shipping in a hundred thousand Chinese to join the fifty thousand Tibetans already living there. As far as he could see, Lhasa, which in Tibetan meant the dwelling place of God, had been converted into one more of the grey smokey urban tracts that comprised modern China.

'There should be something more we can do,' Fowler

said as Kincaid eased the truck to a stop in front of the drab two-storey building that housed Jansen's office. 'You want the water permit records. But they won't let you see them. Not without identification.'

'I may find a way. I know how the bureacrats speak.' Shan stepped out and turned away from the truck, facing the old city for the first time.

'No. Tyler will go. It's perfectly normal. They won't say no to him, asking to see his own permits.'

But Shan could not reply. For there it was, on top of the small mountain that dominated the city. Or rather it *was* the mountain that dominated the city. Its huge lower walls, brilliant white and sloping steeply upward, gave the main structure the appearance of a vast, golden-roofed temple floating above Himalayan snows. The precipice of existence, Trinle had once called the walls in a winter tale, so high, so rigid, so alluring that they recalled for him the path to Buddhahood.

Never before in his life had Shan been afraid to look at something. He felt unworthy to stare at the building. He had been wrong. Something did survive of the dwelling place of God. He gazed down at his feet a moment, wondering at his sudden flood of emotion, then, unable to stop himself, his gaze moved back to the Potala.

'What are you doing?' Kincaid asked suddenly, his hand reaching out as though to catch Shan.

Shan realized that he had unconsciously dropped to his knees. 'I guess,' he said, still in wonder, 'I am doing this.' And he touched the ground with his forehead, the way a pilgrim might on first seeing the holy building.

Most of the old yaks had their own names for it, or were fond of reciting the many appellations given the structure in Tibetan literature. The Seat of Supreme Being. The Jewel in the Crown. The Sublime Fortress. Buddha's Gate. One of the younger monks had proudly reported that in a Western magazine he had seen the Potala listed as one of the wonders of the world. The old yaks had all smiled politely at the news. Now Shan knew what they had all been thinking: the Potala wasn't of this world.

Maybe five years before he could have visited Lhasa and seen the structure as a tourist might, as a massive stone castle, impressive for its size and age and historic role as the Buddhist Vatican. But Shan had not seen it five years ago, and now he could see it only through the eyes of those who told the winter tales.

An ancient priest, the same who had gone out into the snow to die the year before, had first visited it in 1931, when the Thirteenth Dalai Lama was still in residence and again two years later when the salt-dried body of the old ruler was interred in a solid silver chorten in the Red Palace of the Potala. It had been the Thirteenth who warned on his deathbed that soon all Tibetans would be enslaved and would have to endure endless days of suffering. Later the same priest had been fortunate enough to be assigned to the library of the Potala. It contained the original plans of the Great Fifth Dalai Lama, who had started construction of the Potala in 1645 and asked that his death be concealed so that it would not interfere with the work. The old yak had described the plans in detail to his awed, shivering audience at the 404th. Richly worked walls of stone, cedar, and teak joined by hand without a single nail created a thousand rooms over thirteen floors that once held the hundredfold shrines. Only in the third retelling of the tale had Shan understood that the reference was not merely figurative. The Great Fifth's palace for Buddha contained a hundred times a hundred shrines, ten thousand altars, and on them sat two hundred thousand statues of deities. As he gazed on the huge walls Shan remembered the monk telling them they had been built for eternity. Maybe he was right – later Shan had learned that the exterior walls, in some places thirty feet thick, had been strengthened for the ages by pouring molten copper inside them.

Much later, in the Tibetan year of the Earth Mouse, 1949, Choje had visited the same library. Seven thousand volumes of scripture he had seen there, most of them unique manuscripts dating back centuries. Some, he explained in a childlike tone of awe, had been written on palm leaves brought from India a thousand years earlier. In a special collection of illuminated manuscripts, which Choje spent ten months studying, there were two thousand volumes in which the lines of scripture were written in alternating inks made of powdered gold, silver, copper, turquoise, coral, and conch shell. For the Red Guards who invaded the Potala during the Cultural Revolution, nothing had symbolized the Four Olds better than these manuscripts. They had made a public display of destroying the volumes on the temple grounds, ripping many into pieces which were sent for use in Red Guard latrines.

Rebecca Fowler's hand on his arm brought Shan back. 'Tyler should go instead,' she repeated.

'Piece of cake,' Kincaid agreed with a gleam of mischief. 'Been to the Ministry of Ag before. They'll probably recognize me. Kowtow to the big American investor.'

Shan nodded reluctantly, and handed Fowler the canvas bag he had brought with him. 'Give this to your friend Jansen.'

'What is it?'

'From the cave. One of the gold skulls. I asked it to be removed for evidence.'

Kincaid looked at him uncertainly.

'I didn't say for evidence of what,' Shan continued.

Kincaid's eyes widened. 'Son of a bitch,' he said with a grin. 'Son of a bitch.' He accepted the bag eagerly and glanced inside.

Shan pulled out an envelope. 'These are the resumés of

Director Hu's geologic exploration staff. I thought it might be of interest.'

'Resumés?' Kincaid asked.

'Hu has eight staff members assigned to find new mineral deposits. Six of them were transferred last year by Wen Li at the request of Hu.'

'But Wen is Religious Affairs.'

Shan nodded. 'The six have no geology training. They are archaeologists and anthropologists.'

Kincaid stared at the envelope in confusion, then comprehension lit his eyes. 'Shit! His mineral exploration – it's all about looting. He's not looking for mines,' Tyler exclaimed to Fowler, 'he's looking for caves! Shrine caves. Wait till Jansen sees this!' With a huge grin he grabbed Shan's hand and shook it, hard. 'Be careful, man,' he said awkwardly, glancing up at Fowler's amused face and turning back to Shan. 'Really. I mean it.'

The American paused and solemnly reached into his shirt to pull out a white cloth that had been hidden there. It was a silk *khata* scarf, a prayer scarf, that the American had been wearing around his neck. 'Here,' Kincaid said. 'It's my good luck charm. Keeps me alive when I climb.'

'I can't,' Shan said uncomfortably. 'This is not for –'

'Please,' Kincaid persisted. 'I want you to have it. For protection. I don't want you getting caught. You're one of us.'

Shan accepted the *khata* with a blush of embarrassment, then climbed out at the next intersection, praying the faded army coat he had brought from Lhadrung would persuade any onlooker that he was nothing but a straggling soldier who had hitched a ride.

But as he rounded the corner towards the centre of the city, the Sublime Fortress was there again. Lokesh had been there too, Shan remembered, first as a young student who, by excelling at his exams, won the honour of scraping the candle grease from Potala altars. The memories of that first visit, spent in the darkness of the lower floors, had been almost entirely aural. Lokesh related that he had constantly heard the tingle of *tsingha* cymbals but never in a month's stay had he been able to locate its source among the maze of rooms. There had been the high-pitched *jaling* horns blown at the opening of special rituals and the melodious *vajre* bells rung to call monks to the services that seemed to begin every few minutes somewhere in the complex. Finally there had been the twelve-foot long *dungchen* horns, so deep they were like a groan of the earth, and so resonant that Lokesh insisted that their echoes rolled about the lower floors for hours after being blown.

As Shan approached the museum the hairs on the back of his neck stood, the skin tingled. He made two slow circuits around the building, lingering in a throng watching a chess game on the first circuit, moving to a bus stop queue after the second. It was a very small Tibetan man who was following him, wearing a blue worker's jacket and carrying a cabbage. His long, limber arms and sharp restless eyes belied his slow, feeble carriage. Shan tested the tail by rapidly walking down the street three blocks, then sitting on a bench. The man followed on the opposite side, lingering at a vegetable stall while Shan pretended to read a newspaper gleaned from a trash can. Shan watched until he was certain the stalker was alone. Public Security operated tails with teams of at least three.

Chiding himself for not considering that Jansen's office could be watched, he found a public washroom where he removed his coat. Outside, he climbed aboard a bus and got out at the first stop. He switched to a second bus, watching with his ears around his eyes, as a Beijing instructor had once described, meaning watching with every sense, sensing the rhythm of the crowd so he could see where the rhythm broke, watching the way every pedestrian watched the others. It was the ones who ignored the others who were the ones to fear.

After six blocks he emerged back into the sunlight and began walking not towards the street of the museum but parallel to the street, still testing the pavement.

Suddenly there was a loud crack behind him, as though from a pistol. Shan spun about and froze. There, not ten feet away from him amidst the throng of Chinese shoppers and rush of bicycles, was a ragged, unkempt Tibetan with a filthy leather apron over a felt coat. His hands were thrust into the straps of wooden clogs, which he was now clapping together over his head. Someone beside Shan, a plump Chinese woman carrying a jar of yogurt hissed an expletive at the man. '*Latseng!*' she added. Garbage.

But the Tibetan seemed unaware of anyone on the busy street as he left the kerb. He brought the clogs down in one liquid motion and stretched himself full-length on the pavement, his arms extended in front of him. With a murmured mantra he pulled himself forward, moved back to his knees, stood, and clapped the clogs in front of him twice before clapping them over his head and repeating the process. Traditionally, Shan remembered, pilgrims did three five-mile circuits around the Potala. But he also recalled that the government had obliterated most of the pilgrim's circuit, known as the Lingkhor, constructing apartment buildings and shops squarely to block the route after monks had invited Tibetans to protest their Chinese government by creating an endless chain of pilgrims around the circuit.

Emotion overtaking him again, Shan stared helplessly at the Tibetan, who gazed fixedly ahead. Trinle had laughed heartily about the route being blocked. 'The government will never be able to see what the pilgrim sees,' he had said with absolute conviction. He had repeated the phrase for Shan like a mantra again and again with his huge smile until, not knowing why, Shan had laughed too.

An angry shout rose from the street. A youth on a motorcycle was yelling for the pilgrim to get out of his path. A car pulled up behind the man and began honking its horn. The pilgrim was entering an intersection, oblivious to the traffic light. A truck approaching down the cross street added its horn to the chorus.

Pilgrims were sometimes run over by vehicles. Shan had heard guards at the 404th joke about such roadkills. The pilgrim kept moving. But there was something new in the man's eyes. He was aware of the vehicles now. He was afraid, but he would not stop.

Shan looked back to the crowd. Was someone there? No. But did he still have the rhythm of the crowd? No. He took a long look at the Sublime Fortress and stepped into the street.

He moved past the angry drivers, still pounding their horns, to stand beside the solitary pilgrim. With tiny steps he escorted the Tibetan as the man struggled through the intersection. Up on his knees. Up to his feet. Arms in front. Clap the clogs. Arms overhead. Clap the clogs. Arms down. Stop. Kneel. Drop to his belly. Extend the arms. Recite the mantra to the Buddha of Compassion. Retract the arms. Up on his knees.

People were shouting louder, infuriated at Shan now. But he did not hear their words. He watched the pilgrim with great satisfaction, and in the pilgrim saw Choje, and Trinle, and all the old yaks. An odd thought flashed through his mind. Perhaps this was the most important thing he had done in three years. Choje might have suggested that everything that had happened before was so Shan could be there in that moment to protect the pilgrim.

They reached the kerb and the safety of the sidewalk. Without breaking stride or diverting his eyes, the pilgrim spoke in an emotional, uncertain voice. '*Tujaychay*,' he whispered to Shan. Thank-you.

Shan watched the pilgrim move on another thirty feet before the world crept back over him. He glanced up and realized he had no hope of regaining the rhythm of the crowd. Twenty faces were watching him now, most of them resentful. There was no time left to watch and elude. He moved straight to the museum.

He entered along with a tour group, then moved in the cover of the crowds through the exhibits, willing himself not to linger at the exquisite displays of skull drums, ceremonial jade swords, altar statues, rich *thangka* paintings, crested hats, and prayer wheels. He paused only once, in front of a display of rare rosaries. There in the centre was one of pink coral beads carved like tiny pinecones, with lapis marker beads. He wrote down the collection inventory number and moved on.

Suddenly he was at the exhibit of costumes for demon protectors. There was Yama, the Lord of the Dead, Yamantaka, Slayer of Death, Mahakala, Supreme Protector of the Faith, Lhamo, Goddess Protector of Lhasa. And in the last case, Tamdin the Horse-headed.

The magnificent costume was there, its face a savage bulging mask of red lacquered wood, four fangs in its mouth, a ring of skulls at its neck, a tiny, ferocious, green horse head rising above its golden hair. Shan shivered as he studied it, his hand clamped on the *gau* around his neck that now contained the Tamdin summoning spell. The arms of the demon lay beside the mask, ending in two grotesque clawed hands, identical to the smashed one found at the American mine.

It was small comfort to confirm that the hand was indeed that of Tamdin, for the costume in the museum was intact, and in Lhasa, not in Lhadrung. There was a second costume but if it did not belong to the museum Shan had no way to trace it, no way to link it to Jao's killers.

He stared at the exhibit in deep thought, waited for the room to empty, and opened a door. A janitor's closet. He began to shut it, then paused and pulled out the broom and a bucket. He moved slowly through the building, sweeping as he watched the interior doors. Suddenly, and with a wrench of his gut, he saw someone new, a Chinese with bullet-hole eyes trying quite futilely to look interested in the exhibits. The man surveyed the room, not noticing Shan, then gave a snort of impatience and moved with a military gait into the adjoining hall. Shan stayed in the shadows and watched, to his horror, as the man conferred with two others, a young woman and a man dressed as tourists. They left the room at a trot and Shan stepped inside the first door that was not locked.

He was in a short corridor that opened into a large office chamber divided into cubicles. Most of the desks were empty. On a bench in the hall was a white technician's coat. Abandoning the bucket and broom, he put on the coat, then picked up a clipboard and pencil from the first desk.

'I lost my way,' he said to the woman at the first occupied desk. 'The inventory.'

'Inventory?'

'Exhibits. Artefacts in storage.'

'It's usually the same,' she said in a superior tone.

'The same?'

'You know. Two of each piece. One on display, one in storage. In the basement. Parallel collection, the curator calls it. Makes cleaning and examination easier. One upstairs. One downstairs, arranged by their inventory number sequence.'

'Of course,' Shan said, with renewed hope. 'I meant the organization charts. The location of artefacts.'

'In notebooks. On the library table.'

In the small library at the back of the corridor he found a thick black binder, its vinyl covers worn through to the cardboard at the edges. He had already located a section entitled *Costumes* when an older woman appeared at the door.

'What is it?' she snapped.

Shan started, then settled back into the chair before looking at her. 'I'm from Beijing.'

The announcement bought him another thirty seconds. He kept searching as the woman lingered at the doorway. Ceremonial headdresses. Demon dancer costumes.

'No one informed me,' the woman said with a suspicious tone.

'Comrade, certainly you realize audits are not nearly so effective when advance warning is given,' Shan said curtly.

'Audits?' She paused, then slowly entered and walked around the table.

As she saw Shan's clothing a sharp hiss of air escaped her lips. 'We will need identification, Comrade.'

Shan kept studying the books. 'They said to leave it at the front desk. We have much work here.' He gestured to a chair. 'Perhaps you would like to help.'

The woman spun about and disappeared down the hall. *Tamdin*, the book said, Code 4989. Set One from Shigatse gompa, 1959. Set Two from Saskya gompa, dated only fourteen months earlier. He walked quickly to the corridor and began checking the doors again. The third one opened onto descending stairs.

The basement shelves rose from the dirt floor to the ceiling, crammed with boxes of wood, wicker, and cardboard. They were arranged by inventory number as the girl had explained. He darted down the rows, desperately scanning the numbers at the end of each shelf. Suddenly there was a new sound, the unmistakable sound of running feet on the floor above.

He found the 3000 series, and kept running. Then the 4000. Shan pulled a box from the shelves. It held an incense burner. He began to run, and stumbled onto his knees. There were shouts upstairs. He found a shelf marked 4900. A set of golden horns extended from a box. The mask of Yama. Frantically he checked the boxes. They were on the stairs now, shouting. Another row of lights was illuminated, much brighter. Then he had it. *Tamdin*, the box said. *Tamdin, demon costume, Saskya gompa*. It was empty.

Someone yelled nearby. There was a white index card taped to the top of the box. He tore it off and ran away from the sounds of the searchers. There was a door up a shorter flight of stairs, showing daylight at the bottom.

It was locked. He rammed it with his shoulder and old wood splintered. He fell outward onto the ground. As he lay blinking in the painful sunlight someone jammed a boot into his back, then reached down and placed handcuffs on his wrists.

The first syllable of weak protest was still on his lips when a truncheon slammed into his forehead, spattering blood. 'Hooligan shit,' his captor spat before he spoke into a hand radio.

The blood that trickled into his eyes prevented him from seeing how many there were. They were Public Security, he had no doubt, but they seemed confused. From behind him, as he was pushed into a grey van, there were arguments about whose prisoner he was, about his destination. The first two didn't use place names. 'The long bed,' one of them said. 'Wires,' argued another. But a third man joined them. 'Drabchi,' he said, in the tone of an order, referring to the notorious political prison northeast of Lhasa. Prison Number One, it was formally called, where the high ranking officials of the Tibetan government had once been held.

It was over. Sungpo would die. Shan would have new wardens. Eventually, if Tan did not abandon him, he might be returned to the 404th, with five or ten years added, but only after Public Security interrogation and the stay in the infirmary that would follow. Who, he wondered in some remote corner of his mind, would be recruited to express the people's disappointment in his socialist development?

I'm a hero, Shan would tell his captors. I lasted twelve days on the outside.

The blood was in his mouth now, and the pain of the wound began to surge through his stupor. The van was moving. A siren erupted, painfully loud. They were on a fast road, accelerating. He blacked out. Suddenly there was a shout, and he heard the sound of breaking wood and chickens squawking in terror. He felt the van slam on its brakes and heard the men in front leap out.

There were furious shouts from the front of the van. Then someone climbed into the driver's seat and the van was moving in a U turn. The siren was cut and the vehicle made a series of a rapid turns, then it pulled to an abrupt stop. The rear doors were flung open and four hands reached in for him. He was half carried, half dragged into the back seat of a car, which instantly pulled away.

Slowly, with dreamlike motions, he wiped the blood from his eyes and pulled himself up. It was a large car, an older American sedan. The driver wore a wool cap over his head. When they pulled into the broad thoroughfare that led out of town the man dangled a small key over his shoulder. As Shan unlocked the handcuffs the man removed the cap to reveal a head of thick blond hair.

'I didn't know –' Shan began, paralysed by confusion. He pulled out his shirttail to wipe away the blood. 'Thank you,' he muttered in English. 'Are you Jansen?'

The man shook his head and muttered to himself in a Scandinavian tongue as he drove slowly through the traffic, careful not to attract attention. 'No names,' he said in English. 'Please. No names.' On the floor beside him Shan recognized the bag he had carried to Lhasa. The skull from the cave shrine.

'How could you know?' Shan asked after five minutes. Jansen had sunk into a depressed silence. 'I'm just taking you to the highway somewhere. Your friends will be on the highway, they said.'

'Why?'

'Why?' Jansen pounded the steering wheel in anger. 'You think I would have done it if I had known? With the knobs as thick as flies? Nobody said anything about knobs. They said for me to be there, that's all. Need to help the gentleman who brought all the information from Lhadrung.' He shook his head. 'Nothing like this has happened before. Help with the records, no problem. Give an old man a ride from Shigatse, no problem. But this –' He threw up a hand in frustration.

'The *purbas*,' Shan realized. Somehow it had been the *purbas*. The little man he had seen on the street had not been alone. He had been a *purba*, Shan now understood. 'But how could they know?'

'How do they know anything? Like telepathy.'

The knobs had somehow known. The *purbas* had somehow known. Everyone seemed to know everything. Except him.

'Like telepathy,' Shan repeated in a hollow voice. He looked out of the window for a fleeting glance of the Potala as it faded into the distance. The precipice of existence.

'Worst they do, they deport me,' Jansen muttered to himself.

Shan lay back on the seat. He found a paper towel and held it to his forehead. 'There was an obstruction pushed onto the highway,' Shan said, as though to himself. 'A farmer's cart, I think. The knobs got out to clear the path.'

'They told me you need a ride. To wait with my car. Okay, I thought. A ride. I could ask you about the skull shrine. Suddenly one of them runs by. Tosses me a key. For you, he says. Then this Public Security van races down the alley and they throw you inside. Who are you? Why does everyone want you?'

'For me, he said. Did he use my name?'

'No. Not exactly. He said for the pilgrim.'

'The pilgrim?'

'The name the *purbas* are using for you. Tan's pilgrim.'

No, Shan was tempted to say. A pilgrim moves towards enlightenment. All I move towards is darkness and confusion. But suddenly a tiny flicker of light appeared. 'You said you drove an old man from Shigatse? To Lhadrung?'

Jansen nodded distractedly. He was nervously watching the rearview mirror. 'His wife had just died. He sang me some of the old mourning songs.'

Rebecca Fowler and Tyler Kincaid were waiting fifteen miles out of the city, parked at a flat stretch of highway along the Lhasa River where truckers gathered to sleep. Jansen pulled in behind a decrepit Jiefang truck, from which four young men instantly emerged and escorted Shan to the Americans. Shan turned to thank Jansen, but the Finn just nodded nervously and sped back down the road.

The Jiefang pulled out in front of Kincaid and the driver motioned for the Americans to follow.

Fowler was silent. At first he thought she was sleeping but then he saw her hands. They were twisting the road map, their knuckles white.

'It's like free-falling,' Kincaid said, with unexpected excitement in his voice. 'A hundred feet a second. Your heart's in your throat. The world's flying by.' He glanced back at Shan. 'It's them, right?' he asked with a huge grin.

'Them?'

'In the truck. The real thing. It's gotta be *purbas*.'

'I'm sorry.' Shan felt his forehead. The blood was clotting now.

'Sorry? For this day? The whole damn day, it's been

like rappelling down a mountain. You just jump off the cliff and let it happen.'

'I never meant for you to be in danger,' Shan said. 'You should have just left.'

'Hell, we made it out alive, didn't we? No sweat. Wouldn't have missed it. We got 'em good, the MFCs. You sent me to search for what isn't there. Perfect. Playing games with their minds.' He filled the truck with another of his cowboy whoops.

'Dammit, Tyler,' Fowler said. 'Get us out of here. It's not over until we're home.'

'What do you mean, "seeking what isn't there"?' Shan asked Kincaid.

'At the Ministry of Ag. Water resources office moved away in a reorganization. All the files were shipped to Beijing five months ago.'

Going to seek what wasn't there. Shan had forgotten the card from the archives. He pulled it from his pocket slowly, as if it would shatter if it moved too fast.

Tamdin, the card said. *Saskya gompa*. But there was more. On loan, with a date fourteen months earlier, the same date it had been discovered. On loan to Lhadrung Town. There was a name, written hastily and smeared. But the chop at the bottom was clear. The personal chop of Jao Xengding. Below it was scrawled 'Confirmed,' followed by a final ideogram, the inverted, double-barred Y. The same one he had seen on the note from Jao's pocket. *Sky*, it meant, or *heaven*.

Twenty miles past the airport the Jiefang truck stopped on a sharp curve and Kincaid pulled in behind it. A man jumped out, ran to the Americans' vehicle, and whispered urgently with Kincaid, pointing to a side road ahead of the truck. The Jiefang turned around and the *purba* jumped on as it passed by.

Kincaid eased their vehicle into four-wheel-drive and moved onto the side road. 'The knobs have road blocks on all roads out of Lhasa, at repeating intervals. They are steaming. They probably have a special reception committee waiting at the Lhadrung County checkpoint. So we have to detour.'

He drove recklessly over the rough route, towards the setting sun, then abruptly stopped as the distant flickering lights of Lhadrung valley came into view. 'We could go back, you know,' Kincaid announced to Shan with a meaningful gaze.

'Back?'

'To Lhasa. The road blocks are checking vehicles leaving the area, not entering. We could do it. You're too valuable to go back to prison when this is over. You know so much. I can help you.'

'Help me how?' Shan sensed the American's *khata* that still hung around his neck.

'Talk to Jansen. We'll calm him down. Hell, he'll want to pick your brain for weeks himself. He knows people who can get you out of the country.'

'But Colonel Tan. And if Director Hu –' Fowler protested.

'Hell, Rebecca, they don't know Shan is with us. He just disappears. I could get that tattoo off. I've seen it done. You could be a free man.'

A free man. They were such pale words to Shan. It was a concept that Americans always seemed infatuated with, but one which Shan never understood. Perhaps, he reflected, because he had never known a free man. His hand drifted to the *khata* and slid it off. 'You are very kind. But I am needed in Lhadrung.'

Kincaid saw the scarf in Shan's hand and shook his head in disappointment.

'Keep it,' he said admiringly, pushing the *khata* back. 'If you're going back to Lhadrung, you're going to need it.'

Chapter Seventeen

Colonel Tan seemed to read the messages from Miss Lihua and Madame Ko simultaneously, his eyes ranging back and forth from the one in his hand to the one on his desk. In the fax from Hong Kong, Miss Lihua reported that she was urgently trying to book flights for her return, but meanwhile wanted to confirm that Prosecutor Jao's personal seal had indeed been taken the year before. No one had been arrested for stealing the chop, although it was the sort of minor act of sabotage typical of monks and other cultural hooligans. A new seal had been fabricated, and a notice sent to alert Jao's bank.

Madame Ko's note reported that she had made inquiries at the Ministry of Agriculture in Beijing, finding a man named Deng who was responsible for the recordkeeping of water rights. Deng knew who Prosecutor Jao was; they had spoken by phone the week before Jao's death, Madame Ko explained. And Deng had an appointment to see the prosecutor during his stopover in Beijing, at a restaurant named the Bamboo Bridge.

'So one of the monks stole Jao's chop and got the costume. Maybe Sungpo, maybe one of the other four,' Tan asserted.

'Why his personal seal?' Shan asked. 'If I went to all that trouble, and wanted to sow confusion in the government, why not steal his official seal?'

'Opportunistic. A monk saw a chance and broke into the office. An open door or window, and the first thing he found was the personal seal. He got scared and fled. Miss Lihua says it was a monk.'

'I don't think so. But that's not the point.' Shan found himself gazing out of the window towards the street, half expecting to see a truck of knobs arrive to arrest him. There was only the empty car of the officer he had driven to town with. The knobs in Lhasa had known who he was. But they were not coming for him. What had been their orders? Merely to scare him away from Lhasa? To eliminate him if he could somehow be snatched beyond Tan's reach?

'What are you saying?'

Shan turned back towards Tan. 'What's important is that the Director of Religious Affairs lied about it. He told us the costumes were all accounted for. He said he checked.'

'Someone at the museum may have lied to him,' Tan suggested.

'No. Madame Ko checked this morning. No one ever called the museum about the costumes.'

'But Jao would never have ordered the costume sent back from Lhasa to Lhadrung. There would be no reason,' Tan said tentatively.

'Did you ever hear that his chop was stolen? It would be very disturbing for a prosecutor to lose his seal. Something the military governor should have known about.'

'It was only his personal seal.'

'I think his personal seal was accessible to someone here in Lhadrung, and they used it to stamp the card that was later put on the museum box.'

'You're saying Miss Lihua is lying?'

'We need her back here, right away.'

'You saw her note. She's coming.' As Tan dropped the fax on the desk, they became aware of Madame Ko standing excitedly at the door, uninvited but apparently unwilling to leave. She raised her hand and made a quick, victorious fist in mid-air. Tan sighed and gestured for her to enter.

'So Jao was to meet this man Deng in Beijing. For what?' Tan asked.

'To review water permits in Lhadrung,' Madame Ko reported. 'Jao wanted to know who held the rights before the Americans.'

'And Comrade Deng of the Ministry of Agriculture. He had the answer?'

'All the records were still in the original boxes from Lhasa. That's why he was so unhappy that Jao never arrived. Said he spent hours sorting through them.'

'For some stranger from Tibet, he did all that?'

Madame Ko nodded. 'Comrade Jao said that if they found what he expected that he would want Deng to go with him straight to the Ministry of Justice headquarters. A big case, he said. Deng would be commended to the Minister himself.'

Tan moved to the edge of his seat. 'It would have been one of the agricultural collectives,' Tan asserted.

'Exactly,' Madame Ko confirmed.

'You asked him?'

'Of course. It's part of our investigation,' she said with a small conspiratorial nod to Shan.

Tan cast an impatient glance at Shan. 'And?'

'Long Wall Farm.'

Tan asked for tea. 'She acts like she just solved our mystery,' he sighed as Madame Ko left the room in an excited bustle.

'Maybe she did,' Shan said.

'This Long Wall collective is significant somehow?'

'You recall Jin San, one of the murder victims?'

'Jao prosecuted one of the Lhadrung Five for his murder.'

'And in the process discovered that Jin San operated a drug ring.'

'Which we eliminated.'

'Perhaps you forget that Jin San was the manager of the Long Wall collective.'

The colonel lit a cigarette, studying the ember as it burned. 'I want Miss Lihua back here,' he suddenly barked towards the open door. 'Get her a military plane if you have to.'

He drew deeply on his cigarette and turned to Shan. 'That opium operation is finished, fell apart after Jin San died. Drug sales in Lhadrung have stopped. Drug cases have disappeared at the clinic. I was officially commended.'

Shan laid out the photo maps depicting the unexplained licence area, the same maps Jao had seen. 'Can you read these photos?'

Tan went to his desk and retrieved a large magnifying glass. 'I told you. I commanded a missile base,' he grunted.

'Yeshe studied the maps yesterday. The new road. The mine. The extra licence area to the northwest. He was confused about something. This is the licence area for four consecutive months.' Shan pointed to the first map. 'Winter. Snow. Rocks and dirt. Indistinguishable from the rest of the terrain.'

He chose not to speak of Yeshe's other discovery. The computer disks taken by Fowler had indeed been inventories. Half the Chinese-language files had even matched the English files. But the other files had been inventories of munitions, of soldiers, even of missiles located in Tibet. Yeshe's hands had trembled when he gave them to Shan. Together they had taken them to the utility building at Jade Spring Camp and burned them in the furnace. Not for a moment had Shan considered the data on the disks to be genuine. But Yeshe and Shan both knew it made little difference. Public Security was unlikely to be concerned about such a fine point if it found the disks with a civilian. As he had watched the furnace flames, Yeshe had asked for leave to go to the 404th. Civilians were gathering, he had said.

'Not entirely,' Tan observed, and used the lens.

'There's terracing. Probably very old. But you can see traces of it. Faint shadow lines.'

'Exactly. Now, a month later.' Shan flipped to the next map. 'The slopes are green now, faintly green. But far more so than the rest of the mountains.'

'Water. Just means the terraces still catch the water,' Tan said.

'But a month later. Look. The colour is inconsistent. A blush of pink and red.'

Tan silently leaned over the map. He studied it with the lens from several angles. 'In the developing process. Sometimes there are anomalies. The chemicals create false colours. Even the lens. It doesn't always react to visible light accurately.'

'I think the colours are exact.' Shan set down the last map. 'Six weeks ago.'

'And the colours are gone,' Tan observed. 'No different from the adjoining slopes. Like I said, a developing fault.'

'But the terraces are gone, too.'

Tan looked up in confusion, then leaned over the map with his lens.

'Somebody,' Shan concluded, 'is still growing Jin San's poppies.'

Shan hated helicopters. Aeroplanes had always struck him as contrary to the natural order; helicopters seemed simply impossible. The young army pilot who met them at Jade Spring Camp did little to relieve his anxiety. He flew a constant two hundred feet off the ground, creating a roller-coaster effect as they moved over the undulating hills of the upper valley. On Tan's command he banked sharply and began a steep ascent. Ten minutes later they had cleared the ridge and landed in a small clearing.

The terraces were ancient but obvious, built up with rock walls and connected by a worn cart path. Their spring crop had already been harvested. The only sign of life was thin beds of weeds, rising out of the terraces through a carpet of dead poppy leaves.

'The rocks.' Tan pointed to a flat rock, then another, and another, all at regular intervals in the fields, ten feet apart. Shan kicked over the nearest. It covered a hole, three inches wide and over twenty inches deep. Tan kicked a second rock, and a third. They all covered similar holes.

Under a high overhanging rock Tan found a stack of heavy wooden poles, eight feet long. He tried one in a hole. It fit perfectly. In the shadows under the rock Shan found the end of a rope. He pulled it without success, then called Tan. Together they heaved and a huge bundle of cloth appeared, wrapped in the rope. No, Shan quickly realized as it emerged into the light, it wasn't cloth. It was a huge military camouflage net.

The silence was broken by a shout from above.

'Colonel!' the pilot called as he ran down the slope. 'There's a radio message. They are firing machine guns at the 404th!'

Tan ordered the pilot to circle over the prison. There were three emergency vehicles, lights flashing, sitting at the front gate. Four groups of people could be discerned, each clustered together, like pieces of a puzzle waiting to be connected. In the prison compound sitting in a compact square were the prisoners. Shan searched for bodies, for litters of figures being carried to the ambulances, but found none. Outside the wire in front of the mess hall were the prison guards in their green uniforms standing in a crescent facing the prison compound.

A taut grey line of knobs reached around the wire, intersecting the sandbag bunkers. The fourth group was new. Shan studied it as the helicopter landed. They were Tibetans. Herders. People from town. Children, old men and women. Some were facing the compound, chanting mantras. Others were building an offering of butter *torma*, to be sanctified and lit to invoke the Buddha of Compassion.

The acrid smell of cordite laced the air. As the whine of the helicopter engine faded, Shan heard children crying and heard frantic calls rising from the crowds. They were calling names, calling out to individual prisoners inside the wire. Several old men sat near the front. Shan listened for a moment. They weren't praying for the survival of the prisoners. They were praying for the enlightenment of the soldiers.

Tan stood in silence, barely containing his fury as he studied the scene. A dozen knobs were deployed in front of the civilians, their sub-machine guns unslung. Shell casings lay scattered around their feet.

'Who authorized you to fire?' Tan roared.

They ignored him.

'There was movement towards the dead zone,' an oily voice said from behind them. 'They had been warned.' Shan recognized the man even before he turned. The major. 'As you are aware, Colonel, the Bureau has procedures.'

Tan stared at the major with slow burning eyes, then moved angrily towards the warden, standing with the prison staff. As he did so Shan stepped as close as he dared to the fence, searching the faces of the prisoners. Hands appeared from behind him, one on each arm, and squeezed painfully. His prisoner instincts taking over, he flinched, raising his arm over his face, to prepare for a blow. When none came, he let himself be pulled away by the soldiers. The knobs, he realized, didn't recognize him as a prisoner. His hand moved to his sleeve, pulling it down to cover his tattoo.

He stood where they deposited him, staring through the wire. There was no sign of Choje.

The Tibetan civilians pulled away as he walked through the crowd, shunning him, refusing to let him close enough to speak. 'The prisoners,' he called out to the backs that were turned to him. 'Are prisoners hurt?' he called out.

'They have charms,' someone shouted defiantly. 'Charms against bullets.'

Suddenly a familiar figure was in front of him, looking strangely out of place. It was Sergeant Feng, wearing the old woollen shirt Shan had put on him in Kham, his face covered with grime and fatigue. When his eyes met Shan's, there was no arrogance left in them. For a passing moment Shan thought he saw pleading in them.

'I thought you were in the mountains.'

'Been there,' Feng replied soberly.

As Shan moved towards him, Feng stepped forward, as though to block him. Shan put his hand on Feng's shoulder and pushed him aside. There was a priest on the ground behind him, saying a mantra with an old woman. He stopped and stared. It was Yeshe, he suddenly realized, wearing a red shirt that gave the impression of a robe. He had cropped his hair to the scalp.

Yeshe grinned awkwardly when he saw Shan. He patted the woman's hand and stood.

'I was asking about the prisoners,' Shan said.

Yeshe gazed towards the wire. 'They fired over their heads. No one injured yet.' There was a self-assurance in his eyes which Shan had not seen before.

'Damn the fool!' the sergeant suddenly spat from behind them. He began running through the crowd to a cooking fire where a woman was arguing with someone. It was Jigme.

'She won't give me anything,' Jigme said as soon as he saw Shan. 'I told her, it's for Je Rinpoche.' He looked at Shan, then to Yeshe. 'Tell her,' he pleaded, 'tell her I'm not Chinese.'

'You were at the mountain,' Shan said. 'What happened?'

'I need to find herbs. A healer. I thought maybe here. Someone said priests would be here.'

'A healer for Je?'

'He's very sick. Very weak. Like a leaf on a rotting stem. Soon he will just float away,' Jigme said with a forlorn tone, his eyes hooded and moist, like those of a mourner. 'I don't want him to go. Not Rinpoche too. Don't let him go. I beg you.' He grabbed Shan's hand and squeezed it painfully tight.

A whistle blew. The knobs snapped to attention as a government limousine appeared. Li Aidang jumped out and threw a jaunty, abbreviated salute to the major, then strode over to Tan. They spoke a moment, then Li joined the major along the line of knobs, as though inspecting a parade.

Shan pushed Sergeant Feng aside. 'Go to town,' he said urgently. 'Get Dr Sung. Get her to the barracks.'

Colonel Tan stood as if waiting for Shan, silently watching the civilians.

'Why do the lessons come so hard?' the colonel asked quietly. 'After forty years still they don't understand. They know what we have to do.'

'No,' said Shan. 'They know what they have to do.'

Tan showed no sign of having heard him.

Shan turned to him, fighting the temptation to run back to the fence. 'I have to go inside.'

'In front of the commandos' guns? Like hell.'

'I have no choice. These are my – we can't let them die.'

'You think I want a massacre?' Tan's face clouded. 'Forty years in the army and that's how I will be remembered. For the massacre at the 404th.'

The limousine honked its horn. Tan sighed. 'Li Aidang wants me to follow. We must go. I will drop you at Jade Spring. There is a reception for the American tourists. Then final planning for the Ministry delegation. A special banquet. Comrade Li apparently expects to be installed as Prosecutor after the trial.'

They stopped above the turnoff to Jade Spring Camp. Two soldiers manned a new barricade across the road, restricting access to the prison and the base. On it was a sign, in English only. It said ROAD CLOSED FOR REPAIRS. Shan puzzled over it, then remembered. The American tourists.

Before Shan climbed out of the car Li appeared at the window and dropped an envelope onto Tan's lap.

'I have completed my report and the murderer's statement,' he announced. 'The trial is set for the day after tomorrow, ten in the morning. At the People's Stadium.' He looked at Shan with a new chill in his eyes. 'Ninety minutes have been scheduled. It must not interfere with lunch.'

The top page in the file was a handwritten list of names. Shan pulled it out for closer inspection. Honoured guests for the event at the stadium, to be seated on the stage. Members of the visiting Ministry of Justice delegation topped the list, followed by Colonel Tan and half a dozen local officials. Shan saw Director Hu of the Ministry of Geology listed, and Major Yang of the Public Security Bureau. A shiver moved down his spine as he saw an ideogram near the bottom. No name, no title, just the inverted Y with the two bars.

As Shan pointed to the mark, Tan saw the question in his eyes. 'Just the nickname,' he said with disgust. 'He likes his friends to use it. Thinks it's funny.'

'Sky?'

'Not sky. Heaven. You know, god in heaven. All the priests pay homage to him.'

Shan lifted the paper and stared at it with grim determination. The other guest on the podium was the man who had signed the confirmation on the index card bearing Jao's chop he had taken from the museum, and the same man who had signed the note to Prosecutor Jao, the note that Shan believed, but could not prove, had lured Jao to his death.

Wen Li, Director of Religious Affairs.

Chapter Eighteen

Sungpo was moving for the first time. He held the old man's head in his lap, wiping it with a wet rag, sometimes pausing to drop rice into his mouth, one kernel at a time.

'We tried to get a doctor,' Shan said. He felt helpless. 'A town doctor.' But Dr Sung had refused. When he had called to beg her to change her mind she had offered an abundance of excuses. She had clinic hours, she said. She had surgery, she said. She wasn't authorized for a military base, she said.

'They told you, didn't they?' he had said to her. 'That it was an old abbot.'

'Why would that make a difference?'

'Because of what happened at the Buddhist school.'

In the silence that had followed, Shan wasn't sure if she was still on the line. 'An old man is dying,' he had pleaded. 'If he dies we will have no way to speak to Sungpo. If he dies it may mean another will be wrongly executed. And a murderer will go unpunished.'

'I have a surgery,' Dr Sung had said, almost in a whisper.

'Don't give me excuses,' Shan had replied. 'Just tell me you don't want to.' She did not respond. 'I realized something the other day in your office,' he continued. 'You're not bitter about the world, as you want everyone to think. You're just bitter about yourself.'

The line had gone dead.

'Rinpoche,' Shan said softly. 'I could get *tsampa*. Tell

me what you need to eat.' He felt the old man's pulse. It was slow and faint, like the occasional rustle of a feather.

Je's eyes flickered open. 'I am not in need,' he said with a strength that belied his appearance. 'I am looking for a gate. I found doors, but they are locked. I am looking for my door.'

'It's only another day. We will have you home after tomorrow.'

Je said something, so softly Shan could not hear. It was for Sungpo, who understood, and guided Je's hand to the rosary on his belt. Je began a mantra.

Jigme had been allowed to enter the guardhouse, at Shan's insistence. He had instantly retreated to the darkest corner of the cell. When he returned the rice cup was empty. Shan moved towards the corner. For a moment Jigme blocked his way. He looked back and forth from Sungpo, to Je, then relented.

He had constructed a tiny spirit shrine by pushing two headrest stones against the wall and stacking a third on top. Between the bottom stones were half a dozen balls of rice, the pliers from the desk and the wire. They rested on several small bright white papers.

Shan reached to touch the papers and Jigme slapped his hand away.

'The guard, he had them at the desk when I came. Laughed and showed them to Sungpo. Sungpo meditated. The guard threw them into the cell. I gathered them before anyone could see. I must burn them. They are disrespectful.'

They weren't papers, Shan saw as he turned them over. They were photographs. They were a dozen photographs, of three different monks with Public Security officials. With a wrenching chill Shan recognized the monks from the pictures in Jao's files. Each of the first three members of the Lhadrung Five was the subject of a series of four frames. First, standing between two officers at his trial. Kneeling on the ground. Then a pistol held eighteen inches behind his skull. Finally, sprawled on the ground, dead, his head at the centre of a pool of blood.

With shaking hands, Shan stacked the photos and put them in his pocket.

Sungpo was speaking to Je again. A hoarse wheezing laugh came from the old man. 'He says to tell someone we'll need to begin soon,' Je explained. Begin? Then Shan understood. Begin the rites for passage of his soul. The old man's eyes wandered towards the cell door and lingered uncertainly upon the figure of Yeshe, then moved languidly on. 'When you let it drift sometimes it finds its own way,' he murmured, as if a thought had inadvertently found its way to his tongue.

Jigme was at the bars, holding on as though he might otherwise be carried away. 'We could ask him to come down from the mountain,' he whispered to Shan. 'For such a holy man, maybe he would help.'

'A healer?' Yeshe asked. 'Did you find a healer?'

'He's hungry, that horse-headed one,' Jigme groaned. 'Okay, let him eat me. I don't care. Maybe then you can talk with him, maybe then he'll help you save Sungpo.'

Instantly Shan was at his side, pulling him from the bars. 'You found him? You found Tamdin?'

There was a cave, Jigme finally confessed, where the demon slept. 'The hand of the demon was gone, but the old man we brought from the market knew the prayers well. Only villagers and herders came at first. But then one came from above, stepping down the mountain like a goat, on a path no wider than a man's hand. He had left the prayer against dogbite, recited a few mantras, and climbed back up the slope. Even without the old man I would have known it was Tamdin's servant. Because of them.'

'Them?'

'The vultures. They followed as if they were tame, as if they knew he would provide fresh meat for them.'

Jigme and Sergeant Feng had followed Tamdin's

servant for almost a mile up the slope, into a blind gorge near the top. 'When he left with an empty water jug I went in. But Tamdin was in wolf demon form.' Jigme pulled up his trouser leg to show a jagged, weeping wound on his calf, outlined by a row of punctures. 'Hot damn, I run like hell.'

'You could find him again?' Yeshe asked excitedly.

Jigme nodded slowly, looking at Je. 'Let him eat me, as an offering. I don't care. Sungpo will find me in the next life. Fill his belly, then maybe Tamdin will speak with you. You ask him to come down to the valley, for Rinpoche. But there may not be time. Up that mountain, it is far above the American's shrine.'

'No,' Shan interjected. 'There is a shorter way.'

'How could you know?' Yeshe asked.

'Because I know where Tamdin's servant came from.'

The four men moved over the rocks silently, lost in thought and fear, the wind deviling them, the high altitude sapping their strength. They had found the path where Shan had expected, parallel to the Dragon's Throat, intersecting the road behind the rock formations near the old suspension bridge. It rose precipitously up the North Claw for nearly a mile, then struck a course along the crest of the long ridge.

Jigme, who had insisted on the lead, suddenly dropped to his knees and pointed ahead on the path. 'Him!' he gasped. 'The servant!'

Feng's hand slipped to his holster. 'No,' Shan said. 'He will do us no harm. Let me speak to him alone.'

Shan was sitting alone in a group of boulders, the others hidden on the far side, when the man approached. He was carrying a canvas sack over his shoulder and wore two *gau* around his neck. He stopped abruptly and squinted at Shan.

'Hello, Chinese.'

'I am glad it is you, Merak.'

The *ragyapa* headman nodded as if he understood. 'There never was anyone else asking for the charms, was there?' Shan asked.

Merak set the bag down and leaned against the rock beside Shan, his hand on his *gau*. He seemed relieved to have been discovered. 'But who would have believed it? It's not often a *ragyapa* is able to do great things.'

'What is it you do for him?'

'A demon needs much rest. He must be protected while he rests. I was afraid that if I could find him, others might too.'

'How long has it been?'

'That bastard Xong De. Director of Mines. He refused to let my nephew work in the American mine.'

'Luntok,' Shan said with sudden understanding. 'Your nephew is Luntok? The one who climbs mountains.'

'Yes,' Merak said with obvious pride. 'He is going to climb Chomolungma, you know.'

'But how did he get his job if he was rejected?'

'Xong died. People say Tamdin did it. I believed it, because afterwards Tibetans were given jobs at the mine. Permission for Luntok was quickly granted. I wanted to offer tribute to Tamdin. I knew he lived in the high mountains. I kept watching. Then, when Luntok found his hand I knew where to look. I know our vultures. They seek their food on the high ridges. That bird dropped the hand near the Americans. After he picked it up he would quickly realize it was not his usual food. He would have dropped it soon after finding it.'

'Which meant Tamdin was in a high cave near the Americans.'

Merak nodded vigorously. 'At first I was afraid I had disturbed him. I touched his golden skin. But when I felt his power I realized what I had done, and ran away.'

'But you went back with charms of forgiveness. And you have been helping ever since.'

'He was hurt bad, I could see that. Lost his hand

fighting that last devil. So many battles he has had. I returned his hand, and brought the charm, but I knew he needed rest. So I brought them there, to protect him while he recovered from his wounds. I have been taking food and water ever since.'

'Food and water?'

'I know the difference between demons and creatures of flesh and blood.'

'Why would you need prayers to protect you from them, if they are yours?'

'Not mine. I bought them from a herder. Now they belong to Tamdin.'

Shan studied him with a vague but rising sense of dread. 'Do you wish to come with me?'

Merak picked up his bag and shook his head heavily. 'I know you have to do this, Chinese. People tell about how you did the summoning. You cannot turn back.'

Pointing down the path Merak explained to Shan how the entrance was hidden from view, half a mile away inside a small gorge, then shook his head again. 'I don't want to be there when a Chinese tries to enter. You should wish to come with me. I liked you.'

When they found the gorge Shan studied his companions. 'Sergeant,' he said, with a gesture towards Jigme. 'His leg is bleeding again. You need to bandage it.' Shan ripped off the tail of his shirt and handed it to Feng.

Sergeant Feng, staring nervously into the gorge, seemed not to hear at first. Then he turned and frowned. 'You think I'm scared of the demon?'

'No. I think his leg is bleeding.'

Feng grunted, and guided Jigme to a flat rock at the mouth of the gorge. Shan and Yeshe followed the gorge as it narrowed into a small passage, then abruptly opened into a clearing.

The instant Shan stepped into it, the beasts attacked.

The creatures were eating the food left by Merak, but instantly sprang up at the sight of Shan, teeth bared,

402

growling viciously. They were the biggest dogs he had ever seen, black Tibetan mastiffs, bred to defend the herds against wolves and leopards, but much larger than the dogs Shan had seen in Kham. He saw now why the charms against dogbites were so important to Merak. If they had not been tied they would have torn him apart. When Rebecca Fowler had conducted the ceremony at the foot of the mountain, something had howled in the night.

Beyond the dogs was the cave.

Suddenly, like a cold whisper over his shoulder, he remembered the words of Khorda's fortune-teller. *Bow before black dogs*, she had warned. He dropped to his knees, then prostrated himself. The dogs quieted, curious. There was movement beside him. Yeshe was there, speaking in a low, comforting tone, holding his rosary for the animals to see. Incredibly, the dogs lowered their heads and slowly moved forward. Yeshe began to stroke them, reciting a prayer. Shan remembered Khartok gompa. The dogs were the incarnations of failed priests.

Inside, there were torches leaning against a rock. Shan lit one and followed the tunnel as it curved to the right and opened into a large chamber. He froze, for an instant seized with panic. His heart stopped beating. It was looking at him. It was coming towards him, baring its red fangs. He had violated its holy ground and it would take his head too.

'No!' he called out and shook his head violently, as though to release himself from the spell. He told himself it was a trick of the light and, battling his fear, moved forward. The headdress and costume had been deliberately arranged on a wooden frame to frighten intruders. Its finely worked gold gleamed, and the necklace of skulls danced in the flickering flame. Khorda's summoning spell had worked, he mused darkly. But who was summoning whom? Tamdin seemed to be waiting for him.

There were words Choje would want him to say, but

he could not recall them. There were *mudras* he could make in offering, but his fingers seemed paralysed.

He did not know how long he stood, hypnotized by the creature he had hunted. Finally he jammed the torch between two rocks and moved slowly around the costume, in awe of its power and beauty. On the front, rows of disc-shaped emblems had been sewn. He pulled the disc found by Jilin from his pocket. Just below the waist there was a gap where the disc fit perfectly.

A shudder came from behind him. Yeshe had entered, and was feeling the power of the demon. He dropped to his knees and offered a prayer.

Behind the costume was a flat, table-like rock which held Tamdin's ritual instruments. The nearest was a large curved flaying blade with a handle on top. He touched the blade; it was razor-sharp, certainly sharp enough to sever a human head. Special boots over which were mounted gold-plated shin plates stood under the rock. The arms were arrayed on another rock near the wall, one mangled and missing a hand. Merak had reverently placed the broken hand below it.

Shan touched his *gau*. Oddly, it seemed hot. He slipped a trembling hand into the worn leather sleeve of the functioning arm. It was fitted with elaborate levers and pulleys. He pushed a lever near the wrist and a line of tiny skulls along the upper arm turned. He pushed another and claws extended from the fingers. Another set of arms, small false limbs mounted near the shoulder of the real ones, could be manipulated with rings that fit over the fingers of the dancer. It was a wondrous machine, a vast technical feat even in modern times. Certainly it would take hours to learn to use it. But not weeks, not months. The months of training for the Tamdin dancers, Shan realized, must have been for the ceremonial motions, for the coordination of the machine with the complex rituals for which it had been designed.

Shan pulled Tamdin's arm snugly to his shoulder. It

felt surprisingly comfortable, almost natural. The silk lining allowed almost unfettered movement. He extended the claws and found himself staring at them with a feeling of immense power. He worked them in and out. This was Tamdin. This was the way one became Tamdin.

A feeling of great satisfaction began to swell within him. With this arm, with these claws, with this power, accounts could be settled.

A startled gasp from behind him pushed the spell back. Yeshe leapt forward and began to pull the thing from Shan's arm. Then suddenly Shan too felt the darkness and ripped it from his body. The two men stood over it, then in unison looked up. The two black dogs were sitting at the mouth of the cave, staring at Shan with a silent but chilling intensity.

His hand shaking, Shan pointed to three large rose-wood boxes in the shadows. They quickly discovered that the boxes had been designed to transport the costume, one fitted with a post for the headdress. There was an envelope fastened inside the chest with yellowed tape. From it Yeshe pulled several pages of paper, some brittle with age.

The top pages were the missing audit report from Saskya gompa, completed fourteen months earlier and recording the discovery of the boxes in the quarters of an old lama who had once been the Tamdin dancer.

'But who took it?' Yeshe asked. 'Who stole the costume and brought it here? Director Wen?'

'I think Wen knew, but it is only part of the puzzle. Wen didn't use the costume. Wen didn't take the prosecutor's head to the shrine.' He didn't *believe* enough, is what Shan meant. Whoever had used the costume and severed Jao's head was a zealot.

'You mean you think now a monk did steal it?'

'I don't know,' Shan said, feeling his frustration rise like a great lump in his chest. He had expected the end of his long search for Tamdin would have brought him the answers he needed. 'Maybe only the lama they took it from knows.'

Yeshe turned to the older pages. 'A report,' he announced after scanning the first page. 'An anthropologist from Guangzhou. History of the costume. Details of the ceremony, as he witnessed it in 1958.' He paused and looked up. 'At Saskya gompa. Saskya was the only gompa in the county to perform the dance.' He began reading out loud. 'The knowledge of the ceremony was a sacred trust,' he read, 'passed from a single monk in one generation to one in the next.' The Tamdin dancer in 1958 was considered the best in all of Tibet.

'But who,' Shan thought out loud, 'had the costume last year? The old dancer, if he were still alive. Or his student. He would know who took it. That's the proof we need. That's the link to the murder.'

Yeshe read on silently for a few more paragraphs, then lowered the papers and stared at Shan in confusion. Shan pulled the page from his hand and read it. The dancer in 1958 was Je Rinpoche.

A tent had materialized in front of the barracks, a yurt-style structure of yak-hair felt. Four monks were quietly waiting at the gate. Feng pulled the truck to a stop as they watched.

Four knobs approached the gate, carrying a litter. The gate opened, and the monks took the litter, walking in tiny, painstaking steps, wary of their fragile burden. The tent flap opened and they were admitted. An ancient truck, its engine sputtering loudly, approached, brakes screeching, and parked beside the tent. Shan recognized some of the men who climbed out. Monks from Saskya gompa.

Inside, the tent was hazy with the smoke of incense. The old priest Shan had met in the temple at Saskya was bent over Je, washing Je for the ceremony. A second older monk with a brocaded sleeve – he must be the *kenpo* of

Saskya, Shan realized – presided at the head of the litter, which was raised on bales of straw. As Shan and Yeshe approached, two younger priests stepped before them. Yeshe stepped forward, as though to protect Shan.

'We must speak with him,' Shan protested.

They did not speak, but pointed to a space beside a group of monks who sat before the pallet, spinning prayer wheels and softly reciting mantras.

'One question,' Yeshe said urgently. 'Rinpoche would not begrudge one question.'

The priest glared at Yeshe. 'Where did you study?'

'Khartok gompa. I can explain,' Yeshe pleaded. 'It is about saving Sungpo. Maybe even saving the 404th.'

The priest looked at Shan. 'The Bardo ceremony has been started. The transition has already begun. His soul. Already it is lifting out. It requires all his concentration. He can see a small light now, in the far distance. If he breaks away, if he loses it for an instant he could be sent somewhere that was not intended. He may never find it. He may drift endlessly. This monk from Khartok knows that,' he said with a scornful glance at Yeshe.

They sat and waited. Yeshe began saying his rosary, but as Shan watched he slowly lost count and began twisting his fingers, turning the knuckles white. Butter lamps were brought in and lit.

'You don't understand!' Yeshe suddenly blurted. 'He could save Sungpo! We can protect the 404th!'

The *kenpo* turned and stared icily. One of the younger monks angrily stepped towards Yeshe as though to restrain him physically, but was interrupted by a sudden stirring at the door. Low, urgent protests could be heard. The flap was thrown open and Dr Sung appeared. She glared at Shan and ignored everyone else, then stepped to the pallet. The moment she opened her bag the abbot called out and clamped his hand over her arm.

She did not speak. Their eyes locked. With her free hand she pulled a stethoscope from the bag, slung it around her neck and then, one finger at a time, peeled away the abbot's hand. He did not move but did not stop her examination.

'His heart isn't beating enough to keep a child alive,' she said. 'I suspect a blockage.'

'Is it treatable?' Shan asked.

'Perhaps. But not here. I'd need to run tests at the clinic.'

'Just one question,' Yeshe pressed, looking at his watch. 'We need to know. He is the only one who can tell us.'

Sung shrugged and filled a syringe with a clear fluid. 'This will wake him,' she said. 'At least briefly.' She scrubbed Je's arm.

As she bent with the needle the abbot placed his hand over the prepared patch of skin. 'You have no idea of what you are doing,' he said.

'He's an old man in need of help,' Yeshe pleaded. 'He doesn't have to die here. If he dies now, Sungpo may die too.'

'His entire life was dedicated to this moment of transition,' the abbot warned. 'It cannot be stopped. He has already begun to cross over. He is in a place none of us are allowed to disturb.'

Dr Sung looked at the priest as if for the first time, then slowly lowered the syringe and looked to Shan, who moved to the platform. 'You're the one who asked me,' she said. But her confused tone made it sound more like a question than an accusation.

'If he dies today, Sungpo will die tomorrow,' Yeshe said in a desolate voice over Shan's shoulder. 'It will all be for nothing. If we don't have the answer now, we will never have it.'

Shan gestured towards the entrance. The doctor dropped her instruments on the pallet and followed him.

'If it is sickness we should take him back,' Shan said quietly. 'If it is just a natural passing –'

'What do you mean, natural?' Dr Sung asked.

Shan looked outside, past the barbed wire to the long building where Sungpo sat. 'I guess I don't know any more.'

'If I could do tests,' Sung suggested, 'maybe we could –'

She was interrupted by a horrified shout. They spun about. The priests were jumping to their feet. The old abbot was flogging Yeshe on the head with a ritual bell.

Yeshe stood over the pallet with tears running down his eyes. He had injected the syringe into Je.

Everyone was shouting. Someone demanded to know the name of Yeshe's abbot. Someone grabbed his red shirt and ripped it off his back. They were abruptly silenced by the rising of Je's arm.

The arm extended vertically, the hand rotating in a slow eerie motion, as if clutching for something just beyond its grasp.

Shan darted to Je's side and wiped his forehead with the wet rag. The old man's eyes fluttered opened and he stared at the felt above him. He brought the extended hand down to his face and studied it, moving the fingers with exquisite slowness, like that of a butterfly in the cold. He turned and put his fingers on Shan's face, squinting as if he could not see it well. 'Which level is it, then?' he whispered in a dry croaking voice.

'Rinpoche,' Yeshe said urgently. 'You were the Tamdin dancer at Saskya. You kept the costume until last year. Who took it from you?' he pleaded. 'Did you teach it to them? Who was it? We must learn who took the costume.'

Je gave a hoarse laugh. 'I knew people like you in the other place,' he said with a rasping breath.

'Rinpoche. Please. Who was it?'

His eyes flickered and shut. There was a new sound, a rattle in his chest. They watched in agonized silence for several minutes.

Then the eyes opened again, very wide. 'In the end,' he said slowly, as though listening for something, each word punctuated by the wheezing rattle, 'all it takes is one perfect sound.' He closed his eyes and the rattle stopped. 'He's dead,' Dr Sung announced.

Chapter Nineteen

Yeshe stared at the body in utter desolation. The eyes of the old man at the foot of the pallet welled with tears. A voice in the back shouted out an epithet in Tibetan. The priest who had been conducting the Bardo ceremony began to speak with a chilling ferocity, a dark chant Shan had never heard before. He was glaring at Yeshe as he spoke, his invective coming faster and louder. Yeshe stared at him mutely, his face drained of colour.

Shan pulled Yeshe's arm but he seemed unable to move. The attending priest, tears pouring down his cheek, was frantically searching through the hair on the crown of Je's head. If properly prepared, Je's soul would have drifted out of a tiny hole thought to be on every human's crown.

'Get him a bone!' someone yelled from the rear.

'His name is Yeshe!' another shouted. 'Khartok gompa.'

Shan put his shoulder into Yeshe and pushed him out of the yurt. Something inside Yeshe had collapsed. He seemed suddenly feeble and senseless. Shan took his hand and led him to the cell block. Inside, Sungpo was chanting now, a new mantra, a sad mantra. Somehow he knew.

'It doesn't matter,' Shan said to Yeshe, not because he believed it but because he couldn't bear Yeshe to become still another victim.

'Above all, it matters,' Yeshe was shaking now. He stepped into an empty cell and gripped the bars to steady himself. There was a fear on his face that Shan had never

411

seen before. 'What I did – it destroyed the moment of his transition. I ruined his soul. I ruined my soul,' he said with chilling certainty. 'And I don't even know why.'

'You did it to help Sungpo. You did it to find justice for Dilgo. You did it for the truth.' He hadn't told Yeshe about the coral rosary in the Lhasa museum, the duplicate of Dilgo's, the rosary that no doubt had been planted to implicate Dilgo and ensnare Yeshe in the lies. It didn't matter that Yeshe learned of the evidence, because his heart had learned of the lie long ago.

'Your justice. Your damned justice,' Yeshe groaned. 'Why did I believe you?' He seemed to be getting smaller, shrinking before Shan's eyes. 'Maybe it's true,' Yeshe said, with a realization that seemed to horrify him. 'Maybe you did summon Tamdin. Maybe he's been lurking around us all the time. Maybe he used you to create the ruthlessness. He lays waste to everything, lays waste even to souls, in the search for truth.'

'You can go to your gompa. You want to be a priest again, you've shown me. They will help you.'

Yeshe moved to the back wall and slumped against it. When he looked up he appeared so gaunt it seemed the flesh had shrivelled on his bones. His colour had not returned. He was not Yeshe, but a ghost of Yeshe. 'They will spit on me. They will drive me from the temples. I can never go back now. And I can't go to Sichuan. I can't be one of them any more. I don't want to be a good Chinese,' he said. 'You destroyed that for me, too.' He fixed Shan with haunted eyes. 'What have you done to me? I took four. I might as well have jumped from a cliff.' Throw him a bone, the monks had said. 'For nothing.'

He slowly slid down the wall to the floor. Tears were streaming down his cheek. He found his rosary and pulled it apart. The beads slowly dropped onto the floor and rolled away.

Numbed by his helplessness, Shan filled a tea mug with

412

water and handed it to him. It fell through Yeshe's hands and shattered on the floor. Struggling to find words of comfort, Shan began picking up the pieces of porcelain, then stopped and dropped to his knees. He stared at the shards in his hands.

'No,' Shan said excitedly. 'Je told us exactly what we needed to know. Look!' he said, shaking Yeshe's shoulder as he held up a shard. 'Do you see it?'

But Yeshe was beyond hearing him. With an aching heart Shan rose, gave Yeshe one last painful look, then darted out of the building.

When Sergeant Feng and Shan arrived at the market, Feng made no effort to leave the truck. Shan moved straight towards the healer's shop. But he did not enter Khorda's hut. He stood in the alley beside it. A youth in a herder's vest appeared beside him. 'Wait,' the youth said urgently. Moments later he returned with the scar-faced *purba*.

'You don't need to go to the mountain,' Shan told him. 'You don't need to sacrifice yourself. I found another way.'

The *purba* looked at him sceptically.

'I need to go with the food today. To the 404th,' Shan said.

'We don't deliver the food. It is the responsibility of the relief association.'

'But sometimes you go with them. There is no time for games. I know what happens now. Sometimes you leave someone behind.'

'I don't understand,' the *purba* said stiffly.

'The camp of the 404th is built on rock. There is no tunnel. There is no hole in the wire fence. And no one is flying through the air like an arrow.'

The *purba* surveyed the marketplace over Shan's shoulder. 'Have you finished your investigation?'

'I've seen Trinle. Not at the 404th.'

'Trinle is a very holy man. He is often underestimated.'

'I don't underestimate him. Not now. For him the 404th is not a prison. He comes and goes on the business of Nambe gompa. He comes and goes with the *purbas*. There is no one else who could do it for him.'

'And how would we perform this magic?'

'I don't know exactly. But it shouldn't be difficult so long as the headcount isn't changed.'

The *purba* winced, as though he had bitten something sour. 'To take the place of a prisoner would be foolhardy. It would risk immediate execution.'

'Which is why it is a *purba* who does it.'

The man did not react.

'Trinle is sick more than most,' Shan said. 'We have become used to it. Sometimes he stays confined to his bunk with his blanket over his head. Now I know why. Because it isn't him. I can guess how it is done. On agreed days *purbas* help with the food, when the relief association serves meals. One man wears prison clothes under his civilian clothes. When Trinle reaches the food tables there is a distraction. Perhaps he ducks under the tables and puts on the civilian clothes. The *purba* switches with him, and stays in the 404th until Trinle returns. The guards are not fastidious. They don't know every prisoner's face. As long as the headcount is the same, how could there be an escape? And as long as his face stays hidden, what other prisoners will suspect?'

The *purba* stared at Shan. 'What exactly do you want?'

'I need to get through the dead zone. Today.'

'Like you said, it is very dangerous. Someone could be killed.'

'Someone *has* been killed. How many more does it take?'

The *purba* looked out over the market as though in search of the answer. 'Cabbages,' he announced suddenly. 'Watch for cabbages,' he said, and seemed to glide away.

Twenty minutes later as Feng drove through the town traffic, a cart of cabbages upturned directly in their path. As Feng moved into reverse, a second cart suddenly blocked them.

Instantly Shan jumped out. 'This is what you must do. Go to Tan. Tell him he must come with you to the 404th. Meet me at the wire with him in two hours.' He turned, ignoring Sergeant Feng's weak protest, and disappeared into the crowd.

An hour later he was inside the 404th, wearing an oversized wool hat and the armband of the charity, serving out bowls of barley gruel. When half the line had filed past, a bucket of water was dropped on a guard's foot. The guard shouted. The Tibetan carrying the bucket fell backwards, knocking over a prisoner. More guards ran to investigate.

In the ensuing confusion Shan ducked under the opposite end of the long table, which had been draped with a dirty piece of felt, discarded his jacket and entered the line, wearing prison clothes provided by the *purbas*.

Choje was not eating. Shan found him meditating in his hut, and sat in front of him. His eyes flickered open and he put his hand on Shan's cheek, as though making sure he was real. 'It is a joy to see you. But you have selected a troubled moment to return.'

'I needed to speak to the abbot of Nambe gompa.'

'Nambe was destroyed.'

'Its buildings were destroyed. Its population was imprisoned. But the gompa lives.'

Choje shrugged. 'It could not be allowed to die.'

'Because of the promises made about Yerpa. To the Second Dalai Lama.'

Choje showed no surprise. 'More than a promise. A sacred duty.' His lips curled into a weak smile. 'It is wonderful, is it not?'

'Do the *purbas* know, Rinpoche?'

Choje shook his head. 'They want to help all prisoners.

415

It is the right thing to do. But they never needed to know our secret. We have a duty not to tell. It is enough for them to know that Nambe gompa lives, that by helping Trinle they keep it alive.'

Shan nodded as Choje confirmed his suspicion. 'I understand now why Trinle had to go, why the arrow rite finally seemed to work. You had to be certain the knobs acted in public. Once the miracle happened witnesses were sure to come, as word leaked out of the magic.'

Choje looked into his hands. 'We were worried, Trinle and I, that maybe what we did was a lie.'

'No,' Shan assured him. 'It was no lie. What you have been doing *is* a miracle, Rinpoche.'

The serene smile lit Choje's countenance again.

'You know the world will think that all this was to save one soul,' Shan said.

'The soul of a Chinese prosecutor. It is not such a bad lesson, Xiao Shan.'

One hundred and eighty monks commit suicide to save the soul of their prosecutor, Shan considered. Anywhere else it would be the stuff of legend. But here it was just another day in Tibet.

'But you and I know it is not the real reason.'

Choje bowed his hands, the fingers touching at the tips. It was an offering *mudra*, the flask of treasure. Choje stared at it with a distant smile and pushed his hands towards Shan. Silently Shan did as Choje desired, forming his own hands into the shape. Choje made a gesture of pouring his flask into Shan's, then drew his hands slowly apart, leaving Shan with the flask.

'There,' he said. 'The treasure is yours.'

Shan felt his eyes well up with moisture. 'No,' he whispered in weak protest, and clenched his eyes, fighting the tears. They will still build the road after you die, he wanted to say. But he knew Choje's answer. It didn't matter, as long as Choje and Nambe gompa had been true.

'The thunder ritual, it is also part of Nambe's duty, isn't it?'

Choje nodded approvingly. 'Your eyes have always seen far, my friend. Nambe was already centuries old when the vow was made to protect the *gomchen*. Nambe was the centre of the ritual. It had perfected the practice. For a mortal being to make thunder requires an intense balance, the highest state of meditation. Some say it was the reason we were honoured with the protection of Yerpa.'

'Trinle and Gendun, they are masters of the ritual.'

Choje only smiled.

They remained silent and listened to the mantras beginning outside as the monks finished eating.

'You came with a request,' Choje said at last.

'Yes. I must speak to Trinle. About that night. I know he will not talk without your permission.'

Choje considered Shan's words. 'You are asking a great deal.'

'There is still a chance, Rinpoche. A chance to save Nambe and Yerpa. You have to let me find the truth.'

'There is always an end to things, Xiao Shan.'

'Then if there is to be an end,' Shan said, 'let it end in light, not in shadow.'

'They would give them drugs, you know, if they caught Trinle or Gendun. Like spells, those drugs. They would be powerless to resist the questions. They know that. If the soldiers try to take them, Trinle and Gendun will choose to die. Can you bear that burden?'

'If the soldiers try to take them,' Shan replied quickly, 'I too will choose to die.' It was a simple thing, to die when the knobs finally came for you. If you ran away they would shoot. If you ran at them they would shoot. If you resisted they would shoot.

He saw Choje smiling at him and looked down. Shan's

hands were still in the *mudra*, holding the treasure flask, as Choje began to talk.

Twenty minutes later he stood at the edge of the dead zone and took off his prison shirt. He took one step forward. The knobs shouted a warning. Three of them cocked their rifles and aimed directly at him. An officer pulled his pistol and was about to fire into the air when a hand closed around the gun and pushed it down. It was Tan.

'You have less than eighteen hours,' Tan growled. 'You should be finishing the official report.' But as they moved away from the knobs his anger faded. 'The Ministry delegation. They are already with Li. They changed the schedule. The trial will be at eight o'clock tomorrow morning.'

Shan looked up in alarm. 'You have to delay.'

'On what grounds?'

'I have a witness.'

Chapter Twenty

They arrived before dawn, as Choje had instructed. Do not speak to the *purbas*, he had said. Do not let the knobs follow. Just be there as the sun rises, at the clearing before the new bridge.

'There was no sign of him?' Shan asked as Sergeant Feng switched off the engine. 'Maybe he moved to another barracks. He has no place to go.'

'Nope. He's gone. Down the road at nightfall,' Feng said. 'You won't see him again.'

Yeshe's bag had been gone when Shan had returned to the barracks. 'He didn't say anything, didn't leave anything?'

Sergeant Feng reached into his pocket. 'Only this,' he said, laying the ruined rosary on the dashboard, nothing but string and two marker beads. He yawned and lowered the back of his seat. 'I know where he went. He asked how to get there. That chemical factory in Lhasa. They hire lots of Tibetans, with or without papers.'

Shan put his head in his hands.

'We could ask patrols to pick him up, if you still need him.'

'No,' Shan replied grimly, and climbed out of the truck.

There was nothing, just the sliver of the moon over the black outline of the mountains. As the stars blinked out he found himself watching for Jao's ghost.

Another vehicle appeared along the road from town, and eased in behind the truck. It was Tan, driving his own car. He was wearing a pistol.

'I don't like it,' Tan said. 'A witness who hides is useless. How will he testify? He will have to come with us, to the trial. They will ask why he speaks up now, so late.' He studied the dark landscape, then looked suspiciously at Shan. 'If it is a cultist, they will say he is an accomplice.'

Shan continued staring into the heather. 'A group of monks were watching the bridge,' he explained. 'They were trying to cause it to collapse.'

Tan muttered a low curse. 'By watching it?' he asked bitterly. He looked back at his car, as though he might leave, then followed Shan slowly into the clearing.

'By shouting at it,' Shan said. How could he explain the rite of the shards? How could he explain the broken pots above the bridge or at Yerpa, where Trinle and the others trained in the old ritual of thunder? How could he explain the ancient belief that a perfect sound was the most destructive force of nature? 'Not a shout, really. Creating sound waves. It was what scared Sergeant Feng that night he fired his pistol. Like a clap of –'

He stopped. In the gathering light he saw a grey shape thirty feet away at the end of the clearing, a large rock that was gradually becoming the shape of a man sitting on the earth. It was Gendun.

They stopped six feet away. 'This is a priest of a nearby gompa,' Shan explained to Tan, then turned to Gendun. 'Can you explain where you were the night of the prosecutor's murder?'

'Above the bridge,' Gendun said in a firm, quiet voice, as though he were saying prayers. 'In the rocks, chanting.'

'Why?'

'In the sixteenth century there was a Mongolian invasion. Priests of my gompa stopped it from reaching Lahdrung by causing an avalanche to fall on the army.'

Tan glared furiously at Shan, but before he could turn

420

away Gendun continued. 'This bridge. It does not belong here. It is destined to fall away.'

He was interrupted by the sound of a heavy truck speeding on the gravel road behind them. As it skidded to a stop Li Aidang jumped out, clad in military fatigues. He took ten steps into the clearing, then snapped out an order. Half a dozen uniformed knobs began leaping from the truck. The major appeared in the headlights, a small automatic gun hanging from his shoulder. The troops formed in a single line along the road, in front of Li.

A strange serenity settled over Gendun, a distant look. He paid no attention to the knobs, but studied the mountains as if trying to remember them for future reference. He could not control his next incarnation. He might rekindle on the floor of a desert hut thousands of miles away.

'The sun had been down maybe an hour when the headlights of a car appeared,' he suddenly continued. 'It stopped near the bridge and turned out its lights. Then there were voices. Two men I think, and a woman laughing. I think she was intoxicated.'

'A woman?' Shan asked. 'There was a woman with Prosecutor Jao?'

'No. This was the first car.'

The silence before dawn was like no other. It seemed to hold the troops in a spell. Gendun's words were loud and clear. An owl's call eerily echoed from the gorge.

'Then she screamed. A death scream.'

The words snapped Li out of his trance. He stepped into the clearing and moved towards Gendun. Shan stepped in front of him.

'Do not attempt to interfere with the Ministry of Justice,' Li snarled. 'This man is a conspirator. He admits he was there. He will join Sungpo in the dock.'

'We are still conducting an investigation,' Shan protested.

'No,' Li said fiercely. 'It is over. The Ministry will open

421

its trial in three hours. I am scheduled to deliver the prosecution report.'

'I don't think so,' Tan said, so quietly Shan was not sure if he heard correctly.

Li ignored him and began to gesture for the knobs.

'There will be no trial without the prisoner,' Tan continued.

'What are you saying?' Li snapped.

'I had him removed from the guardhouse. At midnight last night.'

'Impossible. He had Public Security guards.'

'They were called away. Replaced with some of my aides. Seems there was some confusion about orders.'

'You have no authority!' Li barked.

'Until Beijing decides otherwise, I am the senior official in this county.' Tan paused and cocked his head towards the hillside.

It was a droning sound that distracted him, as though of frogs, a sound of nature that had not been there before. But then it seemed much closer. In the rising light another priest became visible at the edge of the clearing, ten feet from Gendun. It was Trinle. He was in the lotus position, chanting a mantra in a low nasal tone. Li smirked and approached Trinle, the new object of his furore. Then there was an echoing sound from the opposite side of the clearing. Shan stepped in that direction and discerned another red robe in the brush. Li took another angry step towards Trinle and paused. A third voice joined in, and a fourth, all in the same rhythm, the same tone. The sound seemed to be coming from nowhere, and everywhere.

'Seize them!' Li cried. But the knobs stood, transfixed, staring into the brush.

The day was breaking rapidly now, and Shan could see the robes along the edge of the clearing well enough to count them. Six. Ten. No, more. Fifteen. He recognized several of the faces. Some were *purbas*. Some were from the mountain, protectors of the *gomchen*.

Li turned and pulled a truncheon from the belt of a soldier. He walked along the perimeter with a ravenous glare, waving the club. He stopped at the rear of the circle and pounded it against Trinle's back. Trinle did not react. Li shouted in fury for the major, who moved forward with uncertain steps and stopped ten feet from Trinle. Li moved to his side and seemed about to grab his gun.

Shan willed himself to step between them and Trinle. There was new movement at the side of the circle. Sergeant Feng appeared, with the lug wrench from the truck. It was over, Shan realized. That he had lost was no surprise. But that the 404th, and Yerpa, would be lost was unbearable. He ached for it at least to be over quickly. It would be fitting, he thought absently, if the bullet came from Sergeant Feng.

'Back away,' he heard Feng growl. But the sergeant was not speaking to him. Feng turned and stood beside Shan, facing Li and the major. The mantra continued.

'You old pig,' Li sneered at Feng. 'You're ruined.'

'My job is to watch over Comrade Shan,' Feng grunted, and braced his feet as though preparing for an attack.

The mantra seemed to swell as it filled the brittle silence again. The major stepped back to his men and ordered them to pull the truncheons from their belts.

Tan materialized at Shan's side. His face was taut. He glanced at Shan with a strangely sad expression, then turned to face Li. 'These people,' he said, with a gesture that encompassed the circle, 'are under my protection.'

Li stared at Tan. 'Your protection is worthless, Colonel,' he snarled. 'We are conducting an investigation of you. Corruption in the performance of duties. We revoke your authority.'

Tan's hand moved to his holster. The major reached for his machine gun.

Suddenly there was a new sound above the chanting, the hissing of air brakes. They turned, aghast, to see a long shiny bus pulling to a halt. Windows were being pulled down.

'Martha!' someone called in English. 'They're doing morning services. Get the damned film changed!'

The tourists came out of their bus, single file, clicking their cameras, rolling video of the monks, of Shan, of Li and the knobs.

Shan looked into the bus. The man at the wheel was familiar, a face from the marketplace. With him, wearing a trim business suit with a tie, was Miss Taring of the Bureau of Religious Affairs. She began speaking about Buddhist rites, and the closeness of the Buddhists to the forces of nature.

She climbed out and offered to use an American couple's camera to take photos of them with the Chinese soldiers.

The major studied her for a moment, then quickly herded his men into the truck. Li stepped backwards. 'It doesn't matter,' he spat under his breath, 'we have already won.' He waved to the Americans with an affected smile and climbed in the front of the truck with the major. In moments they were gone. Then, as abruptly as it had arrived, the bus too moved on.

Tan sat down in front of Gendun. Instantly the mantra stopped. Trinle appeared and knelt at Gendun's side.

'Tell me about the woman,' Tan said.

'She seemed very happy. Then – there is nothing so terrible as the scream of someone unprepared for death. Afterwards there were other voices, not hers. That's all.'

'Nothing else?'

'Not until the second car. It drove up an hour later. Two doors slammed. There were shouts, a man called out for someone.'

'Calling a name?'

'The man from below called "Are you there?" He said he knew where the flower came from. He said, "What do you mean I won't need the X-ray machine?" The man above said, "Esteemed Comrade, I know where you should look." The man below,' Gendun continued, 'said he would make a trade, for more evidence.'

Shan and the colonel shared a glance. Esteemed Comrade.

'Then he moved up the slope. The voices were much lower, and faded as they climbed. Then there was another sound. Not a shout. A loud groan. Then ten, fifteen minutes later the lights of the car went on. I saw him, maybe a hundred feet from the car. The man in the car got out and ran down the road.'

'You said you saw him in the lights.'

'Yes.'

'You recognized him?' Shan asked.

'Of course. I had seen him before, in the festivals.'

'You were not scared?'

'I have nothing to fear of a protecting demon.'

They reduced Gendun's testimony to a written statement, which Tan authenticated with his own chop. He did not ask Gendun to remain behind as the monks began to rise and fade into the heather.

'The next morning,' Shan asked as Gendun moved to join his companions, 'was there anything unusual?'

'I left before the work crews arrived, as I had been warned. There was only the one thing.'

'What thing?'

'The noise. It surprised me, how early they started. Before dawn. The sound of heavy equipment. Not here. Further away. I could only hear it, as though it came from above.'

They made a solemn procession into the compound of the boron mine an hour later, Tan's car in front, the truck of soldiers summoned by Tan's radio, and finally, Shan and Sergeant Feng. They drove straight to the equipment shed, where they selected a heavy tractor with a digging bucket and the mine's bulldozer. The machines were already moving onto the dyke by the time the first figures emerged from the buildings.

Rebecca Fowler ran towards them, then stopped and sent Kincaid back for his camera as soon as she recognized Tan. The colonel motioned for her to stop, then deployed soldiers to cut off access to the dyke.

'How dare you!' Fowler exploded as soon as she was in earshot. 'I have a call in to the Ministry of Geology. I'll call Beijing! I'll call the US!'

'Interfere and I'll close the mine,' Tan said impassively.

'Damned MFCs!' Kincaid barked, and began snapping photographs of Tan, of the licence plates of the vehicles, and of the machines and the guards. He paused as he saw Shan. He took another photo, then lowered the camera and stared at Shan uncertainly.

The tractor dug into the dyke where it crossed the gorge, where it was the deepest, where Shan remembered seeing equipment in the satellite photos taken just before the dyke was completed, where one final gap had remained just before the murder. It was twenty minutes before the bucket struck metal, another twenty minutes before they had confirmed that the car they had found was a Red Flag limousine and hooked it to the bulldozer.

The machine churned against the turf, ripping it apart, until it found traction. The engine heaved and for a moment everything seemed to stop. As the car slowly pulled free of the mud, there was an extraordinary sound, unlike any Shan had ever heard, a ripping, unworldly groan that shook his spine.

The bulldozer did not stop until it had dragged the car nearly to the head of the dyke.

Shan looked inside and saw a briefcase.

'Open it,' Tan said impatiently.

The door swung open easily, emitting an almost overwhelming smell of decay. Inside the case were Jao's tickets, a thick file, and a satellite photo, cropped down to the poppy fields.

The trunk was jammed. Tan grabbed a crowbar from the bulldozer and popped the lid open. Inside, shrunken within a colourful floral dress, was a young woman. Her mouth was drawn into a hideous grin. Her lifeless eyes seemed to stare right at Shan. Lying on her breast was a dried flower. A red poppy.

A horrifed moan escaped Tan. He turned and hurled the crowbar into the lake. He turned back, his face drained of colour. 'Comrade Shan,' he said, 'this is Miss Lihua.'

Rebecca Fowler stood paralysed, staring in mute horror into the trunk as Tan moved to the radio in his car. It seemed as though she was drying up as Shan watched, as though any minute she would crumble and blow away in the wind. For a moment he thought she would faint. Then she caught Tan's stare, and the resentment brought her strength back. She began barking orders for the bulldozer to move the car off the dyke, for the machines to start filling the gaping hole, for dumper trucks to be filled with gravel, then began running towards the hole, shouting for Kincaid.

By the time Shan joined her, she was on her knees. Water was rapidly seeping through the weakened dam. With small, frantic groans she shoved dirt into the hole. The tractor arrived beside her and began pushing dirt with its bucket. A trickle appeared on the side of the hole. As the tractor edged closer the dirt under it began to shift. Fowler screamed, leapt up, and pulled the driver away just as the wall disintegrated and the machine lurched into the hole. The back wall held for the few seconds it took for the hole to fill with water, then it too was gone. The tractor was washed into the gorge and the pond broke through.

They watched helplessly as the water hurled down the Dragon Throat, ripping boulders from the sides, collapsing the banks, gathering speed as it dropped under the old suspension bridge towards the plain below in a maelstrom of rock, water, and gravel. Shan became aware of Tan standing beside him. He had binoculars. He was watching his bridge.

But they did not need the lenses to see the wall of water slam into the concrete pillars. The bridge seemed to totter for a moment, like a fragile toy, then it lurched upward and was gone.

Shan remembered the sound of the dyke surrendering the car, the shudder of the earth, the wrenching, sucking, squeezing scream of the mud that had shaken his spine.

All it would take, Je had said, was one perfect sound.

Kincaid, who had darted past the disinterred limousine to join Fowler, now stood by the open trunk, his jaw open, his eyes disbelieving. 'Jesus,' he moaned with a cracking voice. 'Oh Jesus.' He bent as though he needed to touch Fowler, then stopped and slowly straightened. As though guided by some sixth sense he turned to stare at the road leading down to the mine. Following his gaze, Shan saw a new vehicle appear, a bright red Land Rover.

Even from thirty feet away Shan could sense Kincaid's body tighten. 'Damn you!' the man screamed, and began running towards the road, bending to grab stones which he hurled in the direction of the still distant vehicle. 'Come and see her, you bastards!'

The red truck halted, then began backing up the ridge and disappeared.

Tan had also noticed. He was back on his radio.

Luntok appeared, carrying a blanket to the limousine. The *ragyapa* were never afraid of the dead. He reverently covered the woman in the trunk then turned and stared at his friend Kincaid. But there was something new in his eyes.

Rebecca Fowler took a step towards the *ragyapa* engineer. 'Whose workcrew was responsible for the final fill on this dam?' she asked him in a strained voice. Luntok did not reply but kept staring at Kincaid.

The expression on Kincaid's face hardened momentarily into defiance as he glared back at Luntok. But when he looked at Fowler and Shan, standing together near the car, confusion seemed to overcome him. He bolted towards the office building.

Fowler's sigh was almost a sob. 'If my mine was hiding someone's evidence,' she said, 'we could be deported, couldn't we?'

Shan did not reply, and watched as she slowly followed Kincaid. Five minutes later Shan found her in the computer room, her head in her hands, staring into a cup of tea. Kincaid was also there, playing slow, sad notes on his harmonica, one hand urgently scrolling text on the screen of the satellite console.

'It's over,' Shan said as he sat across from her.

'Damned straight. I'll lose my job. I'll lose my reputation. I'll be lucky if they give me the airfare home.' Everything about Rebecca Fowler, her voice, her face, her very being, seemed to have been hollowed out.

'It wasn't your fault. The army will rebuild your dam. The Ministry of Geology will receive an official explanation. This is Party business. They will clean it up quietly.'

'I don't even know what to report home.'

'An accident. An act of nature.'

Fowler looked up. 'That poor woman. We knew her. Tyler took her hiking sometimes.'

'I saw her in the photos on the wall.' Shan nodded. 'But I believe she knew what Prosecutor Jao knew. If Jao had to die, so did she.'

'Someone said she was on leave.'

'Someone lied.' He remembered how excited Tan had

been when he had established contact with Lihua by fax. The faxes had indeed come from Hong Kong. Shan had seen the telephone transmission codes. The source had even been identified as the local Ministry of Justice office. Someone had lied in Hong Kong. Li, who had reported taking her to the airport the night she died, had lied in Lhadrung.

'The satellite photos and the water permits,' Fowler said. 'It was somehow about them.'

'I'm afraid so.'

Fowler buried her head in her hands again. 'You mean I started it all?'

'No. What you started was the end of it all.'

'The end of Jao. The end of Lihua.' Her voice was desolate.

'No. Jao was already marked for murder. They probably would have eventually found a way for Miss Lihua to disappear.'

Fowler looked up with a haunted expression.

'There were five murders really, five that we know of. Plus the three innocent men wrongly executed.' Shan poured himself some tea from a thermos on the table before continuing. After seeing the body in the car he felt he might never get the chill out of his gut. 'It seemed hopelessly confused. What I didn't understand at first was that there were two cases, not one. The murder of Prosecutor Jao. And Jao's investigation. I couldn't understand the murder without understanding what Jao was tracking. And the motives. Not one, not two, but several, all coming together that night on the Dragon's Claw.'

'Five murders? Jao. Lihua —'

'And the victims of the earlier trials. The former Director of Religious Affairs. The former Director of Mines. The former Manager of the Long Wall collective. Then the monks. I never believed the Lhadrung Five were guilty. But the likely suspects never fit the crime. No

430

pattern. Because it wasn't a single man. It was all of them.'

'All of them? Not all the *purbas*.'

Shan shook his head and sighed. 'The hardest thing was connecting the victims. They were all the leaders of a large government operation so they were symbolic of the injury inflicted on Tibetans. The activists were instant suspects. But no one focused on a more immediate motive. The victims were also officials. And they were all old.'

'Old?'

'They were the senior officials in their offices. Very powerful offices. Among them, they ran most of the county. And below each of them, next in line, was someone much younger, a member of the Bei Da Union.' He stood behind the console. Kincaid was calling up the log of map orders.

Rebecca Fowler's mouth opened but she seemed unable to speak. 'You mean the Union was like some sort of club for murderers?' she asked finally.

Shan stood and paced along the long table. 'Li was successor to Jao. Wen took over the Religious Affairs Bureau when Lin died. Hu took over at the Ministry of Geology. The head of the Long Wall collective didn't have to be replaced, because it was dissolved due to its criminal activities. Maybe they didn't even know about it when they started the killing. But when they discovered it generated huge revenues as a drug supplier, how could they resist?' What was it Li had said the first time they had met? Tibet was a land of opportunity. He picked up one of the glossy American catalogues and slid it towards Fowler. 'Most of the things in here cost more than they make in a month on their official salaries.'

Kincaid still sat staring at the computer monitor. He had stopped blowing into his harmonica. His knuckles, gripping the edge of the table, were white. 'You showed him,' he whispered. 'You showed Shan the maps. There were none in the files so you actually transmitted them down for him. You never order maps on your own.'

Fowler turned towards him, not understanding. 'I had to, Tyler, it was about Jao's murder. Those water rights we never understood.'

But Kincaid was looking at Shan, who had moved close enough to read the screen. It was not the computer log for Jao's poppy fields Kincaid was studying. It was the log for the maps of the South Claw. The maps that had revealed Yerpa to the American engineer.

'When we studied the photos taken of the skulls in the cave, we found the one that had been moved,' Shan said. 'Not destroyed, just reverently moved. I thought it meant a monk had been there. But a monk would have been able to read the Tibetan date with each skull. He would be unlikely to tamper with the order of the sequence of the shrine. Much later I realized someone could have been reverent towards the skull but not able to read Tibetan.' Kincaid seemed not to have heard.

'You mean it was a Chinese?' Fowler said weakly.

Shan lowered himself wearily into a chair across from Fowler and decided to try a different direction. 'The *Lotus Book* can be easily misunderstood.'

'The *Lotus Book*?' Fowler asked.

Shan clasped his hands together on the table and stared into them as he spoke. An immense sadness, an almost paralysing melancholy, had settled over him. 'It isn't about revenge,' he went on. Kincaid was slowly turning to face him. 'It isn't about vindication. The *purbas* don't mind committing treason in compiling the records, but they will not kill. The *Book*'s just – it's very Tibetan. A way of shaming the world. A way of enshrining the lost ones. But not for killing. That's not the Tibetan way.' Shan looked up. Why, he wondered, did justice always taste so bitter?

'I don't understand anything you're –' Fowler stopped

in mid-sentence as she saw that Shan was gazing not at her, but over her shoulder at Kincaid.

'I couldn't understand until I saw Jansen with the *purbas*. Then I knew. He was the missing link. You gave the information to Jansen. Jansen gave it to the *purbas*. The *purbas* put it in the *Lotus Book*. You just passed on what your good friends gave you. Li, and Hu, and Wen, you thought they were trying to create a new, friendlier government, to heal the old wounds by helping the Tibetans. You had no way of knowing the information was lies. You would never have suspected, because it had so much virtue behind it. Everyone was ready to believe that Tan and Jao did those things. You even got your friends to donate military food and clothing as a token of their commitment. A truck of clothes went to the *ragyapa* village, which you knew about and felt sorry for because of Luntok.'

Rebecca Fowler pushed her chair back and stood. 'What are you talking about?' she demanded. 'A book? The murders had to do with the Tamdin demon, you said. A Tibetan in the demon's costume.'

Shan nodded slowly. 'The Bureau of Religious Affairs did audits of the gompas, you know. They found the Tamdin costume a year and a half ago. It had belonged to Sungpo's guru and he had hidden it all these years. But he was going senile, and probably got careless about protecting it. Director Wen hid the audit report describing the discovery and, since so many clerks knew about the audit, a shipment was sent to the museum to cover the tracks. But Director Wen never sent the costume to the museum, because the Bei Da Union had met someone who could use it for them. Someone who would never need an alibi for murder because he would never be suspected. Someone who would revel in the symbolism. Someone with special powers. Strong. Fearless. Absolute in his convictions about the Tibetan people. About the need to take revenge for the pillage of Tibet.' Or maybe,

Shan considered, the need to take revenge on the world at large.

'To kill a man with pebbles, one by one. To sever a man's head with three blows. Not everyone is capable of such things. And to use the costume, it would take someone very special. The Tibetans trained for months, but that was mostly for the ceremony. Someone not interested in the ritual could have mastered the costume much more quickly, especially someone trained as an engineer.'

Kincaid moved to the wall with his photographs of Tibetans and stared at the faces of the children, women, and old men as if they held an answer. 'Wrong,' he said in a hollow voice. 'You have it so wrong.'

Shan slowly rose. Kincaid began to retreat, as though fearful of attack. But Shan moved to the console. 'No, I *had* it very wrong. I couldn't believe that such contempt, and yet such reverence, could exist in the same person.' The computer screen still showed the data on the Yerpa maps. It was extraordinary how well the American had come to understand the Tibetans. In its own way, the killing of Prosecutor Jao had been an act of genius. The American had known the 404th would stop work on the road, and no doubt had assumed the major would see that the knobs went through the motions but inflicted no real harm on the 404th. Shan hit the delete button.

There was the sound of more machines outside. Rebecca Fowler moved to the doorway of the room and stared out of the window on the far wall. 'A flatbed truck,' she said distractedly. 'They're taking away Jao's limousine.'

She turned back, her face a mask of confusion. 'Tyler, if you know something you should tell Shan. We have the mine to think of. The company.'

'Know something?' Kincaid said with contempt. 'Sure, I know something. The Lhadrung Five weren't executed. That's how wrong you are. The only ones who died were a bunch of MFCs who should have been executed years ago for their crimes against Tibet.' He seemed angry.

Fowler's head snapped up. 'What do you mean?' she asked.

'The club. The Bei Da Union,' Shan said. 'Li, Wen, Hu, the major. Mr Kincaid was an unofficial member.'

'Someone has to act, Rebecca,' Kincaid interjected in an impassioned tone. 'You know that, it's why you help the UN and Jansen. Tibet has so much to teach the world. We have to clear the slate. We've made great progress.'

'Progress?' Fowler asked in a near whisper.

'Someone has to stand up,' Kincaid shot back. 'It has to be done. No one stood up to Hitler. No one stood up to Stalin until it was too late. But it's not too late here. This is where we can make a difference. History can be turned around. The Bei Da Union knows that. Criminals have to be turned out of power.'

'Can you recognize a criminal, Mr Kincaid?' Shan asked. Without waiting for an answer, he turned to Fowler. 'Do you have a shipment of samples being prepared for transport next week?'

'Yes,' Fowler said slowly, more perplexed than ever.

'It will need to be stopped. Perhaps you could call.'

'It's already sealed. Pre-clearance for customs.'

'It will need to be stopped,' Shan repeated.

Fowler got on the phone and minutes later a truck was brought round to the office door. Shan paced about it as Kincaid and Fowler watched in confusion from the doorway.

'The "me" generation,' Shan said absently as he studied the shipment crates. 'I read it once in an American magazine. They can't wait for anything. They want it all now. With one more murder they would have won. Only the colonel was left. Maybe they were going to take over the mine, too. I think the suspension was partly a response to what Kincaid did with Jao; they wanted to be able to get rid of you if circumstances got out of control. Do you remember what day you received the permit suspension?' he asked Fowler.

'I don't know. Ten days ago? Two weeks.'

'It was the day after we discovered Jao's head,' Shan said, speaking slowly to let his words sink in. 'When they discovered their demon was getting out of control. 'I don't think they had decided yet whether to get rid of you. They just liked to keep options open. Like planting the computer disks and pretending there was an espionage investigation.'

'Tyler,' Fowler gasped. 'Talk to him. Tell him you don't know –'

'No one,' Kincaid insisted, 'did anything wrong. We're making history. Then I can go home and get the attention we need. I'll bring back even more investment. A hundred million, two million. A billion. You'll see, Rebecca. You'll be my manager. My chief executive. You'll always understand.'

Fowler just stared at him.

Shan began unpacking a box of brine samples, each in its own four inch wide metal cylinder. 'Something here was made outside. You ordered it from Hong Kong, maybe. The boxes, perhaps?'

'The cylinders,' Fowler said, barely audible. 'Made by the Ministry of Geology.'

Shan nodded. 'Jao had been trying to find a mobile X-ray machine. He wanted to bring it here I think, or to the Bei Da Union compound. I believe he expected to find something in the terra cotta statues they were selling or the wooden crates used for shipping. But the Union is smarter than that. I kept wondering, what was the point of advancing your shipping dates?' He unscrewed the lid on one of the metal canisters and dumped its brine on the ground. 'It had to be because they wanted to ship as much as possible before the added security precautions for the American tourists took effect.' He did not know what he sought, but he measured the interior depth of the canister with a long screwdriver he had found in the truck. The screwdriver's head was barely visible above the rim. He held it along the exterior. It was six inches short of reaching the bottom. For several minutes he examined the cylinder, then finally found an almost invisible seam. He twisted the container to no avail. Fowler called for two large wrenches. Together they freed the bottom compartment, pulling the ends of the container in opposite directions. Inside was a dark brown, acrid paste.

'This,' Shan announced with a nod towards Tan, who stood a hundred feet away, directing the machinery, 'is what will make the colonel a hero. Murder is only murder. But smuggling drugs, that is an embarrassment to the state.'

Fowler was as pale as a ghost. Kincaid stumbled forward. He grabbed another of the cylinders and opened it as Shan had done, then a third. By the fourth he began to shake. He shoved his hand inside and pulled it out, covered with the thick ooze. 'The pigs,' he moaned, 'the greedy little shits.'

'As you said, you were the only one who was friendly both with the Bei Da Union and with someone close to the *purbas*.' Shan's hand found the American's *khata* around his neck and pulled it off. 'They fed you information about the victims and you got it to Jansen. Jansen knew the *purbas*, so he gave it to them and it was recorded in the *Lotus Book*. But it wasn't meant for the book. It was meant for you. Because they knew you had to believe in what you were doing. You wouldn't do it if you thought it was just to help them advance in office. No. You did it to punish. You did it for your cause. Only with Prosecutor Jao you went too far. It was probably easy to persuade them to entice him to the South Claw. After all, if killing Jao on the 404th's road caused the Tibetan prisoners to react and the knobs to be brought in, your friend the major would always be in control, he could go through the motions without really hurting the Tibetans, right? But the skull shrine. That upset them, because they were taking so much of the gold for themselves. What you did with Jao's head threatened to shut their gold reclamation down. They had to discipline you. Maybe they decided they didn't need you any more. So they went to the hiding place and incapacitated the costume, then suspended the permit. And when you tried to go back to the costume there were guard dogs. They bit you on your arm. Not a cut from the rocks. A dog bite.' He dropped the *khata* on the ground beside Kincaid and looked at Fowler. What had she called Kincaid? The lost soul who had found his home.

There was still a glimmer of defiance in Kincaid's eyes. 'Tamdin is the protector of the Tibetans. The people have to believe again in the old values. That's all I did, protect the Buddhists. We saved them. We saved the Lhadrung Five.'

'What do you mean?'

'They're in Nepal, the others. That was part of the plan. Once they were officially reported as executed, no one would notice if they were actually smuggled across the border. The major got them across. They're all alive.'

Shan sighed and reached into his pocket. Only a slender thread remained of the American's delusion. Shan handed him the photographs of the three executions. By the time Kincaid had seen half a dozen he had fallen to his knees. When he looked up it was not to Shan but to Fowler. A dry sob wracked his chest.

'It wasn't about drugs,' he cried. 'You've got to believe me. If I'd ever thought –'

The tears that streamed down his cheeks seemed to revive Fowler. When she spoke it was as if she were comforting a child. 'Then you wouldn't have put on the costume for them, would you, Tyler?'

'It was Hitler. It was Stalin. You know what they have

438

done here. We're going to change it. You would understand, Rebecca. I always knew you would understand.
Someday you were going to be proud of me. They can't
be forgiven. Someone has to –' He stopped as he saw the
revulsion in her face. 'Rebecca! No!' he screamed, and
collapsed to the ground at her feet, pounding the earth
with his fist.

Chapter Twenty-one

The arrests were made swiftly, Colonel Tan reported. Li Aidang, Hu, and Wen Li had been at their private compound, loading boxes of records into their Land Rovers. The major had gone straight to his helicopter, confidently expecting to fly across the border. But Tan had disabled the machine the night before, and staked it out with a hand-picked squad of soldiers. Fifty more of Tan's troops had been sent to search the Bei Da Union's buildings. It took them six hours to locate the vault built into the old gompa's subterranean shrine. It held bank records for Hong Kong accounts, names in Hong Kong, and an inventory of processed opium paste.

Shan worked all night on his report. In the morning, just after dawn, Sungpo and Jigme were released from the warehouse at Jade Spring Camp where Tan had secreted them. Shan stood at the gate and watched, wanting to say something but finding no words. They did not acknowledge him as they passed through the gate. They refused the offer of a ride. Twenty feet down the road Jigme turned and gave him a small, victorious nod.

Two hours later Shan was in Tan's office, dressed in his prison garb. The phone was ringing incessantly. Two young, well-scrubbed officers were assisting Madame Ko.

'The Ministry of Justice has already decided to declare Prosecutor Jao a Hero of the People. A medal will be sent to his family,' Tan announced impassively. 'They expect arrests in Hong Kong later today. Li talked all night. Tried to make us believe he was in it as part of his own investigation. Gave enough evidence to fill a book. Won't make any difference. A general from the Bureau's office in Lhasa has arrived. They have a special place in the mountains they use for such things. In tomorrow's newspaper the people will be told of a tragic accident on a high mountain road. No survivors.'

Shan was looking out of the window. The 404th was still not at work.

Tan followed his gaze. 'With the bridge gone there's no need for a road,' he announced. 'The project is terminated.'

Shan turned in surprise.

'There is no money for a new bridge,' Tan explained with a shrug. 'The Bureau troops are already moving back to the border. The 404th will not be punished. It starts a new project tomorrow. Irrigation ditches in the valley.' Tan joined Shan at the window for a moment, looking down at the street where Sergeant Feng was leaning against the truck. 'You've ruined him, you know. All these years in my command, and now he asks for a transfer. As far from a prison as possible. Says he wants to go to see if any of his family is still alive. Says he has to go to his father's grave.' Tan gestured awkwardly to a paper bag on the table. 'Here. Madame Ko's idea,' he said. There was a strange tension in his voice, not the jubilation Shan had expected.

It was a new pair of military boots and work gloves.

Shan said nothing, but sat and began unlacing his shoes. 'What about the American?'

Tan hesitated. 'Not a problem any more. The US embassy has already been contacted.'

'Deported already?'

Tan lit a cigarette. 'Last night Mr Kincaid climbed the cliff over the skull cave. He secured a rope to his neck and leapt off. The work crew found him there this morning, hanging above the cave.'

Shan clenched his jaw. So many lives had been wasted because Kincaid had been too hard a seeker. 'Fowler?'

'She can stay if she wants. There's a mine to run.'

'She'll stay,' Shan said as he eased off his shoes and tied the laces together to carry them. He would wear the boots for Madame Ko, and give them to Choje later.

Tan stared at a folded sheet of newspaper with an indecisive air. As Shan pulled on the boots, Tan shoved the paper across his desk.

It was a press report dated ten days earlier. A full page obituary. Minister Qin of the Ministry of Economy was mourned as the last Eighth Route Army survivor in active government.

'I called Beijing. He left no instructions about you. Big housekeeping already done in his office. Seems lots of people wanted his records destroyed, fast. Files all gone. The new staff, no one's heard of any instructions about you.'

Shan folded the sheet into his pocket. It wasn't necessarily good news. With Qin alive, there had at least been someone who remembered him, someone with authority over his tattoo. He wouldn't be the first person to be forgotten in a Chinese prison.

Tan fingered the small brown folder Shan had seen on his first visit. 'Right now this is the only official evidence of your existence.' Tan closed the folder.

'There was something in Beijing, though.' Tan lifted a parcel wrapped in oilskin. 'They didn't find a file, but they found this on his desk, like some kind of trophy. Had your name on it. I thought you would –' the words drifted away as he opened it. On the cloth lay a small worn bamboo canister.

Shan stared in disbelief. His eyes moved slowly from the familiar canister to Tan, who was gazing at it. 'I used to watch the Taoist priests,' Tan said solemnly. 'They would throw the sticks and recite verses to groups of children.'

Shan's hand trembled as he reached for it and opened the lid. Inside, the lacquered sticks were still there, the

throwing sticks of yarrow used for the *Tao te Ching*,
passed down from his great-grandfather. Because they
had been the only physical possession Shan had valued,
the Minister had made a show of taking them away.
Slowly, making his hand remember the motion that once
had been reflexive, he scattered the sticks in a fanlike
movement. He looked up, embarrassed.

'It makes you remember,' Tan said with an odd,
haunted tone. He looked at Shan, his face narrowed in
question. 'Things were different once, weren't they?' he
asked with sudden emotion.

Shan just smiled sadly. 'The set is an heirloom,' he said
very quietly. 'You are kind. I had no idea they had been
preserved.'

He rolled them in his fingers, surprised by the pleasure
of their touch. He gripped them tightly, with his eyes
shut, then returned them to the canister and cradled it in
his hands. For the most fleeting of moments there was a
faint scent of ginger and he felt his father was near.

'Perhaps,' Shan said, 'I could ask a great favour.'

'I have spoken to the warden. You are to get light
duties for a few weeks.'

'No. I mean about this.' He reverently set the canister
back on the cloth. 'It will be confiscated. A guard will
throw them in a fire. Or sell them. If you or Madame Ko
could keep them, I mean until later.'

Tan looked at him with pain in his eyes. He seemed
about to speak, then awkwardly nodded and covered the
canister with the cloth. 'Of course. They will be safe.'

Shan left him there, staring at the sticks.

Madame Ko was waiting, tears in her eyes. 'Your
brother,' Shan said to her, remembering her devotion to
the sibling lost so many years ago in the gulag. 'I think
you have honoured him by what you have done.'

She embraced him, like a mother would embrace a son.
'No,' she said, her lip quivering. 'It is you who have
honoured him.'

Shan was halfway down the corridor when Tan called out from behind him. He walked slowly, uncertainly, towards Shan. The canister was in one hand, Shan's official folder in the other. 'I can't do anything officially about a Beijing file,' Tan said. 'Not even a lost file.'

'Of course,' Shan said. 'We made a deal. It has been honourably concluded.'

'So you'd have no travel papers. Not even work papers. You'll be in jeopardy anywhere outside this district.'

'I don't understand.'

As he spoke Tan's eyes began to shine with a light Shan had never seen in them. He handed the folder to Shan.

'There. You no longer exist. I'll call the warden. You'll be removed from the rolls.' Tan slowly extended the canister, and their eyes locked as though for the first time.

'This land,' Tan sighed. 'It makes life so difficult.' He nodded, as though in reply to himself, then dropped the canister into Shan's hand and turned back towards his office.

Dr Sung asked no questions. She gave him the fifty doses of smallpox vaccine without a word, then made him wait for a booklet on its administration. 'I hear they're gone,' she said impassively. 'The Bei Da boys. As if they never existed. They say a special clean-up squad came from Lhasa.' She found a small canvas bag for the medicine, then followed him into the street as though unable to say goodbye.

She stood, the wind tugging at her smock, while Shan shrugged a farewell. At the last moment she produced an apple. As she stuffed it into his bag he offered a small smile of gratitude.

It would be a long trek to Yerpa.

The Flower Net
Lisa See

'Tense and exciting' *Sunday Express*

On a January morning in Beijing a child skating on a frozen lake finds the corpse of a white man under the ice. Liu Hulan, a woman detective, is assigned to head what will be a delicate investigation. The murder victim is the son of the American Ambassador.

Thousands of miles away, David Stark, an assistant US attorney, boards the China Peony, a barely sea-worthy freighter carrying hundreds of illegal immigrants to America. On board he finds the badly decomposed body of a 'Red Prince', a child of one of China's top officials. The murders appear to have nothing in common until rare plant fibres are found to be coating the respiratory tract of both victims, and the Chinese and American governments agree to work together.

'Mixes illegal immigration, Chinese medicine, smuggling and ancient Chinese customs in an authentic brew that is exciting and informative' *Mail on Sunday*

'An atmospheric, tightly plotted suspense story. *The Flower Net* is a treat' *Washington Post*

City of Ice
John Farrow

'Combines gritty realism with fast-paced storytelling that never lets the reader off the hook' Lynda la Plante

A bomb explodes in a busy Montreal street. A mob lawyer blown apart, an innocent child murdered. Watching and powerless to prevent it is Montreal's most illustrious policeman – Emile Cinq-Mars. Then the corpse of a young man is found hung from a rafter with the inscription M-5 dangling round his neck. M-5, March 5th, a calling card in English.

Linking the two crimes, the detective finds himself in the midst of the Canadian mob. Their new ally is the ruthless Russian mafia, and in particular an enigmatic crime boss known as the Czar. When Cinq-Mars uncovers the identity of a mole within the Czar's organisation, he knows it is a race against time. Can she help him catch the Czar? Can he save her from almost certain death?

In his desperate search through the icy streets of Montreal, Emile Cinq-Mars has only his morality and formidable intelligence to guide him in a world where black is white and white is black . . .

'A deft thriller . . . rich descriptions of Montreal in winter blend well with the bone-chilling plot' *New York Times*

'A gripping thriller' *Time Out*

NOW AVAILABLE IN ARROW PAPERBACK